THE PROUD VILLAGER

ENEBELI O.M.A.

authorHOUSE®

AuthorHouse™ UK
1663 Liberty Drive
Bloomington, IN 47403 USA
www.authorhouse.co.uk
Phone: UK TFN: 0800 0148641 (Toll Free inside the UK)
*   UK Local: (02) 0369 56322 (+44 20 3695 6322 from outside the UK)*

Published by AuthorHouse   03/30/2023

ISBN: 978-1-7283-7990-6 (sc)
ISBN: 978-1-7283-7991-3 (e)

Print information available on the last page.

Author's Anthology: Potpourri Of Perspectives

I am *"The proud Villager"* from both geographical hemispheres with enough urbanization stuff and a magnificent and drilled *"Brains over the barriers"*. *"Foes" (Friends or enemies standing)* abound everywhere one turns, but, with perseverance most torments and backstabbing fuse in a time warp, evoking the timeworn aphorism that *"Sweet are the uses of adversity"*. *"Trust" (The rigours under sadistic transgressors)* cannot be cheaply given when one has *"the pocket pamphlet of wisdom"*. A day with an elite American Marine would make any right-thinking man commit to memory *"Quantico" (The Marines' home)*. No *"Wambling, queasy and hallucinating"* when one works side by side with a Marine because they are tough and obey laid down rules with military precision.

World political rumblings bring about *"The inequality quality in equality"* as the rife bearings of the operators are the *"Quantitative equation of political taxidermists"*. Yes, raw politics attracts assorted and unproven hidden deaths. These are practicable *"Indelible sins of unforgettable yesterday"* that have her plumes, buds, and nodes from unexpected individuals and quarters to grope in the darkness looking or searching for the improbable ladder to exit the dungeon.

Despite the setbacks inherent in life niche, *"Generations of positive knowledge competitors"* grappled with facts and their proven sources to rip *"RIP-Alternative facts"* that are operated like sifting the wheat from the chaff. A theory that is known by most. That again brings about all the *"Vampiric born again consultants"* who defy proven norms to deface and make their irritable deceptive words and actions to further their inebriated and bibulous acrimonies against a once decent and peace compatible society. They invented several codes that included some *"Codes of presidential imbecility"* that attracted much *"Above the subservient breaking point"*.

The voice of the intellectually caged was freed by the *"Amazing Amazon"* with the blessings and elucidation of *"Symbolic symbiotic zero"*, but amid all these stirring deadly times lay *"The abuse of silence and distance" (SAD)* that continued unabated with the palpable offenders "Swimming in jar and gyre" — trapped and sinking to the abyss. The groundwork begins....

"Author's anthology: a potpourri of perspectives" is a sequel to *"The Birth of a New Dawn"*.
EO111414022018MA (ARR) Ex Cathedra Martinet (Enebeli Mike A.O.)
EO224825072021MA (ARR) Ex Cathedra Martinet (Enebeli Mike A.O.)

Recommendation

I seriously recommend this book for University or tertiary English language students, higher secondary school students levels and speakers at functions or occasions and many more. You will be surprised and happy for taking the dip. Nothing good comes easy, which is why as the author of this book, I am making a sound claim of recommendation to anyone that wants to upgrade by adding and replenishing his knowledge. I know the immense help it will be to whoever reads it, with the same passion it was written and passed on. It is like the dispersal of seeds that multiplies with every germination and crossbreeding. I assure you of being the new person of tomorrow's knowledge and a better manager than yesterday. I strongly recommend this book for everyone seeking leisure, past time and as stated in the opening sentence, for it will elevate you to new unforeseen heights. It will be an honourable and unforgettable experience so positively made to advance your knowledge for the good of humanity. Delve and savour. Happy reading.

Enebeli Mike A.O.

Validation And Hazy Bottlenecks

Follow the norms and etiquette of a system so hazy.
    Systems that bottle you up if you allow it.
    Systems marred by bureaucracy and bureaucrats.
    Hard hidden hibernating transgressors of the status quo
    Rejections spur the indomitable and sane to greater heights.
    Thy synopsis is enough self-validation than others running afar.
    Not in the mood to bribe my way through validations and certifications.
    The only plausible and acceptable validation is the I in me for me in I
    The I and Me have jointly spoken and no doubts.
    Fear of external aggressors and intrusions turned regressor platoon parades dimmed.
    Never wait for laziness to turn wrinkles to go.
    Decide comprehensively following the trends at daylight timing!
    Hard variable writers of times understood, why not me or you.
    Get down and burst the retrogressive immaterial balloons home of nothingness.
    The bassoons sounding melodious are the players.
    Some decorated but fake "Pub houses" blindfolded by cataracts and dark blind angles.
    Nothing remains the same — metamorphosis is gradual but happening.
    The voices against literary poisons are here to stay for the good they mean for man.
    Rejection and endorsement are surmountable hurdles in broken "icy" norms.
    I trust me in I and the I in me wholly and conclusively.
    Begging myself, conscience and being are completely out of the insidious, heinous man-made and model equations.
    I own and polish my shoes my way without questions and questionnaires.
    The need for rejection is a self-discerning writer's pedigree seeking his mathematical perigee.
    Out of many lies the most sinister one vanity house. Beware.
    Determination, persistence, and doggedness in thee hold thy dissemination.
    No trusted thoughts and beggarly ways to the knoll. It's you and only you.
    Avoid the hydra-headed truculence that permeates the vicious circle of retrogression.
    Validation that you await does not await you.

EO190024042016MA (ARR) Ex Cathedra Matinet Visier (Mike Enebeli)

Content Summary

The Sahara desert has her most endearing beauty from the air and on land exudes her mixed beauty with incontestable fright to the Lily-livered sojourner. A very vast inhospitable terrain conquered by the invading illegal immigrants from mostly West Sub-Saharan Africa, supported by their peers from the East, North-East and North-West of the continent in search of Greener pastures in Europe. One of those infinitesimal reasons of brain drains in most parts of the affected countries of the continent.

Illegal immigrants are the bravest in any society. They possess the most unimaginable, invincible lethal weapon of all times in their arsenal that could elude all scanning machines ever made and still being conceived by man, all sniffing dogs and any known man-made control checks that have ever existed — which they carry all about undetected and could be used to their advantage anytime anywhere for their daily operational survivals. The Proud Villager called their human deconstructive weapon a "weapon of mass destruction, reconstruction and new construction — Their BRAINS.

Most sojourners who had fallen for the "Unknown" had suffered assorted despicable deprivations of indescribable magnitude from their various governments of the day and cushioned by endless insidious individuals that aid one of the most disrespectful trades women are forced to partake in willfully and mostly by coercion. A trade better called "Jihad al nikah" — Arabic meaning of sexual holy war.

Everyone involved is appalled by events after setting off into the "Unknown" but they still find solace in that distant life of excellence and fulfilment outside the shores of the African continent.

How would their aims and dreams be accomplished? Find out as they give credence to the truth and sincerity of their purpose.

Marketing Summary

The Proud Villager shows a country and continent dichotomized by all humanly negative existing factors and unethical behaviour by entire very hostile host African Northern countries against a people who did not fault except for being illegals. Neighbours who saw themselves as better than their dark-skinned peers of the same continent because of their skin colour. Neighbours who call themselves Arabs to make a clean difference of not being Africans and neighbours that call themselves Africans when there was that need to gain favour and support from those dark-skinned people they so despised. Neighbours that could better be described as insidious and invidious.

The Hoity-Toity, insidious, invidious, invincible planning among people and government officials in most of the Sub-Saharan African and European countries to revalidate, and reinstall systematic slavery and prostitution in very many ways unknown to humanity— in a modern world are indeed very difficult to comprehend to the unsuspecting and unfathomable mind.

Some illegal immigrants who for the want of greener pastures in Europe ended up as corpses, prostitutes, truncated and modelled slaves in their Sahara-bordered countries. A people cheated, duped, enslaved, beaten up, chased about like failed tethered goats, some driven deep into the desert and abandoned to fate, emasculated and emancipated by their Arab Saharan bordered neighbours. Despite all the man-made odds, the Sub-Saharan Africans make all the running facts like fiction out of unrecognized self-pity to show the warmth and rage they are mostly made of. They created bonds of love, hope and aspirations for a new dawn and opportunity — knowing that giving up in the face of those invincible odds would create doom and cataclysm for them and their aspirations. Only a fraction of them would sing *Veni Vidi Vici* just as not all soldiers that go to war survive to tell tales about their experiences — but how? Read on.

Dedication

The Proud Villager is dedicated to my maternal and paternal grandparents, my children, grandchildren, endless great grand children, my dear wife Anny, and my parents who despite their long life like many other family bread winners sustained our household with the meagre they were able to toil for and remained very steadfast all through their God-given tenure on earth, to Adeke Mike and his entire household and with deep heartfelt concern — all illegal immigrants around the world who for the want of the Golden Fleece and other myriads of reasons and intents found themselves webbed up in foreign lands from:-

- Poor governance and negligence with that daily mindfulness of a false dawn.
- Suffered from leaders that exhibited hydra-headed outposts of tyranny.
- Leaders who have vented their spleen and official anger on the common man.
- Leaders who look pious on the outside, but have all the innate coatings and bearings of sarcastic domineering.
- Leaders who detest grassroots combing of facts and events from the popular perspective and agreements with her citizenry.
- Leaders that portray themselves as gargantuan honourable with very inordinate, dehumanizing and dishonourable conduct.
- Leaders whose epithets don't match the torrents of the impostor titles they forcibly carry to the detriment and dwarf the common man.
- Leaders who are just by chance are leaders.

I still dedicate the book as I salute all immigrants that originated from South and North Americas, the Caribbean Islands, the Middle East, Asia and Africa. You are all the bravest of any established community with your resolve to see things accomplished. You have the resilience hidden in your positive plans with your sombre voices, and yet you are the most desperate intelligent human most valuable content — your brains.

To those of you that met their untimely deaths while trying so hard not to be among the downtrodden, I say "Rest In Peace" and to those that survived and still living after those arduous and very tortuous journeys on whatever means everyone may have used to get across, I say:- "Never fail to appreciate daily the good works of God in your life". Pray for the living and dead heroes and comrades unknown. There is hardly any African immigrant anywhere that does not understand indignation, and indentured servitude either through experience or feelings. They all know that no man wants to live and contend with racial profiling, stigma, ignorance and daily total fear of the unknown.

I love you all.

Enebeli Mike Okwus.

Acknowledgement

It is difficult for some people to fit into the man-made status quo. I sincerely and humbly did not intend to make headlines pedigree other than imbibing through a strenuous hard work emanating from my conjecture to inform people all over the world about some more than enough cocooned incidents that had existed for decades (if not as time could reckon) unnoticed, now being made bare to everyone that cares, through a very rigorous narration from my own experience and perspective — first-hand available information. Every human being has that endowed performance with something special embedded in him or her that exudes some inherent golden opportunities. Everyone just needs that gentle and Midas touch to be able to push and discover them cosmically to align ourselves with the trends of the times.

I am truly happy and essentially humbled to be associated with all those that urged me to make my thoughts and experiences count in the unrelenting maze of modern heaps of real-time sharp information techniques. You have all given me the rare but radiating privilege not easily come by on a platter of gold. It is worth mentioning, how you all positively urged me on and on — kept me trudging on seriously but happily on my toes to make my best better with the utmost we could achieve together in the instance. All of you that urged me on through your different ways of support is my team *extraordinaire* from the very first day and remained consistent, supportive and unwavering in your different but substantial professional helpful advice and encouragement. You all gave me a good lighted dark passage at a point I thought the book was almost at a dead end.

Not all doctors take the Hippocratic Oath, because of their professional differences and diversifications — you all that supported me in one way or the other were seriously different but collectively aligned to a side of your common and respective briefing — removing all differences that would have a bore and bugged the reality of my envisaged goal. The success of it all was not preempting me with your entire noble, good and logical understanding of the human strata. You respectfully made me one of the wholes.

On the other hand, you defended me like good lawyers that know their Onions would do — not like lawyers that graduated into dormancy and finds it very Herculean to defend a hungry housefly that perched and proboscises on secreting sore content.

Thank you all for giving me the opportunity and chance to prove my mettle to the wider world. You have all created, sharpened and shaped my views and visions, which have all been realigned to a model modern world.

If I waited to remember every detail of history to seep through, or for every single piece of information before publishing this book, I would wait for eternity with nothing substantial to show. No real-life history is completely exact and pinpoint, as they must have transpired and transcended time in many undeniable ways, but her place of reality in history persists in importance and remembrance.

My special thanks go to all my children, grandchildren, my great wife Anny, my childhood friend Adeke Mike and his entire childhood and to all my other friends who for the sake of space are not mentioned here but saw the wise decision in my good purpose of writing down my overdue experience and thoughts together. Your incessant reminders broke my many years of procrastination.

I am sure that you all mentioned here and every other reader will enjoy reading this book where incipient frustration tamed incivility of some inchoate people on how a man should explore noble enduring believable encouraging lecithin inclement for a functioning world.

Your positive high standards have collectively led my mind to the grandiose passion effervescences that culminated in the birth of The Proud Villager. Once more, millions of thanks to you all.

Enebeli Mike Okwus

Contents

1 Introduction 1

2 Toddling Years 6

3 Asoki-Awoko 11

4 Parachute Landing 27

5 Military Sweeping Decrees 34

6 Misplaced Trust 43

7 Insidious Notoriety 46

8 Godfather Procreating Injustice 62

9 Endemic Corruption 68

10 Desideratum 70

11 Fare Thee Well 74

12 Saharan Drive 85

13 Saharan Trek 91

14 Jamahiriya South To North 116

15 Coastal Life 129

16 Connection Connecting Connectors 151

1

INTRODUCTION

IN HINDSIGHT, RANDY'S STORY HAD BEEN A REMINISCENCE OF ASSORTED BOOK READERSHIP, LIFE actions and scenes that have so much remained indelible with some wonderful ideas combing through his life. Randy saw the illegal immigration across the Sahara as the direct opposite of what was happening between Mexico and the United States of America. Most African Moslems from East African countries head for Yemen and Saudi Arabia because of their geographical location and religious affinities. Some Christians too would sacrifice anything to be in Israel from the Philippines and entire Africa. Randy knew so many people that trusted that country purely out of their religion and wanted to be there because they thought they were God's children along with the Israelites and felt at home if they ever succeeded to get across the border. It is noteworthy that there are many ways and illegal routes from the African mainland to the Mediterranean Sea. It is very difficult to bring a whole long-life story into a sentence but possible to digress and get everything connected randomly as per remembrance and reminiscence. To his late son, he wrote in tears: -

My dear lovely son,

I remember that early morning in Kaduna when the military vehicle brought you back to me lifeless into my waiting hands. I remember the last kisses we shared in your state before you were committed to mother earth. Rest in perfect peace darling and stay ringing bells behind Bivasco till his ever-last day. He committed a crime against an unsuspecting daddy and boasted about it. The man who killed his visitor is not a hero but a coward.

I have been through too much through no choice of my own but still engaged in tough settlings. I bore the cost, efforts, resources and material casualties for the journey and life I undertook from pains that metamorphosed into real-life happiness. Have kept facing things with a mix of patience and urgency that will not be easy to maintain. The sights of all imminent dangers are not lost but it takes the tough man some hard decisions to make a breakthrough. People and some old friends have caused more than enough trouble. New ones must not add to it. One important thing that some human wicked souls do is being quick to inflict pain on others but lacking the genuine courage to experience it. The past is still alive in the present crisis which makes me genuinely trust but never forget to verify. I hate to hide behind my shadow because I want people to know how much I know. When I authorize some friends, they take me for a ride, but authorization is easier to grant than to repeal. Without risk, freedom will not be won. The greater individual freedom and opportunities are being abused to the detriment of others. Before us, we had people, who refused to lift their gaze beyond their welfare. We should debate not suspend the alarm the whistle blower has raised. I have stopped emotional talks because they are unhelpful. We have been serious with issues to a degree. We are coming and want to win, even though it has not happened now, it will surely come to pass soon. The secret is that almost every decision-maker is hoping we would collapse. They have forgotten or don't know what we are made of. Son, we are wiser and have known that Soldiers don't go to war with hope as their primary weapon. In war, one cannot count on his or her enemy to conform to his or her desires. In examining the plan as outlined, whoever has the experience would note serious problems. Our enemies would be surprised at the paralyzing embarrassment we are going to inflict on them. We have to employ our full range of resources. War is no testing ground for petty theories. In war one piles on with everything one had gotten — then one is likely to get what one paid for.

Honey, I further want you to know on your side of the divide that, I have realized that life raises people but reality knocks their feet from under them and character is what one is while reputation is what people think one is.

Son, nothing stays buried forever. Let it be known to you that one of the most populous dark-skinned countries in the world has been placed on the world terrorist list because her son that lived outside her shores and went for terrorist training from his base in the United Kingdom was involved in the unimaginable attempt to blow up an aeroplane over the Atlantic. The United States of America, the United Kingdom and some of her Middle and Far East allies and friends failed to make the list despite their production of homegrown terrorists and the Pakistani Madrasa graduates of destruction. It has been an idealism not cushioned by realism. The terror perpetrators keep threatening securities in all forms and ramifications completely unknown to man.

Oh, O boy boy boy was that name bond for father-son display at play. I need to remind you that Bivasco insulted your home diaspora and the entire community. He had stated that they were a bunch of dunces incapable of rightful educational throughput. He was wrong. He forgot how he had written and begged your father to carve three stamps for him to forge certificates and documents to aid his Uncle Sam's education. If he had done that and pointed one limp finger at your people, did he forget that he would always meet the stone he had thrown ahead of him years ago? Boy, trust your people, he was ignored not because no one could answer him but for he to go where it matters to explain to the elders he had insulted. Love, I if not we will be there when he gets there if he will ever be there. Respect begets respect for a personable human relationship, which Bivasco lacked, lacks interminably and endlessly. Still remember our last kiss as I cuddled your body for the last time in my arms. Be steadfast in your side of the human divide and keep the respect with which we as a family and as a people are noted for.

The unassailable facts are that human rights are often flouted, denied, and have become a will-o-the-wisp. That being so, I am in the position of asking for a reprieve from all I have suffered. I rejoice and take solace in the fact that one could build a new present but cannot build a new past. The past will always be passed for a focused future.

Check out the problems I have gone through honey. We are in an overly sensitive moment and the atmosphere is more than charged. I have applied and used a cooperative, not confrontational approach that would have gone to the root of all problems to no avail. That being so I have made it a point to avoid stress, which boosts the production of the hormone cortisol, which increases inflammation and leads to achiness. Remember that the killers that dotted the lines of our lives cannot all be killed. The braver, effective course is to deny them cause and succour by defusing wider grievances thereby disarming them. They can hardly identify their real enemy. Till then, I wish they stayed lucky with the taxing dilemma that has brought us this far. Incredibly beautiful futility is hanging in the air for our detractors, like the smile on the Cheshire cat. People have been occupying and invading our time. I am not talking about the time taken to listen to all gossip and insolence so dished out to me in the intervening years, not a clock timeline of either recent history or the much longer history for this anachronistic sound but time as something palpable but slippery and ungraspable — like wind or something like the volume of the emptiness that surrounded and threatened to engulf "human perpetrators". I have in so many ways been palmed but still sliding from so many directions at once. I might have lost so much but these are earthly and ephemeral things compared to life. Dubiousness has its historical curiosity. The logical destiny makes a house an existing memory, which is paradoxical. Dear, we do not need to understand time, although we think that we do, but we are living it and living it that we know it will end. Life without a horizon would be intolerable, even if we never know quite how distant that horizon might be.

Honey, despite my warnings to people who have cheated me endlessly, they have continued to behave erratically, apparently without rhyme or reason. Is hard to be used to deferring to the grown-ups and having my views overridden, or simply unheeded. You have made an indelible mark on all aspects of my life and thought without knowing it. Only a microscopic percentage of people know all my life really as a mentor — I mean someone who believes in you more than you believe in yourself. Daddy has seen what everyone else has seen but thinks what no one else has thought — but everyone thinks something different at different times depending on the situations and moods. Any form of management and responsibility for other people is difficult yet; I still instil exacting values and high standards in others and still retain values that make normal human beings.

Everyone has a past like every story has a beginning. I try to open my mind like a parachute that functions only when it is open. There are people, situations or things that one needs to remember, no matter how badly they hurt. One learns from them because if one removes the memory of someone and situation, one would lose the lessons one had learned from the characters.

I am now in a world that is not accepting the imposition of unrealizable demands. I am fair enough to know the solution to some peoples' toughness and intransigence. I need to be where wishes come true because without the right solution one could never go far and there are perils of ignoring bubbles of a kind. No one seemed to listen to my preaching of everyone putting aside lies, prejudices and preconceptions but we must be alert for the unusual and unexpected as we had better think outside the entanglement and come up with an interpretation that can resolve seemingly conflicted phenomena. Many people have been impostors throughout their life. Some give their parents automatic posthumous titles and still heap unwarranted insolence on the very community where their umbilical cords were buried at birth and their mouths were fattened to be real normal humans. Is like biting the fingers that have sweated it out to feed one. Wonders they say shall never end. Boy, it was hard to believe that stoicism held sway in the face of all adversities, and what would have been forced dogmatism for your daddy as a Wonderful Proud Villager that juxtaposed his experiences with the ever-turning and running latent wheels of life and their experiences. They were burgeoning crises I never ignored but handled with the best mettle through my dedications, added strength that converted my subdued pains to victory.

The world had pushed me faster to almost a lightning speed than I can reliably perform but managed to keep to her tempo. It is a dose of reality that brought me face to face with that curve that made the driving differently clear. Boy, you are a face in the crowd. I still visualize your handsome face when you came newly to this world and when you left me in unsurpassable agony that I have managed to dilute. Nature had spoken and we must not contest it. It is time to step up to the home plate of opportunity and adjust the cup of caution. We may pull the hamstring muscle of inadequacy and fall face-first onto the field of failure. Without fear or favour to anyone, daddy needs very consistent accountability wrapped in transparent honesty. We need not create terms of endearment because our interests differ or coincide almost seamlessly instead should give room, and endurance and be tolerant of our divergent ideas or views about life or things. Mistaken consensus is difficult to straighten up. Just getting you informed on how things have gone and been since you left. We will always remain in that eternal love.

Rest in perfect peace and eternity. The struggle continues here. Aluta continua.

Love Daddy.

2

TODDLING YEARS

RANDY WAS BORN IN A LINEAR SETTLEMENT VILLAGE. AS A TODDLER, HE HAD FRIENDS OF HIS AGE group with whom he played *epo moto-Janglova (seesaw game)* on wind-aided fallen trees in the village and stumps with centred fulcrums. They played football and ran with discarded bicycle wheels while they were sent on an errand by their parents. They also had the palm tree trunk scraped to mimic *alupupu* (motorcycle), punching squared sardine cans to make cars that were tied and drawn with a rope on self-constructed bridges and hordes of other children invented games.

Randy's teen friends Kide, Ehon and Magbo always made his days. The mother would always come begging him to come home to eat his food or for some other niceties, most good mothers provided for their children. After some time, his parents started to tell him he would be going to see his aunt with her in a very far away place from home. He did not take it seriously because he did not know what travelling meant and more so did not know that another place existed other than where he was born. Randy did not know what suffering was like in his teen years because the parents provided and cared endlessly like every other parent to their offspring. Though there were not those infrastructures that made the western world glitter like gold, life was enjoyed to the maximum with the unknown and most of the time then-unheard-of western world niceties. People made their life enjoyable by being creative in the very best way they could, and it worked wonders for them. It was cutting their coats according to their sizes without knowing or reckoning it.

They boarded a heavily wood designed *"ngwogwolo" (constructed wooden lorries)* to the West. He could not and did not know how to inform his teen friends that he was leaving. They parted without any words or knowledge that they were not going to see themselves for years or maybe forever again as long as they existed on earth because there was going to be a reason or reasons at every corner to keep it so without any prejudice and enmity. They were children that might never know or remember that they once played together. The ground ran along endlessly with them and stopped each time they did. It was a journey Randy would consider "from the unknown to the unknown" and the one that would open, shape and sharpens his undiscovered itinerary in a world so distant yet around him. All he needed would be the awareness - the awareness that would take decades to grow and mature into his manhood subconscious mind of effervescence metamorphosis.

He grew into what he is today from that very first journey he made with his parents. He cried aloud when the parents were travelling back and leaving him behind with his aunt. Randy got adaptive and acclimatized so fast socially with the environment and made friends that would just be friends in life's memory lanes.

He stayed at home for some years with the aunt with that bellicose childhood freedom because it was customary with one unapproved but bylaw for a child to have his hands cross his head to the opposite sides of the ears before he could be accepted as a pupil in the primary school. It was a very dastard, primitive and depriving way of assessing a child's school-age in those colonial days. He made it fast to school but for those who were not lucky enough, the school was almost elusive because of their biological hormonal imbalance and body structures. Nature was the defining and determining factor added to the ruthless unapproved bylaws in vogue then. Randy would later as an adult think why such obnoxious and retrogressive determinant factors would be used to evaluate school-age and worst still why the people sheepishly allowed it to happen. It was like forcing a log down someone's throat - it was the sub-human strata of inhumanity to man that were not merited by innocent children and their parents.

The iron curtain exists in the mind of those who believe in it. It is only a feeling and an illusional connotation of deprivation. Anywhere you are, is where you are. Randy is born of incorruptible and glorious subsistence farming parents. His parents were always on the right side of the law. Even though they had to struggle for life's necessities on daily basis, they gave their children the endless and unlimited freedom to follow their unimaginable serene and courteous life. That meant catapulting them into carving a niche for them. The parents may not have been educated but they knew the positive rudiments of living and human interactions.

He started school as a little boy living with his aunt in Onudoh town at the age of six and later transferred to his home village where he had hardly lived before this time. After two weeks in his new class, he was given a promotion to the next class. He tried to force himself back to the right class, but the teachers and the headmaster concerned made it clear to him that he would remain in the upper class. He grudgingly accepted and later found it was not as difficult as his mates had speculated. Before he went to his village from the city, he remained in primary one for three years because the mistress who taught his class was very humorous and never treated them harshly while in the next class, he was promoted to was a teacher that utilized much corporal punishment to get his teachings and knowledge across to his pupils. Randy out of fear remained in that class and the guardian never knew what was happening in the school and to Randy as a pupil. The number of extra years he spent in his first-class straightened his primary educational standing to have warranted the double promotion he gained when he went to his native village for the first time.

As a pupil, he had all-around training and joined many social clubs in the school. Amongst them, was his membership of the Boy Scout and choir membership of the school.

They sang on Sunday catholic mass services. They were taught and forced to memorize catechism. He was not too good at doing that then. The problem he had was the change from the Yoruba language to his native language catechism. It was then easier for him in the Yoruba language, but who was going to understand him where Yoruba was not spoken. It was no shock to him when he failed his first catholic baptismal test. Before his second trial, the idea of the catechism question and the answer was abrogated. He was so elated at the edict that nullified the question-and-answer sessions. He was baptized but had been told categorically before the baptism that they must bear any of the saints' names. He chose David and Samson for baptism and confirmation, respectively.

The idea of the saints' name being chosen was a disservice to his African identity and affinity. The Reverend who made it mandatory and compulsory for them to bear saints' names bore none. His name was Coey. His name never existed in the Holy Bible, but he wanted some other people he could deceive to bear names of recolonization and lost identities. Who was fooling who in God's name? That was an open daylight robbery on the cultural embodiments of a people.

A name is a code of identification and one should be allowed to bear whatever he or she likes. The idea of willy-nilly was mental recolonization religiosa. Randy had never seen a Non-African bearing a typical African name from his place of origin, but the Reverends thought their African names were not good enough or what to have warranted his dogmatic appellation. Maybe it was done or recommended for their easy pronunciation, but Randy on his own could pronounce all names — no matter where the person came or hailed from. Pronunciation was one great problem Europeans, and most Americans have with African names. He preferred to be called and asked his African name, the meaning, the pronunciation and how to write them than forcing him to bear foreign names he does not know how they came into being.

As children, they played lots of moonlight games till late at night. They felt so safe, and their parents knew that those were the days one did not bother oneself with security around. Before now he played football in almost all the streets and compounds in his village of the old. The football game endeared them to one another in the best of spirit – no wonder his village stood as one of the local derby champions amongst the adjoining villages.

They went swimming, descending, and climbing the hills that shielded the river from the lonely forests. Birds and animals chirped away sonorous and melodious sounds in the serene surrounding. Children then knew dangers but never thought about them and they hardly came or befell anyone of them. When it ever did they were together to comfort and console one another.

Every child wanted to be seen as a model for emulation hence they mostly woke up that early to go to the river to fetch water in groups for their different families in abundance before it was daylight. This would enable them to be punctual at school. Sometimes they went to fetch water from the river and go to school to sweep their apportioned morning manual labour before returning home to get ready for school proper. A civil duty they all carried out with glee. There was no way or the chance to play truancy, and if anyone did, were heavily punished by teachers at school and at home by their parents. No child wanted to be saddled with such humiliating and shameful punishments.

Since most of their parents were subsistence farmers, they practised joint but individualized farming called *Nkeli (a small garden likened to a farm)*. Here they allocated portions of land to themselves, the land they don't know who owns which portion and they hardly completed the farming cycle. They ended up setting traps to catch rodents and other little animals that strayed into them. At one point, most of the traps instead of catching animals caught snails. Randy was the last to catch a snail amongst all the kid farm owners there. When one of the kids met a spitting cobra in his trap, he ran for his dear life. The news ended their farming operations there. No one went back there to harvest whatever was planted. They knew and had seen on some occasions when a cobra is caught by trap the other sex waits around in defence of the trapped one. Whoever came around is almost blinded by its white sticky venom. The cobra has the power of spitting for some meters targeting the eyeballs. If it gets the eyeballs, it gums the upper and lower eyelids, and this is very dangerous when not given a real-time treatment.

They were young and knew all the tricks of the forest and how to survive in them. They knew all through emulations, simulations, and age-old stories. They never took anything for granted as realism was the bane of their real existence.

Christmas and New Year celebrations are held in very high spirit and esteem. Parents bought or shopped for their children from their meagre savings. They bought new clothes for their children and made the best meal available for the festivities.

As a child, he was a member of the catholic choir group. They sang and visited families after the twenty-fourth of December mass service. They sang going from house to house and door to door till about 05.45 hrs of the twenty-fifth of December. These were mostly during the civil war years in his home country. The years that lacked homogeneity in the citizenry's daily plans overlaid and over-imposed structural adjustments by the marauding *muje muje (listening to only forward ever commands)* soldiers in their spheres of operations. They were tin gods in his village and beat people indiscriminately and threatened to kill whoever did not sheepishly obey them. They enjoyed everything in the name of "on active service ". People in Randy's village were forcibly asked to serve them, and they stayed in peoples' houses without paying any rent. Randy's father was almost beaten to death because he dared to ask a soldier that was in all facets human like him why one of the wife's basins of water was commandeered. They beat and stripped people naked in broad daylight and gave people cow dung to eat and urine to drink. The *Naija (a worldwide sobriquet for Nigeria)* soldiers of the Ninety-something battalion that came to his village were barbarous and abyss power drunk. In their so-called intrepidness, misbehaviour and nonchalance toward the local people, they feared going to the war front that was so close to the River Niger delta areas of his now Ukwuani river-based areas. They were impostors and deceptively a figment of their human imaginations. They bore names they could not defend and did things they could not own up to. Things have changed now in the country and no one dared intimidate the other because he carried a gun or because he did his or her job with a gun that everyone

9

contributed through tax money to purchase. The war to Randy's understanding was not fought only by the soldiers of the different branches of the force, but by the collective efforts and individual contributions of the citizenry.

Before the civil war, they danced and paraded masquerades. This was synonymous with yuletide periods. Randy was one of the people that directly wore and carried the suffocating carved wood called masquerade around his face because he could dance and had enduring power and stamina. They travelled by trekking around to the adjoining villages dancing and collecting financial gifts from those that fancied them and their dances. They did these for years before the civil war broke out. No one in the dancing team got a dime from their dancing parades and sojourns in those years of good yuletide celebrations. Nothing was ever shared amongst the child dancers. They danced and toiled for people without conscience but apathy and the heart to cheat them.

Instead of making gains from the gifts, one family whose son happens to be a member of the dancing team cheated and never gave anyone the chance to speak or demand what belonged to the group. Apart from their child in the group, others meant nothing and true to the situation the other children did not complain. Only in later years did it dawn on Randy and others that they were grossly cheated and duped. The same cheating and duping would be repeated when he was in the Choir and Boy Scout movements for the same type of house-to-house and door-to-door singing celebrations, respectively. What a time for obvious and deliberate calculated dupes and cheats of the first order on innocent children.

3

ASOKI-AWOKO

RANDY RECEIVED HIS COLLEGE INVITATION FOR AN INTERVIEW LETTER AFTER SCHOOLS HAD RESUMED for the year. He was so elated and worked so hard to see himself successful in the intended written and oral interview examinations for prospective students.

After he had received the invitation letter for the interview, he became a bit restless and completely engulfed with what might become of his fate in the so much valued test then. He concentrated on his studies since he had finished his primary education and awaiting his college admission.

As the days approached, Randy would go to help the father on the farm and study tirelessly in the evenings. He had felt a hole created in his life that needed to be filled to get even with his much-respected friends who already were in different colleges. One was a good child if he could go beyond his acceptable means of physical working tolerance to help the parents on the farm. Neighbours and every other person around watched a child's behaviour as he grew and made silent and discreet records about him. The girls were highly watched and rebuked if they derailed or were involved in any moral decadence-related behaviour of any form. Generally, the children never wanted anything that would get them into any bad books and as such behaved well before they were ever called to order. Things sounded immaculate but some amongst them still displayed inconsistent and deplorable moral laxity that perplexed the population.

Randy would perfect the bits of help on the farm for the father to be happy in rendering the needed financial help on the day he would be travelling for his college interview examination.

When Randy reached the college compound on that eventful day, the candidates were ushered into the different dormitories for the next day's examination tests. The list for these new entrants came from the State Government well organized and coordinated awaiting list. Before this invitation, Randy's supposed classmates were already studying for about eight weeks presumably. The new entrants would need some catching up and lots of ground to cover the difference created by the unavoidable dichotomy.

As luck and intelligence would have it, he passed the examination that included English language Civics, Geography, Current affairs and primary mathematics (known as Arithmetic).

After his admission year, sports were added to show the physical fitness of all intended new students. It was no mean feat to be a student in those days when things were so rigorous, and the best always went through the drills and hassles. Those who made it knew they were truly amongst the best in whatever field of their chosen endeavour. It was a time of meritocracy and indigent support for some of the best students in the school. One of the friends he made during the interview examinations failed and had to retake the exam the following year — Randy saw him many years later as a respected and successful educationist.

Randy resumed school after the midterm break. The new intakes were assigned to the school dormitories freely in the first few days and were assembled for final balloting into the college houses after some weeks. The house prefects assembled the new intakes and write as much equitable number of ballot papers in the right number of the intakes. The new intakes were asked to choose and open their papers. Whatever house was written on the chosen paper held by the new student was where he will spend the next five or rest of his schooling years as his abode. Randy had gotten used to his Clook house but on this ballot day, he would go to Goon house as per his chosen ballot paper. He did not like it initially but with time became very happy with the multicultural ethnographic composition of the house as the years rolled by.

Internal and external houses were created after the merger of Mareeree College with his college. The population got swollen and the students felt better with the new status quo. As the population got swollen, the old Modern school on the outskirts of the town was turned into Gwoon and Akenzor external houses. Other external houses were along old Agboor / Asiabah road. Students enjoyed the homogeneous, association of their single educational purpose of togetherness and learning from one another.

Students were made to clean their environment and immaculately dress their beds for official inspection. The students did everything with unquestionable allegiance. It would be a problem for any error to be traced to any student or his accredited manual labour portion. Cleanliness competition was held weekly without any prior notification and, thoroughly supervised by any of the controls and checking masters without fear or favour. It was a profoundly serious and happy thing seeing Randy's house win the Shield that was always awarded to them through their house captain at the Assembly hall dais on Mondays. The other house beat their house sometimes to the second position, but Randy's carried the weekly competition plaque more than the other houses. It was noble and pride to be associated with the winning house. Is like winning and being presented with an Oscar award.

At the inception of Randy's studies in the school, the senior students were so militant, intolerable, and indifferent to pain. Junior students would be fagged to submission and when any of them proved stubborn and resistant, the other senior students of the same grade would come to aid the senior perpetrating the act into subduing the junior on the scene to obey their own. It came to a time Randy wanted to go back home for the fear of being fagged to death and more, so everything looked strange for him. He could not comprehend the new ways of life in the school and the mannerisms of the senior students. The new students were called names like *apo, apele, apokapos, (fagging names created by old students) meaning literarily that the new students were in deep slumber when the old students were in school.* All sorts of things were said to castigate the new intakes and other junior students. Randy still remembers one of his classmates who was then a family man telling him that he was leaving the college because of the ill-treatment. True to his quest, Pauletto Oohile left unannounced, and the principal would not have known why he left. Randy will not tell anyone what Pauletto had told him about the fagging fears. He felt so bad to see his juniors in age mistreat him and call him very derogatory names. Randy felt for him and almost acted like him too, but for sheer luck that intervened in his case, he would have gone back home too.

The difference between Randy's school and other schools was that the Principal never allowed corporal punishment among the students and members of the teaching staff. He allowed students to punish themselves like in the military echelon to affect maximum discipline in the school, but not corporal types. Other punishments that were not corporal were worse than corporal in themselves. The seniors and some tutors used them with wanton disregard for the disaffection of the junior students.

After the first term, Randy got used to the system and the created fears in him about the seniors atrophied. He made some friends among his classmates and could relate better with some seniors with time.

The teachers assigned to his college set were all dutiful and probably the best teachers Randy would have used their substantive analogies till adulthood. They were so dedicated and loved to do what they knew best then. Amidst the good teachings by the teachers, laid some bad teachers who always wanted to disgrace, oppress, and dwindle the integrity and the promising light of success for some of the students.

The principal Dr Oaye was a very good administrator and had the wherewithal for multitasking and the associated job peripherals. Mr HO Izhai — popularly known as HOJ then was very respectful and loved by all the students. He never treated anyone with disdain and acrimony like Mr Gue who always relished in his opposite stance. Gue was a nonconformist and a sadist like Mr Abmen. Mr Iamu made students in his class jurisdiction serious. He would conduct impromptu tests and made a borderline for passing the best student. He promised those that passed his tests a good grade in their final examination. True to his words — students who enrolled on his subject would pass it without problems. Messrs. Abosu and Ojizu had their seriousness, smiles, friendliness, and thoroughness with physics lessons. They both made physics look like a child's play. Mr Baigie had deadly looks. He had some very insidious bad manners towards the students. No one wanted any confrontation with him because he never knew the pains other people's children were in by being away from their parents. Mr J2 Joda was nicknamed "delinquent" by the students because he always called any erring student a delinquent. He taught religious knowledge and was too abrasive and insulting. He loved punishing students and savoured doing so. Mr Adenor was nice and made the students love history and physical geography and other lessons he taught. Messrs Obenu and Oogu were authors of some useful paraphrases that made the students pass their terminal and final examinations. Mr Siomhense was nicknamed "Anthill", but Randy specifically called him "Anthill of the Savannah" — a term culled from one of those books he read on the side of his accredited syllabus. He was harsh and had very militant behaviour. He punished most students for any flimsy reason without verification and fatherly forgiveness. He was very high-handed like Gue and Joda. Most punishments he meted out to students were ill-blood based. He loved sending the students out into the bush to fetch some anthills on very flimsy excuses like Abmen would send Randy to bring him some bamboo poles from the bush for no good reason other than wanting to show that he had gotten his polytechnic certificate and was teaching students he thought will not be able to get to where he was. He was a very myopic teacher with a hatred-coated heart. Tropical bushes are infested with some dangerous and poisonous creatures of which the town was no exception. Those tutors that punished some students by sending them into the jungles to fetch them anything without due regard to their safety and life were just dumb with their psychopathic misuse of anachronistic powers. All the bad tutors seemed to have had a competing hearts to show who was more wicked and feared by the students. They forgot that they were planting the seeds of discord for their tomorrow relationship with their future ex-students. Years later, Randy still viewed those tutors as brainless brats without any good judgment of the Dark Age. In the modern world of today, they would have smelt their coprophilia till forced to swallow them. They were too inhuman to the children they were asked to teach and eventually cared for. How could a physical educationist prevent a student from wearing his country's national sports colour on a game's day? Stupid. Arrogating the needless to make a substance in the public domain.

Mr Oobia would remain the students' *primo uno* geography teacher. He engaged the students in one of the most advanced gears of learning in the college. He gave more than enough extra lessons to his students free of charge. He was a committed teacher and worker. Randy's schoolmates set still try to fathom out his unrivalled and tireless ways of imbibing his knowledge into them. He was a genius of a kind in a different world he was with his students. The students were so advanced in Geography even though they were in a junior class. They could pass the senior examination with ease if they were allowed to sit for it. The students later heard it as a rumour that Mr Oobia was going to leave on scholarship for a master's degree program at a university somewhere hence he was almost getting the set of students he loved and was loved in return with passion for advanced learning (even though they were in a junior class). He got Randy's set ripe and ready to control the subject all through their stay in the college — years after he suddenly disappeared from their learning radar. His disappearance never affected their knowledge. They would always talk about him and what he had taught them. All the teachers that followed in the subject found they had no job to do apart from physical geography that Mr Adenor rounded up for the students. Mr Oobia was nicknamed ITCZ (meaning - Inter-Tropical Convergence Zone) by Randy's class while others had other names. The name will resonate thirty-four years later between two direct classmates who for those intervals of time did not meet. They embraced and rode in the same car talking endlessly about their past life in the college and mostly about Mr Oobia's extraordinary knowledge of consistency and unalloyed respect for the students. It was then that, Randy would get to know as a confirmation of what he had heard from his old friends in the college that Mr Oobia had become a professor in one of the respected citadels of learning in their country.

Randy will not forget the arrogance and irretrievable abuse he got from Mr Abmen. He was a Polytechnic neophyte that was intoxicated by his emptiness and inconsistency of purpose. One day, he was announcing the result of other schools in the Eastern States of the country then, when Randy in support of his announcement commented by saying *Ekuhkuh*. The word, in reality, meant nothing but just a way that the schools in question were indeed good. An empty exclamation drew trouble. That was it. He punished him by asking him to go to the bush to fetch some bamboo poles from the bush and in another encounter, he asked Randy to walk out of his lesson classes. Randy as matter of fact preferred not being in his class and found his presence very nauseating and retrogressive. He was a teacher that was intelligent enough only for himself but lacked the inherent knowledge transfer to his students. He was in his encysted world and had a lacklustre human relationship and believed in authoritarian anti behaviour — putting students down with ignominy and disdain. He left the school better for the students unnoticed. The students were happy at his French leave and did not bother asking after him. He had opaque connections to their progress with unrivalled acrimony. Students nicknamed him "Madman" but dared not make him hear it. He was an instrument of unwarranted fear among the students he taught.

There were other tutors in the school that were conscientious with their lecturing and ever ready to help the students overcome their difficulties at any point of educational challenge. These included Messrs Ioyah, Aasun, Cizie, Eddagbon, Areery, Momdu, Mrs Oshola, Mrs Oaye and one Agricultural science master that was nicknamed Dascoria because of his interesting gestures and demonstrations to show what he meant at any point after using some jaw-breaking botanical names that would aid the students to pass their practical and theoretical examinations which demanded much of the terms he used. The possible last in the lineup with the tutors that taught their class set would be Mr Okhaime — a lively instructional communicator the students nicknamed "Dichotomy". He knew his Onions and respectfully taught the students using sometimes what the students called "Conc grammar". These words were so much and brain-racking that one of them stood out prominently — with which the students nicknamed him. He was lively and loved by all the students.

Generally, the tutors were so dedicated while a few others trampled on the realities of that time. Their dedication to their jobs was cumbersome with polished finishing as some of them believed in extreme and concocted allegations to assert their ephemeral positions on the students.

Once the tutors in their designated syllabus led the students, they read well ahead on their own. No wonder most of Randy's classmates had their London General Certificate of Education and the External West African Examinations Council Examinations in their third year in the college. It was a time of positive academic rivalry and competition. Students loved to read and made the very best of the result they could. It was the time when students would cram Shakespeare — Julius Caesar, Professor Wole Soyinka's — The Lion and the Jewel, H.O.N Oboli — Geography, Principles and practice of education by J.S. Farrant, Stone and Cozen – Biology to name but few of the many. It was a time when if any student was asked any question, he bubbled and dished out answers like they were the authors of the books they read. Notable among the students that passed their great results in class three were Joika and Jogoenla. Jogoenla would pass his Advanced level examination in class four — a feat no one surpassed amongst the set but passed after they had graduated.

They had many brilliant students in Randy's set and he will keep singing their praises years after they had graduated from the college. It was a set no one student was able to take the same examination position twice for the duration of their five years college course. It was competition at her best amongst the students. There was no animosity, but they encouraged one another to aspire for greater heights in the maze of knowledge and understanding. Everyone strove for academic recognition. Years later, Randy would doff his hat for most of his classmates adding the needed seriousness for their academic ingenuity. Notable amongst them were: Posai, late Tomjeyan, Javandma, Andaemo, Abdumed, Esowan and lots more for a set that excelled in educational wonders for life careers in later life. If Randy failed to mention more academically talented students is because the list runs to mean everyone in the set. It was a set to be proud of, a set to always remember, and a set to always seek to meet even after those years of educational togetherness. No one was an academic drone and weakling. Randy remembers only two students dropping off the line set for the duration of their five years stay in the college. The remainders won the race on an equal academic footing till the end of the course.

Randy was a cognitive and social noisemaker in the class. When the list of noisemakers for the day was written without his name on the list, its authenticity and veracity were put into question. His class monitor always added his name just out of "might is power". He was older with better body structure build-up than Randy for any confrontational settlements. He always settled for the younger students in the class to make his daily list of noisemakers and it was so without quarrels and questioning till their class set would become seniors in the college. The older students were so infuriated and loathsome of the noise, which came in the form of murmuring in the class with his other younger class friends to the point that they arranged a fight once for one stout Fikhine to fight with him without the class reporting to no one. It was a calculated design to shut Randy up from noise-making that made him stronger in the end. Randy had gotten a small misunderstanding with Fikhine that boiled down to Fikhine dwelling on their age difference and his podgy body structure warned and was poised for a fight which the school authorities never allowed — but the older students in their class would this day validate it in unison — saying "two of you should fight — we will not report and no one should report to the school authorities or any of the school prefects". Randy's intestines and liver started to fail him but his younger friends urged him to accept the challenge at stake. He accepted it and the fight started with no one hailing. The older students called for silence and urged Fikhine to make sure he beat Randy well to make him learn the hard way. While Fikhine was very sure he could beat Randy, he never trusted the

Goliath story. Fikhine started throwing some hot punches at Randy that made the older students happy. The older students with maximum joy and happiness heralded every punch on Randy. The younger students would not let go. They urged Randy on and on as Fikhine pummeled him. He got more than enough punches from Fikhine but fate would set in the next few seconds to decide who would be a winner in the fight. Just as Fikhine tried landing another deadly punch, Randy dodged to the best of his reflex action and landed the only punch that would silence Fikhine and his supporters. The punch landed on his lower lip, tore it and made blood gush out through the rupture at a rate that made the older students stop the fight while the younger students were jubilant — but Randy's body was aching from Fikhine's deadly punches. They quickly called for the fight to end by opening the windows and doors. From then on, Randy would talk without fear and his younger friends in the class would be bolder too, but the names of noisemakers' list writing continued as usual and unabated by the monitor of the class Patwinda. Randy saw the monitor some couple of years after they had graduated. They boarded the same public cab. The meeting made Randy's day because he reminded the ex-monitor of his disregard for the truth. He told the monitor he knew he was a noisemaker but was not as frequent as he made it look like or sound in those years. While Randy laughed over the past, the ex-monitor was feverishly and fervently serious with silent belligerence and unwarranted shame about what Randy could not discern, but it was not his concern to ask or know what was going on in his life or bothering him. Randy was just fine and happy with seeing him again after those years of childish exuberances.

Once they became the custodians of the rule of law in the school, the monitor had no power for his insidious daily list. It was a system the students called "Government hand over". The senior students always handed over to the next set to theirs to be able to concentrate on their final examination studies. The students nicknamed night or all through the night studies for examinations as burning the midnight oil or popularly known as *awoko*. Once the system had been handed over, the outgoing students would have no say anymore in the running of the school system affairs till their last day of graduation.

The power they say corrupts. The excessive type misleads and inhibits the vision of reality. As new custodians for the Government of their intended time's pulpit and dais, some of them started to act militantly — exerting their collective influence on the junior students. No wonder Randy would be involved in a collective discipline of some junior students that would boomerang. Some of the newly elected officers were involved in some shouting at some junior students and Randy happens to have added a voice of cognizance to theirs — that boiled down to one particular junior student drawing a knife on some of the seniors. It almost involved an accident on their way to the dining hall in the afternoon. The school authorities viewed the incident with all seriousness. The new schoolhouse prefects in Randy's set that orchestrated the incident were let go because they felt it was inglorious to punish one of them publicly. The so-called floor members' names were insidiously compiled to make the ugly list. It was a new Government of the day and the euphoria with which it came would soon fade and atrophy into reality and oblivion like every other set he had witnessed in the college.

Randy had been in the school for the fifth year and knew how certain things played out to the conclusion of the school. Rumours started to fly around as to what was going to be imminent the next Monday at the Assembly Hall. The rumour was that a list of seniors' names had been compiled for punishment concerning the incident of the previous Friday. Randy started to question inwardly why his name would make such a list of which he knew that he did not start any shouting but was only shouting in support of his mates. The rumour and the subsequent exoneration of the house prefects who perpetrated the acts of the incidence would be proven at the Assembly Hall the next Monday. As a student, one needed to accept the decision of the Principal and his subordinates hook and sinker. The principal delegated authorities to those who sidetracked the naked truth and misused justice when it was needed most. No appeal and defence was needed before these colossal anarchists of the moment. Whatever was levelled against anyone was so, believed and accepted willy-nilly.

When Randy sensed and evaluated the rumour that had been in the air, he was engulfed with how he could minimize whatever punishment had been designed for the chosen day. The news got imminent every minute of every passing day — corporal punishment had been recommended. He was in no place to prove the veracity of the rumours but had to act intuitively against the impending misfortune and demise he found his support for his prefects on that fateful day boomerang on him. The rekindle and the backfire effect of the incident grew to no bounds in the college. In reality, the incident was a hollow case that bore no injuries or any record and recognizable effect — other than the ephemeral shouting of junior-senior misunderstandings that never ran deep at heart but always bore the hallmarks of every New College Government handovers of which Randy considered a collective childish college exuberance of that day. The authorities had their different colonial mental view, which would not be tolerated in the modern, democratic and technological blissful world of today. Their notions were biased and irredeemably sour in the sense that no one was invited to give any statement in self-defence. They just had their kangaroo court wherever and meted out punishments without due regard to the rule of law. It was crude but acceptable out of sheer fear of age and time.

They say that in every rumour, there are some elements of truth. The talk of the incident resonated in every corner of the school from that Friday till Sunday evening with a constant inevitability. Randy braced for the worst — come Monday. On that day, the names of the purported scapegoats were announced publicly at the Assembly Hall — and the offenders asked to come forward. It was like the modern-day beauty pageant parade before the other students. They were all standing at the Assembly pulpit while others watched them as the sinners of the moment — but the real sinners were aside among the students watching the innocent being paraded. The principal announced their offence and pronounced their immediate public punishment. They would be thrashed fifteen times on their buttocks as each one of them lay face down on the Assembly antiquated, oval table. Some members of staff sat around the table and the students would watch with glee and mixed emotions. It was a message they sent to other students but unjustly. What they did was reminiscent of the flogging of an offender in some religions but the leaders of this religion to some reasonable extent allowed the accused to offer some defence but in their case, it was completely the opposite.

The flogging was carried out as specified and delegated. As rumours had been circulating about the intended punishment, Randy stuffed his buttocks with many short pants to alleviate the intended resultant and concomitant pains. After Mr Joda (alias delinquent) had finished with the flogging, he called Randy and asked him to remove his pant publicly. Randy never hesitated but kept removing while the students counted in elation. He had seven short pants on. Mr Joda repeated the flogging all over again on his bare skin. It was a sadist and very devilish order imposed on Randy and unchallenged by any member of staff. Joda was completely bereft of ideas that were not for intimidating and subjugating students. He raped all due respect that was destined humanly for the students. Randy would for years nurse that injustice and hatred against Joda for that public assault cum ill-treatment. The pains were so excruciating and would be the most inhuman, dastardly, and sadist decision ever carried out on him before then. In addition to the flogging punishment, they would have to do some manual labour which made them lose one week of their much-needed studies. It was a disproportionate and unfair punishment that would not have ever been thought about or carried out on those framed for the list. The authorities openly and brazenly flouted the application of any layout or acceptable laws in the instance. They were satisfied with their medieval inklings on the students that were seen as plebeians in their small world of "obey before complain" — which meant subjugation. Who would complain after serving an unjust punishment, and to whom, and for what? There was no use running when one runs on the wrong road. The authorities were not ready for anyone to be right or openly challenge the status quo — one could therefore run on the right road feeling justified, but made to face the wrong direction that would never reach their insidious characterization of any of their passed and sealed judgments.

When Randy would partake in their school tribal meeting held at Mr Obenu's abode, he would be angry with him for being part of the seniors' punishment. He clearly would not want his person to be part of the assumed misbehaving student. Randy was too void to make any defence in the instance, but would years later regret the hook and sinker nature of his acceptance of the punishments and maltreatment. It was like a broken China that can never be mended. Mr Obenu was Randy's House Master and knew him well enough to comment on him and all that was needed then was always taciturn to any tutor's comments. One was viewed, as being recalcitrant if he ever challenged the status quo — but the judgment strata without any chance of defence were indeed rotten to the core and highly abhorred by Randy. Much as the students abhorred the system it was the accepted norm of the times then. Randy still remembered Mr Obenu's comment on one of his terminal examination reports "Noisy but Intelligent". Randy would not know about his love for him as a student until he had graduated from the college. There was that incident when he came to Randy's village on a visit to a friend when both would suddenly meet. Randy went up to him after he had made his presence known to him and prostrated to greet him as a mark of accumulated African respect. They exchanged some little current domicile information and what was going on in their lives — but more was going to come from Randy's side to his ex-school tutor and housemaster. After the exchange of greetings and information pleasantries, Randy left but was called back after he had taken some few distant steps away from him. He had praised Randy's educational ingenuity as he strode away with his host doubting and surprised at the positive comments. He called Randy back for more in his presence. Since then, his host would tell other people in the village about Randy's educational mettle and capacity. Randy was unassuming and detested people who were and raised their shoulders for no plausible reason. His village had so many unsung academic and sports heroes. He loved to talk about them all, but the nation would lose all their talents to societal man-made blind and inescapable hordes of the reason for non-utilization.

Many things happen to teenagers and Randy at this point in his life was no exception. In the early parts of his studies in the college, he had enough Casava to subsidize the not enough food on the college menu. Processed cassava was locally called *garri, (Manihot Spp — ground cassava)* but the students nicknamed it *asoki, Antioch in Pisidia* and sometimes *saint saviour* etc. *The saint saviour* name came about the student's private augmentation with some days, not enough boarding school food that barely sometimes filled the students to survive the day's intestinal requisition needs. Almost every student brought *garri* privately from home to checkmate hunger. When his *garri* suddenly finished, he would seldom in the presence of some of his classmates help himself with those who still had. Everyone saw him and he never did it without the knowledge of someone being around. One night, he was surprisingly called for a house trial after their evening studies. The case was called by the house prefect Asan who had planned his witnesses' team against Randy seconded by Anum, Ekweren, Kabson and a host of others. Kabson was the most vocal of them all, while Mr Wihuenbor (alias - Author) was intelligent and quiet all through the proceedings. Mr Wihuenbor did not see anything wrong with what was being taken as a serious matter but kept quiet all through the duration of the case while Kabson fumed to create empty fear in Randy. Mr Wihuenbor did not want to be an outcast from his classmates hence he was around all through the proceedings that lasted as long as the seniors wanted it to be till their kangaroo court fake and gang-up verdict was pronounced and heard. He was asked why he took *garri* from some students without their permission and that does he know what that amounted to? He could not believe what was happening. It looked as if he was in a trance but answered that: "he had really taken *garri* twice or thrice in the presence of all the assembled witnesses and house members but that people also took his without letting him know about it. He was quickly asked to shut his mouth. He obeyed out of sheer childish reasoning. Dafabor and Jatags were the crown witnesses against Randy and he never nursed any grievances against them all through their college years — but Randy's perception of the case would change and deepen in his adulthood. He was made a laughingstock, his integrity chastised and grossly abused. All the people involved against him were his seniors in age and could get him ostracized if some instincts of pugnacity were called into action. He accepted the passing of the case against him. It was an easy court of the prearranged verdict to shame him into submission, which he refused to yield to in his tactical own way. The reason for the case and subsequent punishment that followed was because Anum had asked Randy to be his boy service as a senior which he declined by action — as no junior ventured to say "NO" to a senior's demand for such a request. It was a norm Randy hated but could not fight alone. He settled for his way of saying "over his dead body". When he held his ground and there was no way to intimidate or incriminate him, the seniors ganged up to help one of their own — the housing case that did not change his will — even after the pronouncement of the punishment that: - Randy should wash the house toilet for a complete school term. The toilet was a human removable type. The excrement was taken by the school employed night reputable carriers and dumped on a site. The toilet oozed with an indescribable smell that made any stomach go paroxysmal. The petulant and belligerent seniors had won and the insidious but colic witnesses who were his direct classmates were made closer in ties with them. Their testifying against him did not change his stance, stand and belief of descending to serving any senior in any capacity. Randy once said that "If only time could be rolled back, he would have challenged their kangaroo schoolhouse court" to free himself from their clutches, but unfortunately, time moves on to create more beauties and fatalities that will keep regeneration of the human circles more perplexed. For them, Randy had been subjugated and disgraced before everyone and would carry the shame to silence him, but it never worked. Randy would hear decades later that Dafabor was involved in a case of incest culminating in his societal outcast. It was an anathema of an act that was unheard of in his town. He got the sister pregnant but luckily lost the baby. The girl with all her beauty lost face, dignity, and respect in the community much as the person that got her pregnant.

There was that midterm break when Randy remained on the school campus. Most of the students had travelled home for the short break. Within this time, came a very strong storm that carried away the roof of their hostel based in the old Modern school. The incident involved two college external houses based therein. The storm and rain came strongly parri-passu amidst the heavy tropical lightning with the roof removed to create aghast feelings. Fearing the worst, Randy in his swim pant and the late Ugbai ran to make the report to the principal who in turn ordered the school driver to make sure that he packed all the students' belongings under their control and watchful eyes to the old and existing part of the College's Model Primary School. The long building was shared equitably by both houses that had been hit by the calamity. The students who stayed in the school during the break made sure that nothing belonging to anyone was lost during the transfer. Randy respected the fast and workable track of the Principal's decision — maybe that was why he had always been the head since the inception of the school. He considered all the elements of any case that will soon change to most of the annoying decisions ever made in the school after his glorious retirement that was never announced to the students. Dr Oaye would have merited the eulogy and send-off party the students would have thrown in his honour if they had been informed. His departure left a void of incalculable organizational deficiencies till Randy set would leave the school.

Mr Ogbame became the Acting Principal with the retirement of Dr Oaye. Things changed a lot under him, but he would be relieved of the post after some weeks of deputizing.

Mr Ceekmit would assume the leadership of the school as the new Principal. Under him, things got almost upside down. He would always wear his long black pants with a white shirt atop. He never changed his dress. Students wondered if he ever had another wear apart from the same, he wore every day. He was insidious and tele-guided those he entrusted the school's activities to because he did not live on the school compound. He delegated most of his duties to some of the tutors who could not run the status quo unlike when Dr Oaye was in command and made sure that everything went very well with the students. Some of the animalistic set of tutors went on a damaging spree of the students existing codes of conduct. The laid-out rules were flouted flagrantly without due justice and respect by the uncultured sets of tutors the students nursed fits of anger and secretly hated for their hell stands. There were shortages of rations and when students reported, they would be shunned and castigated by a delegated tutor who always called them "delinquent". Randy experienced it one evening and had to settle for his *Asoki* for dinner. Mr Delinquent would not even offer any apology for the students missing out on their already paid-for food. He ended up being called what he called the students completely and vilified with reasons by the students as Mr Delinquent Joda.

As Randy sat under an Umbrella tree enjoying some fresh tropical breeze, he would reminisce over an incident that would have defaced his name and personality in the college. There were that one of the many drivers' wives that liked him so much which he regarded in principle as the senior sister. The brother-sister relationship would be cosy each time she was patronized by Randy. She would make sure Randy had enough of whatever he bought from her. He bought mainly "Arachis hypogea" *(groundnut)* from her door-mouth shop ware display to get his *Asoki (soaked garri)* rightly down his alimentary functioning. She liked Randy so much because of his resemblance with his junior brother of the same age. The nostalgia endeared him to her till one day when the worst would come to get them pit-a-pat.

One Saturday afternoon, Randy went to buy some Arachis hypogea from her on his way from another hostel. They exchanged pleasantries as usual on his arrival. She went inside her house as he stood waiting for her to return and bid her a good day but when she emerged from the house after some few minutes, she smiled broadly and asked if Randy saw the money on the table as she had left. Randy answered in the affirmative that "he had seen it but did not know how it managed to vanish from the table" she said that "but she had left him alone there as she went into the house". She was right but there was one fast action that eluded both of them "an oversight that only luck could rarely find or detect. She would dwell on her point of Randy being there alone, but he would also deny not taking the money but seeing it. Luckily, Randy had only the money with which he had come to buy his Arachis hypogea and had paid her before the incidence came between them. It was the very first time that Randy would see her fuming and suspicious of the inevitable act that could be perpetrated by any inconsiderate juvenile. Randy's side of the story was almost nullified and thrown to obscurity, but he will not let his testimony also go.

Meanwhile, there was one of Randy's hostel schoolmates Joruaye who had come to buy something there when the incident and drama started to unfold. Randy's fear of disgrace and castigation increased on seeing Joruaye. He was Randy's junior by one year but very mouthy and satirically eloquent. If it was true that Randy had removed the money in question, he would go to the hostel, broadcast and chastise him beyond the needed veracity? The social conduit broadcaster he would have been to the other students engulfed and overwhelmed Randy with hidden anger, but he could not leave the scene for the fear of being branded a thief. Randy asked the woman to search very closely and deeply, as he stood motionless, bemused, and angry. She checked everywhere and could not find the missing money. They both knew the exact amount, but where was the money. Joruaye will not leave but kept quiet about what the outcome was going to be. Randy felt bad each time they made eye contact. Joruaye's demeanor spoke of "you will not say anything as my senior in this school anymore "you are a light-fingered brat". Randy could sense his thought, which beyond all reasonable doubts was true of his insinuation. Randy was indeed very Sceptical when the incident was leading him to the college campus. People would believe what they wanted, but he knew could not influence their thoughts for the best from the realities on the ground. Much as he envisioned the worst-case scenario, he knew he was completely innocent but would only be absolved if the core truth of finding the money were met. As the woman saw her little son standing by her, she spontaneously asked him what he was holding in his hand. The little boy would just keep quiet as the mother forced his hand open to see what he was holding. When the little boy's palm was opened, there was the long-sought-after money intact. The amount was exact, and the discovery was made right in the presence of Joruaye. Randy had an unimaginable heave of sigh. Anger welled in him, but he said nothing in the instance. He was happy inwardly, thanking his luck. The name damage that would have fallen out of the incident had been salvaged. The woman started to apologize for forgiveness but her newfound conciliatory and placatory tones after the discovery seemed to have added to the dysfunctional incident. Randy had made his decision never to have anything to do with the woman. Randy stopped passing by her place and even though he did, did not look in her direction till he graduated from the college. Joruaye who would have been the bad news disseminator went up to Randy as they both walked back to their hostel and said to him "you see, you see that woman, you see what people can do "if she did not find the money in her baby's palm of which I am a witness, she would have branded you a thief". He was right but the news would have been over-blown by him on that dry hot afternoon day when students relished and relaxed much with their "Asoki" to cool down the heat effect set off by the blazing tropical sunshine. Randy was the next to the money, but the fast fingers of the little kid created an oversight that would kill their long-time friendship cushioned by what would have been Joruaye's graphic denigrating descriptions of that day's event. Randy thought that had he left the place as the woman went inside her house, no one would have believed him because he was right on the scene and spot on which Joruaye would have capitalized to complete his intended damage and destruction of his character, humility, and personable nobility. His aims got a stillbirth that fateful day that Randy was saved by Mother Nature's natural laws of human existence. Randy would not have gotten any defence but only denial that would have been baseless and useless. Luck sometimes works and saves.

The downtrodden see fully the inconsistencies of any governance and devise ways to wade through what they cannot readily change as a way of life. Progressions in the yearly promotions into the higher class made the ugly experience in the college more manageable. As the students grew older in the school, they start to see things from a more mature perspective and get bolder to handle issues.

The college functioned on an all-around discipline and respect for constituted authority for whatever life had gotten to give and shape their views. They were academically sound and had lots of sports brass of international standard. The college always waived the first term's examination for the students because of their preparations for the school's inter-house sports. The students were made to undertake some cross-country races every morning to keep them fit for the upcoming event. The students would run between fourteen and twenty kilometres to some of the adjoining villages led by some of the college's best athletes. Like every other person, Randy made the race each time they went running the distances.

Before the day of the event, students would be asked to fetch sticks, bamboo poles, palm fronds, palm leaves and some creeping stems that were used as ropes. The aforementioned items would be used for the erection of a canopy where all the invitees and dignitaries would be seated. The musical group was invited by the school authorities to grace the occasion on the "D" day. Schools far and near were invited to contest the best of sports spirit in the relay race that would be the day's climax of the event.

The college would be electrified and agog with people during the events of the day. Students will dress fine and clean, and wear some happy smiles before the visitors of the day. Once the school authorities would not hire a band to play but instead asked the different school hostels to compose a song that went with the name of their houses. It looked odd from what the students had known always and experienced yesteryears. The students did as they were directed, and it went just well with some displays and added colours by the school's Man 'O War group.

This was the college Randy had started his studies with all glee and interest and almost absconded because of the fagging and derogatory statements and comments from his seniors that became suddenly so interesting to him that he hardly took cognizance of the odds of the moment and what would be next. He had grown to maturity at heart and in reasoning. The pains, agonies and sombre moments would mix homogeneously with his studies for which he treasured so much. Much as they had so many drawbacks, they still considered the college a positive builder of human idiosyncrasy with attendant character delineations.

Randy's set wrote their final examination with some of his classmates nursing accrued malice against the school authorities. When Dr Oaye retired from being the principal of the school, the subsequent deputies and principal developed a nonchalant attitude to the day-to-day running of the school. In addition, was the way and manner some of the tutors conducted themselves in a manner that became terrible and unacceptable. Joda, Gue, and a host of others became too recalcitrant, adamant and unbending to reasoning. Most of the students started to sleep without having their share of ration from the dining hall, a meal they had paid for and no one in the school listened to their complaints. The case became very peculiar and pertinent to the finalists that needed that food much to survive their *"Awoko"* *(excessive applications of wit to read longer than one could bear for an examination or test all through the night).* The inefficiency dwell on so many factors that culminated in the blind anger of the finalists that would develop within the ugly period that would have set off an imminent indescribable carnage at the end of their final examination.

When his college set finished writing their final examination subject which happened by chance to be Religious knowledge, the vice principal summoned them for a meeting which was held near the long school building near the Lawn Tennis court. At the assembly, the deputy principal said "you are all gathered and complete here today and luckily after your Religious knowledge subject" a subject that has given and taught you morals to shape your faith and denomination, you might never be completely gathered in life after today, your graduation comes up in the evening and you should all be cool-headed and the good students you have always been" Then came the salvo: - He told them how some students amongst them had planned to set the college ablaze. The rumours had gone round and he had to nip the problem in the bud. Randy could not phantom where the plan had originated and those involved in the planning. Everyone looked at the other in doubt and disbelief. He continued in a mellow and friendly tune. This was one of the harsh men who directly or indirectly supported the whims and caprices of some of his heady staff against the students now toeing a fatherly and friendly line to avoid a dooms day tsunami catastrophe in the school. He ended the meeting with "you are going into the world where you will experience much more than you have seen all the time you were all in the four walls of this college" I wish you all good luck and we meet at the graduation ground in the evening". Everyone dispersed with mixed feelings with no one in mind on who was planning what, but the anger seemed to have rightly welled up in all intending graduands. The accumulated effects of bad governance of the downtrodden commoners were at each other's throats in an intersection of unideological disarray and malfeasance.

Before the final papers and passing out day, all the finalists had made their private arrangements on how they would leave immediately after their graduation on the night of the last day. It was God for us all and everyone for himself. Those students from Randy's area of the country had arranged a cab they jointly paid for. The driver of their cab arrived at the college well ahead of time. They arranged their personal effects onto the cab before they went for their graduation ceremony at the school's Lawn Tennis court. Once they were issued with their testimonials, they left and reached their villages before the dawn of the next day (except for those students that came from outside the state.

During the presentations of the evening events, the principal made a long speech eulogizing their college set but would elaborate on using WAEC as his guiding rules. WAEC in reality means West African Examinations Council but on this day he meant - Warning - Advice - Endurance - Courage. They were the words he elaborated and dichotomized one after the other as a paraphrase guide to the entire graduands. Those who did not get the meaning and sense of the words for that evening must have lately digested them in later years. The meaning of what the Vice-Principal and the Principal said that day had an ephemeral meaning for Randy. He would grow older to relate more closely with the meaning as he ran the invincible life's race. These were words that were used in sending them into the unknown empty wide world to fend individually for them. Randy felt those words and statements, as he grew older. Those statements to him looked fresh as if they had been spoken the previous day, their meaning sinking more and more into him at every passing day of his life. Randy saw these statements so compelling and overwhelming that he longed to see any of his class or schoolmates again. These people he considered his best set of friends contrary to what existed in a modern world of deceptions and misunderstandings. Most modern-day associations were fair-weather friends based on indiscernible life, cantankerous associations and murky materialism.

4

PARACHUTE LANDING

ONCE RANDY WAS HOME AFTER HE GRADUATED FROM COLLEGE, HE WAITED FOR HIS GOVERNMENT posting at his station. He would be posted to his area of the country where he assumed the post of Instruction Communicator for some years before exiting for further studies.

While teaching, he applied for other jobs with better pay and respectable conditions of service. He did not like the solitary-like features of the job he was engaged in. He attended an interview at the State Capital with one of the State Ministries. He met one of his direct classmates at the interview centre. They socialized and were happy to meet themselves again. The disarray in the interview centre was so much that, they lost contact almost immediately with the crowd with the inefficiency and ill-conduct of the organizers. Randy's name was on the list but was neither called nor interviewed. People milled around not knowing what to do. In the end, the organizers had taken a bribe and filled the job opening spaces with names they knew and asked all other applicants to go back to wherever they came from. Randy could not believe what had happened but had to accept the inevitable outcome.

Then, there was another interview invitation letter for him after some weeks for the post of Air Steward with the National Airline scheduled for the capital city. He commended his invitation for the interview but the thought of boarding an aircraft for the very first time overwhelmed him. He travelled to their State capital two days ahead of the interview date. Some family friends accommodated him for one night at the State's capital on his way for the interview. He showed up at the airport and tendered his letter of invitation for an interview to the check-in counter and his name was added to the flight manifest. He was treated as one of their own at the check-in counter. He was issued with a complimentary ticket that would serve his to and fro trips for the interview.

On the day of the interview, the interviewers made a caricature of Randy even though he knew he was qualified for the advertised post. He was made a laughingstock when he was called inside the interview hall. One of the interviewing officers asked him if he was a sportsman, Randy answered in the affirmative and the other officer interjected asking what type of sport Randy liked most. He told the panel he liked Football best and they wanted to know his skills, he also added that he was good at goalkeeping. The mention of that football position made the teasing worst. Randy would be asked to demonstrate how he would act as a goalkeeper if shots were played from different directions to the post. Randy started to jump like a jittery kangaroo before the panel. The panel started laughing at him till they had their fill of fooling him for the day. No single challenging question was fielded from his college curriculum and required abstract knowledge of the substantive post in question. They were still laughing when one of them managed to send him out. He never heard from them and was not worried or expecting anything from them. They had given him his result to see physically. The interview and the insulting panel never bothered him in any sense for a second thought. He was more concerned with his free flight but had gotten an eye-opener in a good society where some filthy people operated with reckless abandon and nonchalance against meritocracy. After all, no experience was useless. No matter how bad an experience would be, they were sometimes needed to get through life's travails.

No one ever knows what befalls him tomorrow and "never say never". Randy was very free-minded and associated so well with the human strata around him. For him, it was "since we existed free on the same planet and place, he had no boundaries for their cohabitation". He associated freely with members of the staff and children in the school. His newness to the encysted and cocooned world may have made him gullible and defenceless to some forms of human acrimony and concocted accusations. There was his contemporary's daughter who was fond of Randy along with others that whom he joked. He smiled with everyone with no boundaries and sinister attachments. One day he asked the girl in question with her junior sister to drop off some brooms for him at his doorsteps. Some weeks later, the junior sister told the mother they had gone to Randy's place to drop off some brooms at his doorsteps. The mother will not tolerate that and must have switched the story for some more sinister designs as she related it to the husband.

One day as Randy lay sleeping at night, then came a knock at his door with a voice so sharp saying "open the door so many a time and furiously". The difference was that he recognized the voice and opened up to find the unbelievable. The husband had come with both daughters to make charges against him before his landlord and his wife, and in the presence of his classmate that they both were posted together from the college to the school in the village. They were trumped-up charges in fairness to his thoughts and predicament. He had accused Randy of seducing his daughter. Once he had levelled the accusation against Randy, his defence fell on deaf ears. He was fuming and warned Randy, in the end, to hand off her daughter. Mr Siku was an aged man and had convinced the Headmaster who hails from the village with him about what had transpired. Randy kept his cool but was too angry at what had happened, something that never crossed his mind in the light it was being seen or viewed. It was all a false accusation of which Randy knew how he got to know. Randy had fallen out with his wife to a level that he stopped visiting Mr Siku and his family. The wife had disrespected Randy some weeks earlier but for fear of family or personal confrontation, he decided against the daily visiting of the family and leaving together in the morning for work as a group from their house. He did not complain but went off the radar of that daily family school affairs contingent. It was on this basis that the wife who already had been nursing unproven malice against Randy had reported falsely what had transpired in a negative sense and light to the husband. She instigated her husband to threaten Randy with submission as he had done.

Randy from that point stayed clear of the family way, even though when it had some official connections, he would employ some tactical maneuverer to evade them all.

Randy forgave their ignorance wholeheartedly and visited the family when he went back some decades later. He had seen the girl in question in the city some years after he had left their village with a baby strapped to her back. They greeted but never spoke for more than two minutes and went their different ways. Randy would hear how the woman in question was involved in mass adultery against her husband. The daughter married and got divorced and the parents rested in perfect peace years apart. Randy still considered them good for they acted within the limits of their anachronistic knowledge and understanding as against what is in modern-day vogue of special understanding and sociable strata. The ideas of hiding and seek or unnecessary preventive measures are now a thing of the past. Positive freedom has come, grabbed, used, reused, and kept till death do people and the free world part with it.

As a teacher and new graduate from his college, he taught informatively. When the senior class was preparing for their final examination, the Headmaster appealed to some of the teachers to upgrade the knowledge of the pupils. One day some of the pupils were disturbed as he lectured them. He asked them to stop distracting the class several times, but they will not listen. It got to a point that he asked them to leave the class for some time to effect sanity. When Randy would peep outside to call them in, they had absconded only to re-emerge as he was going home from the free lessons with Machete. The duo had planned to get Randy beheaded. Randy had no defence of any sort against this unpremeditated attack, but his body reflex and split-second decision made him carry his bicycle up for cover. His friends, who were with him, saved what would have been a dastardly, cold and premeditated murder. After disarming the boys, Randy out of anger wanted to fight back but his accompanying friends quelled the imbroglio.

A day after the incident, one of the boys in question went to import one mercenary from one of the nearby villages called Adeje. The old vagrant of a mercenary had hidden at the footpath end of the road entering the town expecting Randy and his colleague to show up from their rented apartment. Once they were out to the public footpath, the man accosted them and behaved as if he needed some directives from them. He finally asked if Randy was the teacher that had some misunderstanding with one of the boys the previous day. He gave Randy a thundering slap as he answered in the affirmative. His friend Mr Andaemo rolled up his sleeves and started to display to his amazement of Randy some pugilistic acrobatic techniques. Randy tried to fight back but his ex-classmate and contemporary ruled the moment. After they had been waylaid and fought for their lives, they continued their walk to school and made a formal complaint to the Headmaster.

It is customary in the village not to go to the police to make reports of any incident except the Elders of the village had treated the case exhaustively without a reasonable and reliable solution found to ameliorate the situation or aggrieved parties. If one was not satisfied with the outcome, he could then be allowed to proceed to the government of the day to register his or her appeal.

The Headmaster hails from the village and both teachers that were attacked by the atrocious mercenary were from other villages far away. The headmaster wisely and secretly went to the Divisional Police Station with Randy to register the case with a promise to come back if the case was not well handled back home but if all went rightly, they would not come back for anything.

The case was called with the heavy sound of the horn blowing called *Oduh (town crier signs and name to assemble the people to towns square for meetings and deliberations)*. The case was tabled before the entire village with witnesses around. One man was missing in the multitude – the mercenary. He did not come for fear of the inevitable against him. The case was settled to the contentment of Randy with the crown witness being one of the pupils in the crowd now Barrister Frayibo. His question to the Elders was "who is the aggressor and who is more powerful against the other "the man defending with a bicycle or the man with a machete ready to dissect his victim"? The answer was too obvious and made the Elders call for final consultations and deliberations known as *"ije umeh" (the final deliberations preceding the final judgement of any case)* with the inner caucus for the final decision on the case. The right judgment had been made and announced. The pupils were all reprimanded and heaps of blame made and directed to the absent criminally-minded mercenary. Randy did not need to pursue the case further and thanked the Headmaster for his quick intervention and foresight.

Since Mr Siku and his wife had had problems with Randy over their daughter, his Landlord's wife had been casting some suspecting and discerning eyes on him. She had one grown-up daughter amongst many who was in the early years of her secondary school education. She always came home to get herself prepared after school and get back to whatever activity she had daily in the early evenings. Suddenly, the mother started to accuse Randy of him dissuading her from marriage. Randy did not understand what was going on and from where the question and accusation held root. She asked Randy to hand off her daughter because one doctor Bue was asking for her hand in marriage. She continued shouting "this teacher from Uuno, please leave my daughter alone, allow her to marry. Please! Please!! Pleeeease." Randy had no defence other than to watch her in consternation insult him to her fill. Randy neither reported the incident to the husband nor another person. He was fed up with concocting accusations emanating from unscrupulous and unanticipated quarters. The only thing Randy was able to say was "I never wooed your daughter and have no idea about the marriage thing you have just said". It was after the incident that Randy travelled home to report everything to his family. He had been made a subject of too many concocted and insidious stories. The endless fabricated stories attracted all types of suspicion. The fact that these accusations kept coming and he failed to treat them with disdain created some effective weapon to plan his exit from the town without any remorseful acclamation of unrestricted and unproven evidence against him. He made it so for fear of creating enemies around him. Despite the strings of wrongful accusations, he still managed to forge a light string of relationships with them. Randy did not dwell on the wrong side of history. Decades later he visited the town in search of his landlord and wife for a better reunion but would be told they were late. Randy could not deliver the gift he had bought for them but was able to get connected with their children after he had been given the directives on how he could trace one of their children. He did and maintained the relationship with the entire surviving family. As Randy met the most senior of them all and narrated his experiences with her mother over her, she apologized for their short-sightedness and that life had to go on amongst the living. Randy just told her; otherwise, he bore no animosity against any member of their family. They were all lovely and caring people despite their shortcomings.

After all the major incidents in Randy's station, which he saw as human confusion and manmade insecurity, his senior brother went with him to apply for transfer to another station in their Local government headquarters. His senior brother had the appointment planned and asked Randy to meet him up at the Local Government School Board. He asked for permission to go the next day, but his Headmaster wanted to see his lesson notes before excusing him. Randy had been an amazingly fast and concurrent writer. He bent down and wrote his lesson notes in a few hours and passed the same for the Headmaster's endorsement and approval. Once that was done, he excused Randy but asked him to collect all mails destined for the school on his return. Randy knew for sure there would be at least one letter for the school, his transfer letter (if no other was there for delivery as requested by the Headmaster).

Brothers converged at the Divisional Headquarters to seek a purpose. The Officer at the helm of affairs then Mr Efere was good enough to make things fast to Randy's elation. He was transferred to one of the best Model schools in the Local Government Area that will decades later be converted into a college. Randy returned to hand over his letter of transfer to his Headmaster. The Headmaster scornfully congratulated him for the transfer, but it was just a shadow action. He had teamed up with Mr Siku to get Randy demoted in-class teaching rating classification. He never called Randy to ask after whatever he heard or was told about him but went ahead to get him ostracized for all the farce and unproven stories against him. The entire school got wind of the transfer and while some sincerely congratulated him some like Mr Siku shame faced and half-halfheartedly did. As they conducted the morning assembly, Randy left them all for good. It was a respite from an entanglement he had suffered for too long in a village he almost lost his soul to the children that settled misunderstandings with weapons.

Randy made so many friends in his new station and was far from any man-made and concocted problems. His fellow teachers were friendly as much as the school pupils. His new station offered more opportunities for life progression than where he was transferred from. The cosy atmosphere around him brought the very best out of him. His co-teachers commended his attributes and dedication. The new Headmaster eulogized his personality and interactions with everyone in the school. No one here ran haywire and berserk with concocted stories to get him unpardonably smeared. When one of the State School Board Inspectors visited the school for their unannounced inspections, Randy got the best-graded attestation. Much as the goings were good, that did not get his head swollen. He felt he was just himself doing what he was supposed to do but in hindsight and reflection, he became proud of the man he had been. He knew the future was bright but did not let the light get him blind.

He later resigned his appointment to further his education in the capital city. The city was highly and densely populated. The transportation system in the city was good but the unnecessary infrastructure and human congestion made all commuters extremely uncomfortable. The tinkered buses and the minibuses were known as *"Molue" (tinkered metal body buses for mass transit used in Lagos areas of the country)* and *"Danfo" (converted mini buses for more passenger spaces used for mass transit)* respectively were the main commuting auto types plying the city roads. Private taxis and some unmarked private cars are known as *"Kabukabu" (private cars used by their owners to carry passengers in the metropolis)* and added to the mass transit movement augmentation. There was a lot of chaos and deafening noise in the city. The pollution was easily visible in the sky with the obscured sky-scrappers in the background. The air was stale and humid to an almost unbearable state amidst the well-connected fly-over bridges over the lagoons cushioning and intersecting the city.

Lagos is a beautiful city by all standards but lacked maintenance then. It is a city comparable to any other world standard model and in modern grading. Thieves and pickpockets operate in the city with reckless abandon day and night despite the draconian laws passed against their nefarious acts. No wonder, no one dared shout "thief" in any of the country's cities. The shout (if at all) is like soldiers adhering to the blow of their emergency whistle for assembly. If anyone is caught stealing and an alarm is raised in the form of *Thief! Thief!! Thief!!! Or Ole! Ole!! Ole!!!*, at an extremely high decibel to instantly call the attention of the people around for help from the victim, there would be alert and whoever could help tries. That could only happen when the thief or pickpocket is unarmed. These happened daily basis, but when it comes to night and daylight robbery, people never tried being heroes. Everyone ducks for his or her life in the instance. When thieves are eventually caught by chance in the absence of law enforcement officers, they do justice on the spot to the thief. The justice was wearing a necklace — this means wearing the offender an old tyre with kerosene doused on him before setting him ablaze. The people believed the law enforcement officers would not carry out justice equitably after the offenders are reported or released to them. They come back and perpetrate the same acts repeatedly. The release and subsequent counter stealing made the people lose faith and trust in the police. Sometimes, the police are seen as aiding and abetting sins against society. Nowadays, thieves or robbers make some long and sustained plans to achieve their aims. They use months planning and perfecting their "D" day modus operandi. Randy had heard some unverified stories of operational tactics on banks amongst the people, which they use to destabilize the status quo.

Randy hated the idea of getting a human being doused with any inflammable liquid and set ablaze without due justice even though it bothered on such crimes as stealing.

Nowadays, thieves know that people hardly went about with cash and do not keep cash at home in reasonable quantity. The robbers or thieves resorted to stealing from banks without (in most cases) maiming anyone in their operations. No commuter carries huge physical cash around. Transactions are done on papers and signed in the banks that are confirmed for end-of-job agreements.

5

MILITARY SWEEPING DECREES

AT THE END OF RANDY'S STUDIES IN THE CITY, HE CRISSCROSSED THE LENGTH AND BREADTH OF THE country searching for a job. It was an incomprehensible itinerary for him. The unplanned movements would lead him to live temporarily in two major oil cities of the nation. The more he made efforts to secure one the more it looked elusive. At a point, he decided to return to Lagos for a lecturing appointment in the computer school. He taught Communications, Cobol/RPG Programming and Data Processing Technique there for about a quarter of the year. While lecturing, he attended some interviews. Prominent among them was the one with the National Oil Company.

The letter for the other interview he would have attended for the post of Analyst Programmer at the University of Benin did not reach him till it had come and gone. The interview letter went to his address in Warri as he was lecturing in Lagos and there was that very unsavoury situation of no phone to get him informed about the interview. Then, there was no good communication to pass on information for a follow-up. The only way was by letter writing, letters that crept like a snail, sometimes misplaced, missorted, miscarried to wrong towns and addresses and could get lost. The envelope was intact when he received it months later. Randy got to know all that happened in the interview centre when he met one of his friends in the oil city of Warri. He had gone to visit one of his schoolmates in the computer school that was working with one of the Banks in Lagos. It was then he told Randy after he had asked one of their friends that, "Jofua was working with the National Oil Company, and that he just went some days back to resume training". Since Randy sat for the same examination and interview with him, he had used his Warri address because of his going around the country in search of a job. He made his way directly from the bank to the headquarters of the National Oil Company to request his result. The officer in charge was good enough to check the result out for him. He looked at him with a smiling face and said, "You are successful, and your letter of employment has been sent to your Warri address". Randy thanked him and went straight to the computer school to tender his resignation in a manner that would aid his financial cushioning. The proprietor of the school paid in arrears and would not be happy with Randy if he heard he was going for good. Randy devised some stories, which made his accrued salary be paid the same day. He left for Warri the next day morning. He met his letters and had to report for training. Randy reunited with Mr Jofua when he reached Warri. It was there and then that Jofua started to relate how he had gone for the Analyst Programmer interview at the University of Benin. He had heard Randy's name being called several times to be interviewed but, he was nowhere to be found. He, Jofua stepped in to tell the interview Panel that he knew Randy and that he had not seen him come around for that day and that he convinced them that Randy might not have received his interview letter otherwise, would have been around. He was asked if he knew Randy, and he said "yes", I know him so well, he will not be here since the time has gone this far". They embraced one another again to show the long cumbersome affiliation and affinity between them.

Randy had applied for the post of Oil Production Programming Technologist but was switched to Refinery Operations, Boilers and Wastewater treatment units of the Power Plant department. The next day, the training coordinator Seme documented Randy and sent him to his department to commence his training with the other staff. Randy enjoyed the courses as they developed into greater strata with their different linings.

All the departments were assembled in the only Petroleum Training Institute in the country. It was a special Business school that has all the attributes of modern-day equipment for all the branches of Petroleum studies. The tests and examinations they sat for all through the course were challenging, simple and interesting for him. The staff was there purely because they merited their positions but there was that term used to make meritocracy a child's play. Some parts of the country were designated as Catchment areas, which prompted some of the staff to be recruited with less knowledge of what was to be learned in the training and carried out in the Refinery plant. These set of people flunked the tests badly and disgracefully, but they stood the best chance for promotion and advancement in the country. Meritocracy was flouted with ignominy and the safety of the equipment and staff was not duly considered. An Italian contracting company oversaw the theoretical part of the pieces of training while a Japanese firm took charge of the practical pieces of training. The difference between meritocracy and favouritism showed under the Japanese knowledge microscope. The Japanese instructors will not accept ninety-nine-point nine percent as a good result. They wanted to see everyone making a hundred percent listing in knowledge. They felt bad with some aided catchment staff but could not do anything about it. The government had spoken, and it had to be followed to the letter as specified in their gazette.

Randy never had to redo any of his tests under the two International consortiums. Some basic courses took place in Petroleum Institute Warri while some main courses were arranged for the Karefinery, and the town where every trainee will converge after they must have all ended their training. The Power plant operators were the first set of trainees to leave the Warri training centre for the new Karefinery to commission their unit and the first set of staff to engage in direct official work before their other counterparts joined them. Randy's unit worked along with their Japanese counterparts for the commissioning of the power plant units.

After the commissioning and working for some time as a panel operator for his unit, Randy had an interdepartmental transfer from the Refinery to the Pipeline division of the National Oil Company. He found his new job challenging and interesting. There was lot to learn and committed to memory for very fast system operations and monitoring. He would however be a master of the job under the good teachings, guidance, and directives of Mr Nademe. Nademe was Randy's primary school classmate that engineered and aided his crossover from the refinery. They had reunited at the training centre in Warri and knew they would be meeting again in Kaduna when they would finally be on their job units of the company. It happened and friends would be friends again and better placed in trust as adulthood checked and crept into them.

Not quite weeks after Randy had crossed over that he would be nominated for further training in Nederland. Nademe happens to have been in the first batch of the trainees and Randy in the second. The second batch was made up of six employees. The training company had made particularly good plans well ahead of their arrival. It was in the middle of the biting winter months that they arrived and had to be issued with some heavy winter wear that made them look like astronauts after dressing to go outside. It was an all-rounder training in structure and workability. One of the trainees in their group got sick before the end of their official time. He returned weeks later after getting fit.

Their flight vessel to Nederland was the National carrier KLM. It was Randy's first long haul and his first intercontinental flight. They had a day flight on a day the weather was so clear and turbulence-free. The conditions and coupled with Randy's sitting by the aeroplane window made him watch life below in their tiniest mode of formations. The Sahara Desert had so many colours that intertwined with one another to give credence to her natural beauty. Randy kept his neck in that position most of the time till the early winter weather swallowed his view underneath the aircraft.

One of the teachers from the training company noticing Randy's positive progressions in his understanding of the training jokingly requested he stay back while others were gone. Randy declined the offer with a wry smile. He had declined but knew that if he got serious with the teacher, he would have made it possible for him to stay back. It was one life offer Randy would regret later in life to have shelved aside despite the glaring chances associated with the request. He later considered it a loss of toto-lotto he won but later lost the ticket for claiming the prize. He will not accede to the demand for him to stay because his Government had spent a fortune this far to get him trained for the technological advancement of his country. He, Randy was part of that collective advancement of what they did not want to betray. He would use the resultant knowledge to upgrade his practical knowledge whenever he returned home to his other colleagues but the powers that be strata in his station would alienate and fizzle out his newfound technological knowledge into a minus zero operational ambiguity. It was a system where invincible hurdles of digression, careless attitude and nonchalance arising from sheer indiscriminate disregard from a brazen bad planned management organizational structure existed. The same system still existed and has become a cankerworm in the status quo of the company fueled and funded by the Government of the day. It is one of the reasons why in that country some of the refineries stopped functioning. Now the country that had three refineries and would have capitalized on their chance to get more just in a short time started to privatize their chances and ended up in shrewd crude export overseas and in turn buying the finished products back into the country. Some oligarchs and power brokers invent what profits them with wanton disregard for the masses. How could a population survive on two dollars per day reckoning? Randy felt the pain and shame the country had been drawn into.

While Randy was with the National Oil Company, he graduated from Pennu to Gaspen Labour Union strata. He was the first entire Northern zone senior staff Gaspen union, secretary. He was returned unopposed because of his intrepidness, tenacity, sincerity and openness to other matters. He had before then a stint in the same post in his zone. He realized later that unionism in his country was a waste of time. Union leaders were easily stigmatized, profiled, persecuted and caused endless pains in various forms. When that happened, all members hate to fight for their fighters for fear of losing their only connection to the world of survival. The blessed assurance job, and till their kingdom come yours obediently jobs. They end up in serfdom because they are afraid of change. It is just the direct opposite of their counterparts in Europe and elsewhere outside Mother Africa. If people do not believe and cannot fight for change and cannot be bold enough to stand by those fighting for them, their lives and future are doomed, if not in the short term, surely in the long run. Randy had always believed in fighting for justice rather than dying in perpetual subjugation, massive oppression, and extremely uncomfortable tailgating.

Randy trusted the working mechanisms of his mental pulleys. He had no fear of doing the right things at the right time. Much as his understanding and trust on the job never waned from the local official technical managers' misdirections, they felt threatened by Randy's rants and presumed arrogance. The local management on that note started to make some insidious traps and invincible hurdles to get him derailed. Randy was thought to have known too much and had chains of informants within the organizational structure. The entire staff trusted him highly and revealed more than enough shady deals the leading officers perpetrated against the company to him. He would never reveal or compromise his source of information since he was entrusted with their official welfare. The branch management feared this setup and he knew exactly what they were up to. Since they knew that Randy had no godfather in the company to cushion his unionism and position from their insidious designs, and when they would finally carry out their sinister formatted agreement, he found himself standing alone. None of the union officers tried to defend his rustication and all other members of staff just looked morose and indifferent. Randy heard and read years later that; his Chairman Delomo ran into a worse problem with the Government of the day. He was detained along with Manire and many others over the super welfare plans for the Oil company staff that they all started fighting for before he left. He hardly went to the root of the matter again to know how they must have ended their engagement with the Government. He had had his and gone off the radar of unionism. After all, he was the first target and victim of a decadent system of "see all and say nothing, swallow it hook and sinker to die or live if you are lucky".

Randy must have lost with the company, but it was better to go into a greater and better world unprepared than into a Government prison where one hardly survived those harsh and intolerable human conditions, and if one did survive would be silenced in all forms forever. The worst is that the person will never be the same again biologically. One's body structures would be exposed to invincible calibrated dangers that would take luck to survive if one had the means to get medical attention otherwise the invincible decapitations would ruin or kill the victim in the end. Most managers at that time were incompetent and impostors. They relished in duping the company's lifeline, survivability and risk management systems. The thwarted and mismanaged systems were carried out by the officers and their accomplices to sabotage the efforts of whoever was conscientious with his or her duties, but it bothered much on the technical staff more than the Human Resources department. Most of these problems came from the Head of the Human Resources department Mr Gui and Mr Eju on the petroleum operations front who had so many skeletons in their cupboards. Mr Gui always made the transfer of aggression arising from his marital and domestic affairs to people he knew or believed were standing against his dubious ways while Mr Eju had no operational ability to run the staff under him. Both managers were like leeches and saprophytes on the knowledge of the officially downtrodden. Both managers would insidiously accuse Randy of meddling with the political system in a concocted query. These ran for months with their constructive dismissal. Randy knew what was coming and was ready for it unapologetically. He knew he was right and will go with his head raised as a victor over devilish men in a corrupted and smelling system. The managers were Randy's detractors that allowed their emotions to overpower their intelligence.

Randy did his job diligently with certainty. The laboratory Chief trusted him so much when it came to calculating petroleum interfaces and batches. He was once asked to discontinue his annual leave because the system was expecting their first Venezuelan crude through their system to their station in the Northern part of the country. Randy had gone to visit some of his friends in the southern station of Warri. When he got into the Radio Room to greet his colleagues in the Northern station, the voice he would hear after the greeting was that of the Operations Superintendent. After exchanging greetings, he asked Randy to cut short his annual leave that, the station needed capable hands to track and receive successfully the first Venezuelan crude to the Northern station from Warri southern station. It was the very first time his intelligence and the good job would be acclaimed and certified but for their self and post-aggrandizements. Randy obliged and immediately left Warri for his village. He told his parents why he was cutting short his annual leave. They wished him well in his chosen field and life.

Randy left the next day for his station and resumed duty almost immediately to the adulation of the Operations Superintendent and his supervisor Puruk. Puruk was a dedicated supervisor like Nademe. Randy could communicate and knew much about Petroleum dispatching from Nademe. Randy's working with him made him align better with Puruk when he would replace Nademe as the supervisor. Before the arrival of Puruk, Kibeeman the American who was contracted to run the system with Nademe and others, Randy had been taught much of the systems operations and calculations much as Nademe had imbibed more than enough information into him. Kibeeman was a workaholic that treated his counterparts with respect as to the man who succeeded him after his departure. Dakays who succeeded him was arrogant, an incriminating renowned faultfinder who because of his uncooperative attitude was transferred to Pipeline Headquarters. He displayed his unfriendliness and uncooperative attitude to the Station staff there and ended his contractual attachments to the company there. Randy could handle any situation and challenges unsupervised before the arrival of Dakays but his archaic systems and unnecessary faultfinding made him always lock horns with him. It was a department one never messed up. The department required an exceedingly high knowledge combination and multitasking attributes because of the overall sensitivity of what the job entailed. It was knowledge and safety first to all. It was not a job for the weakling and lily-livered.

Randy had copied the information about the Venezuelan crude from the southern control station when he was asked to cut his annual leave short. On resumption, he recalculated the operational flow again and reconfirmed most of the numbers. Reconfirmation of numbers of varying degrees and summations was the base ethics and tactics for the job. The Chief Laboratory Controller was very elated to see Randy come back to resume duty for the new challenges ahead. Randy's love for his job rose from when one of those past batches of operational handlings was saved from product contamination. He was on night duty with the laboratory technician around. The laboratory technician seldom comes for night duty unless the station expected an interface that was being tracked during the nighttime.

On this fateful night, Randy had recalculated the interface time of arrival when he resumed his night duty. He informed the laboratory technician and the kapipeline system's operators with added assurance. Both departments always trusted Randy's calculations and were happy to be on the same shift with him. The Kapipeline operators would transmit their timing and loggings to Karefinery operators for necessary operational actions. The Karefinery made her calculations much as the Kapipeline made theirs too but there would be counter and counter refusal of mathematical adherence as the night wore on. The refinery department had to liaise with the Pipelines department and compare times to know when the head and tail of the interface will reach the Kapipeline sampling Bay to avoid contamination. Interface not well calculated and well cut or segregated causes petroleum products contamination, which in turn causes lots of explosions and blowouts to the unsuspecting end users. Adulterations are rife among roadside sellers too. The quest for gain and lack of knowledge of the danger petroleum products posed to the layman on the street causes a lot of problems for the end-users too. In an exceptionally large country like Randy's, the government depends on the good segregation job of the products by the Pipeline Oil Operators to minimize accidents and causalities to the teeming population.

This night would mar or make Randy's linear line of progression on the job. There would be so much demand and test for his accrued knowledge from the most unexpected quarters of officialdom. After giving out his shift instructions to the night duty station operators and the laboratory technician, he went to his petroleum dispatching office desk to monitor and control the crude line and finished product lines via the customary radio communications. The radio had remarkably high atmospheric interference at night making communication almost impossible between stations. The night wave interference made stations not do the right things at night, but the experienced dispatchers and operators knew what was happening with the hourly rate and what sub-stations were involved. Experience superimposes the radio communications at night. There is no luck in Petroleum dispatching — the worker is the human sensor where there is equipment failure. One needs to look for the problems and get them solved before it becomes hydra-headed. In an advanced world of modern technology, desktop computers, cell phones and other cornucopia packs of assorted gadgets must make it possible to eradicate what used to be communication problems.

The refinery crew on this particular night and because of the sensitivity of the Venezuelan crude started to make endless calls to the Kapipeline operators and the Kalaboratory technician to keep to their Karefinery time calculations. Several times they asked the Pipeline night shift workers to go to the sampling bay and they will in turn call on Randy for confirmation. The calls became nauseating that they had to be referred to Randy for agreement. Randy gave a standing order to the operators and the laboratory technician, "don't listen to anyone except to the daily and shift revised written instructions edition from me" tell the refinery staff that your dispatcher has given you your daily and shift instructions that you are adhering to as a rule, and that anyone in doubt should contact the dispatching department of the pipeline unit". They trusted Randy's operational instructions and when the refinery would call them again, they told them exactly what Randy had instructed them to do. When Refinery night workers could not take it anymore, they became jittery and belligerent and called Randy at about 02:00Hrs to tell him that the interface was at hand and that they were coming to make the operation as was necessary with the Pipeline night shift workers. Randy objected to their demand and asked them to take things easy, that the interface was still too far from their projected time. He told the contracted British accented man that the interface head was going to be in the station at 06:00Hrs and would be followed by the tail some few minutes later. He added that should any problem arise from his calculations and decisions; he should be held fully responsible and accountable. He said by his calculation, it was due at 00:00Hrs but it was past two-ante meridian and Randy was still telling them about four hours away to wait. The British man tried in vain to exert his expatriate positional power in vain on Randy. Randy was sure of his calculations and will not bulge or look for any uncalled-for directives. Randy told him quietly that he knew his onions added to how he had been on the job and how he knew the rudiments that applied to all intricate situations, like the night in question. Randy was undaunted and asked Mr Eonu the laboratory technician to go back to his duty room and never take any order or instruction or heed any hysterical call for any change of time. After all, he was working directly with him Randy. The Buck stopped with Randy on the shift. The same instruction was passed on to the station operators on duty.

From then on, the Pipeline department was in control while the Refinery department got jittery and had to come with their operational entourage fidgeting and looking dazed. They went to the laboratory technician and station operators to talk about the event of the night, which culminated in their inviting Randy for the baseless meeting. Randy repeated all he had talked over with them on the phone. Before Randy left them, he knew the error the British man was involved in his wrong time calculations. Randy asked him two questions about his calculations but his answer to Randy was grossly faulted. Randy did not want to embarrass him as an expatriate but reiterated his position and instructions before leaving. The pipeline staff on duty had not seen Randy work with utmost authority and assurance like he did that night. The Refinery staff reluctantly left after that. Randy knew what was on their mind but did not bother about their decorous deadly plans against him should he fail his interface time. He smiled at what he knew they did not know about the system's calculations. If he failed, they would accuse him of not listening to their superior knowledge and level more incriminating charges against him. When they left, everyone started to ask what the Refinery staff thought they were. Pipeline staffs in the instance were no pushovers or dummies. They knew their individual designated jobs beyond all reasonable doubt and how to get them done to a very meaningful end. One of the staff said, as they drank tea, "They don't know you". Randy smiled as others seconded the eulogy.

Randy's success on the job did not make him pompous nor did it make him arrogant. At 05:45 Hrs, he called the laboratory technician to get ready and leave for the sampling bay and informed the station operators accordingly too. The refinery staffs were already around before his final instruction for them to be at the sampling bay. They went collectively to the station's sampling bay. No sooner than they had started sampling, the interface arrived at about 06:02 Hrs. and the tail followed some minutes later. Tanks were switched accordingly and successfully. As the operation went on, everyone looked at Randy in uttermost amazement as if he was from outer space.

The British expatriate came over to Randy and shook his hand and said publicly "you are intelligent and know your job very well, I have all respect for you and for whatever you truly stand for, thanks for a job well done". As he praised Randy so too did his night shift Kapipeline colleagues. The news went around like wildfire in the station. The powers that be in the station did not like it but had no open way to circumvent the truth. They embarked on the worst against Randy but the Lab Officer will from then on seek or consult him for all interface arrival times, even when Randy was going to be off duty or make a daily handover of shift. The system "two Dee" stations would also request his calculated times for eventual interface arrivals to their respective stations. Randy had become versed on the job and made the right projections. Good things they say, don't last out unbalanced controlled times. Much as Randy knew he was dedicated to his chosen field of endeavour with all gusto, the head of the human resources had avowed secretly to politicize and jeopardize his trail of successful endowments. They had the power over him in their belief that Randy oscillated without a connector. Randy was a loner without any certain godfather. Queries started to follow one another on flimsy excuses but the truth was that they were based on his being a strong member of the workers union. The officers arrogated more than enough unwarranted powers of evil against humanity. Randy still wondered why queries in Oil Company would have any political lining and leaning or, at worst, anything to do with the political structure of a nation. The electioneering campaign in the country was done outside all official premises of any functioning office, be it private or governmental. They were insidious, concoctive, and lacked the merit of being juxtaposed with the political attributes that existed at the time. They were corrupt all through their brain and in their heart of hearts. There was nothing Randy could do against a military dictatorial system that had decree set in place against ill-treatments, unwarranted and constructive dismissals. Randy's case had been secretly discussed and passed for the worst at the headquarters awaiting the doomsday. The waterloo came and he ceased to be extant in the company. It was a gross misuse of official power that had prevailed over innocence and sincerity backed by military decree number two at the time that avoided redress in any court in the country. Any aggrieved government official was not allowed to go to the court to contest any injustice meted out to him or her and for a redress of any kind. It was cancer the military used to infect the noble at heart citizens of a nation they forcibly drew with a chain against their collective will on their potholed roads of backwardness. It was a, take it to hook and sinker system and the National oil company took advantage of the decree as one of the Federal government's parastatal entities.

From then on he knew that anyone could be victimized and that no one was indispensable for any reason. He went in search of new jobs and was ebbing away in quality and substance as the years went by. He started to hide from persecution and from being trivialized. He could no longer make ends meet and had to curtail and shrink his abode. His fair-weather friends started to gossip about him while only a few stood by him and still remembered what he stood for. They became friends today and enemy tomorrow. Some friends like Dili, Baroh, Sifo and very few others stood by him while most looked the other way or pretended not to see or know him whenever he was met outside. It was the loath-some time that would drill him through the hardest mills of life to keep him shining like gold in later years.

6

MISPLACED TRUST

HE OUTWARDLY LOST HIS PERSONALITY, DIGNITY AND RESPECT. HE LOOKED TOO INFINITESIMAL TO be reckoned with then. His son Eony died and no one among his old friends and family came or sent messages of condolence to him. He understood that life was not for the lily-livered but for those that stayed focused and decided on targets. He utilized his self-made hard discovery. "We came to this life alone and will go back alone". The more Randy failed the more he got extant at heart. Nothing pulled him down in his worst of times and predicaments. He had learnt how to meander through his problems but lacked the financial wherewithal but trusted he would be out of it. When under these tantalizing mirages of circumstances many conflicting thoughts arise. It would be up to one to get these cornucopias of ideas weighed, sifted and sanitized to make the best decisions that will put one forward a step ahead in the present.

After some years of his constructive dismissal, he got employed as an Operations Officer with an Independent Petroleum Marketing Company in the ancient city of Sokoto. He had much to do as per the demand of his post for the company, but the Director of the company settled for the unaccountable dispositions of his brother who had no oil ideas and experience to superimpose Randy's authority on the job. Randy had a heap of files to work on but the director's brother will not give any account of his transactions needed for updating the files. There was daily gross rape and erosion of authority on Randy's position and personality from the day he resumed duties till he was dumped. Randy worked there only as a number while the director's brother did the job crudely with unacceptable, unaccountable misappropriation away from the official norms in the most disagreeable financial structural imbalance and non-commitments.

The director would not trust Randy because of his religious biases. He made him work on public holidays and made sure he was locked out from all company official information. Much as that would be, Randy was never worried but wanted a way to get out of the messy situation. It was a family business rolling down the slopes with no sequestered forthright directions.

The director was one of those prominent people in the society that upheld and exuded outward religious chastity but behind the scenes ruffled his sanctity in the infested smelling spirogyra-laden mud. He was always fondling the non-compromising office secretary in the office. The secretary objected endlessly to his immoral amoral conjugal moves to her, telling him about her boyfriend Ansilova always but the official power broker will not let go. That continued unabated till Randy left for good. When Randy would go back years later to visit, she had left out of desperation for another job. Randy knew years later that the director's actions were part of an international moral menace and decadence. He had seen the same in many countries as some people accepted and approved of it as a natural obedient structural instinct of conjugal attestation and association. Some managers or people at the helm of official affairs took advantage of the unprotected and the willing to misguided ephemeral moments of the victims' lives.

When things got worst in the northern city of Sokoto, he was enticed by his family to fall back home, an agreement he hates to give hindsight and still regrets conforming to after so many years. Randy would not dwell on the murky happenings or things that transpired then but were enough to have involved hatred between him and members of his family. Those days he spent at home bordered momentarily on exceptionally agonizing woes. He realized that there was no family without their misunderstanding and malfunctioning points in variations unacceptable to them to create a fracas.

Things had fallen apart almost irretrievably to a point only the brave can reset for continuity. It was a soaring sour sore of a situation.

He had gone through some unsavoury moments and acrimonious life that was not of his design. He forged ahead during the thick and thin of the life-infested battles and tribulations. Randy left for Lagos and later to the northern part of the country. As time wore on without any mercy and success of securing any job, he started to contemplate so many things on how to get his sandwiched position better, but most paramount on his mind was how he would exit the country. Enough was enough for his foreboding.

During this time, he met one of his childhood friends Jekilo in Kaduna. Jekilo had come from the United Kingdom to visit his family in his home country and got stranded. Randy would have helped him out of his entanglement if he had the means but was out of a job before they met in the city. The flame of old friendship started to blow and blossom between them. One day, Jekilo told Randy he was going back to London after so many months of trying to garner some money. Randy asked him if he could help him to repair his malfunctioned camera that he bought from Holland years back. Jekilo accepted and asked him to bring it to him. The arrangement was that he would get it serviced or repaired before posting it back to him. Things will always happen in very unexpected quarters. Jekilo left with Randy's camera and never stayed in touch with him till after about ten years. Randy afterwards got domiciled in Germany and travelled to England on a visit. Before then, Randy had gotten his number from his ex-niece with which he communicated with Jekilo about three times to let him know he was coming on a visit to the United Kingdom. Randy eventually met him but did not ask after his camera anymore, but he guessed he knew what was on his mind that he did not want to voice out. Before they left Jekilo's abode, he asked Randy what he thought about their joining to own a joint business venture. Randy gave him some quasi look and answers to hope in him but needed to project his hindsight and cogitate thoroughly sifting all that mattered before asking further and hoping for anything that will bring them together business-wise. He had met the stone he threw years ahead of him. Once a cheat, they will remain a cheat in so many forms.

7

INSIDIOUS NOTORIETY

AFTER HE HAD LOST HIS JOB MONTHS BACK IN SOKOTO, HE RECEIVED A MESSAGE FROM HIS HOME village that the money owed him by Bivasco was about to be paid back to him. He was not happy in any way at the news. He had more than five years back on trust, as neighbours and childhood friends have given Bivasco some thousands of dollars for him to pay his school fees from far away from the United States of America, but Bivasco ended up utilizing the money for his self-aggrandizement. The dollar was then selling at sixty-seven US cents to their national currency on the international market bank rate transaction. Bivasco enjoyed Randy's sweat and toils only to pay the money back from the States through the father after the national currency had lost more than about ninety-five percent of its value in the international market. The family would beat their empty chests because their criminally-minded son had sent the money for repayment. His immediate senior sister at the crescendo of the money palaver engaged in insulting Randy's mother indirectly but in town cry mode. She had no element of shame to have town cry on her myopic assemble. It was pure and sheer ignorance that transcended the family lineage. They were shortsighted and overwhelmed by their deficient economic calculations. They lacked what mathematical financial values equation meant. His people were psychologically blind and failed to see the heinous magnitude of what their brothers and sons had done to trust as a human value. The family failed to realize that both brothers had set Randy and his children on a slow, silent crippling death that would take years to stabilize if they ever survived the two brothers' devilish insidious designs. The family would have known better that, what Bivasco and his brother Biwo had caused another man along with his homestead was an agonizing and unpardonable crime. Their effrontery was an abyss. It got to a zenith without any known or recorded apology from the direct perpetrators and the family in general.

Bivasco had gone to India from where he went to the States for further studies. After some years, he came on a visit to his fatherland where he rightly belonged. He got stranded after some time. He could not go back to continue his studies in the States. When Randy came home from the city where he was working with the National Oil Company, he met Bivasco and was happy to reunite with him as childhood friends. They exchanged mails while

Bivasco was in India. He would sweet-talk Randy with his stints abroad. They discussed what it would take Randy to be there to study. After all Randy had always had plans to go abroad to study and his childhood friend would serve as a better ladder to throttle his wishes into the right gear and get going. The discussions meandered till the financial breakage of what was needed. Randy had the money and assured Bivasco he would go back to his station in Kaduna to fetch the agreed and required amount for him to effect the payment of his one-year school fees on his return to the States. He had been Randy's friend and neighbour since childhood. Randy had no reason to doubt him, he believed he would carry his message to a meaningful end but, unknown to him that he was on the off to his demise. He was unknowingly asking Turkey bird to vote for a Christmas, which was very impossible for what the ominous result would be. Randy went back more than a thousand kilometres to his station to fetch the money and later added some thousands through the junior brother Biwo. The idea was for Randy to have enough money on arrival to the States as a freshman in the university.

Bivasco returned to the States and was in contact with Randy. He would claim to have secured admission for Randy but would not send in the originals of the different letters of admission. He finally sent some photocopies of the letters of admission, which could not be used to secure a visa for Randy's travel to the States. The American Embassy office in Kaduna marked his passport out of further official processing of his documents for non-availability, submission, and confirmation of original copies. They were right doing their job. Randy was now tied to fate. He could not pay new school fees for his secured university admission to read Aeronautic Science at Embry Riddle Aeronautic University at Daytona Beach-Florida and to major as a Commercial Pilot at the end of his studies, but his money was tied down or confiscated thousands of kilometres away by Bivasco and could not be reached again with time. Bivasco had put his friend in a worst and most pitiful dilemma. Randy's educational plans had been tied down as Bivasco started lying and relishing in his dubious craftiness. The truth and reality started to get around the air. Bivasco had boasted before returning to the States gleefully about how he had conned, cheated, and duped Randy. On that note, Randy went to Bivasco's junior brother in Lagos to demand a refund of the money he had given to him to remit in addition to the money his brother already had in the States. Biwo claimed he had sent the money to his brother in the States but when Randy would demand the evidence and proof of remittance, none was shown to him and none was presumed to be forthcoming. He now knew something was amiss but was too late to give a good chase to right the wrong. Bivasco denied ever getting any additional money from his junior brother. Randy did not believe any one of them anymore, but said, "whatever was the case, the money was with both of them but Biwo had to give his part back". It took some concerted efforts of the village head and some family deliberations to get him paid back in patches from Bivasco's junior brother. Randy had gotten their shrewd, cover and screw-ups divulged, annotated, and understood. The relationship between friends and families got sour to an irredeemable level, Bivasco and his brother Biwo had created a feud among once very happy families. The once happy and easygoing families drifted and thawed apart. The two brothers had created a human gorge that will never metamorphose into a flat plane. They had caused intractable goose-pimple they will in years pretend they never knew the source. It was pure inhumanity to man.

As Randy communicated with him, he would sweet-talk him acting as if things would be all right within some days. It was not surprising, therefore, when Bivasco will ask Randy to carve three different school stamps in the country for his private certifications. Little did Randy know he was aiding and abetting in forgeries of very high magnitude. Randy regrets the action years later for having done what he did even though he would have gotten his way through Bivasco. It was partaking in a crime unknowingly. Randy was not as wise as to stay clear off the crime of that time. He felt he was helping a friend in a foreign land and so much in need. Randy realized that he could help any of his friends but surely not with certificates and forgeries. The stamps were neatly carved, packaged and posted to Bivasco in Fremont-Ohio State.

Randy thought about why he would have been registered continuously for fifteen years in one of the American Southern States' higher institutions of learning for his first degree. He could not graduate within the normal duration for Engineering and that was probably because of his mental instability condition which he was diagnosed with and medicated. He is still under the mental imbalance qualification in fairness to Randy's human summations. When he finally finished at the university, he had a similar problem while attempting to get his stillbirth master's degree. Not only maybe was he having problems with English language competency, which was very compulsory and highly required and demanded by prospective employers but also his academic diminishing returns were deeply questionable. In places like Texas, there is a standard written English competency examination required of any Technical, Engineering and Pharmacy students. Companies made it compulsory by protesting to all Boards that accredits Universities because most of the graduates of those standing and qualification were finding it increasingly difficult to write amazingly simple technical reports when they were employed. The course must have held Bivasco hostage or back and if he ever passed it must have paid somebody to exchange face and personality for it. When he eventually managed to graduate, after that long stint at the university and applied for a job at one of the largest and most noble conglomerates, he was not offered a job and people hardly knew why it was so. All the people heard later was that he protested to the Equal Employment Opportunity Commission alleging discrimination on the part of the conglomerate. The Conglomerate relented and offered him the job. The Conglomerate reversed its decision not to hire him after the intervention of the Equal Employment Opportunity Commission. Despite his being employed, the Conglomerate must-have in the first instance called the University and made appalling discoveries that dwell on his duration of schooling, repeated many courses, poor grades, stay on extraordinary circumstances and most of all disability act to protect people that are handicapped citizens from being discriminated against. If the Conglomerate had the above information about his mental imbalance and he did not acquit himself properly during the interview process, in that case, the Conglomerate would have been forced or compelled to reverse their decision based on the disability act, which forbids and protects the mentally disabled or handicapped citizens from discrimination. In another development, he claimed to have passed a series of American and British professional examinations "some at first sitting" but when the official list of all professional engineers licensed roster in the State of Texas was conducted, it was discovered that he never passed the said exams (if he ever enrolled for them). The claims were all figments of his imagination, which the Board of Licensing surely knew nothing about if they were to be personally consulted. Randy thought that Bivasco's mental condition as things went on prevents him from knowing the truth and reality around him.

The same Bivasco will after so many years go to Randy's village to get one of the old headmasters convinced that he attended the primary school there and request to be issued a testimonial of school attendance. While he had his way getting issued, he never attended the school in question. He attended the opposite local government religious movement primary school contrary to his claim of attending the Catholic primary school in Randy's village.

Bivasco's junior brother was more than a decade later involved in swindling an innocent associate of their family who was travelling to the States to meet his brother. Biwo asked for some money to call his brother and get him informed that the person in question would be coming at a particular time and date. The money was given to him, but he never made any call but devoured the charged amount. He assured the man in question that the brother was aware of his coming and arrival time in the States. When the man now a tested war veteran Captain Valiant in the American army arrived, no one was at the airport to receive him. He called Bivasco to inform him about his arrival, but he was as surprised as the newcomer into the country. He was angry about the unannounced arrival, but the brother had swindled again but this time alone. Swindling, duping and deceptions had always been their trademark. Trades and traps which unsuspecting persons would always fall prey to. More than three decades later, Bivasco still got someone in the States duped and travelled to his native country. There is no how anyone could wash the nose of a dog to get clean. Endless lies, dupes, credit card financial siphoning acupuncture, stealing and other possible ways of circumventing stated laws had become his trademark and had over the years been perfected against the status quo to all unsuspecting innocent people.

The computer age has brought the best way to get around with repository information dissemination. Bivasco will use this medium to lie against anyone, castigate and put to use some criminal instincts. He told lies about Randy's village online and was involved in many other concocted stories that were faulty and summarily fallacious. Randy would not go into the history of his prattles online, but one thing stood clear about his lies about Randy's village, the man Bivasco wrote about that his house was burnt by Randy's people was in-law to the village by tradition and one of his sons happen to be Randy's college mate. What Bivasco did not know was that one of the old man's sons had gone to steal some tubers of yam from one of the village inhabitant's barn and was nabbed in the process. The owner of the barn, seeing him commit the crime, raised an alarm that did not go down well with the thief. As the owner's voice got higher and higher alerting the people on the nearby farms, the intruder approached the owner and stabbed him to death. He escaped. When the youths of the town will hear what had transpired, they got angry and swooped on the family house. The thief had provoked an already orchestrated case between his father and the community. Their house was razed down in anger as a vengeance for the man that died prematurely and senselessly in the hands of a thief. As he tried to escape, he was caught and handed over to the police later.

Bivasco claimed to be a champion of Randy's language, the language he is completely devoid of writing tenses with grammatical unevenness. His assertions are unlimited. Hear him talk about girlfriends and childhood friends.

The people he holds dear, as his childhood friends don't know him that well. He started associating with them as adults but surely not as children. As a child, Bivasco's contact and association in Randy's village was about fifty meters radius. He would be lost in a maze of his cocoon after the mentioned perimeter. He is not in contact with those that know him as childhood associates. Childhood meant growing together and sharing a lot in common as children till adulthood. Only but very, few merited the ascertained qualities and could talk about his being and existence.

On the girlfriend front, he was way back behind any of his mates, but he boasted and lied about his forays in adulthood. Bivasco could not talk to any girl to the best of Randy's knowledge but the only one he would muster some wasted boldness to approach living in the opposite local government area to Randy's. She fell for Bivasco for the simple reason that he was ready to live on the shores of their country. She must have anticipated joining him someday **as a been-to.** It was less than a week stint of an affair between them before he left for India. Before Bivasco would come home again she was already respectably married but he will not let go. He lured her out of her matrimonial home as long as he was around and each time he visited the country from the States. He became the catalyst that broke the poor woman's marriage but remained unchanged at the end of the incidents. It was indeed a sad, sorry and disheartening situation prompted by coated evil fornicating tendencies embedded in Bivasco. He always carried a tax return copy of his official document to show women what he was worth to be able to get a woman as a girlfriend. It was his certificate to get across to women who hardly knew his debilitating and retrogressive qualities.

His junior brother Biwo under the command of his father and with the police commander dealt ruthlessly, mercilessly, and unforgivably to one Todi. Todi was a son of the soil who got involved with one of Bivasco's immediate senior sisters. He had gone to visit her in their house because they were in love but was temporarily kidnapped by father and son in their house. As he tried to leave, he was prevented from doing so freely. Father and son pummeled him to a submitting level and a police officer that incidentally hailed from their area of the country working in the village was corruptly invited to take Todi to the station for whatever concocted reason they must have established against him. He may have been charged for fake trespass or assault or battery with needed extinguished love burning light under the charges. Their father had sworn to never allow the daughters to get married to any of the natives of the village where he had adopted their place as his home for decades. While he did that, no one was interested in seeking the hands of her daughters in any form of a lasting relationship. He was only giving his wishes, which the town's people did not reckon or tally with their interest and personifications strata and sedimentations. His boys found it Herculean to get along or have the town's women not because there were no women but because they could not then, and most parents loathed their stand and incontestable negative family idiosyncrasy. Their father was selfish with her daughters and lacked cooperation with the village people. Most of her daughters ended up either partially married or not married at all except one that was made to marry against her will and wish. Bivasco bulldozed the one that was prepared to live through her love and affection with her husband and children out of her matrimonial home. What a shame of a social outcast and misfit. It was an irony of history when he lost his wife and settled for one of the village's daughters as a woman friend. Randy asked what if the villagers or the family involved were to raise an eyebrow about his taking one of their own after his draconian treatment of the daughters to avoid getting along with the villagers years before. Randy thought that he would have known that what was good for the Goose was equally good for the Gander. The villagers were receptive and had nothing to complain about and never nursed any animosity because they knew that two wrongs could in no way make a right.

Bivasco had a child he was forced by law to pay a monthly child support stipend but does not know where mother and child were for a long time. He will not care about them but will be engaged with some Internet freaky girls that will on different occasions promise to get married to him but ended up duping him because of his nasty and uncanny behaviour they could not stomach. He was always dumped after they had had their fair share of his criminally made and assembled booty of yesteryears. He had lost the ill-gotten money many times to different women much as he had made happy homes to lose from trying to eke out living and love as a family.

When Bivasco claimed he knew Randy's village in out, he forgot his migratory attachment to the village. Randy always wondered why he would dwell on the claim. He had bought a plot to build his house on a disputable piece of land. The purchase of the land would highlight his lack of knowledge of the community. The man who had sold the piece of land to him was himself a migrant to the village. He would have known better were he rightly informed as he always claimed to have known the community so well. Randy always wondered where his knowledge of the community lay.

His prattles and vaunts may have contributed to his reading for his degree in a long but unquantifiable length of time and shows his remarkable sign of indolence before being catapulted by his forged and inglorious stolen luck. He has created more enemies and lives in enmity with most if not all of his ex-school and classmates. He is not in the good books of anyone Randy had known him with. When Bivasco is told anything, he goes around to get it magnified negatively and never stops his filthy mind from painting everyone inordinately bad. He wrongly sees himself as the saint re-incarnate.

Bivasco is capable of any devilish foundation. One would not wonder why he used someone's credit card and social security number to amass thousands of dollars of credit insidiously. When thieves and criminals commit crimes, they forget there are always tracks to reach them. Yes. He would be nabbed when the credit card company will send in their bills to the wrong transacting person. He had callously and devilishly used another man's official information to commit a crime punishable by the law of any democratic decent society and country. The cat was let out of the bag because the buyer and user of the credit card that was Bivasco defaulted. The ensuing investigation was traced to him and almost took him behind bars but for the quick intervention of his only surviving parent and the parents of the aggrieved party back home in the village he was saved from what would have brought him to justice and silenced him forever with a long time visit to penitentiary confinements. His record would have been unforgivable and indelibly dented. It was in the same state that he was distributing numbers to married women on dollar notes in Houston Texas. He cannot go to Houston Texas for any reason to socialize freely and even if could only sneak in and out for maybe official reasons. He made himself an anathema of the people.

He caused some community problems that will take years to beg for him to be taken back into his maternal fold. He is a destroyer, not a builder.

He is always involved in some kind of fraud with the social security numbers usage of anyone that had stayed some time with him through the green card lottery win. He has no conscience of any kind, had not gotten any and will never get any.

Bivasco unknowingly relished the wrong fact that no one from Randy's village was a member of the ethnic Internet club he belonged to pride himself as a false son of the soil. He started to post false stories, misrepresented Randy's village geopolitical affinities, quarrelled with anyone that called him to order and disrespected every member of the club. He never made his feasibility studies well to have arrived at his assumed and stillbirth conclusions. Many elites were more qualified and better behaved than he had thought of Randy's people. He demeaned members of the club and made monstrous acclamations about his monthly take-home at the club. He feigned his entire living and refused to think purposefully about those juggling and invincible ladders he used to catapult himself to impostor status of his extant ephemeral present.

He has wrongly disseminated his lies claiming he was an *"Exbiasojafra"* (ex-Biafran soldier). He was never military personnel and never fought any war. He had always been an impostor in every aspect of his life. Randy never saw him with a simple catapult as children. Catapult was the easiest weapon any child could carry about to shoot at birds and some dangerous reptiles. The only person that could claim to be *Exbiasojafra* is one retired Pilot who happens to be a family associate of Bivasco's extended family. Capt. Chipado was that valiant ex-military officer that fought on the side of the *Biasojafra*. As a teacher, Capt. Chipado taught his school pupils military marching and was displayed when there was an inter-school march parade competition at the Local government headquarter. Randy was there to watch the beauty of military marching being displayed by teenagers. Randy was proud of him as their teacher and told everyone around about who had taught them. More people asked after him from Randy and he almost ended up talking about the history of the man who was on that fateful day making history. His school had dwarfed the other schools in the March Past parade and became the talk of the town.

The country that was destabilized and polarized caused everyone to go to his or her side during the civil war. A comeback movement everyone made for *"Osondu"(running for one's life)* and *"Sa fun iku"* *(run from death)*. It was then that Bivasco and his family went across the River Niger to their side of the country and remained there till the end of the civil war. No one ever mentioned his being anything registered or gossiped about something related to the military service for the nearly three years he was away with his family across the borderline. The mother had refused to go with them but when their father divided the children, one was extra, and he threatened a division of the child to press her to follow him and the entire children as a family. In the melee for life, Hon. Chaks bought his workshop from their father. It was the money that would get the entire family into safety from the marauding *muje-muje* soldiers that were lurking on their heels. Decades later, Bivasco claimed completely the opposite, his father's house and shop were destroyed by the war. Fallacious. They sold their house to make extra money that would sustain the family from Randy's village to theirs. The same Bivasco would claim in his Internet club that his people across the Niger River are better than Randy's people. There was no base and reason for that comparison. One never insults a group because one from the group is rotten, arrogant, and full of misconceptions. He might have his reasons for being one-sided in his Judgments but he was not able to explain or clarify why his people would attack or try to daze the convoy that carried the junior brother's corpse in the middle of the night near his village.

Randy's people will never conceive or plan such an intimidating attack on innocent visitors that have come from afar to pay their last respect to the deceased. He was asked to make a do with that advertisement that talk about the clearness of differences between commodities. It is called the seven-up advertisement. They say never speak ill of the dead but that is just sentiments. Everyone will die along the terraces of life, but one leaves a legacy for whatever one does or believes in. People should be courageous enough to speak about the living and the dead sincerely, boldly, and truthfully. After all, every day that passes brings us nearer to our graves. Randy would not be surprised to hear from some close family associates about how Bivasco's cousin had insulted his junior brother in death. The junior brother Biwo had dishearteningly dissuaded a personable would-be suitor to his sister. He wanted Bivasco's brother to die the second death in death to show his maximum anger on what he did before leaving mother earth. Randy had no prayers for evil-minded persons. He tried to re-write history that does not fit into time, his personality, and his profiles. There are certain things and traits people outgrow or stop doing before adulthood but Bivasco remained the same in adulthood as a child. Randy thought and always wondered why he would still be that bragging, mouthy and arrogant brat he had always been into adulthood.

When you expect Bivasco to be humanly responsible is when he cocks a snook at civility. Randy had expected him to know before adulthood that, etiquette demands from everyone that, political, conflicting, or personal points of view should not be expressed within the limits of acceptable and responsible self-control while preventing or heading off every impulse and spiral of violence. He is always the first to tell people their weak points and use it as a launch pad to laugh at them or their demise, but he forgets that he has more than enough loopholes with which people could use against him. An example of the many loopholes is when the maternal grandfather Kaseeboom raped his first cousin's wife and on his paternal side was classified by his cultural peers as malicious social untouchable photocopies. There was a time someone who knew him so well in Randy's village called him the loathsome and forbidden loaded names. That triggered his going about and around those who he felt knew his extended family members so well to ask some of them if they were what he was called. It was anathema and whoever he asked would never clarify their family position for him because even if it was true, no one would like to tell him the truth or give the right answer in the instance. When people say, "I don't know or say that I have never heard about that", it means whoever called him whatever name knew what he was saying and knew the family lineage well and meant whatever he must have said. He always castigated people in the diaspora when they are bereaved that for one reason or the other could not travel immediately back home for wake keepings and internment but when his father died, he emphatically told a close acquaintance that he was not going to travel because he just arrived from home. It was an irony of history that he toed a line he criticised others for. Everyone wondered why he could not go home with his much-vaunted billion-dollar earnings. It showed his ignoble mouthy acclamations that lay bare his real impostor positions. His influence is a facade. He paints a very disturbing picture of people and the unknown.

He had approached Randy's niece for some immoral conjugal affairs with his fake innocence. The innocence he had used as bait would run against him. Randy's niece asked him" if he Bivasco does not know her and if he was coming to make his round of complete three hundred and sixty degrees". She continued "are you not Bivasco, the man that duped my uncle and went about rejoicing at your deceptive willowed senses of coverage, you wanted to make my uncle captive of your atrocious designed system, You failed in all your bids against him and he is forging his life in Germany just like you are doing in the United States". Bivasco was undaunted and continued to ask for Randy's where about and still feigned the notion of whose Randy's niece was. It was Bivasco's first time to know that Randy was not where and in the position he had thought he would be. He must have been flabbergasted by the discovery but hid his uttermost surprises. He had expected to hear the worst news about Randy but the real news must have broken his negative and sadist expectations. The only bad news he did not get that day was the loss of Randy's son that arose from his delays in the school fees transaction and the subsequent confiscation of the money beyond and in years of the acrimonious atrocity. The little boy had passed away from the Bivasco's resultant factor and must have spoken about his not forgiving him for incapacitating his daddy. The child had gotten a sting from Bivasco's poisonous arrows and eyes him with all hatred and stench in his heart. Bivasco had prematurely deprived him of his life, the baby is crying in his grave for justice and expecting to singlehandedly make a case from the other side of the human divide against the man that stood in his way in life. The baby would have been man enough to be an adult. Randy soothed the situation and tragedy with "Aluta Continua". If only Bivasco had sent Randy's money back at the time things went so sour for him, he would have been able to fight for his son's life but there was a situation of impecuniousness made worse by seizure incapacitation. It was indeed a heartless hold back against all demands and appeals made by Randy to get his situation and that of his son salvaged that fell on cello-taped deaf ears. Rest in perfect peace Eony.

Arrogance and respect cannot be juxtaposed in a society where one thinks twice before talking to people. Anyone who does not accord respect and love to his fellow-men is doomed and so is Bivasco. No one would say that the entire village was bad because of a single incident that reflected on very few people of the entire population. The same would go too that not all brothers would slap their brothers on the day of their marriage right in the presence of the bridegroom and court registry officials overseeing the tying of the knot but Bivasco was slapped by his junior brother on the day of one of his many marriages right before all who were in attendance and hardly held together afterwards. Bivasco's arrogance had taken him very deep to a point of no return. In one of his arrogant exhibitions at his father's village, he had a physical loading for some pugnacious engagements and broke his victim's head very viciously. He was arrested and detained by the police for causing some bodily harm and damage. The same month, he returned to the States to make a life notable disgraceful transfer of aggression to his maternal peers on the web after his paternal forum members had called him a societal outcast and were picked by some members of that forum for wider circulations.

When Randy will travel for the first time to the States, he unconsciously said as the flight took off "Bivasco, there you are and here I come, America, you denied me is the America I am going to without having to apply for any visa, nothing remains same forever, life revolves on dynamism but it is static for Bivasco". Randy smiled broadly and cast his mind many years back in retrospect about all that had transpired through and from Bivasco. Randy at that point almost shed tears for his late son but held them back tightly with his throat drying out. Randy asked for a glass of water and said silently "Bivasco, this world is quid pro quo and meant equally for everyone but whatever anyone does is auto and individualistic, pray curses don't give you tears but you must change your cataclysmic behaviour innuendos".

Randy in hindsight about what had transpired between him, Bivasco and his junior brother came to a sordid conclusion that "a promise is a comfort for a fool" but on a second thought consoled himself that Randy was not that as acclaimed and ascribed to the boys next door's shameful and recriminatory actions. He also realized that everywhere one went was where one is as he always upheld. The brothers Bivasco and Biwo and of course brothers in crime had enjoyed their years of another man's sweat but have taught the victim that hatred does not leave room and space for anyone to be fair and composed, instead, it makes one blind and closes all doors of thinking.

The way and manner Bivasco had turned the good inventions and intentions of modern technology into a medium for castigating well-meaning people in a virtual world made Randy think he is afflicted with a non-hereditary genetic disorder. Everyone has got a past with every story having a beginning but is not so with Bivasco. He failed to realize that apathy is the greatest danger to the human future. Much as that would be, people should never let the future disturb them because they surely and undoubtedly meet it. Whatever Bivasco has metamorphosed into financially came from Randy and has not gotten the blessing due to a genuine way of life. His relish and vaunts are tantalizingly ephemeral. They went into a crime so early from their beds at home and were supported by every member of their family. What a blind reasoning family.

Bivasco wanted to annihilate Randy through his insidious and later celebrate what he would have branded as "backwardness". He relished in his exhilaration and negative hopes about Randy that the bad promises he had gotten about his plans to defraud him would soon start to see him eroding and denudating. Bivasco was wrong. Randy never believed in negative energy that would make his efficiency drop before a lily-livered people. His courage and generosity did not fail him in this instance. Both of them Bivasco and Biwo had no excuse, defence and no justification for their actions against Randy. The incidents happened, as Randy was not oblivious of the genuine and man-made risk that was going to be created by them. It was very insidious. They had knowingly designed and created the joint iniquitous atrocity and associated inimical conditions. Randy was patient and knew they would with time reap the seed of discord they have sown.

After the entire incident, Randy allowed them to go into a world where he devised his novel tracking systems. He surreptitiously tracked all their movements and activities without having to input any draining calories. They wore his infrared transmitting *Pizzini* chips.

As children, Randy, the brothers, and other friends collectively danced at yuletide times. The family cunningly at the end of every dance confiscated the money the children made without any conscience. Randy would have learned from that but what has an innocent little boy got to think about open and harmless daylight robberies carried out on innocent children who instead of sharing their hard-earned toiled for money, concentrated on the food and new dressings for the Christmas day and the associated festivities? The family's hallmark had always been their deceptions and deceits. They are a collection and bunch of self-configured, chronic, ardent liars with insatiable abyss greed. The family had negative longings with superficial and meretricious linings carried over in life by both brothers. They all existed as a hotbed of disdainful back hitters, high-profile criminal activity against innocent children, and syndicates with styles skirting the law.

Randy said, "you could know someone for years but still discover something you never knew or noticed before". Is like going out with someone you cannot vouch for or tell people about. Bivasco was full of fulminating loquaciousness with uncontrolled idiocy and short-sightedness. The Internet club members would not need him on his temerity and the unmitigated gall of conducting time. No positive changes are too late for any man to make in life. One has gotten the choice to do that but Randy guessed people like Bivasco would rather decide for the wrong side of history. Gangsters and miscreants find it so hard to change except when the law forces it through them. He escaped the law when he would have been forced by it to make the right and positive consenting changes.

Bivasco had given him breathless anticipation but in adulthood, Randy considers himself a survivor, triumphant, indefatigable, and unbeatable with their murky hurdles. Randy had driven through his fears and tears but, even when people try to be careful, they make mistakes. If one is not comfortable with the loving hand you have dealt with him or her, please fold as soon as possible, in Randy's case he was cajoled amidst the dangers of Bivasco's hands. Randy failed to realize the enormity and seriousness of the situation, which he Bivasco needed to secretly step on to get to the ladder. Randy pushed himself into a blind alley by not being able to decode Bivasco's nefarious intentions. It was a one-step with tightly hidden implications.

Bivasco would offer a piece of advice or tell you what to do and make a fool of you in the end. Randy was supposed to have been leery of him before it all happened but for the intervening years thought he must have become a changed man, but he was dead wrong. He only knew him better than best after the incidents unfolded. Randy held to the saying that said, "The true and candid measure of a man is how he treats someone who can do him complete and absolutely no good". Randy did not see Bivasco anymore since the day he gave him money until the pages of telling it all and how it was truthfully and sincerely recorded in the flood of indelible oozing ink being swallowed by papers in retrospect. They behaved outrageously to Randy. It was a horrid, terrifying, degrading, and humiliating experience. They opened a Pandora-box of boiling dissent not oblivious of the human life involved. They wanted Randy to be useless and at worst dead but instead of that he lost his son in the heat of those trying years. Bivasco is the type of man that will not accept the responsibilities of history. He has that undeniable reality of misguided hopes. He now in adulthood toes an unpredictable fault line that will swallow him on an unimaginable quake.

Bivasco, his brother Biwo and some members of their family are a very close-knit criminal fraternity. They cannot out-fight any resilient man in life's penultimate position — which goes for the worst for them. Randy thought over the years that the negative glands they exuded must have dissolved and atrophied but was wrong. They went on solo manipulation of people as a way of life in adulthood. Bivasco has always held a mirror to delusion and made people of his Internet club members a captive audience before his complete technological virtual rejections. He is an excuse maker with the energy of a slug and the spine of a jellyfish. Randy considered him a non-inclusion from all distances to any group of life mountain climbers. His fortifications and unethical conduct will not prevent his potential doom.

Bivasco's sadist, corky and endless searching behaviour of sniffing for news about other people, magnifying anything he hears, backbiting, will not allow him to reach the Promised Land and even if he cannot match towards it. He did not know that happiness he locked against Randy sneaked in through a door he never knew existed in his filthy and worst of minds. Randy might have left the past behind, but the past certainly and surely has refused as a rule humanly possible to let go. The past is always there to remind one what one did that was right and what wrong one did too. Randy believed in people submitting sometimes to their weak points but warned against making one's problem another man's or border on people's way and life. While Bivasco's calculated dupe and stealing tricks caused Randy numerous setbacks, Randy turned the entire retrogressions and shortcomings in the end to the relocation of purpose with harmonic balance.

Bivasco ought to have known that integrity takes discipline, where impulse takes none. It is rare and special thing to find a friend who will remain a friend forever. He chose and preferred to be an enemy to Randy but will be harder if he chooses to confront him again in life's sojourn. Randy by choice preferred to keep his distance to allow the proverbial sleeping dog to lie. Despite Bivasco's ranting and vaunts, Randy upheld that the lowest form of wit in any man is sarcasm and it takes a fool like Bivasco to remain sane. Curing him of his invincible malady will be worse than the disease in him. Whoever deals with him must live with confronting the pains and digest the concomitant utter despair. His evils built on stony lies and long fingers are a style too cunning to be easily understood and discern. He and his brother inveigled Randy into their complete confidence and went ahead to do the worst that bordered on his lifeline and immediate family.

Randy saw the blood-sucking brothers as no more than a conspiracy of beggars that are haggling to save their lives but were blind to larger human concerns of which Randy was the victim extraordinary. They lacked sincerity, nobility, and accountability by all standards.

Randy gave Bivasco his final summation and understanding with one sentence of wisdom:- "Winning is without value if victory is unfairly, dubiously and dishonestly achieved". Cheating is easy, but Randy is sure it certainly will not bring pleasure to asinine Bivasco.

Many bad friends abound like Bivasco in so many sour and misleading ways. There was another cataclysmic incident years later that involved him and a friend he held so dear because he felt they shared a common interest in language and cultural affinities. His insidious actions, unverifiable, unpalatable character and incognito behaviour broke them apart when life agitations went sedimented on the truth and sincerity scales. Hear what transpired between them: -

Koland had from his premonitions from the blues accused him of meddling and flirting with his girlfriend and junior sister over the telephone. When he confronted him with the accusation, he tried to set Koland's ill thoughts and wrong judgments aright on the phone, but he disconnected before he could make him see the reasons for his wrong and uncalled-for actions. He tried to phantom where he had gotten the wrong information, he was using against him. He drove from his place to meet Koland for a talk over the issues he raised and make amends despite the outright outrageous provocations by Koland, but he rebuffed him. He called him when he reached his house area to meet him for a talk, but he instead of being a man chose to threaten him with unlawful arrest on the phone. He asked him to get away from his place otherwise he would be arrested. He laughed at his folly and idiocy. Randy asked himself why he would be arrested on a government-approved road and more so for reaching out to him with an olive branch. That was when he felt his unwarranted cumulative provocations. He came so far with peace and for peace but was thwarted and rebuffed by Koland. He had no alternative but to go back to his place of abode.

When he returned to his place, he called some well-meaning people who knew Koland to make the report of his accusations and experiences with him. One prominent acquaintance to him called Koland's girlfriend to ask her if Randy ever approached her in any amoral setting. Koland's girlfriend failed to answer the question without any good reason being adduced for not supplying the much-needed answer. His acquaintance pressed her to give an emphatic and convincing answer of No or Yes to either incriminate or exonerate him, but she circumvented the answer thereby complicating issues the more. She had the answer but refused to tell the truth. It remained so till he relocated from the city.

Koland had met her girlfriend at a bar in their village and in the process of their relationship had a child that culminated in their secret but official cut-and-nail marriage of convenience. It happened after Koland had been involved in a gigantic and well-coordinated financial embezzlement where he worked in Austria. The company had entrusted him with their company cheque and accounting systems with a free hand and access to manage but he betrayed the confidence reposed on him when trust mattered most with his evil machinations. He secretly designed and executed his evil plans with the writing and cashing of some millions of Euros with the company's cheques from their account. He suddenly became a company director and magnate of his own company with a business associate. With time he fell out of favour with his business partners who knew so well how he had gotten his ill-gotten wealth in Austria.

Meanwhile, he was married to an Austrian woman but had in absentia contracted another marriage with the newfound bar girlfriend in a marriage registry in his home country. Original bigamy was put into place. Koland kept the Austrian woman in the dark about his nuptial activities and grand landings. When Koland fell out with his business partners, one of them attended his extramarital bigamous marriage from where he secretly recorded the marriage ceremony which he later sent to Koland's office in Austria and in addition asked the office to refer and check out a particular date that Koland had perpetrated the heinous financial juggling raid and rape of the company's account with a particular cheque that the details had been submitted along with their report of the incident. The particular cheque that was cashed on the mentioned date in their reported petition said it all. The company investigated every detail therein and found the entire veracity of the information so supplied to the company by Koland's business partner. The subsequent investigation culminated in Koland being sacked, tethered and sentenced to some years of imprisonment with hard labour in Austria.

He was released from prison after serving his term. Since his record had been dented and polluted in Austria, he headed to Munich in Germany where he started a new life. His other but secret reason and motive for the relocation was to ensure the casting and right balancing of his bigamy. He took up another job and got himself enmeshed in a disgraceful official credit card usage for his self-aggrandizements in Munich. He was supposed to use the credit card for his official approved transactions, but he ended up with it to satisfy his personal and greedy ego. He was dismissed with ignominy.

While he was in Munich, he paraded himself among people with lies that magnified his endlessly deceitful, impostor position and character. He borrowed some money from a female colleague who rightly documented the deal and agreement, but he reneged from the agreement that made them go to the court for redress. Injunctions were passed accordingly to affect the immediate repayment of the money in question from the incontestable evidence before the judge of the day. His lies had no end but were very linear in the arrangement. He once told Randy falsely how his father had nursed and nurtured through his mother a one-time accused but unproven ex-coup plotter in their village, and that he was interviewed by a cable news network in Munich. The lies were so nauseating and an upsetting indignity for him without boundaries. He once asked Randy to unbelt when the police noticed he was not wearing a car seat belt inside Randy's car. Randy asked him why he should unbelt and he said so that they would be the same before the police officers. Randy could not believe what he was up to till then but later got to know him better with his assorted miscreant packed full behaviour.

As things went on, one of Koland's brothers raped the sister of his girlfriend in their country. The family tried in vain to cover up the incident, but Koland's girlfriend made everything known to all and sundry.

When the girlfriend turned, the wife years later was eventually brought to Munich to join Koland, Randy related to the family as people that hailed from the same area back home in their country without any reservations. She even went to visit him to pick up the pair of sports shoe gifts meant to cushion her from the debilitating winter she was exposed to. During her visit, Randy did not indulge in any dirty talk or was ever involved in any amoral leaning with her. She was not gotten close to or touched for any reason, but he wonders endlessly why he was accused of flirting with her and Koland's sister. The sister graduated into one of the soft occupations that carried some women of easy virtues to nowhere. Randy knew much about Koland personally but got most of his double life dealings affairs through the girlfriend turned wife. Koland always castigated her by calling her and her family witches' domain without reservations. A statement so hurtful and disgraceful privately, as in a relationship and worst with strangers and visitors being around.

He later knew that it was because Koland had so much misrepresented himself publicly and socially with his negatively refined impromptu lies among all and sundry that he found a very cogent but wrong reason for a biased coated wrong cause to break off from the fake friendship. Before the incident happened, he had already known him as a very chronic, unrepentant, and ridiculously recirculation liar, more so and worst of all, a financial guzzling light-fingered man.

His actions with bigamy prompted him to leave Germany for Canada. The Austrian wife never knew he was married to another woman from his country of origin. Koland always found reasons why his Austrian wife should not visit him in Germany. He always travelled to visit his Austrian family to soothe their feelings and save him from being nabbed by the laws of one-man one-wife law of the continent. He remained neck-deep in bigamy till he relocated to Canada from Germany. The distance increase was only an increase in time and succour till the beans would be spilt and the cat let out of the bag. The imminent and realistic doomsday will always loom over his head. It could only be postponed but nemesis will catch up with the insidious hearts and minds of an impostor.

He once almost broke off with his countrywoman now called wife in Munich but managed to set their official but unapproved marital relationship straight again. Randy had heard that: "Koland and his latest country woman wife had said that what happened between them and him was long past with the intervening years and that it was an old issue worth forgetting but for Randy, it is a living memory down the lanes of life that can never be atrophy. Randy does not share their ideas of time, lies and insincerity. Randy always thought that: "if only She had answered the question thrown to her over the phone through Randy's acquaintance, then he could be in a better position to think along in same line a bit with them. Randy thought that they have enough children now to protect their truth. A No or Yes that Randy did not do what he was wrongly accused of but her mum's mouth would always leave that gorge of pain for an endless feud that might be very incriminating.

They say that "if one carried a monkey from Africa to England, it certainly remains a monkey." Koland in Canada still got himself immersed in insatiable financial misappropriation and endless fiduciary gourmand in his place of work. He was placed on company suspension from his duty post through so many months of exhaustive investigation and sacked in the end. He went about lying about the truth. He returned to Germany with his entire family — exposing and submitting the glorious and open-ended blissful Canadian future of his innocent children to tatters. He would always be that endless liar and pilferer of a kind that lies about and hides as Ostrich does.

8

GODFATHER PROCREATING INJUSTICE

At the time Randy would go home to answer his family's call, he had almost become a figment of his imagination. He managed to trudge on but deep down in him, he was dilapidated, truncated, famished with no reasonable and reliable course life direction. This was the time he realized that there was no meritocracy in his country. Somebody in most cases was somebody in the country, if only he had a godfather to cushion or back him up in every field of human endeavour. He had gotten the baptism of official powers that be to uphold that meritocracy existed nowhere in the country.

He tried to join the army in the northern part of the country through a friend but the officer in charge, a colonel demanded some bribe to include his name on the list of potential recruits. Randy had not gotten the requested money to satisfy the demand of the officer but promised to get back to him. He tried again and was asked to go to his home state from where if he were eventually recruited would be transferred to the military depot in the north for the commencement of his training. He travelled to his home state where he reported with the required documents. There was chaos, unwarranted drills, and indiscriminate and senseless whipping of some potential recruits with cow tails called *"koboko" (dried horsetail turned into a whip)* at the recruitment centre. It was pure callous and asinine mistreatments of people who had come to lay their lives in defence of their fatherland. Those without backers from the government like Randy were senselessly whipped out of the barrack premises by some of the drug-addicted soldiers. Some had smoked marijuana and topped it with *"sapilo-aqua" (hot native dry gin)* drink that gave them a concentrated irrational feeling of nonchalance against their fellow countrymen. Randy had been rushed out of the race of recruitment for not conforming to the system of bribery and godfather adherence. The soldiers had painted a very disturbing picture of who they were to him, to the unknown and the unsuspecting leaders of the nation. At this time, he had weakened in strength. The world had beaten him to a near pin-fall submission, rendering his influence in life a mere facade rather than real.

Randy tried to join the Navy but was repelled for the same reason but without any whipping. The naval officers were really intelligent men with the right touch in public relations. They may have not recruited Randy but he was respectful of the fact that they followed to some extent the rules of recruitment, and engagement which went deep enough to get polluted in the end by the laid out negative standards of bribery and godfather message attachments.

There was no job and Randy had gone and done enough in any conceivable circumstance to secure any type of job but would not get one or be allowed to show what he was up to, in any open position. He was on his way in one of those private junketings and saw an advertisement again for an air force recruitment exercise coming up nationwide. He went to his home state where all the potential recruits sat for a competitive selection examination under the scorching sun and on a bare green field in the front of the laboratory department of the state air force headquarters. They were asked to come along with their faeces sample after the examination, for the next day's continuation of the exercise. They had been medically tested physically and outwardly before the examination was conducted for the fit and strong candidates. The next day, the result was announced and those that failed were given the marching order. Randy was first and one other candidate from his local government area came second. The air force needed only one person from Randy's local government area. The second person Suwutu felt so bad and cried back to Lagos from where he had come for the recruitment selections. As that day passed, the remaining candidates were asked to come back for their medical results and to partake in an oral interview. Randy had passed till this point and was still Sceptical of what might befall him on the ladder. Before Suwutu went back to Lagos, there was an air force officer in the recruitment station that hails from the same village as Suwutu. When he saw the result, he came directly to Randy to ask him where he hails from in the local government area of the state. Randy told him and he started to talk the language to him to sweep him aside for Suwutu. He was very disappointed when Randy seemed to talk the language more than he had expected. He gently went up to Suwutu and told him that he had no chance of beating Randy out of the recruitment. He told Suwutu that, Randy was first, had better height, qualification, and working experience and had passed all the required tests till that point of the expected oral interview. They were very good comments that would soon go down the drain. The news made Suwutu look downcast but cried back to his sponsor in Lagos. Suwutu had reported the entire case to his sponsor. The sponsor Paise went crazy and very angry after she had heard that two people from her local government had outperformed everyone in the state and possibly in the country and none was given a chance for advancement. She was a very highly connected woman of substance. She knew the big wigs of all military strata in the country. She placed a call to the head of the country's air force command to report the incident and that she wanted Suwutu's name included in those who were going to report for military training in the air force base in the north. Never doubt the power of any woman. They possess the powers that could melt some men's hearts. She employed the best strategy to fight the immediate injustice. It worked to her designs and needs and for the man being salvaged from the debilitating claws of injustice.

On the next and final day of the recruitment, Randy went for the oral interview and was deliberately failed. One of the officers on the panel asked the other panel members if

Randy had a sponsor and the question was directed to him too, Randy said no one because all that were selected had letters of recommendation from highly placed military personnel all around the country. One of the officers on the panel looked into Randy's eyes and said, "You have no sponsor – get out and go". Randy respectably walked out from the denials and manmade failure.

One of the newly recruited recruits had come with his sister to do the human connections for him. The sister was a good charming pretty lady that would keep any man gazing all day into her eyes for that natural feeling of any healthy man. She served as the senior recruiting officer all the days the recruitment was organized. The brother went through on that, immoral and corrupt practices. Randy was not surprised to see himself and Suwutu flunk in the end, it was the wrong but acceptable norm of the corruption-laden society where they both lived. A system that will not even, allow for a free and fair election but allows money to the soil every positive design of any human assemblage.

When Randy would go back to the northern city of Kaduna where the air force headquarters was located, he went to one of his extended family members Innope in the city to inform him about what had happened in their state capital Benin City. He would listen to Randy but had hardly believed him. Any sane man would have disbelieved it too, but the true context of the embodiments of what made it so hard and a show up to people's rare and stark realities was the way it happened — who would believe that someone with the first position in an examination failed? Surely nobody. Except all the candidates failed, which in this instance was not the case.

Innope worked as a chartered taxi driver and sometimes worked as an attached chauffeur at the airport and five-star hotels respectively. Unknown to Randy, he had a very cordial relationship with Paise who patronized him on every visit to Kaduna. Innope asked Randy to accompany him to the airport to pick up Paise and Suwutu. It was on their way to the airport that Innope told Randy how he had known Paise and confirmed Randy's story about the recruitment at their state headquarter as being true. He continued to tell Randy that, she was coming in the company of Suwutu who had taken the second position in the competitive air force recruitment test in Benin City, and that Paise had gone to collect all necessary letters from the country's Chief of Air force Staff commander to effect Suwutu's commencement of the training in Kaduna air force base. Randy accompanied them to the air force base and watched Paise hand over Suwutu to the base command-training officer. Randy saw his position go physically in his presence to another man but was happy that the insidious cheating of his local government was at least halted and righted. Sowutu looked into Randy's eyes and, turned to follow the training officer in the direction of the other recruits. Sowutu must have had mixed feelings over a rotten system of which he had become an official and part from the day he was accepted as a soldier for the nation. From that point on, Randy interacted better and more closely with Paise. She tried to find Randy a job but nothing about her efforts came to fruition. Randy would know years later that the efforts to find him a job were thwarted by insidious Innope.

Innope had sent a letter to his senior brother through Randy who incidentally was an air force officer in Lagos. Unfortunately, Randy did not go as expected for some obvious financial reasons. He safely kept the letter to take it along anytime he was ready to make the journey to Lagos. It took so much time that he forgot all about the mail. The letter got lost inside his flat after a very unplanned long-time journey to Lagos. One day, Randy went about cleaning every nook and corner of his flat and found the letter under one of his sofas. Randy had always been very sincere but out of humanly premonition and intuition, a thought asked him to open the letter. Innope had demanded the letter back, but Randy told him that he had posted it to the senior brother in Lagos. He found it too bad to tell Innope he had lost it and that reason would cause unnecessary ill blood between them. When he found the letter again and based on the reason, he had conveyed to Innope, he curiously opened it and read it. Randy was surprised and overwhelmed by goose pimples. The content was sore and acidic against Randy. Innope had given Randy his death sentence to carry to his senior brother to deliver to the Golgotha. He had advised his senior brother to avoid helping Randy in any way possible and that Randy was the architect of his misfortune, it went on and on. Randy thought about the entire content and cast his mind back to see if there was anything he had done to warrant such an insidious treatment. In the first place, Randy had not solicited any help from the senior brother and did not need any in the instance. Where the officer brother lived in Lagos was almost out of town. Randy will never conceive any notion of going to him for anything but Innope thought about the contrary in his filthy heart. Innope was one man Randy held so dear and made sure he bought him so many gifts when he went overseas for his petroleum training but here, he was castigating the man that respected him most. When the going got too harsh and unbearable, he was the one Randy would sell some of his household property to at a giveaway and regrettable prices. Randy always wondered why he was being castigated and spoken ill of. Randy would come to know he had spoken ill of him to Paise to get her demoralized. Paise had asked Randy some leading questions that made him trace the link of helplessness from her. Innope had fabricated lies Randy could not decode but they were there to melt with time. The time that would bring unspoken guilt and shame to Innope and the time that will not let Paise and Randy meet again in the physical. Randy heard of Paise's death in the hands of assassins in Lagos. So many rumours had been attributable and adduced to her death but Randy held her as her confidant. She was shot and killed with her son watching inside her car. The son was said to have begged the assassins to spare the life of her mother, but his pleas fell on deaf ears.

Randy did not quarrel with Innope or made the content of the letter known to him. Randy held on to the letter for as long as he remained in the country. He posted it to Innope's senior brother when he heard that, he had been transferred back to the Kaduna air force base. The postage was made from overseas through Innope's private letterbox in Kaduna to his senior brother. Randy thought about what it would look like to receive a letter after so many years from the writer directly to the receiver. Randy wondered if the letter ever arrived as scheduled. If it did would mean more than enough to two blood brothers Randy held in very high esteem without any blemishes. Randy will see Innope after more than ten years again when he visited his home country from overseas. It was a reunion that was not so cordial and friendly, but the human aura spoke it all between them. He had spoken ill of Randy a few days to that day but there and before he was that man he hated so much with passion for no reason in his house after those long-enduring years. He must have cast his mind on the letter he wrote that read **unedited**:-

P.O.Box 1234
Kaduna
12/2/91

My dear brother

Please kindly forgive me for not writing you uptill now for I was intending to come but the present situations is disallowing me. Can you <u>belive</u> that I hadn't completed children fees and their textbooks up till now? And as I am writing you, my car was <u>hitted</u> in the church <u>premisess</u> and I hadn't enough money for the <u>repars</u>. If you can send me five hundred before the month ending I will be grateful to God. I was glad to have received the forms on the second day of the posting. Thanks be to God. Thank you dear I had wanted us to <u>discouse</u> things in figure.

My dear brother, Becareful and beware of Randy and his <u>problemes</u>. Figure <u>discoursion</u> <u>pleas</u>, See you when I come and May God guide us all in Jesus name Amen

Innope

NOTE:- the letter continued on page two after signing off on page one. It continued:-

I heard that many Airforce <u>personals</u> will be going on retirement even as from now. What is you faith?, before thinking of helping he who don't want to stop doing wrong things.

(And the letter ended). Syntax and every other error are Innope's and not the author. The author only reproduced a jargon that was well interpreted and put into the right place in history and posterity.

The above letter has confirmed that Innope had had several conversations and discussions about Randy with his brothers and sisters, for Randy noticed their behaviour and some of the sisters scornfully made a caricature of Randy's state of unemployment. Randy knew but laughed at their linked stupidity and endless idiocy. The result of who sleeps at the side of the mat is better settled when everyone has taken his or her place at night to sleep. A proverb worth aligning with.

Decisions are made based on lots of actions and reasons. When Randy had made so many frantic efforts to get reemployed into the labour market for some years without any success, he swore never to do any job that came his way. His decision was borne out of necessity and explosive frustration arising from the sale of some of his property to make ends meet and for the obvious reason that he had no godfather to keep his leverage in the polluted society. Randy believed in meritocracy as against godfather system enshrinement. This time in question, godfather had eaten too deep into the fabrics of the nation with varied tribal racism that had grown unchecked. Both had grown into unstoppable, unconquerable, and indomitable enemies of the society and were seconded by unquenchable corruption in almost everything the citizenry did. It was a way of life. One was seen as an idiot or stupid if he or she failed to join or assuage the protection of corruption. The only thing that held the nation together was sports and their formidable oneness which Randy thought would equally thaw and erode with times denudating effect. His nation spoke with one voice on unity but lacked the good leadership to better the lives of her citizens. The one voice that has become divided and disenchanted, from a growing dispirited and disgruntled populace. The people easily got disintegrated along tribal or ethnic divides but there still existed some well-meaning citizens who suffered the same fate as Randy. Some of these sets of people always met torture and government-organized imprisonment in the hands of the powers that be. Some people were killed or forced to emigrate by the military high handedness and chastisements. The system then was, take it or leave it democracy. Elections are won by nominations guided by employed gangs of miscreants shouting and sputtering endless balderdash on their opponents with loss of lives. The ballot box was just a decoration or formality and figment of world-recognized democracy's imagination. Is like the way communism still holds sway in the former Soviet Union and those that dare to challenge the authority and status quo of the government of the day that is installed in cosmetic but hated democracy are taken and dumped in Siberia or maximum-security prisons around the country.

9

ENDEMIC CORRUPTION

RANDY HAS COME TO THE HARD CONCLUSION THAT CORRUPTION IS ENDEMIC WORLDWIDE IN different forms from manmade situations and adduced to several mismanaged situations. The balkanization of Mother Africa in 1886 in Berlin did not end sensibly on paper but went ahead with the looting of her booties in all forms and the degradation of her people worldwide. The Continent was called a dark continent and tagged third-world corrupt governments in all facets. Randy came to the sunny discovery and wondered who must have created or invented the disapprobation. Randy thought about what had made Africa that had contributed immensely to the technological advancement of other continents with their needed minerals for human advance and developments, yet the term third world is still adduced and ascribed to the continent. Randy had always asked which entities comprised the first and second worlds. It was a stereotype of a name embedded in corruption and racism against a continent that had been siphoned and left to bleed to death but survived the chronic tests of the economic times.

Corruption is not tied solely to the assumed third world country but most if not all countries on the world map. All politicians like most policemen in every country are deeply and cancerously corrupt too. There is no particular country to be made a scapegoat for the world ills of the moment. Every nation is guilty of mass corruption in different forms. A politician in the States once put out a vacated position that was meant for a democratic election for sale and some members of parliament in Britain were involved in the highest official financial misappropriation case ever heard in the history of that country and government. The same things happened and are still happening in Russia, China, Japan, Korea etc. It has led to some leaders committing suicide, yet that of a particular continent is magnified and trumpeted like SARS and cancer outbreaks. People who speak against these ills are seen as anathema and clogging the free wheels of progress and continuity. Africans have the perspicacity to understand the new world order and will not kowtow to playing the second fiddle in the comity of nations. Randy thought that it will be nice for those who stigmatized a particular continent with contempt and waive of hand to rethink in the modern age by removing the pecks in their eyes before asking others to do the same. There is no sainthood in parliamentarian, and neither is there any in democracy. The only thing both offers publicly are the freedom of expression and openness against totalitarianism and oligarchy which are hook and sinker systems. We as humans try to be just humans with democracy leading the others but no one is corrupt free and proven from all available evidence and experience. There are many compressed truths and lies that take decades to have their blowouts. No nation should demean or brand the other "anything" with devilish intents. Truth and love should reign supreme over all conceivable evil machinations.

10

DESIDERATUM

RANDY HAD EULOGIZED HIS HOME GOVERNMENT FOR SENDING HIM ABROAD TO TRAIN AS A PIPELINE controls and dispatching specialist. His arrival abroad would open lots of hidden and unawareness in him. He knew that as humans, we are endlessly seeking and searching for life's fulfillments that do not border on prestige and money then. The fast-revolving world for Randy needed to be matched with the substance that will be beneficial to his employers and life with all he might meet on his life sojourns. From the day he stepped on *"kpotoki" (olden days name for light-skinned people that most liked to call white people)* soil, he would go in the quest for greater heights. Success brings many interesting things but could blur some analogies and beliefs in man. These situations were broadened by his new awareness. As the quest broadened so too did his needs broadened to the positive insatiable point. The quest would either be directed positively or negatively to give credence to its utility and foster some of the development of mankind in whatever way it evolved.

Randy's continued resilience took him to Lagos where he met one of his types who had been in the trade for job searches around the country. He still would not know how they had met by chance and started to discuss the sorry situation they had found themselves in. Everyone around started to divulge his utter situation in the little gathering of the disenchanted citizens. One of the men around had told the gathering how sordid things had gone and needed some respite to rethink how he could mend his disintegrating life. Randy was of course in the same situation. It was after the impromptu meeting that Randy decided he was going to leave the shores of his continent. Some of the suffering masses around had hinted how possible it was to get moving through one of the inhospitable terrains on foot. It looked like a child's play in vogue as he narrated the details bit by bit on how it was possibly done and what was involved. He even started to mention friends he knew that had gone and some that had made it to and fro with historical successes. Randy thought of it as a voice of dissent from one famished citizen among the mostly famished population. He thought it must have been just a tale and ploy to soothe the presence and console the needy people like them, but there was a sense in what everyone said, it was only left for those that would find it informative and useful for their advancement. The elevation was there but hidden to

70

the heart that saw no meaning in the stories. Only a few would believe that and the few that believed that would soon come to half the number and half of that would sail on. Those that would sail on might not have the willpower to accomplish what it takes a man to meander through creeks of nature and man-made problems. The results are gotten within a very long-time span. To Randy, the stories had stuck and taken a firm root. He had memorized every detail as they spoke informally to one another. After all, he was a particularly good geographer. When he got home, he told the ex-nephew and his friend what he had heard and that he was going to embark on the journey. They welcome the new information and development with open arms and started to find their own transport money to face life's travails.

In a world where Embassies in the country asked people to produce almost impossible but fat account figures and inexplicable documents to be able to secure visas to leave the country, citizens also devised a means to thwart them. Getting those needed documents became a problem for the common man and when found must have been forged by touts. Sometimes, some of the embassy staff collude with the touts who are highly connected to those in secret and high places of the society to dupe the ordinary man in his quest for progress and advancement. There were some embassies in the country where when one wanted to get an appointment for any transaction online, one never finds a free date. All dates for the whole year must have been allotted but if one could pay an exorbitant price to some touts at the gate that in turn would connect the embassy staff to give out date to the payer then he would be rightly fixed with invitation letter without any forms filled online as required and specified. Lots happening at some of the embassies if not all. Most embassies hide under the cloak of diplomacy to treat people with disdain, disrespect, and affront. If one does not meet those impossible and impracticable demands of the embassies, his or her application is either rejected or marked or stamped and the fees non-refundable. All in the name of checking and controlling the influx of illegal immigrants into their different countries. If it were so all along, there would not have been the slave trade and the evil intent of colonialism. Randy said, "If after milking and siphoning African wealth, why are they being inhuman to Africans by refusing them to be in their place as they have been in theirs". On that note, people started to find ways to go overseas with the circumvention of the atrocious and demeaning requirements of the embassies. People started to learn different specialized and perfected ways to get around the demands of the embassies to qualify for a visa. These documents were disgusting, nauseating, and retrogressive for the common man. Randy was still a novice at this time to what was going on. He later knew it all and through the right way from friends who were caught up in life like him.

As days wore on, Randy's ex-nephew's friend, Taof kept close contact with him. Randy was getting ready for the unknown dark cave paraphernalia but was intrepid in his quest and desires. Taof relied wholeheartedly on him without any hindrance and believed in Randy's ability to pilot him along. Randy was older and dared to shelter him in the event of any unforeseen circumstances but who knew what awaited them in the instance. For Taof, he was sure of his itinerary with him but deep down in Randy, he knew he was courting

Mephistopheles or "whatever inevitable", but he was ready and, for the onslaught wherever it was going to lead him at cost undaunted. His tenet was "better to die on the battlefield as a man than die miserably, dishonourably and cowardly at home".

Before Randy would think about the journey, Fenbrabi had impregnated one young girl that lived in the same compound as him. The young girl lost her womb during the abortion of the pregnancy of her own volition and without any prior notice to Fenbrabi. They lived in the same compound before his elder brother Panbi parked away on another street some meters away from the old place. The girl's elder brother who she lived together with, took the matter very seriously to a point of threatening court action against Fenbrabi. When the matter started to get so serrated with the elder brother to the girl pointing at the sepsis conditions, Randy waded in through one of his confidants in the city. He asked Paise to wade in from the state of the matter, but she considered it a ridiculously small case to handle. She asked Randy to meet the girl's elder brother with her message that read: "tell him that her sister was responsible for her bad state which we truly sympathize with but holding your Fenbrabi responsible was a miscarriage and travesty of justice in the instance if he wanted to go to court or whatever way he wants to get a wrongful redress, the family of Fenbrabi will come to answer through that means". The family in question was Paise and Randy to come forward and use the firepower they knew to get Fenbrabi out of the hook the girl's elder brother wanted for him to face unjustly. Randy and Panbi went to meet the girl's elder brother in their place of abode and tabled the matter with Randy delivering the message word for word as directed by Paise. The message sent ended the case without Fenbrabi's parents hearing or knowing anything about what had happened.

Randy set out to leave the country unannounced with his ex-nephew's friend through the northern part of the country. Randy was domiciled in the northern city of Kaduna but was frequent in the south because of job hunting. The day after their arrival to Kaduna-Zaria, they left for the northern neighbouring country Niger. They were subjected to searches at the border and asked to produce their visas. Randy told the officers that they did not need visas as citizens of the regional community to get around in their country. The officers did not see the truth and pretended not to know the truth or were well informed enough about their claims of being citizens of the economic community of the West African states union. The immigration and customs officers at the border demanded financial bribery to let them through the border control. They had been searched and nothing incriminating was found on them but will not let them go freely. They had seen that Randy and co had enough money and wanted their piece of cake willy-nilly. As they stood their ground, the officers asked if they were going to their northeastern border town of Arlit. They answered in the affirmative and were issued with the uncalled-for visa after their palms had been greased with some bills and bundles of cool cash. It showed the ill feelings of Randy's country northern neighbour Niger nursed against his homeland. The officers in question were uncooperative and unfriendly till Randy and Taof left. Their Modus Operandi differed from Randy's homeland border checks on citizens and foreigners alike. The officers were unreasonably meticulous about people they knew and understood did not in any way constitute a security risk to their country. The experience was so upsetting, degrading and disgraceful. Others could go without thorough searches as have been carried out on them and their luggage.

What baffled Randy most was the way the drivers changed their cars' number plates after crossing the border. The drivers carried the number plate of Randy's country registration and in the no man's land between both countries; they go into the bush and get another plate number that bears the registration for Niger. The drivers were sure and noticeably confident that they would not be questioned about the crime. The drivers said it was a way of life along both countries' borders. The drivers are patient with the time it takes to check every passenger by the border post officials.

It was the first time Randy would travel out of his country by road and, he was not enjoying it, but they would trudge on. After some hours' drive from the border, they reached Maradi from where they will make a connection drive to the northeast border town of Arlit. The connection was not as easy as had been said and directed before they arrived in the town. They started to socialize with the people of the same plan that they had met. The people they met were going the same way as them but had temporarily been stranded or had not gotten the liver to continue the journey as per their interest. They were mostly Anglophone members of the West African community from different countries. Randy and his ex-nephew's friend were ushered into one of the houses. Here, Randy met an acquaintance that was so shy to see him come to their dilapidated domicile and worst of all, what being there meant from thousands of kilometres away from home. Her shyness came from the fact that she was one of those girls that carried themselves shoulder high before any man. Randy sensing her feelings, assured her that, he was not going to let anyone know he had seen her and what trade she practised surviving. He kept his promise over the years. He believed that the act of keeping people's secrets makes them confide in him. It makes one command respect, nobility, responsibility, trust, dignity and reliability.

11

FARE THEE WELL

ONCE THEY WERE WITH THE PEOPLE THEY HAVE MET, EVERYONE AROUND STARTED TO INPUT STORIES they have heard about that made the core of the journey to Libya and finally to Europe. The stories were diverse and endless into eternity. The worst of the stories centred on any man choosing to use a woman for financial income. Under this theory of survival, the man acts as the banker pimp to the union and serves the woman as a house help. The system was in one of the European countries with those men or people called "Puree-boys". Randy hated the system of turning a woman into a money-printing machine, which some of the men always said they wanted for practicalism and had them for their belated and horrible intentions. As Randy loathed the Slavic theory and needs of the union so too did he hate all they did in the name of human survival in a foreign land. Prostitution was the last thing Randy wanted to get himself mixed up with in his plans. In the new order, the woman was supposed to do the job while the man acts as a shadow husband. It was better called pimping a system of procuring or pandering. These things and plans were discussed freely without any shame and conscience. For them, it was the in-thing and had to be done whichever way, for those not partaking are thought not to be man enough to be men. Randy would later come to see healthy men rollicking and relishing the proceeds from some women from Africa without morals and etiquette with their weaker halves into Europe. The men had no conscience as they went about soliciting for men openly to sleep with mothers of children back home that did not belong to them, daughters of other men like them and sisters of other men they in turn called their women. It was a despicable, execrable and unspeakable way of life that most seemed to have loved and enmeshed themself uncontrollably. It was an eyesore to see one of these ladies and think of one girl or woman in one's own family going that way. It was irreparable societal damage in those days.

Randy had promised to visit them on his way back, but it never was going to materialize as planned. The nauseating sight made the intended realism of ever seeing them again unattainable. There was so much information gathered from those Randy had met with his Taof before going back for financial reload. Taof and the new woman had started to talk about where and how they would pass the night and much more, things had started working out for them amorously. There was at least that love in the air between new lovers no matter how long it lasted or short-lived. Of all the information Randy gathered, one of them sounded too bad for him to put up with but while he detested it some people loved and savoured it with endless gusto. It was the idea of continuing the travel with a woman as a partner and using her as a source of income. Randy asked them to call it Pimp which none of them would agree as being the truth. Randy considered it a last resort for the lazy and lily-livered men. Prostitution was the last thing Randy wanted to be associated with or involved in. Irrespective of his thoughts, others saw it and used it as a way of life. Some of the women hated it while some relished dearly in it.

Randy had now realized that the money they had on them was only a pittance from what they would have had for the entire journey. Since what they needed was contradictory to their budget, Randy volunteered to go back to his country leaving his ex-nephew's friend behind in Niger. Randy's acquaintance, meanwhile, had been looking at Taof amorously as they entered the house. Randy needed only a few words to request her to take care of Taof as he went back to financially reload from his country of origin. Taof on his part loathed the idea of going back with Randy for some obvious and ominous reasons.

Members of the house escorted Randy to the garage the next day. On their way, he advised Taof to travel anytime he was able to continue the journey. He asked Taof not to wait for him because people always had different lucks, and everyone has to take his or her chances in life. He deliberately did not advise Taof against taking any woman along. Taof was old enough to decide on his own, whether to go with one of the bevvies of women domed triangular hole money printing machines or not.

Randy returned to his country of origin through a bush part from the Niger border. It was an open burnt-out arid land with tantalizing mirages. Randy had no problem with the trekking across the border. He had his passport on him in case; any immigration official of any of both countries accosted him. The only motive for his trekking across the border was because he wanted to use the same stamp, he had gotten on his passport from the Niger border officials to re-enter the country the way he had come back into his motherland. He loathed going through thereafter he had experienced extortion in the hands of the immigration and customs officials of the Niger border crossing.

Randy spent some months gathering anything he could financially. At this time, he had told the ex-nephew all that had taken place and what stage of the journey the friend was in and why he could not come back with him. The ex-nephew understood better why his friend would not venture backtrack. Randy told them the story bit by bit to make them understand what was involved. Their hearts grew fonder for the unknown circumstances and discrepancies that marred the journey everyone considered simple with the ordinary running of a common pencil on the drawn-to-scale nautical miles on the map. Randy and the people he was educated about the journey would later know in some months that they were playing with their glorious lives on the back of a marauding Tiger. What they thought was a fairy tale before then had been confirmed as being real and they started to beg to accompany Randy on his next trip out of the country. He agreed and they started to map their plans for getting out of the country. They agreed on a date after much and thorough discussions. Randy knew what the entire journey entailed and would not risk coming back again for any reason. He had embarked on lecturing them on what and how to answer immigration officials tersely at their border control posts. He spent the next few weeks telling them how intelligent these officers were even on their worst of days with their laden cum filled heads and bribery thoughts. Verbosity with them could land anyone in the most unexpected place more so in a foreign land where the culture is almost contradictory and opposite to theirs. The bottom line was, to listen carefully and understand what is being asked. Answer directly and never give any contradictory or an answer beyond what had been asked or requested as an answer. The discussions went on for days and daily deep into the night. By now they had mastered everything to recitation point. The ground had been prepared and made fertile for the crops to grow.

Randy's ex-nephew in the company of his friend Kele started to look for money with which they will pay their way through and along for the journey. At a point, Randy's ex-nephew planned to get her mother's golden bracelets and necklaces to sell and raise money, but Randy vehemently discouraged the wrong idea. The ex-nephew then always took Randy's advice. He did not carry his plans out, but he and his friend Kele managed to make up some lies to get their respective families convinced to get some money for themselves.

Once they had gotten the money, they embarked on the journey to the northern city of Kaduna-Zaria where Randy was based. It had rained so much that day with the entire street getting swampy and cars splashed the muddy remains of the mixture on innocent passers-by. The trio left unannounced but Randy's other nephew Osik who could not muster the financial support was informed. He had been advised to keep it a closely guarded secret till whenever time made it possible to get feedback from them. He was highly trusted, and he kept the secret as was directed. The journey lap to Kaduna-Zaria from Lagos was trouble-free and heart-warming. They reached Kaduna-Zaria in the morning of the next day. Everyone tidied up and relaxed for the day. In the evening, Kele and Randy's ex-nephew Fenbrabi went to have a stroll with Cafor and eventually passed the night at his place. They were both in high spirits amidst the cosy reception they had been given by all they came in contact with in Kaduna-Zaria.

The next morning, they set out for Maradi. This was going to take them across the border of their country into their northern neighbour country of Niger. Randy had planned to get through the border as he returned to the neighbouring country while Fenbrabi and Kele would board a cab across the border. Randy's passport had been stamped on his first travel to Niger and getting across the border means he had not been out. Fenbrabi and Kele boarded a taxi that would take them across the border. By now, they had understood the hidden and embedded consequences of any mistake they would make that could derail their journey plans.

Everything in the border town garage looked new and confusing this time around. Randy made sure that both boarded the cab before setting off on a motorbike across the border. The once arid areas between the borders had been turned into farmland and, had grown into thick vegetation that was higher than the height of any conceivable tallest man. Randy asked the bike man if there was no danger of anyone hiding in the vegetation to commit some atrocity against unsuspecting and innocent people who were on a business of looking for their daily hard-to-get bread, the bike man encouraged him to mount and told him that it was free passable land, more so a no man's land where no visa was required of both countries' citizens. As Fenbrabi and Kele left so too Randy and the bike man ride off through the farm road. The bike man would take Randy to the border and, another man, a guide would pilot him through the streets and finally to the main road. Randy had some premonitions that something was going to happen, but he had to go. He saw people still meandering through some of the bush paths with their wares and cargoes. By this time, Randy's heart had gone berserk. His heart was throbbing at a crescendo unimaginable till the vegetation swallowed them. He was more in the negative than positive. As Randy was on the bike, he started to think that the bike man could be the bait and a collaborator with some of the fake or real border officers. Randy knew the country so well with most of the things that went on behind the scenes to appease some of the officers' devilish designs. There were times if not always when some people connived to rip off innocent and unsuspecting people in many inconceivable ways. There are times one knows unavoidable impending dangers would come but cannot shield them off from coming to pass. As they rode on the sandy path after about one kilometre with Randy still expecting the worst that might befall him, there came a sudden and thundering sound from the spokes attached to the wheels of the bike. The bike veered off the path and the rider and passenger fell in different directions without any remarkable injury. Two men immediately emerged from the bush and claimed they were immigration officers. The men had made their unrecognized presence felt and relished in their odd behaviour. They requested for Randy's passport and searched all he had on him. The officers were now having their field day on Randy. As the officers did their illegitimate job on Randy, the bike man pretended to be sympathetic and assist him. All had been planned and well-coordinated. The bike man was an officer himself and they knew they were wrong to be involved in what they were doing but who was there to question their authority in the bush where no one knew what was going on. That pathway was solely for them and their victims.

Everyone fears danger when it does not exist but once accosted by it, the onus is to face it boldly, squarely, and intelligently. Never entertain any fears in the face of any danger. All fears atrophy in the face of any danger. Combat any danger bravely and see what result you achieve proving your intrepidness. That was exactly what Randy did in the instance of the self-imposing and unapproved road blockade set up by the brutish bush immigration officers.

As the officers relished in their flagrant and unacceptable behaviour toward innocent citizens, Randy thought about Fenbrabi and his friend who he thought must have crossed the border and waiting for him on the other side of a new country. Randy would have asked for their identification cards but thought that it will spell doom and painful mishandling for him in the bush where no one was then watching the goings-on. The fake officers had seen an earlier immigration stamp that Randy had used in travelling out of the country. They were hell-bent on making trouble and creating further problems for Randy because they had seen the bulk of the money, he had on him and wanted to apply the law wrongly to have a share of it. Randy thought how this set of fake broad daylight marauding thieves could be reined in but it was impossible at that moment he was leaving the country and would not like to delve into what will cause him an unnecessary delay. The fake officers knew that position and capitalized on it. The officers had asked Randy if he knew he was leaving the country the wrong way. Randy told the fake immigration officers that, it was a free border that did not require any citizen of the regional zone and others that had any reason to cross the border to be disturbed, challenged, or molested, he called the attention of the officers to all that were crisscrossing the border and internally nursed why the bike man was not being quizzed along with him. Randy got very rile but handled the situation with some wry smiles to tarry and confuse the officers. They were working on themselves with telepathy of a kind.

The money the fake immigration officers had seen had gotten their heads swollen and will not let go. They asked Randy to strike a financial deal with them before they would let him go. As the situation got worst, Randy thought about Fenbrabi and his friend who by then must have been at the mercy of some unknown dangers. Randy thought as usual that, the duo must have crossed the border and felt jittery at the non-arrival of their main pilot. If Randy did not arrive early enough, it will raise some concern and unwarranted suspicion at the border town. He had no option but to accept the deal they proposed. He gave them the needless financial bribe amount the officers had imposed on him to assuage the situation and try to catch up with the denudating time. He knew the duo would be running up and down in a taxi trying to locate him for their onward journey to Maradi.

The fake immigration and customs officers allowed Randy to leave with the bike man after they had completed their looting clearance circuit. It was an ordeal and officialdom that would harden Randy before any real or fake border officials in years to come. The journey from that point till when Randy disembarked from the motorbike went well and trouble-free. The biker had navigated the thinly populated vegetation till he reached a man in the field. The bike man stopped somewhere and trekked some distance together with Randy before they met a man inside the farm that claimed he was the guide. The guide set his charges and immediately set off on foot with Randy into the village. In this business of border "*hikihiki*" (*entering and exiting countries through unofficial ways without travel documents*) you never bargained so much, the guide has all advantages over the customer. The guide just pointed to the way for Randy and asked him to go straight till he gets to the main road. It took Randy a few minutes to trek into the village and to the main road.

As Randy waited patiently to meet Fenbrabi and his friend Kele, one man Randy had recognised went up to him to ask him where he was coming from and to identify himself. Before the man would identify himself, Randy told him that he knew him and that he had personally stamped his passport at the border when he came into Niger. Randy knew his visa was still valid and indefinite. The Niger border officer this time was on a covert operation. He was in the midst of some people when he spotted Randy and went up to him immediately, he was sighted from afar. Randy handed him his passport for confirmation of his claim about the officer stamping and signing his visa. The officer was incredibly surprised for a foreigner to have known him after some months. The Niger officer ended up chatting with Randy and wanted to know where Randy was going, Randy said he was going to Maradi but was waiting for some friends. The Officer had forgotten that he stamped Arlit inside Randy's passport, even though he had inspected it on the spot. Randy may have made him take things lightly after telling him about when they met the very first time at the border. Randy nursed a brief bad thought on why the Officer should question his freedom of movement but swallowed it. Little did the officer know that Randy had just emerged from the no man's land bush path to avoid their extortion and exorbitant financial demands which in a way Randy had paid for on his countryside of the border.

Randy had wondered during his first visit how almost everyone was involved in Petroleum trafficking right under the nose of his country's Federal designated security personnel authority. Illegal trading went on unchecked with reckless abandon. To Randy, nothing was illegal there since everything went on without anyone being surprised and baffled. He now realized why the border officers condescended to collect bribery with a much more reckoning force to be part and parcel of the decadent system. Bribery is endemic, a willy-nilly with added nitty-gritty at both border posts. The officers of both countries had the official powers of the gun with them. Law enforcement officers compromise and cooperate to commit crimes against innocent citizens.

The briberies and tortures at the border reminded Randy of an incident that involved one policeman and a civilian at one of those many nefarious checkpoints erected to extol money from people. It went this way: the victim was waived to a stop at the checkpoint, which he obeyed. All his documents were right and the car was in perfect working order but the policeman who controlled him would not let go because he asked the policeman what he had done to warrant the unnecessary checks. The policeman asked him where he had gotten the money inside his car. He told the policeman he was just coming from where he had gone to withdraw some money from the bank. He showed the constable the withdrawal form to make the questions less, but the evidence triggered off a domino effect. The constable got angry that; he was a challenging officer of the law with big grammar. The victim asked why his human right was being infringed upon, but he got more and more into an unpardonable position. The constable realizing, he was talking to a court clerk who had connections in higher places, got angry and told the victim, "you are lucky that this is happening in the daytime, what do you mean with human rights and who is denying you of any right? "Shut your mouth" if this were to have taken place at night, I will sacrifice your life and declare you an armed robber, you want to tell me you are learned and connected to high places and above the law, you want me to lose my job, I will waste your life now if you talk again to me." The victim fearing the constable's binge and inebriate state cum warnings tarried down morosely and accepted the police officer's demands. He bribed the police officers and quietly left the scene. After all, he has fought and wisely decided to run away but to fight another day, if he ever chooses to face them again, but must be sure is not nightfall and has to be where there are many people to garner supportive evidence for survival.

Fenbrabi and his friend appeared in a cab from the direction of Maradi as Randy stood by the wayside. The duo had been searching along the road for his presence as planned. The cab they were in turned swiftly and Randy joined them to drive to Maradi. The Niger plain-clothed immigration officer had hardly seated himself with the people he was chatting with when he saw Randy boarding the cab. He waved Randy goodbye from the distance. Randy did not waste any time boarding the cab as it could bring about another flurry of unnecessary questions and controls of Fenbrabi and his friend.

The trio arrived at Maradi safely and trouble-free, but the way was still far from the planned and scheduled point. The people Randy met on their arrival started more stories again about the continuation of the journey. They realized that the more one travelled northwards the more the stories got complex, diversified and the more experience one amassed to circumvent some dangers. They were gory, astonishing stories that could make one's mind skip and spines freeze. They were stories that would thwart any positive mind into retrogressive life. Randy and his ex-nephew had decided against all odds to move on, come what may. Randy saw the surprises on the faces of the people they met in Maradi when they told them they would like to advance in their journey. When the people on the same journey route but temporarily stranded in Maradi or were there for the fear of advancing saw the intrepidness in Randy and his entourage, they started to tell them what and what they knew about the way ahead. Most of this news and information was gotten from those that discontinued the journey out of fear, impecuniousness, and other unavoidable human failings or setback. The dangers were imminent but had to be confronted in whichever way humanly possible. There was no short way to success except when it borders on a toto-lotto luck dip.

The same day that Randy and those accompanying him reached Maradi was the day they were lucky to get transport to Asamaka. The people around had told them that it might not be possible for them to travel same day, but luck was on their side. There were already some passengers before Randy had arrived from the border to Maradi. Their inclusion that evening would make for a full cab load. The old, stranded passengers had advised Randy and his entourage to go to the law enforcement department in the town that will in turn authorize their travelling to their preplanned destination. To the best of Randy's knowledge, they were supposed to be visa-free to anywhere in the country with unrestricted and open-ended freedom of movement to anywhere they chose to be within the country. Randy wondered at the imbecility and nonchalance most of the officers of the law had displayed right from his country's border to Maradi in the hinterland. Freedom here was re-calibrated to denials, oppression, and suppression. Unknown to Randy and co, the officers had known about the desert travels and were busy exploiting innocent and uninformed travellers. The stranded passengers were their conduits and informants to would be potential northwards proceeding travellers. If they missed anyone, they would resort to using the phone to intercept the driver that may have carried anyone without settling their unnecessary visa that was astronomically tagged at a cost so much. These stranded passengers were gangs and brigands who had formed a brigade ring of dupes and cheats. The officers' little powers were magnified and arbitrarily used to oppress the innocent and the poor who could not in any way challenge their authority, but even if one knew his rights, he could be victimized by the officers in question. They were all in a place the victims lacked the knowledge of their language, the ability to refuse coercion and to fight back their unwarranted extortion. Complaining or fighting back in the face of the injustice meted out to intending passengers was out of the plans and thoughts of the progressive minds. The officers were allowed their field day. After all, their counterparts in other adjoining states' borders were not better by all official sedimentation and human vituperative vilifications.

The people Randy and co had met in Maradi were jobless and living mostly from the prostituting women. Randy could not stomach what he had seen and what was still happening. Most of them had been there for months without any idea of when they would be able to go forward or backwards and worst still their destination. Randy settled for an immediate march on into the unknown. The people they met knew how to apply and used discouragement to persuade the intrepid and willing go-ahead travellers effectively. but only the frail at heart would listen to them. Their endless advice did not work with people like Randy and co. Randy was the true moving factor for the group. He wanted to get away from the nauseating and eyesore he had witnessed in Maradi and maybe to meet more but still have to get through them.

Randy smiled as the news of the cab for the journey was confirmed. The best accompanying news was that they would be travelling along with an extremely popular driver involved in ferrying people across to the northern city of Asamaka and, well known by all checkpoint law enforcement officers along the way. The officers on the way would find it difficult to drop anyone at the barriers with the presence of this driver, Randy asked "but for what reason would anyone be dropped or asked to discontinue a journey an adult had planned for him or herself". Randy had thought that Niger was a country where all things were possible and could happen to any visitor or foreigner with what they had experienced first-hand in his first and second visits without the outside world knowing. Everywhere in Maradi town looked dusty, desolate and abandoned. It was good to pass through town but lacks the fairness of human habitation.

Randy, Fenbrabi and his friend Kele were escorted by the new touts from the law enforcement officers to the driver's place after the un-required visas were paid for and issued to them. The touts feigning good character asked them for some money to make ends meet. After they had paid the driver, they gave the boys some pittance money. They were so happy getting what they had received from Randy. Randy wanted to get out of Maradi as quickly as possible. The boys remained with them till the driver loaded their luggage into the cab and arranged them in a special formation inside the car. They were arranged in a way that will not raise any suspicion before the officers manning the roadblocks. The officers at the roadblocks would be sleeping by the time the driver would be driving through the towns along the way to Asamaka. Randy exchanged names and addresses with the boys. They had promised to meet again and in better condition, but that moment would never come again. Their meeting was just by happenstance and would remain so. Randy and the boys had only temporarily gone through an emotional encounter even though they had met some hours back.

Before they went to the law enforcement officers for their visas, they had asked after Taof and the woman he was handed over to before Randy went back to financially reload. They were told that Taof was gone, and the woman had travelled out to some unknown place.

Travelling creates some affinity and sometimes a conducive atmosphere to make friends with different types of people and is the best degree a man could use to advance living life without prejudice and animosity. It opens one's eyes to things unimaginable, things one could only meet or see in particular places at a particular time. Is like the breaking of a cocoon and being part of the whole. It teaches organization and the oneness of the best between people from different backgrounds.

It was already dark when they left Maradi for the northern town of Asamaka. The driver drove for hours without any gallop and any town in view. They were half asleep and woke up intermittently because of the bodily contact and inconveniences in the overloaded small cab space. They were always expecting the unexpected at any of the many checkpoints. Law enforcement officers manning the different checkpoints stopped them about thrice on the way, but the driver always spoke for everyone. No one apart from the driver could speak the official and local languages of French and Berber respectively. The driver was a momentary Messiah for all his passengers. No money changed hands through the entire journey to Asamaka. Randy was surprised at the friendliness of the night officers. They were truly human and respectable but maybe due to the long night duty they had done before they reached them. Night duty wears one out.

They reached Asamaka in the morning of the next day from Maradi through Agadez. They were met by a new set of stranded people. The men and women here were closer to the action of the onward travelling than the Maradi people. No sooner had they emerged from the cab than they were surrounded by the people there and started to make friends. They were engaged with stories with fulminating loquacity improbable flow and disbelief. They had heard the stories in Maradi but it had been progressively upgraded with a clearer picture of the events and circumstances that brought the situations about.

Randy could not believe what he saw in Asamaka. Almost everyone they met here looked dejected and abandoned. One lady managed to take them into her one-room apartment. Like in Maradi, all the women in Asamaka were prostituting while some of the boys around fetched and carried water with stick bars on their shoulders for their prospective buyers, and this was not a daily and secured job. The woman they were in her place ushered them in because she thought they would be stranded and stay together as others did, then wallow in the same predicament and at best could travel with them as a money-printing machine. She was wrong with her assumptions. Both reasons she may have had were wrong with Randy's position and his entourage. The woman started to suddenly receive visitors; people were coming to see those newcomers to the town. There were three men, and any free woman could take from the extra two to make for a temporary husband of convenience, but Randy and others were not in for that mess of a situation, they wanted to go. It was a forward ever movement for them to their desired destination, "Libya". No going back and no delay of any kind that could be avoided. The people they met in Asamaka would have known better from their forward-ever actions and responses to them.

The visitors to the woman came with different discouraging stories and the worst was the financial account for the journey. After the calculations, Randy discovered they had not enough money to continue the trip. He had learned from Maradi on his first trip that people needed to carry enough of their physical and highly valuable belongings, which could be sold for cash to cushion them financially in the time of dire need and to continue the journey perse. Here was the opportunity to put into practice one of the hard realities of what he had heard and learned from the stranded people's stories and voices. Randy felt too decent to live the type of life people were living there and did not want to be consumed by it. The idea of taking a woman along was thrown at them once more by the romantic women and warned them of the danger of leaving without one. They hammered their reason home that, the repercussion of not going with women would be very deadly and endlessly agonizing. Randy did not understand the woman matter being injected into the travelling forward and how it was being operated other than that, the embedded prostitution therein. There was more to it but only an insider who Randy did not want to become would understand it. Fenbrabi and Kele were not in the mood for it either. The trio had hatred for it and stood their ground amidst the unacceptable convictions from the women. They all needed a free journey far from women's ordeals, strangulations, and problems.

As they realized their short of fund to continue, they decided to sell off some of their valuable belongings to raise the needed money. Randy on his part sold his portable radio, expensive woollen winter jacket, Adidas top, down sportswear, and lots of other valuables. Fenbrabi and Kele sold the things they could too. Randy had bought all he had sold from Rotterdam some years back and was painful to see them go in such inexpensive pitiable conditions. The lady they had temporarily lodged in her place for some hours bought the radio before taking Randy and co to the Stranded people's market where all items and materials had the same price and value. The buyers knew everyone was stranded and profited from their extremely poor position. The rock bottom price seemed to have been agreed upon by the natives before any ware or material was brought to the market. There was no appreciation for anything that came to be sold in the market. It was a crude customer service treatment of taking it or leave it affair. Randy and co needed the money so much and wanted to leave the same day of their arrival in Asamaka. They gathered their money together from the sales.

Asamaka is a lonely, dusty and flies-infested town. Foreigners who were using the town as a transit point were more than her original citizens. The foreigners built makeshift houses called "Bukoki" (makeshift houses made with woven sacks for packing e.g rice or beans or garri). These were houses made of old torn woollen sacks and cellophane products that had been used for export and import for food packaging, to just name all the odds of a mixture that were supported with tiny slings and tiny sticks. These structures were erected on open land without any top to act as a roof. The inhabitants were lucky that it hardly rained in that area of physical geographical location. One could easily see what went on inside the *Bukoki* make-shift erected open-air settlements. It was like living in an open field and making love openly to people's view. None of the people Randy met there was ashamed of their position, character, and behaviour. They believed it was a better life away from the different countries they were coming from. Randy hated the living standards and wanted to disconnect from it as fast as he came to Asamaka but he did not know what the next station and future held in stock for them. Leaving was better than staying in the *Bukoki* flies-infested slum. By Randy's reckoning, things were getting uglier and nastier with every progress they made northwards of the continent.

They had been discussing how they would advance since their arrival to Asamaka. They have kept all deaf ears to all forms of standstill persuasion discouragements and had sold all their valuables to be able to continue to their intended destination. A determined man sets challenges for himself. The woman showed them where they would have to come to board vehicles in the evening to Arlit as they returned from all wares one price market.

They went to the hollow and very sandy assembly point called the garage. There were some law enforcement officers on hand to make sure that there was orderliness and that every intended passenger paid his fare before being ushered into the open jeep.

True to Randy's plan, they were leaving to the dismay and bewilderment of those they had met there that day in Asamaka. Every one of them that witnessed their arrival said, "they had not seen anyone come and leave the same day". It was the same statement that echoed in Maradi. Randy thought that "human beings could do anything if they had the right determination for accomplishment to continue". Laziness and dillydallying on issues regurgitate failures. The focus should always be the bottom line and watchword for success. No wonder they would be able to make it through all the discouragements, retrogressive traps and gorges of speculations.

There were some people they met at the assembly point with, whom they immediately started a friendship and had to help them out to complete their fares for the journey. It was an overly complicated journey that would need a close-knitted sort of friendship and camaraderie. It would be abominable to be an island unto oneself. People helped themselves in their time of dire need. It was like soldiers going to war. They love and help one another to safety if only they could and depending on the circumstances.

12

SAHARAN DRIVE

RANDY HAD THOUGHT THE JOURNEY TO ARLIT WOULD LAST SOME TWO OR THREE HOURS, BUT IT WAS a wrong and improbable assumption. The drivers moved in convoy in a scattered parallel formation to avoid blurring the views of one another and to reduce the vehicle agitated Sahara dust inhalation by the passengers. Another good reason was to help one another should there be any vehicle break down among them. They travelled all night to avoid the daytime seething Saharan heat. The drivers had only one stoppage at night for the passengers to relax their crumpled legs and have some refreshments in the open desert. The passengers had been asked to sleep anywhere they chose in the open terrain. The first stop in the desert had acted as baptism for an endurance test for the journey and the continuation of it from subsequent yet-to-reach main locations. From available stories, the journey they had made was only the tip of the iceberg compared to what was looming ahead. The people they met at Asamaka had told them how to survive in the desert. Randy had bought *"Bidon" (a water container covered with sewn woven sack parts to cool the water inside of it against the fiery and tormenting temperature of the Sahara desert)* at Asamaka and sewed an old sack around it to hold the cool temperature of the water content long enough before it goes warm again with the desert heat.

Randy had expected their jeep to run on a free and tarred road since they left Asamaka but contrary to their expectations it continued on a dusty open Sahara Desert. The terrain was getting colder and colder as they drove on. He could not immediately make out why there was no designated or constructed freeway. It was his first time travelling in a rocky, sandy and dusty environment. Everywhere was wide and open-ended to infinity. It was based on these thoughts that Randy realized that they were too far away from home and in the middle of nowhere. Randy said, "This was the Sahara Desert" one of the most inhospitable terrains on earth". It was at this time that, the danger of what they were involved in started to sink into him, but those thoughts were ephemeral and failed to represent his truly respected compiled purposeful intentions. Randy was no weakling. He would take on any meaningful challenges that would yield good substance or results. Risks are worth the importance of their recognizable gains and Randy was making one worth it for him and his children. The politics of godfatherism in his home country pushed him into experiencing the risk he undertook firsthand. If the leaders of his country had made it to the standard of what they see overseas, millions of his countrymen and women will not be prone to going to *"Abrucheri"* (*Ghanaian name for abroad*). African children turn their backs on their countries because the leaders turn the anvil on their citizens' heads. To this end, the people endeavour to avoid being obliterated from humanity by sometimes fleeing the consequential looming onslaught. Fears atrophy when the danger becomes imminent.

They reached Arlit the next day morning after an all-night drive from Asamaka. Arlit had little or no infrastructure to offer and no one seemed to inhabit the place in the middle of nowhere. It was only a border post to mark where a country ends at a particular point of geographical terrain. Arlit is one of the roughest, deadliest, and most inhuman borders on earth by Randy's reckoning and it has all the adduced attributes. If any passenger cannot pay for the next leg of the journey out from there, he or she was instantly sent back to Asamaka for his or her safety and health precautionary measures. Anyone left in Arlit would die in some hours after being abandoned. There was no means of any conceivable livelihood there. It is a border post without any city or village nearby. The only structure in Arlit was only the junk and rickety law enforcement post. Randy saw Arlit as only an existing name for a border. Randy nicknamed it "the empty Siberian cold landscape of Africa." They were asked a few minutes before they drove into Arlit to have their breakfast. Everyone at this point ate his food absentmindedly. The tendrils had drooped from the body of the plant and so were all the passengers from their morphological assemblies. Everyone looked morose and famished at this point of the journey. The willpower gauge was dropping fast, but they cheered one another to sustenance.

They were checked individually as in Asamaka and loaded unto four open-body land cruisers. The officers there told them that they were from that point human contraband goods, the reason being that all the passengers were living in an area of the continent where they could still waive visa demands by the law. They were now going into another part of the continent where they were supposed to have a visa before entry but were going the *"hikihiki"* way. Randy thought about the term "contraband", and he shook his head on identifying that the odds were against him and others. From that moment, his passport was invalid, he could be treated like an animal and could die any moment without anyone knowing his whereabouts and if he ever ended up dying, there would be no flies or any vulture to scavenge on his decaying body. These creatures knew more than humans that life did not exist in that area of the continent because of the excessive and unbearable temperature.

The temperature was still picking up for the day when they left Arlit and all those that could not pay for their journey were quietly returned to Asamaka. As a rule, not propounded by anyone but by Mother Nature, the ones travelling did everything almost as a family right from the word go. The passengers comprised of different people from different countries with a common purpose of breaking and shattering the invincible iron curtain. The goal was simple but exceedingly difficult to accomplish and achieve.

The drivers moved their jeeps with the most terrifying deep throttle down in parallel convoy. Randy started to reminisce on the contraband term they were referred to as being.

The thinking gave him a simple clue at what had happened at the said Arlit border. The law enforcement officers of both countries of Niger and Algeria connived with one another to allow the passage of goods, mostly foreign-made cigarettes and people that are smuggled through the desert across their common borders. Ingizim was the other notorious and atrocious border opposite or alternate Arlit on the South East Algerian side.

When Randy and the other passengers had driven for hours non-stop, they started to wonder where they were driving. Everywhere was open and undulating. There was no sign of any life apart from them in the middle of nowhere. The journey seemed endless and interminable. No one among them could tell when the lap of the journey was going to end, it was running into unbearable eternity, but they only knew and constantly called the name of the next destination.

Tamanrasset

One of the jeeps developed a minor fault that was quickly rectified. During the fixing, some of the drivers started to view the open and desolate distance and space with their powerful binoculars. That goes to say that while the border law enforcement officers sabotaged the acclaimed constitutional laws in place, the inland law enforcement officers tried to some reasonable extent to do their official jobs rightly. After all, there were so many bad eggs in the police and other forces that thwart the effort of the good ones. The question is how many were true, sincere and noble? Some military personnel sometimes deliberately kill their own purely out of ill blood or on planned mistakes and pretend to be mentally maladjusted. Some commit crimes and circumvent the course of justice, while some act as investigators and still pervert the course of justice in many ways known and unknown to man. Things happen among and between all the branches of the forces in peace and war times. What Randy had observed and seen at the border was not different from what happened in many unaccounted-for borders all over the world. Randy's thinking about the inland officers' sincerity in trying to parade the desert would be proved wrong or right in days to come.

Randy looked at the endless vast and open land from his position speechless and said suddenly "the desert was exactly the opposite of the Seas and Oceans". It was like standing or sitting on a boat in the middle of the Ocean. It lies endlessly with chains of tantalizing mirages. The drivers used the movement of the sun, aided by their mastering of the terrain and other discernible geographical structures to get their directional bearings. The drivers were masters of their job and Randy respected their ingenuity and knowledge. They cared much about the vehicles because the lives of everyone on board depended on their functioning.

In the early evening of the day, they left Arlit, they were driven into one of the numerous rock formation enclosures after many hours of a continuous throttle of the vehicles. The drivers disembarked and went behind one of the rocks and emerged with full jerry cans of petrol to refuel the vehicles. Everywhere was silent under the ravaging and unforgiving heat of the Sahara Desert. Everyone had to be silent because no law or constitutional rights were respected by any of the drivers. They had shown it and only the fool will challenge their authority in the middle of nowhere. Whatever they did or said was right in the instance. Robberies and jungle justice pervaded the entire Sahara Desert. Whoever had the power could kill the weak and powerless without any repercussion. Many Arabs criss-cross the entire Sahara Desert carrying military weapons. If there was any war or any uprising that freely served them weapons, the Sahara will be almost impenetrable to visitors. This is because it will be awash with assorted weapons of indescribable magnitude. Robberies and unreasonable killings would become the pastime of the people living in the enclave. Lots of crimes were committed against humanity in the Sahara Desert. An incident happened before the refuelling spot: It happened when the minor fault had been rectified. The driver in which Randy was travelling in his jeep had asked them to sit in a particular formation even though he knew his passengers were packed like sardines, ten people and all luggage at the back of an open body jeep racing uncontrollably more than any best formula one driver and without anything special to hold on to. The drivers warned everyone to hold tightly to anything and that anyone that bounced off the jeep would be lost forever. It was exactly what they preached. They had no value for the people they did not know and were undocumented in any case. They were the lords of the human contrabands. The bottom line henceforth was "total submission and obedience". They looked gentle but were heartless Lions in human skins. Never mess up with a Berber in the Sahara Desert. These are the *"ogwugwudada" (the name of the Berbers and Fulanis who seasonally came to southern Nigeria to sell their native medical wares)* guys you find come on a visit to some countries in West Africa. They are mean and mean to the core when in their natural domain and habitat. Human life does not mean anything to them and mostly when one is not of their religion. Religion has disintegrated the world to a very confusing crescendo. Most religious leaders that preach purity are even involved in pornographic practices, but their followers see them as sanctified and puritanical Saints. Randy will say, "Tell me now, who is fooling who". Most religious leaders fool their unsuspecting followers by preaching one thing with a Bible or Quaran in one hand but still have a very murky, insidious, and distractive sense of an image on the other. The world saw what was discovered in some leaders' houses when there was a revolution in some of the Arab countries. Alcoholic drinks, nude pictures etc., but the governed are deprived of the same in the name of leading by example. False and feigned examples to the unsuspecting sheepish and dogmatic followers revealed by unexpected happenstance. Where lies the purity in the instance? The uninvited truth surfaced to take her rightful place in the history of their different countries.

One of the passengers on Randy's vehicle Eda challenged the driver who had asked him to stay in a space too small for him. The driver did what he knew best as a desert marauding kingpin. He slapped Eda before he could utter any statement a second time. It was a very demoralizing slap that got everyone into his right senses. He warned Eda that, he could be dropped on the spot and abandoned to die in the middle of nowhere. Eda had on his part been pompous and bullish to almost everyone before then. Everyone secretly sympathize with him but was alerted to a new dawn of warning for the dangers of any more misbehaviour from any of them.

Late evening of the same day they had left Arlit, the drivers stopped in a valley and made a fire for cooking. They killed a goat, which was roasted and shared among all. They baked some bread in the desert sand without any smoke showing or moving around. The drivers have gotten some savvy techniques of doing their things in the desert to elude detection from the authorities. They dug a hole deep enough in the depression and balanced the pot on top to prevent the smoke from spreading around. In effect, if some law enforcement officers were around, they would not be able to pinpoint their position. They knew all the areas where they could easily get some tiny feeble sticks to make fire and points where animals and man shared water in the desert aquifer.

The way and manner the drivers behaved gave Randy some concern but did not want to make his thoughts known to other passengers. As the drivers are stubborn and unbending to normal human reasoning, Randy started to think about what to do to at least instil some sanity and discipline into their cancerous smuggling brains. Randy knew that there was no room for any disobedience for everyone, but the drivers respected him from the inception of the journey, noting how he comported himself gently.

After they had eaten their goat meat with couscous, they started to tell some fabled stories in languages both parties hardly understood. Randy realised the disrespect from the drivers was going on at an unimaginable and unacceptable magnitude; he started to perform some hocus-pocus African tradition that made them reverse their thinking about the passengers they were carrying. At the time the performance was over, the drivers stood straight with their passengers. The humiliation and disrespect of the passengers had been deleted from their blood-sucking hearts and thoughts. They were surprised at the way someone could handle fire without getting burnt. They knew from that point that, they could be outwitted and deleted if need be in the middle of nowhere like they have all along thought about their passengers. Negligence had been terminated on their path but Randy and co wanted a safe and good ending to the travelling and unfolding drama. Everyone was happy about the performance as it restored dignity and sanity for all once more and before the desert smugglers.

Unknown to all other passengers, Randy harboured a wave of very strong anger and dislike for further maltreatment of any other passenger. He had what it would have taken to defend them but did not let them know about it. He kept his cool and patient till an ugly situation would arise. Randy wanted a danger that would go beyond slapping before he would hold them spellbound with unimaginable displays that would have to astound them to their bone marrows. Luckily, they escaped it with the new respect they had ushered into their ephemeral friendship. Randy only decided to give the drivers the dose of what they thought they knew too much more than anyone else.

While Randy displayed to set the hearts of the drivers in the right place about them, some other passengers tried to imitate him and, in the process, got them self-injured but never allowed the drivers to know they were in pain. Randy had warned them against imitating him but some of them foolishly tried what they did not know how it functioned in a world hard and very deep to understand.

The drivers arrived with their passengers in Tamanrasset after two days they had left Asamaka at uncontrolled speed. The journey had looked as if they were going nowhere but it had a defined and definite end then. The drivers secretly dropped the passengers in a desolate area with very scanty vegetation and undulating high rocky and sandy hills.

The desert has so many beautiful sceneries with endless wonderful, physical and natural geographical formations. The features are endless. Randy felt like reviewing his physical geography and map reading lessons in the college. He did not notice any geographical realizations or the feelings on the faces of any of the passengers that occupied their jeep throughout the journey from Arlit to Asamaka and till that moment in Tamanrasset. Randy seemed to have been in a world only he knew what was revolving around a multitude of people. His heart and interest were most of the time centred on the lessons he had received on the subject many years ago. Randy remembered all his former classmates in the college and how all of them enjoyed the subject and made exceptionally good grades in all the associated branches of the subject. He deciphered and knew every rock or sand formation he saw in the desert. He would then praise and pray for all the tutors that had taught him and other students of his heydays. They were all dedicated tutors apart from a few disgruntled and arrogant ones among them. These were the physical features they taught them that none of them the teachers have ever seen themselves, but they were right in their ability to imbibe the knowledge unto a third party. Randy praised his understanding and what the past had meant to him with his educational background. He had connected the past fully with the present and it gave him a temporary respite from the present agonizing cataclysmic moments. Education and travelling are synonymous with knowledge. They are two inseparable but intertwined worlds.

13

SAHARAN TREK

WHEN THEY DISEMBARKED FROM THE JEEPS, THE DRIVERS POINTED IN THE DIRECTION OF THE TOWN for them to follow before speeding away. Randy had a blue twenty litres water can for refilling the smaller ones. It was too big to be dragged along from that point. The twenty-litre can would give their position out to any law enforcement officer and would also inconvenience him personally from easy mobility. Randy managed to pull the water-filled twenty-litre jerry can up the first little hill away from the road to avoid arousing any suspicion. Once he had crossed the road and down the hill on the other side of the bush, it was abandoned. They started to trek in the direction of a Good Samaritan who redirected them to which direction led into the town. The place looked like a farm. They followed through into the town. The Good Samaritan knew obviously what status they had and must have seen lots of people in such dire situations before from the way he acted and directed them. He was good-natured and receptive. Not everyone in a race or people is bad. There will always be the bad, the good and the ugly among them. It is the bad ones that attract insults and curse against the whole. The whole is forgiven because of the few good ones too.

They followed the path and walked calmly as he had directed them. He left them immediately after he had passed his compass knowledge to them. He would be accused of sabotage were he to have been seen with them. They all dispersed and went along in different directions but with a common goal of entering the town. It was the last time some of them would see themselves in the rat race for life. What do they expect from a journey they had been branded as contraband? It meant that they were illegal aliens with no defined status of any kind and should expect the worst of anything in everything.

They parted as the roads and footpaths parted but managed to see one another trekking in the same direction. Within some distance, the terrain started to rise nauseatingly, and people started to lose sight of one another. The rising terrain was turning now to hills and boulders making them vulnerable. They had left the bracken that gave them some cover and succour to move. They needed to tread softly and slowly from that point. They were hungry and had to climb the mountain to her apex. They had to be careful to evade the eagle eye of the security personnel overlooking the mountainous terrains.

When they parted ways, Randy made sure he was in the company of his ex-nephew and his friend Kele. They had reached the zenith of the mountain and could see the town from the top. Randy knew it was not going to be easy to get down, but they must and have to. Their destination lay bare before them with the inherent dangers. The affinity, oneness, unity, cooperation and conglomeration had waned and atrophied among the once passenger family before they got atop the mountain, but Randy and his entourage remained with the same bond with which they had left home together.

Randy, Fenbrabi and Kele hid under the rock with the sun blasting her energy out on their sore bodies and intact souls. They could see two other guys Gozchi and Gese from the distance but were well hidden from being seen from the foot of the mountain. Randy had warned everyone to be very careful from giving out their position from careless movements. It was daylight and no one had the chance of descending without being seen from the distance. They were all scared because they did not know where they were going and what would befall them after their descent. One could be descending and get caught or arrested by the law enforcement agents and who knows what fate had in stock after that. All wanted safety but the open-access was hard to juggle, assess and access. The declivity was steep, rugged and dangerous but was the only way to get down to the foot of the mountain. Descending looked simple and easy a task to accomplish but beneath the simplicity lay incalculable and unforeseen detrimental dangers. Randy thought "someone had to break the ice to get the simmering fears off others' minds". His thought was to get his entourage going by being a model and an example in the instance. He was ready now for the first position to descend the mountain, but he asked who wanted to go first. No one was ready for the daylight descent instead, wanted it under a bit of dark cover to be able to elude the security personnel thought to have dotted the area. Randy had assessed and seen the invincible fears on everyone's faces. He internally made up his mind to be the first but chatted with Fenbrabi and Kele. Randy said, "I am going first — whatever happens, you guys should be careful — if we are through it, we will meet sometime and somewhere inside the town". They agreed and while Gozchi and Gese looked on from under the rock, Randy waved them goodbye. Randy was equally afraid of the uncertainty that might befall Fenbrabi and Kele in his absence, but he had to go to show them that it was possible to advance from that flight height on foot to the foot of the mountain.

When Randy looked downwards, it was too far to face but what had to be done had to be done in all fairness and fast. He started to ponder on how he could get down to the road without being seen, which person he was going to meet in the town, and how he would be able to reunite with his ex-nephew and friend. Those questions bothered him, but he pretended not to have any substance. Fenbrabi and Kele believed in Randy's talent and trusted his intrepidness, which made the moment a time not to show any weakness in the face of the imminent odds. They all had to be men and men they were. The journey was not for the insurmountable, weakling and lily-livered but the surmountable, indomitable, intrepid, and extant forthright thinkers.

Randy looked into the eyes of Fenbrabi and Kele. They all knew the meaning of the look. He did not waive them goodbye as he did to Gozchi and Gese. He turned away from them and took the descent first step. The mountain started to control his centre of gravity at a pace he could hardly manage, he was running on bare rock surface that at the bottom of the mountain carried some thin sand to cushion the base of the mountain. Randy's gravitational control from the top of the mountain was automatic. He reached the base safely and looked back to find the people he had left atop the mountain so small to be considered humans in the distance but could be discerned with a powerful binocular as used to be the case with the law enforcement agents. It was at that point that it dawned on him that the ex-nephew and his friend would survive what he had just gone through. He could not believe that it was him that had made the descent from the unbelievable height. Any skydiver would prefer to fly from that height with a parachute and quietly land at the base. The quick and direct descent was not the healthiest but was the only way and method left for getting into the unknown desert town.

While Randy was still atop the mountain, he had decided which direction he would follow on getting to the base of the mountain but once he was down, everywhere looked strange and misleading. The cardinal points at this time were irrelevant and obfuscating but in a split-second decision, he opted to walk to the left-hand side of the tiny road he reached from the top. He made that decision because the right-hand side of the road had Tyre marks and must have been Police vehicles trailing or tracing some illegal immigrants into the town.

The best motor engine to drive around in the desert is any four-wheeled activated car or vehicle. Any car short of the mentioned qualities is doomed on the endless and vast sandy terrain.

Randy crossed the sandy road from where he had descended to the edge of the town and made straight for the rocks that looked like a burial ground. Nature had designed the place to deceive man into wrong thoughts. Randy had expected himself to get through the area and into the city with very minimal problems. It was the road that the drivers that brought them from Asamaka must have driven through into the town. He was sure because he had seen it from the mountain on the far-left-hand side of their direction. After traversing the road, he headed for the rock's cover but his "*hikihiki* survival techniques" would fail him abruptly for having wrongly decided on his chosen direction. As he reached the flat beautiful rock areas, he was suddenly accosted by two young military officers who undoubtedly had been stationed there to patrol and seek people like him out. While anyone in that part of the world could take laws into their hands and do whatever they liked away from the government of the day, Randy thought otherwise and better that, "who would not like to guide or effect a safe security for her citizenry"? None.

The two officers did not understand the English language and neither did Randy understand or talk their local Arabic language. They started to talk in very incomprehensible, porous, unimaginable, and adulterated English. Randy had to force himself to understand with gesticulations at a cost to get himself freed from them. They introduced themselves as policemen without any identity but for their guns that could easily be used in that desolate

93

and deserted surroundings, Randy mellowed but doubted what a government representative would be doing in such a place. They started to say: Money! Money!! Money!!! Jib! Jib!! Jib! Then they switched to the French language saying: L'argent! L'argent!! L'argent!!! And reverted again to English: Money! Money!! And finally, to Flusse! Flusse!! Flusse!!! In Arabic but all was about extorting money from Randy. He told them he had no money on him. As they were trying to question him further, Gozchi and Gese suddenly appeared, and the officers were amazingly fast at apprehending them. As the military officers concentrated on both arrest and questioning, Randy quietly went off their human radar detection. When they turned and did not see Randy, one of the officers held on to Gozchi and Gese while the other searched for him in the adjoining rocks. Randy noticed that there was no way he could go far or elude them on the vast and open terrain without being seen from where he was hiding. He came out immediately from his hiding place and told the officer he was extracting some bodily wastes under one of the rocks nearby. He did not want an ugly or worse situation to develop from an already bad one. The officers would be very angry and maltreat him if it was discovered he wanted to run away from them without yielding to their already made demands. Randy prayed quietly for the officers not to ask after where he had deposited the foreign bodies otherwise, he would be taken as a teaser and liar. The officers matched him to meet Gozchi and Gese. They pretended not to have seen or known one another before. They searched their small baggage and found nothing of value. When they searched his body, they discovered he had two photochromic-medicated glasses with golden rims. They tested them on the ridges of their nostrils and demanded them. Randy's eyes were not that weak then, so they capitulated on that single reason to confiscate them for the place of the bribe money he could not offer them. The two officers were down-to-earth certified official desert robbers from their mannerisms.

Randy only used the expensive eyeglasses to escape being robbed of his fare money for the onward journey. He had his money right and intact on him while the official robbers had touched it without knowing what it was. It could only be found, with an x-ray machine but where was the x-ray machine to be used on the dusty ground and surrounding to find out what was embedded on a part of a piece of luggage? He had sacrificed his expensive glasses to protect his last hope of advancing his cause. It was a pyrrhic victory that allowed them to let Randy off the hook to get into town through the rocks.

Before Randy could leave, Gozchi and Gese were trying to be stubborn to the officers. He spoke to them in Pidgin English that: - they should play it cool with the officers before they get into intractable and regrettable consequences that made Papa Madiba go through with the number RI 46664 for twenty-seven years in Robben Island. They were not informed enough to get what Randy meant. It was highly coded for their understanding. Then, Randy reframed the statement and advise them again saying "you guys better be careful with these gunners before they call for reinforcement that will land everyone in gaol, that only eternity will know when they would be released or freed". The message sank into them and the officers shared Randy's glasses one apiece right under his gaze. They were elated to allow all of them to go after the appease with subsequent ameliorating human libations.

They wandered along the tiny dusty road aimlessly, but they were moving and just moving to a destination unknown. After some meters of trekking, they saw a Good Samaritan they considered their own and laid their problems bare before him. He quickly understood they were just coming into town. He assisted them into a house. The owner of the house was from the Niger Republic called Suam. He was a kind man with real human feelings. He assured them that he would be able to make the required contacts with drivers that smuggle people across the desert but would be at a later date. Randy came to understand that Suam was a trolley and lived his life in the business.

On the night of their arrival to Tamanrasset, Randy was happy to be where he was but the idea of not knowing where his ex-nephew and his friend were that night gave him so much concern that he remained damp and unsettled at heart. Randy was not prepared to testify for another man's life as enmity, quarrel and other forms of misunderstandings are bound to arise without any meaningful cogitation from whatever statements one might have to adduce to any cause of whatever must have happened. Randy did not want to go back and tell stories he would not know what had happened and how it all began in their respective families, even though they were full-grown adults. Randy thought maybe he had been deficient in situational management but if anything, ever came up negative, which he prayed seriously to avoid and never to experience, he would be good enough to understand the honest misunderstandings and mistakes of intended parties, but he did not bargain or wanted such a situation. He needed success and thought he would have it.

Some people who wanted to continue their northward bound journey came to visit Suam the night Randy arrived in Tamanrasset. They had been in the town for longer than three weeks or more. The rule was to look for passengers that could be loaded like sardines at the back of the open-body land cruisers without due consideration for their lives as a full consignment. Suam later went out to find how many more new people were in town to ascertain the true position of the passenger reckoning. Suam knew where to go and seek passengers since it was his full personal official trade. For him, he had already seven contrabands in his house to add to whatever he would get from outside, but the drivers were the deciding factors. When he returned, he cooked, and the visitors augmented the food with their home-based delicacy.

The contraband visitors spent the day hearing and telling stories among themselves. Sometimes, the boys went berserk without realizing their discernible illegal immigrant status. They had so many petty quarrels and misunderstandings that were quickly settled. No one understood the other, but everyone had a common goal or purpose. Forward ever and away from the death base of the scorching heat. They always thought their next port of call would end their ordeal. They were all right, but the true answer lay years away and ahead.

The news and stories the human contraband had heard in Maradi, Asamaka and Arlit had been re-ignited for their substantial deeper understanding and realities. The printing machine case re-surfaced in Tamanrasset. The second Good Samaritan they met in Tamanrasset was involved in the woman turned money printing machine business. He had blamed Randy for coming that far without taking a woman along to print money for him. Randy smiled at what they called the printing money business; it was prostitution renamed. The women are taken into very secret and remote locations from where interested men would be solicited by the business husbands from another remote location. It was a highly punishable offence in a land where it was called *"Haram"* (*Arabic term for —forbidden*) and their women were almost tethered out of all norms of the modern-day civilization. The citizens who loathed the woman business like the plague were the greatest and ebullient patrons of the illicit trade and yet pretended not to like or be involved in the instincts of conjugal deflations and perforations. The men who had their human female machines would secretly and discreetly solicit for a man to go discharge his content into the waiting tanking of the human money-printing machines. The natives always asked in their local language *nta fi madam?* (*do you have a woman?*) It was a risky business as a security man could as well burst the ring with the same question. The businessman-husband knew how to identify them as a precautionary measure — but even then, many of the officers of the law partook directly in the immoral-intertwined acts of the illicit business. The law enforcement agents and the immoral crime perpetrators were all culpable. Only that one side used the law to cushion and cover their oozing and intolerable malfeansances.

On the second day of their arrival to Tamanrasset, Randy went out with one of the old people into the town. The old person in town had assured Randy that he would find Fenbrabi and his friend at the *"travail"* (*the French word for work*) ground that day. Randy was already Sceptical about his assurance but took it as a half-measured truth. When he got to the area, there were so many people milling around. It was an area the Citizens of the country came to hire illegal immigrants for some cheap and menial labour. It was real slavery re-made and re-enacted to suit modern-day freedom in a democracy. When the Citizens drove by, the illegal immigrants would chase the car in droves for space and job allotment. Prizes were never discussed. The worker accepted whatever he was given with meals provided within the working period. Randy could not believe what he saw at what everyone called *travail* ground. It was a gory and awful sight of a scene filled with able-bodied men looking so haggard and frail. Most among them were emaciated so much like Randy from the desert heat inputted dehydration. Randy heard them shouting *travail* each time they saw a prospective and temporary slavish job giver come by. He now knew why the area was so-called *"travail* ground". All the illegal immigrants lined up on both sides of the road. Randy had not gone there in search of a job but in search of his ex-nephew and friend. He wanted to see them and get off the ugly scene with them as fast as he could. As he got around patiently and unsure of their were about, his ex-nephew and his friend called his name, the voice was unmistakable, Randy turned in the direction of the voice, they were together and safe. Randy breathed a deep heave of sigh of joy and strong relief. They all got together again after a night of separation. They left the chaotic scene together and exchanged experiences of the previous night and the descent from the mountain overlooking the town. They never went back for any reason to the *"travail* ground" again till they left Tamanrasset.

Randy took them to where he had passed the night while the exchange of the previous day and past night experiences continued between them. They were so happy to have reunited. Randy was happy that they did not encounter any problems like him getting into the town. Safety was one of the reasons for the split on the mountain. The realization of the situation called for it and it had worked as planned. Randy introduced his ex-nephew and his friend to Suam. He was not surprised to see them with Randy. He had already been briefed about them the previous night as he was debriefed for the journey plans too. They spent some days inside the house hibernating and holding on tenaciously to what they had. News had it that the last two laps of the marathon journey would be more arduous and dangerous. They could not wait to get moving on and on.

After almost two weeks of waiting at Suam's house, they became jittery over the interminable and endless silence of not knowing when they would possibly be part of a full contraband load for the next journey to Djanet. Like every other day, their host went out purposely to make inquiries about when the passengers would be complete to enable them to embark on the journey. They wanted to leave Tamanrasset behind at all costs for the next port of call no matter what awaited their fate there. The Police chasing of illegal immigrants in Tamanrasset was incessant, uncomfortable, and gave them lots of nightmares.

The Police had started to make arrests of some illegal immigrants and could be their turn at any moment. When people were arrested, they would be driven back to Ingizim. As earlier said, Ingizim is the opposite dusty border town to Arlit in Algeria and Niger respectively. Both borders are a thriving haven for smugglers. Any valuable found on any illegal immigrant when arrested is confiscated before being released or taken away for deportation. If released, could be re-arrested another day by chance and treated the same way as the last or deported back to Ingizim. The women were spared when caught or arrested because they were involved with hawking their wares as women of easy virtues but the police officers preached that their religion forbade them from partaking in oneness with a woman of which they completely were part. That was why there were many hidden cases of incest among the population. For the girls to remain a virgin, they indulge in unimaginable self-defiling with their men.

When the Police officers discover where any illegal immigrant lives, and he or she manages to survive being arrested or deported, a change of abode is affected to avoid a recurrence and the incessant threats that follow from the officers. The officers go back for some conjugal freebies. It was a cycle of torment for the immigrants. They systematically punished and robbed illegal immigrants in the name of doing their official government-approved jobs. Randy never heard about anyone being beaten up in Tamanrasset – Algeria amidst the intolerable behaviour the policemen exhibited. They were the only official corporate thieves in uniform.

One day, their host, Suam, returned from outside to break the much expected and needed news to them. The drivers had asked him to collect their transport fares from them and that they should be led to a secret and desolate location from where they would be picked up. They were happy that they would be continuing their journey the next day and leaving behind the Tamanrasset police terror.

None of them had a good sleep before the next day. The sleeplessness was due to the anxiety displayed by each one of them. The anxiety centred on the police. Anything could happen in between. They had paid and could be sabotaged. That would mean getting arrested and losing the money paid upfront to the drivers and the trolley Suam.

The day they had waited and expected so much had come at last. Things started to happen so swiftly and fast the previous day. They had their breakfast and had some minutes rest. Suam asked everyone to get ready. He marched them through some dark alley and between some dilapidated mud buildings to arrive at one quiet grass-laden building. It was from that point that they were whisked away by the drivers. The Land cruisers meandered through some rocky, dusty, and undulating terrains. The ascend brought them to the knoll of the mountain that looked like a cup holding the liquid content in it. It was indeed an exceptionally good spot with so many rocks that gave them good cover from being seen or discovered. A spot they dared not exhibit any freedom. The rule there was "hide and hide properly till thy kingdom come".

The drivers stopped abruptly and asked all of them to disembark. None of them knew where they were and dared not ask or speak out to the dangerous Berber drivers. They had tasted what it was like to travel with them and no one in the group wanted a repetition of what they had seen happened to Eda to happen to him. Everyone took "unalloyed "*kpamu*" *(local slang meaning to keep quiet and avoid trouble)* from the sheer disregard and disrespect the Berber drivers exuded to their contraband customers. The customers in the instance were guilty and completely wrong for their silence and if they dared ask any questions would be worse off. What a situation and predicament. They just obeyed the instructions from the drivers sheepishly. The desert slap on Eda had rekindled its devastating effect on the contraband passengers once more. Randy said, "these *ogwugwudada* guys are mean to the core" see how the actions of some set of their people are having a chain reaction and effect on people weeks after the real actions had taken place". It was like the devastating effect of a nuclear meltdown having a domino effect on some of them. The drivers told them that, they would be coming later. They did not specify which time of the day they would come back to pick them up, but they accepted every instruction from them with all equanimity. The desert was no place to play human rights and democracy when one is an illegal immigrant or emigre. People always tried to play it cool to get going with their lives. The smuggling drivers were the kings in an empty land that runs without boundaries for kilometres. It was in the city and towns that legitimate government laws worked for desert citizens of the Sahara. While the legitimate government rules her citizens, the drivers rule foreigners in their "might is power world". There was no rule of law in the desert with foreigners patronizing these types of heartless human beings. The sellers here are always right and the customer is obedient to the core for the fear of being subjected to any ill-treatment or losing his deposit at any point of the transaction. The drivers were deadly men on a deadly mission. They forced everyone to yield and yield everyone must without any questions.

Randy and co. were no strangers to the desert in the enclosure the drivers had dropped them like a bunch of disposable baggage. They had already been baptized expecting their manly confirmation as recognized desert warriors of a kind with the next step and move to their destination. They would be desert warriors and soldiers of peace with their next obstacle crossings. Soldier warriors without any feasible weapon but only positive brains to advance the unity and help mankind in any way they could with time. They would be acclaimed as the people with unimaginable endurance at the end of the natural crossover tests. The last test was coming and looming in the unknown distance. They had heard enough stories and were ready to be initiated into that entity reserved for only the strong and brave. When, where, and how was just a matter of time, culminating in where expectations outweigh real situations.

They had been dropped very early on the mountain and it was past midday — none of the drivers had come to tell them anything about the intended journey. They were totally in the dark and confused more than they had been left in the morning with the instructions that they hardly understood but obeyed. They had nobody to turn to for any information. Suam could not be reached, as there was not any form of telephone communication then. If anything happened, no one among them would be able to identify any of them because the drivers wore and wove scarves around their heads and faces leaving only their eyeballs open. They knew how to control their tidal air through their scarf covers. Their true identities were always concealed in the name of religion, which on the contrary was supposed to be for protection against the desert winds that carried so much dust and sandy particles.

Despite their misgivings, they trusted that the drivers would come back to pick them but when was the big question. They decided not to mind the delay if they showed up to pick them up afterwards. They trusted that despite their arrogance, they were sometimes nice and humane people. Business with them was real with a sign and seal of trust and understanding. Every human being has gotten his or her agreeable downturns that should not exceed his or her human tolerance. The agreement was a quid pro quo, and they are bound to carry their side of it to fruition. Bound as the business says but they could renege without expecting any confrontation or accusation from anyone among them.

They stayed on still hiding under the rock and shifting with the movement of the sunrays. As they shifted, Randy remembered the daily movement of the Sunflower with the movement of the Sun. They were now hungry under the rocks and started to eat some of the food meant for their travelling but still had enough to last the journey. As they waited in endless expectations and hope, Gozchi and Gese asked Randy what he meant by all he had told them in Pidgin English when they were all accosted by the police in the rocky area of the scanty bush of Asamaka, after their descent from the mountain, with what Papa's something meant, Randy knew he had the sense, but had forgotten the substance, but knew what Gozchi wanted to ask him. Randy smiled knowing then that Gozchi and Gese never understood what he meant at the rocks place. Randy asked him if he had ever heard about Nelson Rolihlahla Mandela, he answered, "oh hoo" shouting and said "of course" who does not know him? Randy corrected him saying that "they all have heard about him but don't know him". Gozchi smiled at the correction and said that "Randy's correction was true, but he would connect what he had said to what he had asked him". Randy told him that "Papa" meant Mandela in his code for that day, but he should remember that his fellow South Africans called him Madiba. Randy told him that he had read somewhere that Mandela's prison number was 46664 and the RI code he used before the number stood for Robben Island and was his coding to make them understand his pidgin code. He asked Randy to know the full meaning of the RI. Randy told him it meant Robben Island where he was imprisoned for twenty-seven years. Hence RI 46664 was used for both that day. Randy cautioned them not to mix the meaning with Rhode Island in the States. He asked Randy how he had expected him to know anything under that stress invoking and marauding policemen that had everyone spellbound in the rocks place. He said the advice was good but could not readily be comprehended at that moment. They had acted on guess and impulse to Randy's advice rather than understanding him, but it worked out as required and advised.

As the day wore on, and every one of them was getting tired and famished from the effect of the blazing sun, their silence was punctuated by the sound of what seemed like a car coming in their direction from the distance towards them. They were not sure if the sound was that of a police patrol team or the ones for their drivers. Randy asked everyone to hide from the view of whatever was coming toward them atop the mountain. They all went deeper into the rocks like cats. No one would have known there were people inside there apart from those that had taken them there. They made good of their accumulated survival desert knowledge experience in the instance. Randy peered out from under the rock to see four land cruisers emerge unto the rocky terrain. They all noticed at once that they were the drivers who had dropped them off there to be baked a little to submission before the journey started. It took them some seconds to talk over the seating formations and groupings with the drivers. One man was missing from the group that had come together with them from Asamaka to Tamanrasset. No one knew where he had gone or what had become of him with the living or travelling out of Tamanrasset. Randy had seen the missing man last as they climbed the mountain that overlooked Tamanrasset town. New people had joined them now to form a complete load of human contraband. There were no new stories other than the ones they had heard and committed to their memories from Maradi till Tamanrasset. They would discover in days to come if they had known it all or not, after all, there was no harm in a trial.

They were driven from the rocky mountaintop to a place that looked like a farm, but the desert structure of that terrain still bore beautiful level scenery. The drivers asked them to disembark once more from the vehicles. Everyone alighted as instructed except Gozchi. He had followed them either out of sheer mistake or for the fear of being abandoned in the bush. He never gave his reason to anyone for following the drivers or acting contrary to their instructions.

When they finally returned, Gozchi started to relate what he saw the drivers did away from other passengers teeming eyes. Randy had heard about how these drivers and their peers called desert warrior formula one driver had performed some rituals before embarking on the journey. Gozchi told them how he had seen the drivers in the distance making incantations and performing some magical wonders with indomitable vigour. He claimed to have seen the drivers suspend themselves in the air with incantations. Randy believed him but wondered on second thought if he had seen an apparition or a nightmare. Randy knew of some magical things that the guiding laws and principles would not permit anyone doing or partaking in it to reveal whatever he or she has seen to avoid the wrath of the gods.

They embarked on the journey in their different vehicles with a zoom-off that sent the desert dust into the air and formed a dense shade behind them. They were ready for the attendant smudginess of the journey. They ran throughout the night and had an open-air stopover in the middle of a valley as they did on their way from Asamaka to Tamanrasset.

Despite the desert's inhospitable scorching sun of the day, it was always very cold at night that they required blankets to cover themselves. The Sahara Desert had gotten two direct and opposite weathers that could deceive the first-time traveller going through her terrains. The other notable problem of the desert then was the venomous reptiles, scorpions, lions, and other dangerous animals. The snakes and scorpions assume the colour of the desert sand making their hibernation exceedingly difficult for a man to easily find them against their attacks but the colour keeps them away from being preyed upon by larger animals. Randy did not think about the dangers because they never existed in his mind. Randy only realized this after he had seen someone that was stung by a scorpion in the desert as they passed the night in the open. Luckily, he never heard of anyone being bitten by a snake but, the danger was always there as it could happen anywhere they habited.

They drove for so many hours and had a minute's break for some little refreshments. Tea was served to everyone and they were asked to put out the fire before restarting the journey. Before they restarted, he compared the ways these drivers did their things with the Arlit and Asamaka drivers. They were the same in character and general management of identical situations. They made a fire in a valley or depression and knew how to hide and circumvent the law like the past drivers. Same smugglers of a kind that never drove on government-recognized and approved roads.

If the drivers ever went with the speed they used in the desert on a normal road, there would be many indescribable accidents. The drivers just throttle the gas pedal down without any consideration. The space was wide and endless, with no road signs to be followed or obeyed. They only raced at parallel and alternate formations. It was better to be seen than told how they drove.

Before the late evening of the day, they left Tamanrasset, the drivers stopped at a point almost similar to the one they had seen the Asamaka Tamanrasset route drivers use to hide fuel. They disembarked from the jeeps without any information to their passengers and walked behind one of the rocks and emerged with some iron military-coloured fuel cans. They refuelled the jeeps and continued the journey to Djanet.

After the refuelling, Randy thought over the events that had unfolded before him from Maradi till that point of being in the middle of nowhere to refuel. He knew now that these drivers lived from professional smuggling of wares and people across the Sahara Desert. They had made it their custom and way of life. They were masters of their geographical areas and surroundings. Randy wondered how they could know where they had hidden their wares or things in the vast area that spreads as far as one's eyes could see in that sea-like land that everywhere looked almost the same. Randy considered them genius but that was what happened to people when they are born and bred in a place or area.

After the refuelling of the vehicles, they drove for some hours till the late evening and stopped to pass the night as usual in a valley. The drivers made a fire and had some tea while the passengers had some light refreshments. The night was cold and almost unbearable. Most of the passengers had no blankets and those that had had to share them with others. Despite the sharing, it was not enough to ward off the biting cold of the Sahara Desert.

At dawn, they extinguished the fire as a rule and drove on in the direction of Djanet. Before they left their resting place, the drivers had told them that they would soon be arriving at Djanet and that everyone will need to trek across a place where the jeeps will not be able to carry anyone with the loads therein across. No one paid substantial attention to the news until it dawned on everyone later. The journey had taken them so many days to reach where they were, and they wanted to reach their next destination Djanet and think effectively for the next and last lap to Libya. The journey continued till they reached a place with impenetrable dunes. The drivers told them that the place and spot signify the nearness to Djanet. Everyone was asked to disembark from the vehicles and walk through the vast and open distance. Before they reached the place, Randy pondered how one could not ride on as a passenger in a jeep that was meant to subdue all terrains at a particular spot of the Sahara Desert. He wondered and expected what will trigger such human management. They finally reached the dunes after some hours. True to what they had told them, it was all white sand with exceptionally fine texture turned into an exceedingly high hill formed out of the sand dune. They had seen the entire terrain from their vantage point. They were all asked to disembark from the vehicles to reduce their weight. As they ascended the gentle hill from their direction, the jeeps drove on and at some point, had to be helped by pushing to affect a forward movement out of the dunes by the passengers. They pushed and pushed till they reached the descent side of the sandy hill. Every step was swallowed by the fine texture of the sand. The weights of the jeeps were too much for the dune to carry. It was no area to drive slowly. The drivers just throttled on and on to accelerate fast on top of the sand. It was at that point that Randy knew that it was a difficult job for the drivers to get across the dunes and worse for the passengers.

They discovered to their uttermost consternation from the top of the hill how steep it was. Trekking on the dunes was almost impossible to do without enough effort and power being applied to get through. The sand always drew one back while climbing and worse still while descending on the steep side. There were minute and hidden thorns inside the sand, but no one was hurt even though any one of them was hurt by any of the thorns, there would be no complaint and no one was in the mood to be sentimental. They knew it was not going to be easy for them all but had to make it out of the sheer need for human survival. It took them some reasonable time to climb and descend the dune. It was a task that none of them expected in such a measure. They were all tired and completely famished to a degree that they consoled one another for hope and comfort in the end. The drivers eventually crossed the dune and waited for the passengers at the dune endpoint.

In their type of desert travel, there was no way anyone could get a nap inside the jeeps because one was constantly shaken and rocked with the attendant gravity of the jeeps.

They drove some considerable distance for some hours and reached the outskirts of Djanet at midday. The drivers as a rule dropped them inside some very beautiful rocky area and pointed to a direction for them to follow into Djanet. They were warned and instructed to get into Djanet at nightfall. It was contrary to when Randy had reached and entered Tamanrasset at the same time of the day. Randy came to understand better why the nightfall bottom line was added to the instructions the driver had given to them. Djanet is situated at the bottom of a mountain.

These were the days when cell phones were not in vogue and reaching anyone was always by mail or very hard to find telegram machines. Osuam had requested a note to show that they reached safely and for him to use it as his certificate for human smuggling accreditation. The note he, Osuam will in turn be used to convince any would-be prospective human contraband cargo, ready to be ferried across the seething Sahara Desert. The note will bolster his position as a potential human cargo freight handler.

Osuam was nice to them and was in a business he wanted those he had helped to advertise his position for others to patronize him. When they all disembarked from the vehicles in the rocky area, they went haywire and started running in the direction the drivers had directed them to follow. The drivers started to call for a note from anyone of them, but all calls fell on deaf ears. Some of them felt the contract was finished between the drivers and them. It was like setting a captured wild animal free into the wild again. The subjugation, highhandedness and intimidation were all over with those sets of drivers. Randy felt it would be a disservice to renege on what they had promised Osuam at the end of the journey to Djanet. Randy took some steps back to meet one of the drivers and asked for a paper with which he scribbled tersely in the English language "we reached Djanet safely, "thanks for everything". It was signed and carried the language of authenticity in a French colonized country that talks Arabic. All another succeeding human contraband will understand the writing and what it meant. Randy considered them marks of bravery.

Once Randy had written the note, he hurriedly followed the others deeper into the rocks for cover. As they made their way through the rocks, Randy discovered they were old paths being extensively used by people like them. He wondered how news travelled so fast and far enough without any telephone. They had heard about this journey thousands of kilometres away without any telephone. Those that travelled halfway to most of the different towns returned to tell tales and those that completed the journey added to what the notables told, which made a complete sense of purpose to be given viable credence. They were a traumatic assembly of ideas and experiences.

As they went further into the rocky areas, they saw some writings on the rocks that had been written by those that had followed the same way in the past. Some were freshly written while some were old but they were easy to distinguish as it hardly rained in that area of the Sahara desert. Suddenly, they started to see Djanet from the distance and realized immediately that they were on top of a very high mountain with Djanet on her foot. The mountain overlooking Djanet is steep and very rugged while in Tamanrasset the mountain was high but the slope was smooth and slippery. The vegetation leading to Djanet was scanty compared to Tamanrasset, but the rocks offered better cover than in Tamanrasset. The mountain offered genuinely nice hiding places from possible law enforcement officers' detection and the scorching sun's unforgiving rays shone on the group.

They all took to different safe positions but could still communicate silently among themselves. Everywhere was silent like a graveyard. One helicopter flew above their position as they were hiding. Randy asked everyone to keep quiet and avoid movement of any sort. The Pilot must have seen the drivers that brought them but not their human cargo. They must have decided to carry out the reconnaissance flight above the rocks just in case there were people like them in the rocky area. The flight aroused the adrenalin in them, but they remained mum and motionless all the while the flight circled their position. The rocky footpath must have been the only possible illegal entry point into the town and deserved to be patrolled by any means the government thought wiser. They had taken cover just minutes before the helicopter came to their position. They were all lucky and happy for that time of the day. They could not cook anything for the fear of arousing any suspicion either in the distance or from the air patrol officers. They settled for their fast-food packets that kept their enduring longevity.

In the early evening when the sun had assumed a low curvature, they all agreed that it was time to descend into the town but who was going to lead the way? Randy did not wait longer than necessary after the consensus that they should make their way into the town. Once Randy, Fenbrabi and his friend Kele led the way, the others followed. They saw for the very first time the full view of the town as they wanted to descend from the top edge of the mountain. The view showed a terrain that was going to be extremely difficult to navigate into the town. The town was too far below the top of the mountain with jagged rocks of all sizes. There were old footprints on the rocks to show that people had been utilizing the rough edgy footpath. There was no place along the descent route to stand for even a second. The rocks had shapes that no one could stand for any rest atop them. Others followed Randy as he trudged on. There was no other way other than the single file way that took everyone down the sharp slope. It was a bit of daylight when they started the descent but by the time, they were halfway, it had become dark. They groped the remaining distance carefully to avoid injuries on their toes because they still had the long trek from Djanet to Libya to make later.

Meanwhile, their legs were shaking terribly after the descent from the mountain. They were very afraid of being seen by security men as they descended from the mountain. There would not have been an escape for any one of them if the law enforcement agents had spotted the group. There was nowhere to run into or hide from the law at that point. Randy looked at the mountain from below and could not believe he had just come down from such an incredible height but people who had heard about mountains in that area told Randy that, the real climbing would come in the next lap of his journey to Libya. Randy was told that the only difference will be that he will be climbing all through as against his complete descent from the current mountain. They were ready for whatever it would take to reach Libya. After all, not everyone that set out for the journey made it through. Some went halfway and returned while some died in the desert of known and unknown natural and human causes respectively. There hardly were natural causes that were not exacerbated by the effects of the travelling exhaustions.

As they managed to descend into Djanet, they started to hear some foreign languages from some of the houses they passed by. These languages were clearly understood by some of the members of Randy's group.

There was that man who saw them climb down from the mountain that asked them to follow him to his place of abode. The man seemed to have been informed by the drivers that had dropped them off inside the rocky area. The way he was on hand to receive them showed a closely-knit network of smuggling rings and chains. His being at the foot of the mountain at the nick of the time spoke volumes. Randy thought that it was not a coincidence of the way he behaved, but what drove him to be where he was and what he did to achieve it till that moment of his life history that was in the making. He surely was an insider and a gang member of the extended inner caucus secretive smuggling chain. He led the way while they followed. He was a native but could manage some broken English. Randy guessed he must have learned the language from human trafficking associations and interaction with human contrabands that have been streaming across the Sahara Desert for years. The people who heard their footsteps in the dark started to call out to them to join them. Randy knew that the area was completely inhabited by those who had been in the town like them. They surely were not natives because natives will not live in those very ugly shanties, they had seen on their way in. The guide that had seen them from the foot of the mountain asked them not to answer the different voices and comments that were coming from the darkness. They obliged. One statement that caught the attention of the group was "you people don't want to come here, but I bet you all that everything you guys are carrying, both money and other items will be ours tomorrow morning". It was said with assurance and resonating confidence. Randy and others did not understand what warranted such free but confident statements. They gave the comments waives of hand and thought since their guide had asked them not to have any fear but consider the talk as some form of prattle. While the guide must have asked them to get going with him, Randy thought about the certainty, boldness and fearlessness with which these brigands spoke from the dark. He trekked on with others halfheartedly. The talks from the dark were so mesmerizing but life had to go on as planned or continue in disarray to be patched later as the conditions might arise.

When they reached the guide's makeshift house, he made sure the group cooked themselves some food. They told the guide they wanted to leave the town the next day. He assured his visitor passengers that they will be able to leave the next morning as early as 03.00Hrs. They quietly ate and slept but had been warned before then about how houses were attacked, and the inhabitants robbed at night. This happened to mostly the houses that have received some newcomers like them. The warning and news sent their spines and adrenalin to shivers. There was no way to avoid it if it was destined to happen to them, but they clung to the collective luck that saw them through. Everyone started to hide things without letting the others know where and what was being hidden or done to evade the dreaded night marauders should they decide to strike as had been said, foretasted, predicted, and expected. The guide went out briefly to make the journey contacts and returned to tell them that they will be Libya bound at the appointed time and told them what each person had to pay for the guide escort services across the vast Saharan terrain.

Their host woke them up at the appointed time and asked for the fees from each one of them. They paid and some other guides joined them at the house. There was no wasting of time. They did not sleep enough from the previous day's forced sunbathing on the rocks on the mountain, but they had to do what was right to advance their aspirations and plans. They followed the guide and his entourage as they trekked on. They crossed the tarred road and walked towards one imposing mountain that looked bluish on top from the distance as the night started to break into daylight. Everyone called it Mount Hoggar and pretended to be intrepid enough to conquer the climbing without any fuss and fears. The truth was that no person that passed through Mountain Hoggar did not trip a bit in respect for the Mountain. If not for anything it must be for her endless discipline of all the people that dared to tread on her.

As they crossed the road into the other side of the road and continued the bare sheet eroded plains, the guides hurried them up to make sure they were not seen by any law enforcement agent in the town. Everyone was supposed to be sleeping at that hour of the day they were trekking out of Djanet. They trekked for about three hours before they started to experience the dawn of a new day. It was a straight road to one of the highest mountains in Mother Africa. Suddenly they branched off from the straight-line way into some tiny footpaths that led to the foot of the mountains. Before the branch-off point, Fenbrabi had lost his shoes to cataclysmic wear and tear. His pair of shoes submitted too quickly to wearing off on the undulating rocky sandpaper-like terrain. He told Randy he was tired and could not continue while his friend started to vomit some green substance caused by uncontrollable exhaustion. Randy pepped Fenbrabi up saying that he should remember that he was doing it for himself and the entire family and sympathized much with his friend Kele. Randy hammered his reasons why Fenbrabi should continue trekking, sighting the mother as his main reason to go on. Now that Fenbrabi's shoe had worn out and could not trek on bare feet on rocky terrain, Randy offered him his bathroom flip-flop to continue the journey. Randy's shoes were producing their drawbacks at a rate unimaginable from the trekking. The trio will be going on bare feet if luck ran against them on the rough and inhuman terrain. Their change of direction from the straight road brought them into the undulating mountainous terrain that was eating away their shoe bottoms at an alarming rate. At this point, the terrain started to rise gently and considerably into hills. They knew that they were getting nearer and nearer to the much revered and talked about a mountain. The Hoggar is cumbersome, arduous, and Herculean to climb but calorie-sapping to accomplish. The trekking went into a thermostatic crescendo with everyone breathing like a racing horse. The guide walked faster and faster as he carried nothing on him like his customers. The guide customers carried recommended a complete surviving kit that negated their centre of gravity of which did not matter to them. One either followed or else he will be left behind but some people among the group asked the guide to soft-pedal because the people they were leading were from another part of the Continent that had a different terrain that was completely contrary to theirs. Randy now had come to terms with why many had died trying to puncture the invincible iron curtain. Many heroes had fallen on that desert with no substantial inkling and linking information to their various families. Even if anyone knew who died, people always kept mum for fear of being accused of being made a lead to whatever that had happened. Most people preferred to look the other way when anything happened. No one wanted to be involved in any family affairs surrounding any case of death in the Sahara Desert.

Despite Fenbrabi's and his friend Kele's drawbacks, they were still very much in contention with the group's trekking troops.

One good and humble man from Mauritania was in their group. He had become Randy's friend inside the jeep in which they travelled together from Tamanrasset to Djanet. He acted as a noble man and to be fair enough a learned gentleman. Mauriman was a responsible, gentle, and soft-spoken man. He showed respect in everything he did with anyone. He understood English and could get along with most of the people he was part of.

As the climbing of the big mountain continued, Randy heard his name reverberate with much echo below. It was a voice of hopelessness and despair from someone that needed his hope and aspirations cushioned. The voice was chilling and recognizable. Randy listened and the voice came on with almost a last strength. The voice had been calling "Randy! Randy!!, You are leaving me, wait for me, please wait! I will die here, please wait for me". Fenbrabi and his friend Kele called Randy's attention to the voice they had heard. Randy did not answer but waited patiently for him to catch up with them. When Mauriman reached their position on the mountain, he was drenched in his sweat and had gotten sore toes from injuries he sustained by kicking his feet on the rocks. He was exhausted and panting but Randy urged him on. Randy gave him some soothing words that acted as a placebo but realized that if he was left alone and behind from that point on, he would pass out and his death will haunt him Randy for the rest of his life. Mauriman knew no other name among the group other than Randy and that alone endeared him to Randy's heart.

Not quite long that he had reached them, the group were attacked by armed robbers. The robbers started to throw stones at the group and streamlined them forcibly into a rocky valley. Everyone was initially asked to lie face down and keep mum. One of the robbers who had an AK-47 sub-machine gun went atop a very strategic rock to stand while others operated on the defenceless group. The robber with the Kalashnikov ejected the magazine out of the rifle bullets compartment and showed the loaded rifle magazine to the group from his vantage position. He was in essence telling the victims that what they were doing was no child's play and that anyone caught trying to deceive them would be killed on the spot. The bullets were reflected in the magazine compartment and no one needed to be told further what the robbers meant and wanted. They were real and could not be ignored or disrespected. There was no moral decency from the robbers. They spoke clean English and demanded that if anyone from the group being robbed was from a particular tribe in Ghana that he should step aside. One Mohammed and some others in Randy's group stepped aside and were asked to show their identity cards as proof of what they had claimed. The robbers inspected them and spoke the local Ghanaian language to them, and they replied. They were given a VIP treatment while others and their little hand packs were ransacked to their birth suits. They checked virtually everything to ensure that no valuables of any kind on the victims eluded them.

Before the searching went on, they were all asked to submit their money and valuables on them. The robbers warned that if anything valuable was found on any of them later it would amount to not living to tell the stories of their experience to the wider world. Randy knew the robbers meant bloody and I don't care business. Randy whispered to Fenbrabi and Kele to keep straight and patient with events on the ground.

Randy had taken a knife from Tamanrasset to confront any would-be desert marauding attacker, but it was the very first thing he buried into the desert sand as he lay face down. The knife was no match for those glittering fast-moving pyrotechnic bullets. Randy continued to think about how on earth he would have engaged the firepower of a Kalashnikov with a small kitchen knife. They were two incomparable and incompatible fighting tools or hardware implements and would have been foolhardy to ever conceive of using them in the instance. The robbers were superior for the occasion against the innocent and defenceless group.

When the robbers were throwing stones at them to get them into the valley, Randy was amazingly fast to hiding his little money under a little rock. As they were being robbed at the forced designated assembly point, he remembered how on one of those types of an occasion when one innocent virgin in the company of one young man was publicly raped and battered by the robbing gangsters. Dozens of rapes had taken place on that route to Libya with reckless abandon. The robbers never considered the use of condoms and did not mind if they contracted any sexually transmissible disease from their victims. They were heartless and fearless to the point of committing a gentle and subtle suicide. The robbers came with bad wear and worn-out shoes to exchange them for good ones from their victims. They will share some expensive food and other items with their owners. Randy saw them as petty and hungry thieves who lacked bearing in life. They checked the *Bidons* thoroughly to make sure nothing was hidden inside them but let the water go untouched. Water was the lifeline of anyone travelling through the desert. Randy never heard of anyone being killed during a robbery as long as the person obeyed and conformed to the dictates of the demands and wishes of the robbers. The robberies were an intractable problem that no official of the government will ever hear about or be informed of. The victims travelled on unapproved routes and met whatever they did not merit or bargained for in the hands of the robbers. The desert as previously said, was too wide and open to whatever direction one was seeing or looking at it while in the middle of it. It was endless with many look-alike features. No wonder, Randy could not retrace his hidden money after the robbers had had a feast day on them and asked them to leave. Everywhere looked the same and if he were to bend down to move his money or anything, he could be fired upon and eventually murdered in cold blood. Fenbrabi and Kele asked him not to venture to search for the money because the robber with the AK-47 was still standing at his strategic point to make sure everyone left the scene.

Randy lost the money to the Sahara much as the thieves did too. Randy could not speak for his Mauritanian friend. He was robbed too like every other person but what surprised Randy was how the robbers will rob such a man in such an improbable and despicable state. He did not come from the robbers' exempted area and had to go through the collective suffering.

As they trekked along the undulating winding rocky paths, they saw some makeshift graves of those that had died on the route. The graves were marked with piles of stones that were used to cover the dead person. It is so done because there was no way a normal grave could be dug in those areas. The ground was rocky and no implement could be used to dig in. The hearse was only dumped on the bare ground to rot away without flies and vultures around to even scavenge. Hence stones were used instead to mark any fallen hero's place of last breath. The weather was extreme in that part of the desert. They were sights unimaginable in a modern and model world.

Authentic sources had it that the guides always planned the robberies. They were in touch with the robbers to let them know when people will be travelling with them and when they will leave the town. They arrange where the robbers will stay to carry out their nefarious acts on their victims that eventually are the guides' customers. No wonder the guides were asked to stay aside with that particular ethnic tribe from Ghana and watch their customers being mercilessly robbed with impunity and ignominy.

Like in the words of those that spoke the previous night with certainty and fearless assertions that "what Randy and his group were carrying would be theirs the next morning came to be true of their unalloyed claims" They got all they planned for without shedding blood but hard memorable fears infused into their victims that will be so bad for hindsight. It was what it was for what it will remain for those that care to think about the way they followed through with who and why it was made.

The climbing of one of the highest mountains in the Saharan desert commenced immediately after the robbery with extra stamina needed to push through each one of them. Many in the group had reached the apogee of their endurance level before they reached there but everyone had to trek on. This meant that the robbers knew the best place to position themselves for attacking innocent people on the route. Randy seriously feared for his Mauritanian friend's life. Randy and others in the group had close eyes on him, urging him on and giving him some pep-up talks to soothe his waning, deteriorating health and stamina. The climbing and trekking were getting too dangerous and unbearable every passing second on the unapproved way. Randy secretly did that because he was equally afraid for Fenbrabi and Kele but both seeing how the Mauritanian looked must have suddenly and spiritually replenished their power to move on.

They reached a stage where they started seeing the ground below as if they were in an aeroplane. It was simmering, foggy and blue below the mountain base. It made an indelible mark on Randy's mind. Randy thought about how he had years before flown above the sufferings he was going through. He reflected on Bivasco who had contributed to his messy life and continued the ascent to unknown Libya. Randy devised a means to conquer the height. The best way was not to look back and downwards. He asked everyone that cared to look straight to their targets picking their steps from movements of the taking off of their feet to the landing of their feet. It worked and by now they inadvertently left the Mauritanian friend again.

The rocks in the desert thawed to produce some explosions that looked as if there was a war being fought in the distance. Randy thought there were some soldiers or some robbers in the wings waiting to rob them of nothing except their *Bidons* and little fast foods. They started to hear more of the explosive sounds all around. Simple Geography and physics solved the problems for their fears. They were rocks exploding under the impact of the desert heat. It was a reaction of the heat of the day thawing the cold temperature that had developed overnight. The sounds were incessant and heartbreaking to those who did not understand the simple earth crust geographical formations and fragmentations.

At some of the crossing points from one tip of the mountain to another, only a tiny flat plank that did not consider all weight was placed for people to cross over to the other side and there were many of them like that that dotted the entire route. Randy just crossed but tried to look down after crossing, it was really and sincerely like watching from an aeroplane window. Randy thought they were all playing with their individual respective one life. The journey was not worth it if one died at any point but worth it if one was able to get through the entire length and the entire length meant beyond Libya. They continued the trekking but certainly at a flight height with underneath them from the mountain top looking very foggy and the ambient height so clear as was always the situation and condition in real aeroplane flight. It was a practical experience of human wonder that was on display for all to see.

As they kept their climbing tempo, a voice called Randy's name again from the distance below. This time the voice reverberated with a stunning decibel. Randy did not need anyone to tell him that his Mauritanian friend was in some trouble again. Randy waited till he managed to cover the distance between them. In that journey, one never took any step backwards. Everyone saved and conserved his energy for the reposition of needed stamina in every stage of the journey through the Sahara Desert. When they reached one of the dangerous flat plank crossings, they asked their Mauritanian friend to get in between them. Fenbrabi and Kele crossed over the flat plank while their Mauritanian friend went next and almost fell into one of the gorges that had some endless crevasse at one end of it. As he was falling, Randy grabbed him on his long pant in the nick of time and looked down where he would have fallen. The fall would have been like sky diving without a parachute. He was lucky and so were they all happy that the worst was luckily averted from happening to their friend. Randy repositioned him and asked him to look straight to make the crossing. It was the only way to pass through to the other side of the same mountain and he had to be encouraged to make it through the flat plank at all costs. He tried it and went on gradually atop the plank and in seconds was at the other side safely. No one made any comment because they thought they still had more of the same situation to get through. Before the last dangerous crossing, he was not the same man Randy had known from their Tamanrasset jeep to Djanet. He was completely ruffled and famished by the events of the day. As the incidents took place, the guide was busy climbing the mountain like a goat running on a hill. He had gotten his money from his customers and did not care about their welfare on an inglorious terrain. The flat plank connections of some parts of the mountains came on some more times and they made sure the Mauritanian was helped across till they came to the final top of the mountain. The top had a small connection to an edge with the same flat plank that everyone climbed to a very flat surface on the other side. Kele was the first among the trio to get to the flat surface of the other side. He was followed by Fenbrabi, their Mauritanian friend and finally Randy. They gave one another hands to be able to make the last climb to the flat ground that lay atop the mountain. The entire group were assembled after the climb. No life was lost in their group, but it was not easy either for any of them no matter the pretence and bravery some people displayed at the end of the climbing.

They continued the trekking on the flat terrain side of the mountain with less stress but tired from the long hours of mountain climbing. The flat terrain looked like the terrain they had seen all along their journey from Asamaka to the much-talked-about mountain Hoggar. They had climbed the mountain for almost five hours and continued for about two hours more under the scorching and baking sun before the guide asked them to have some rest under some rocks. It was a stop for them to have their breakfast. They had all toiled and endured so many hours in one of the most inhospitable and unfriendly terrains in the world. They cooked in their different assumed areas of the resting place. They refilled their *Bidons* and were asked again to assemble for the continuation of the journey. Everyone rounded up whatever chores that were left and bounced back to the Libyan trail.

After some hours of trekking from their first place of rest, they saw some people coming toward them from the distance. Both sides approached themselves cautiously. The guide did not mince words to alert everyone that the people coming in the opposite direction were desert robbers. There was nothing they could do other than unanimously tell the guide to inform them that they had been robbed and had nothing more on them than their *Bidons*. As the distance between the group and the new group of robbers grew thinner and thinner so, too the disillusionment on their faces grew. They were defenceless and open to any conceivable injuries should there be any unreasonable and despicable act against them from the new robbers. The worst for the people being led was that there was never any way there was going to be any law enforcement officer to defend or track the robbers and best for the new robbers and the guide because they had all gone too far into the desert that no law enforcement of any kind was feasible and probable. Finally, the inevitable happened. Both sides met themselves. There was no way they could avoid themselves. If one side ran away, the other will chase after the group and vice versa. If the robbers are not able to chase all, they could start indiscriminate shooting innocent people that will not matter to them in any way. They wanted to avert the latter option for the fact that it was safer and protective of the sickly among them homing in on Libya. No one wanted a debilitating scene created with collateral damages littering everywhere. If shots were fired, they will ricochet and travel with the deafening speed in the open terrain. As the guide spoke with them in their local dialect, they talked collectively to rub their hands together like in prayer begging the robbers to let them go freely. Those who understood French talked French and those that understood English spoke it but all went for begging for safety, otherwise, there was nothing more to rob from the already robbed. The robbers agreed and allowed them to continue their trekking toward Libya. They had survived another would have been a deadly onslaught. In the late evening of that day, they rested and passed the night like in their former truncated travels in the desert. The heat at that time was subsiding to give way to the night's extreme cold. Everyone rested but stayed very close to one another to avoid the guide leaving them at a point so dangerous that they will not know which direction to head toward. They had survived another traumatic day looking forward to another unknown day.

As they rested, Randy made a reminiscence of the events of that day on the mountain. He thought about the Mauritanian's condition. Thought that: what if he had died before that time, how will he have felt as he thought about it? Randy heaved a sigh and knew that an excessively big danger and bad news had been averted for the Mauritanian and all in the group. He remembered the previous day when some people were talking about their money and the things belonging to them that the robbers had stolen from them. The next day brought fresh ideas about the thieves. The new colleagues that joined Randy's group from Djanet reliably got the information about some of the robbers. They knew them but would not say anything for the fear of being murdered in cold blood in the simmering desert. Someone from the group knew some of the robbers. He said the robbers had been there in Djanet making their dirty money at the foot of the mountains by preying on innocent and poor victims. True to what Randy had thought, the guides liaised with the robbers and the extra people with him were to be able to ward off any attack from the customers that might want to pay him back in his coins. The guides aided and abetted atrocities against their customers but feared their vengeance and revenge at the end of the journey. The guide feared the repercussions and hence he had extra men that acted as bodyguards for him to prevent a fallout with him at a point where the contract terminates. From that point on, everyone will become the master of his destiny and fortune. He will announce it and disappear with his bodyguards. One of the people among them knew the man that handled the gun. He said he was a Ghanaian and some of the ones that searched them while the gunman stood on the strategic rock were equally Ghanaians. He said the robbers knew that the old ones that had spent weeks in Djanet among the group had no money but the new ones who just came into Djanet and left almost immediately were the ones they stifled to get all valuables they could lay their hands on from.

The second-day trekking from Djanet was a bit better because they did not have to climb remarkably High Mountains like the previous day. It was smooth sailing under the heat wave. They trekked for some hours and settled for their meal under some of the rocks. Water was nearby and they refilled their *"Bidon"*. Most of them had injured toes that they had inadvertently stumbled against some rocks. Injuring one's toes on that terrain was a sine qua non with an intolerable sine die coating. After their meals, they were assembled to continue the trekking to the Libyan border. From that point on, they started to trek freely on the footpath that was very unmistakable. People's consistent usage and movements along the rocky pathway had made it recognizable and indelible to follow unaided by anyone, but they still cared for their Mauritanian friend. The group had disintegrated into grouped numbers of varied sizes of people with a common mission. Randy luckily had another man that joined them. He was a Ghanaian called Mr Ghariya who had passed the route before to Libya as a guest worker. He piloted them along and was telling them stories about Libya. There was that imposing mountain called Hamada di Mui suk in the Amsach Mallet area that had a human face from the distance, which signalled the nearness to Libya. Randy's immediate group relished in his experience and kept to the tempo of his trekking speed. At that moment in time, the guide had gone far ahead of them. The reasons being to assemble and stop everyone at a particular area till his own chosen time of the day when the group will be allowed to proceed on his terms that no one in the group dared to challenge. Otherwise, if the law enforcement agents of the country caught anyone in the group, he and his henchmen would be discovered and arrested and they will be charged accordingly for human trafficking and attempted murder. Charges that were taken very seriously by any government of the day and some of his passengers like Randy knew it was true but unspoken of.

The entire group assembled in the late evening and everyone aligned with what direction he was going to take. Randy's immediate group aligned with the Ghanaian man Mr Ghariya who had since their last meal piloted them so good with stories about where they were going. He was by far better than the guide they paid to get them across.

The guide and his bodyguards pointed to the distance and said," that is where you are going to, we are going back from here". His bodyguards were all around him sensing trouble and very ready to defend the indefensible. They were wrong to have even conceived the idea that his contraband desert passengers would or could fight. No one among the group was fit enough to even fight a newborn baby let alone make problems after the arduous and agonizing days they had spent in the desert. Certainly, no one but they were only afraid of repercussions that existed but were not going to be fought over. The guide and his bodyguards were only chasing their shadows that never existed in the early dark evening of that agonizing day.

There were no parting greetings. Everyone was simmering with unspoken and debilitating anger over the ugly and unwarranted experiences. As the guide rested with his boys, they left them and started to trek in two different directions to the light beams. While a group trekked on to Ghat another one went in the direction of Albaraghat. It was already dark but an early evening movement for them. There was no timepiece but was about 19.30Hrs central European summertime.

Their new pilot Mr Ghariya had told them that they must trek the entire distance under night cover and that there was no changing that fact and that if they were unable to do that, they would all end up being *"Kalambush" (to arrest)* and remanded in the *"Zanzu" (prison)*. This means being arrested and remanded in the prison.

They say the words of our elders are words of wisdom. A wise man hears and gets wiser. These are based purely on life experiences. Since Randy had aligned himself and others with the Ghanaian who had been to Libya before, they decided to follow every of his instruction and directives to wherever he was going to land them on their first entry but his destination like theirs was nowhere but the same. He had exceptionally good compass guidance into the town right from when the Djanet group broke into two under that peach darkness. Everyone walked fast to beat the deadline of the night cover. People started to kick and stumble over stones and rocks in the dark with no one screaming or complaining. It was like nature flogging everyone and warning them against voicing out their pains. No one wanted to be seen or arrested by the Libya law enforcement agents. Everyone's endurance was infinite and total. At a point, no one consoled the other for any injury and pains sustained as they trekked along the dark footpath except for them Randy, Fenbrabi and Kele. Their closeness will not allow any one of them to see one another suffer any kind of setback on the way. The trio were together in pain and happiness till that moment.

Whatever one saw at any distance in the desert must be kilometres away from him. When the guide and his bodyguards pointed in the direction of the town they were going to and told them he was going back from there, they had no option but to accept. The contract had ended, and they were seeing the town only to realize later that the distance was only a tantalizing mirage and a complete deception of their nautical mile's knowledge. They trekked all night with Mr Ghariya directing every step of their way. He was better, friendlier and a better heart brother than the guild, but it could also be because Randy and others understood him in an international language common to all in the group. Ghariya asked them not to be afraid of anything, that there will be wild dogs barking when they approach the outskirts of the town and will get louder when they enter the town, and that no one should fear or try to run away from the dogs, that they will all keep walking till they can enter one of the farms and take cover, but from there, everyone will be on his own. They heeded his unequivocal advice and trekked on.

As they approached the outskirts of the Albabaraghat town, the inevitable started to happen. The dogs started to bark in all directions endlessly. It was like they had been ambushed and will be dead in seconds to come. Randy was not afraid, and neither were the others, but it was an ugly scene to be part of. They had been forewarned and seeing it happen only added credence to what information that had been passed on to them by Ghariya.

As the barking got louder and louder, they walked faster but with fast checks to ensure none of the dogs was on their heels. They were almost at the end of the last lap into a Libyan town. Randy and others were happy that their Mauritanian friend had made it through with them in his worst state. Randy thought about the Mauritanian being lucky in the Libyan country. People from his country were all visa-free to Libya under the umbrella of one regional Islamic religious enclave. His Mauritanian friend will not be an exemption hence

Randy advised him to find someone or a place to get enough rest and recuperate before embarking on a journey to anywhere he will choose to go. Randy forecasted that there was not going to be any trekking again from the very first town in Libya except if the unexpected happened. Randy's forecast will be proven right or wrong with time. The Mauritanian friend was happy too to have been able to make it through the stifling Sahara Desert heat.

14

JAMAHIRIYA SOUTH TO NORTH

THEY ALL PLAYED BY THE RULES AS INSTRUCTED BY GHARIYA. WHEN THEY PASSED THE AREA WHERE the dogs were barking, they made their way into the farms to get cover in the sparse vegetation. Before they made it to the farm, Randy and his group saw one of their people that had been living in Albaraghat. He advised them to subdivide themselves into twos and threes because group movement attracted easy and quick arrests. He continued this time with a warning to the newcomers, you better get going now and fast before you are *"Kalambush"*, that there was what was called "Catch! Catch!!" of all illegal immigrants that were going on in the town. Randy understood him perfectly but had a second thought about his comments and advice. The man who had just advised them was equally an illegal immigrant, the only difference was his coming or arriving earlier than them to the town and had known all the nooks and corners of the village to master the environment and gain the practical knowledge on how to meander through them. The situation was serious but would have been laughable scenes of a theatre were it not for their newness to Albaraghat. He had given them the first two Arabic words they will hear and understand all through Libya country. The words were registered indelibly in their memories. They moved on and a few minutes later they landed on a farm.

Right inside the farm, everyone took cover in confusion not knowing what to do and where to go from there. Ghariya asked everyone to find his way into the town and wished everyone good luck. As they lay down tired and exhausted from the previous night's marathon trekking that took them almost twelve hours to complete, they heard the screeching of some police jeep Tyre screeches and sounds. They also saw from the bush how some dark-skinned people were being chased like animals and others enjoying the show of oppression, subjugation, and submission. They did not know if anyone was arrested in the melee but could hear the glee with which some inhabitants and citizens enjoyed the show. These set of people were very callous and hardhearted with no consideration of any sort. Sadists in human skin that even in the worst-case scenario will defy exfoliation. Randy knew that despite the ugly momentary moments there would still be the good ones yet to be met and interacted with. Nothing lasts or remains forever. Things were bound to change whether one liked it or not.

The farmers came to meet them on the farm. They could not communicate with the owners of the farm, but Randy was sure it was not the first time the owners of the farm were seeing people like them appear from nowhere on their farm to hide from the law. The farmers gave them some water to drink and later some food to eat. Randy wished years later if he could only see and still recognize that good-minded farmer that treated them humanly without any strings attached. That farmer showed that there are still the good, the bad and the ugly in every country of the world. The language barrier will not be there anymore if it was possible to ever see and recognize them again. Randy always thought about how many people like them that that farmer must have helped unconditionally in exchange for that golden word "*Shukran* and *Afon*" *(thanks* and *my pleasure)*. Words better translated as "thank you to someone" and the person replies, "never mind or it is my pleasure".

When they had hibernated for some hours, they found the courage to venture into the town. When they entered the town, everyone started to look for where they will stay for the next private and possible plan. They looked like professional street beggars with no bearing. Randy by chance went along with Mohammed and Zeit after Fenbrabi and Kele had gone to find a place where the inhabitants will agree to take them in. Mohammed was one of the people that were not robbed because he came from that robber's designated tribe in Ghana. Zeit on his part had been to one of the Gulf States before and as such knew how to speak the local language that Mohammed used him on arrival to Libya like an umbrella to shade himself from his newness to the country. Mohammed engineered the person that they all had taken temporary refuge to kick Randy out because he was not a Ghanaian. Zeit did not see the good reason for that demand but could not challenge the ill blood and unwarranted revulsion against Randy. The man they had taken a few minutes refuge in his place started to talk one of the local Ghanaian languages with Mohammed and their eyes and countenance revealed the meaning of what they were saying, but Randy was undaunted and unruffled. Suddenly, Zeit joined them to try to evict Randy but he stayed on with plans to leave as fast as he could. Mohammed was a young person with very sadist, acidic and unpardonable bile. Randy wondered what he was going to be if he ever had any chance over a people anywhere, but he knew one thing some of his people from their area of Ghana did for a living to be robbery and possible killings. The open desert result was there for everyone to see and make a very lasting impression on those that experienced it. His people displayed it in the Sahara Desert, and he could be any day anytime and must be more ruthless than his peers of the Sahara Desert foot path Vikings. If Mohammed ever did, he would kill without mercy and boundary. Randy did not want to leave without seeing Fenbrabi and Kele. They had asked Randy to wait for them and any wrong move will make them miss out themselves. Randy asked Mohammed, Zeit and the old occupant of the place to take it quietly with him because he was going to leave in a few minutes, but he will not accept any appeal or force eviction and that after all, they were all have the same status. Their goal was for Randy to get out and be arrested by the police to their delight and happiness. Randy told them that he was only standing near their door and was not inside with them, but they kept pestering him to leave. Randy stood there to be able to see Fenbrabi and Kele anytime they showed up. He was taking a risk to be in his position, but it was the only way to get them back as a group.

Meanwhile, Fenbrabi and Kele were still where they had gone to negotiate with a man that owned a garage that needed their mechanical experience. They will work on a commission basis for the man while an existing accommodation will be given to them. As Mohammed, Zeit and their host grew very belligerent of Randy's presence more and more, he saw Fenbrabi and Kele call out on him to come along because they had seen a place, they will all stay together. Mohammed, Zeit and their host were all inside the room when Randy was being spoken to about the accommodation. Mohammed acted like his peers who robbed and attacked innocent people at the foot of the mountain in the Sahara Desert in Libya. Randy was not surprised at the way he acted along with the others. They were still inside when Randy left with Fenbrabi and Kele and never saw them again. The monsters must have been surprised at his French leave and must have thought about the worst-case scenario. Hurrah, he had been *kalambush* to their designed gusto and delight. Wrong thought for a lucky man.

The trio made their way through the unpaved streets of the town to where Fenbrabi and Kele had secured a place for them to start life in Libya. Three people already lived there before the three of them came to join them. They all became exceptionally good friends from the first day they reached there. The old inhabitants of the garage Johnne, Edisoh and Sonnie told them the story of what had happened before their arrival and all they had heard from people to inculcate in them all that must be handy and memorized for their daily existence in a land their type was being chased everywhere like an offensive dirty dog. From the first day, everyone did what he was supposed to do. While Sonnie and Randy did some under-priced jobs, the others were engaged in their mechanical trade. Some of the so-called technical trades' men were truly impostors and ignorant of what they claimed they knew but they had to survive on and through the knowledge of some others that knew the trade. It was done by watching and fixing because someone says to do it this or that way. The owner of the garage never knew there were only two mechanics amongst them and the third had never worked on any car on his own apart from his theoretical work in the school. Randy knew the secret of the manpower constituency of the garage mechanics but feigned the knowledge values of not knowing what they always knew and thought he never knew. Randy believed in everyone surviving and succeeding in life's maze assignments be they assisted or unassisted. Randy smiled at the goings-on internally and watched how everything went undetected. The road to success was extremely narrow and bumpy. It is occupied and walked through with any convenient tool that must not affect other peoples' life.

They were well fed by the garage owners and to some extent protected from being assaulted around their domain. They never ventured going outside their domain for the fear of being arrested by the police. They knew how to meander and manoeuvre when the need arose. Everything was done in a jiffy if any of them had to go out.

Things got to a head when the police started to go after illegal immigrants in Albaraghat and Ghat. Johnne and others had a little meeting one night and devised a means to curb the danger of the group being suddenly arrested at night. The garage was situated at a place that made them gullible and easy access for possible arrest in the middle of the night. The idea came because of the "Catch! Catch!!" that was endlessly going on and the stories they heard from other people around and Ghat made it sound like it was going to be their turn any moment but mostly at night. They decided unanimously to continue to pass their nights in the adjoining uncompleted and unroofed building next to the garage. Henceforth, they retired at the end of the day into the building. There were no doors of any kind, but they used planks to divert the knowledge of any would-be intruder. No one will know that six gentlemen were inside such a dilapidated building cramped like sardines in one room. They came out early in the morning to avoid raising any suspicion. They were lucky that none of them snored to jeopardize their safety at night.

One night, one of the owners of the garage came for whatever reason he had but met the garage intact but deserted by the inhabitants. He knocked at the door and talked as if to expect anyone to open the door from inside, but nothing happened. He entered the house and garage and found that all their things were inside. He said, "The inhabitants had not gone anywhere but must have gone to visit someone somewhere in the town". They refused to let him know that they were around as he knocked at the door. They knew that night that they had made a particularly good decision and choice of positional defence. Randy guessed the owners must have been surprised and demoralized at his not meeting them that night. He finally must have thought that the inevitable arrest lurking at the heels of the occupants of his garage must have caught up with them or that they must have moved on but it will be too early for him to speculate any move out of town in the instance. When the owner of the garage came the next morning, he must have been astonished to meet everyone intact and happy as usual. When he told them that he was around the previous night and could not find any of them, they told him they had gone out collectively to visit a friend. Non-existent friends.

The journey towards the iron curtain is segmented. The traveller gives his breakdown and how he manages it. The journey involves getting to a place or town and working menial jobs to raise money for the next move. If one attempted to move and failed, the money for the trip was as good as wasted which always culminated in a begin-again process. Most people toed that line not because they did not plan well but because of luck and external human factors. The external human factors superseded the associated natural luck. Different people more than toiled or had their unfair share of life to get through the iron curtain. The iron curtain is a feeling, invincible wall, aberration, and a connotation of deprivation made to ward off those who believed in symbolic life as against saprophytes. When the saprophytes had milked their victims dry and turned their back on them to die or live as they would. The symbiotic seek a fair share and a redistribution of looted things by whatever method available to achieve it. The only way was by marching forward in whatever way or method available to puncture or erase the so-called iron curtain in any possible way amenable to one's acceptable designs by chance or luck, and most of them succeeded in doing just that, while many retreated or died in quest of stillbirth accomplishments. It reminded Randy years later about a prime minister crying over a lost son in the Sahara Desert. A desert that many had passed trekking to somewhere unknown to them, and to a point where their strength could take them in a day and for days. It was the same desert where many heads had fallen proudly unheard of, unpublished and unrecognized. Randy laughed at the sycophancy of the world they lived in. Helicopters, soldiers and other unimaginable government humans and machines were drafted to do a track and tracing of her son in the desert. He was later recovered, and the news media billowed and went red with a heavy anvil to hit the attendant news. Those at the top don't know what the poor man suffers to keep afloat as normal human beings daily for years and till death. Apart from those that have seen the harsh realities of life and had made all the steps to be at the helm of affairs, many that are at the top are completely ignorant of the little things around them. Some of the important personalities that had gone through the ladder of real leadership with ideas to carry all peripherals of the human touch are people like the first dark-skinned South African President and the forty-fourth president of the United States of America. They have seen the sufferings of the common man firsthand and know how it feels to be one of the suffering masses.

In Ghat they got to know that everything one did from there on was through "connection". Nothing was done without connection and for every connection one tipped a connector for the connection and the lazy job and information. Randy saw what went on as a very dubious way of cheating and duping by some unscrupulous die-hard criminally-minded persons involved in the trade. There was no way most people could circumvent the connection thing and so they accepted it as a norm. It was like if you cannot beat them in this case satisfy them and go but do not join them. There was no need to join some disgruntled bands of brigands who had no iota of good feelings for their comrades. The connectors were dastardly in all facets and everywhere they existed as middlemen. People met connections everywhere and in everything, they wanted to do. It was a hardship created by the cheats to add to the suffering masses' already existing deplorable conditions. One of Randy's friends said, "let those connecting keep connecting till one day, they will find themselves connecting through prison gates". The statement made Randy laugh wildly that some tears ran down his cheeks. The connectors were crafty and managed their conman ship very effectively with their Libyan counterparts. The connection was inimical but the people who operated it were more than inimical, dreary and dastard because they did everything to rip people off their little and hard-to-get money.

After about two months, they started to think about moving northwards to any of the coastal towns. Most people chose to move to Benghazi or to the capital Tripoli called by the natives as Tarrabulus. They were the largest cities in the country situated along the coast and the cities where foreigners could easily mix up with the population. Foreigners avoided small cities to elude law enforcement agents that still in some ways troubled them a lot. The police enjoyed chasing undocumented foreigners like a rabbit around town while others watched with glee. This happened in all the towns and cities. There were roadblocks to controlling the movement of people from one town or village to the other. The country was a wide but free controlled and patrolled prison for all foreigners.

There was that government bus that plied the Tripoli and Albaraghat route that could only be boarded through connection. It was an ill-designed trade by a fellow illegal immigrant to thwart every hard-working person from making a self-planned and straightforward progress. One needed to connect a connector who will connect another connector that knows the driver or talk with the driver to give out tickets to all those that will be connected for the travel. Randy could not believe why they erected the monopolistic hurdles that were compulsorily made to dissuade a direct mercantile transaction. That being so, they opted to meet one connector called Alhaji Albaraghat that hails from Ghana to make plans for their boarding the bus at an undecided date. Alhaji Albaraghat had carved an unpopular pimp kingpin ship for himself in the boundary town. He dominated the bus connections services connections, which probably had made his moving northwards unthinkable. He connected with a lot of people that failed but still managed to find their way to the coastal cities. He will inflate the price of the bus fare in agreement with one of the unscrupulous natives and get it cushioned and signed by the bus driver. They always had prearranged cash and delivery talks before the arrival of the duped passengers. They will seal the agreement and Alhaji Albaraghat will settle the entire deal as agreed among them in his most foul and broken local language before the driver will allow the passengers to board the bus.

From all accounts, the drivers themselves aided and abetted in the connection game and businesses. That person could board the bus did not mean that they would be sure of getting to their destinations. There were so many security barriers erected along the tarred desert roads that if one was not lucky, he could be made to disembark from the bus as a foreigner. The law enforcement officers never cared what became of anyone that was dropped off the bus after that. Foreigners compulsorily made to disembark from the bus could be given a very good beating and robbed if ill luck creeps in and more so on a very bad day could be sent to the prison for an indefinite period.

Alhaji Albaraghat gave them their bill, which they all paid happily in the evening preceding the journey. He asked the passengers to report at an early hour the next morning. That night, they were all sleepless and thinking about what could happen in between the payment and boarding. They had heard about how some people paid their money to connectors and ended up with one problem or the other that made them eventually lose their money and could not make the travel. In a worst-case scenario, one could be denied boarding right completely and have no one to report to. Everyone assumed the mantle of the law. Libyans say they are *"sawasawa" (equality)* meaning that everyone is equal before the law but with the exclusion of the foreigner's human rights touch. Foreigners were like rats and could be kicked out anywhere or place at any time without being questioned. Foreigners from West Africa possessed only the valued good quality of their physical and stamina-packed-oriented labour. After that, they were only comparable to a four-letter word.

It was morning as directed and they went to the bus station assembly point to embark on another *"hikihiki"* movement. A term coined to describe the way and manner people did things away from agreeable norms or a transaction done in the wrong or right way that does not conform to the laws in place. In this case, it means doing the right thing without letting the law know that you are beating her for your advantage to survive in life's rat racing. As they assembled themselves, they could not find Alhaji Albaraghat anywhere nearby and no one to direct them instead the youths of the town started to chase them around like goats meant for slaughter. Their main aim was to rob them of their pittance and hard-earned money at that early hour of the day. The entire alley was dark, and they did not know the tiny streets that had no approved town planning. It was an embarrassing and very disgusting situation, but they had to keep running from the marauding invaders. They managed to finally assemble and decided to try and find where Alhaji Albaraghat lived in the town. They tried but did not know his where about till one person among them managed to retrace his abode. When they got there, they met him with some women in a land where sleeping with a woman that was not one's wife was anathema and better described by her people as *Mamnual or Haram (forbidden)*. He asked them to go to the bus stop where he would meet them at his convenience. There was no seriousness and urgency in his handling of Randy's group. It was later that they got to know why he would not leave Albaraghat town. He acted as a distributing funnel for the women who came through the desert and a valve opening the supply to the natives and men around. The police knew him and what he stood for in the community. He would distribute the women and their accompanying men to potential customers. He never disappointed the latter group. It will be sincere to say that anyone that came into Libya with a woman was highly hidden, respected and given a free accommodation along with his woman who in turn paid in kind interminably. In most cases, the women and their men were well sheltered and cared for. The prostituting women had started from Maradi to Albaraghat and will continue, as they were all well aware that they were making their desired impact for hospitality services along the way and among the people. The people too as have been said, hate to be seen or see others talking freely and openly about the "V" triangle business indulgence which they have immersed themselves unashamedly in the practical mechanics of it. The law says, "don't do it but they do it without letting the law see them doing it, even if the law sees them doing it, they will deny it because the custodians of the law too were involved, in this case, the pot cannot call the kettle black because they have committed equal offence knowingly". What an irony of history and disbelief. Those who preach piety in that part of the world deceive themselves first before the world. Events there were better seen than heard through reports.

When the bus arrived from Tripoli, Alhaji Albaraghat emerged like a magician from an unknown hideout looking very ruffled, smudged and unkempt. He did not apologize for all the ordeals Randy and his group had gone through in the hands of the filthy-minded youths of the town before his sudden appearance. He had vanished from his place after Randy and his group had left his place. He rushed Randy and his group to the bus driver to get the overcharged boarding pass issued. As said earlier, one was not sure of getting to his destination till he reached it safely and disembarked from the bus. Every member of the group paid the fare that covered each one from Albaraghat to Tripoli. Randy's heart was pumping faster and racing at a lightning speed than expected as he boarded the bus with the other passengers. He was having a premonition that something was going to be amiss on the way but did not want Fenbrabi and Kele to know how he felt despite their marathon prayers the previous night against anything negative happening to them when the journey will start. Despite the prayers, they had been pursued and chased like aimless chickens right a few minutes away from their abode. They had decided to leave and had to go. It will be better to brave some minor problems and get them sorted out on the way away from the town than remain cocooned longer than expected. They had had enough of the seclusion and wanton disregard for human life in the hands of some of the natives.

There are four checkpoints from Albaraghat to Sabha, which no foreigner is very sure he will be able to get across on a bus. The crossing of the four checkpoints brings all foreigners nearer civilization and further away from the open prison system escape. As the bus driver left Albaraghat, they passed the first checkpoint unchecked till they reached the third in Sardalas. The bus driver was waived down and asked to park aside. As the driver positioned the bus properly, Randy thought that the worst-case scenario they loathed was going to take place in the middle of nowhere. The signs were coming in different forms but the worst for the day was in the making without any defence. The officers were going to force their will down their throats hook and sinker without any mercy. Randy and the entire group summoned unimaginable courage and answered every question that was directed at them. The military officers were all in mufti but carried AK47 sub-machine guns strapped to their shoulders. It was no surprise to Randy as everyone carried a gun without any problems because they believed that any citizen should be able to answer any national defence call at any time.

In the end, Randy and his group were all asked to disembark the bus. They were subjected to indecent bodily searches and their lightly packed bags were ransacked and valuable things removed. Randy lost his aluminium chain along with one condom he had picked after where they were robbed inside the desert sand near the foot of the high mountain. They started to beg the officers of the law to be allowed to continue their journey, but their pleas fell on deaf ears. The officers refused vehemently and asked them to trek back to the next village they had passed. Randy and his group did not understand what the officers meant. The more Randy and his group begged the more they said in a shouting tone *"bara ni, bara, emshi, emshi – emshi"* (leave here, leave, go, go etc) one of them was so belligerent and continued at the top of his tone *"bara, walahi talahi kasumobilahi, bara ni, nti miquois bara"* (go away, truth to my heavenly father, go away you are bad please go away), as he said those words he picked his AK47 sub machine gun and waived the group with his left hand to leave in the direction they wanted the group to go but Randy continued begging the officers. By the time he had his gun in his hand, Randy was alone with the officers while the others had already started retreating in fear to the village. As the officers saw the tenacity in Randy's appeal, the angry officer asked him to move back with a wave of his hand and cocked his AK47 gun with the safety pin turned to off position. Before he cocked his gun, Randy had taken some steps back. The next action was without a warning and to get Randy scared by firing the gun into the air. Randy did not need a fortuneteller to follow others into the village as directed by the officers. He had given the group their warning shot and any other talk or pleading with them will invite the most unexpected. As he shot into the air, Randy dived for safety and scraped his thigh on the rocky desert surface. The diving would have been useless had he aimed anyone directly. It was like any other part they had passed, and they were still in the same terrain but in a different direction. There are times human beings are overwhelmed with fear but when sufferings exceed its designed heart space, fears of all sorts will atrophy. There is no situation humans cannot handle. It only depends on the categorization of what people as individuals can stomach and accept as fitting to one's agreeable system. Randy did not look back again after the shot had been fired and his empty dive for cover in an open and clear close range from the bullet discharging mufti officer. They marched for many hours in a group back to the next village as directed by the officers. The trek back to the village was not easy for them. The distance was far without any water to drink, as is the case for any desert trekking. The soldiers knew what they did and had their hidden agenda for doing so. Luckily, none of the travellers collapsed on the way. They were lucky to have gone through the designed hell on earth for them.

On their way back to Sardalas, they started to plan what they should do to avoid getting stuck there. They met some people in the same position as them who were living in Sardalas. They were in one area that looked like a farm with one uncompleted or vandalized building. Randy and his group looked for one of the free rooms to occupy. There was danger sleeping in that type of place but it was the only available free place and roof over their heads. The dilapidated building did not offer anything good for their safety and robbery was every minute of the day imminent and a rampant pastime for the natives. They were defenceless and will always submit to people that carried guns like their house keys. Gory and sorry situations for them in an abandoned building tucked away on a farm in the middle of nowhere. Randy analyzed the security situation and wrote it off but told everyone they were there and will come out unscathed purely out of natural luck. They managed to cook, ate and rest but were always shocked when anything went a little louder than necessary. The indescribable decorum of the place and the vicinity showed the danger everyone was open to whenever anything sinister or bad would happen.

No sooner had they made it through midday than some natives came around to look for some passengers that would like to be ferried across the checkpoint where Randy and his group were made to disembark from the bus. They were trolleys that none of Randy's group members trusted but what had to be done had to be done and done rightly and fast enough to get out of the unwelcoming environment. The trolleys made plans with Randy's group and others that cared to be part of the trip. They paid with their last money and remained jittery all night. They thought about the situation whereby the trolleys failed to show up to pick them up at the appointed time in the morning. They will be doomed. The experience would be catastrophic and humanly unbearable. When the trolleys had left, they made some dinner to eat and started to think about how they were going to beat the deadly checkpoint in the morning. There was no way they were going to make ends meet in Sardalas if they failed to advance to the next town Ubari. It was an unspoken truth and reality, but they all pretended not to be bothered by the hard facts on the ground. The trolleys asked them to get ready at 04.00Hrs and that they had no plans to wait for anyone not ready before their arrival.

At 0400Hrs summertime, the drivers drove into the defenceless and hollow complex. They arranged Randy and his group like stolen goats at the back of their open-body land cruiser jeeps. They were all covered with a tarpaulin with Randy and his group holding the edges to avoid being seen easily by the officers if any of them were to be standing. They held the edges extremely hard amidst the heavy wind gusting speed of about a hundred and eighty kilometres per hour that tried to give them away to any prying eyes or views. The drivers were specialists and must have been in the smuggling business for a very long time. It is equally possible they agree with the barrier keepers. So much connivance among the natives against innocent illegals who hardly understand the setups and gang-ups to milk them dry in patches and stages of their truncated progressions. They neither behaved nor acted like newcomers into the business. They slowed the speed of the jeep down as they approached the checkpoint and suddenly revved the engine, as they were a few meters away from the checkpoint. The officers had kept the barrier open and were busy sleeping when their driver sped past. Randy could see them through the tiny torn tarpaulin holes at their checkpoint makeshift office. Nature had taken its toll on their nocturnal efficiency to Randy and his group's advantage. Randy was at a vantage point inside the jeep and saw the officers very clearly in a relaxed position that portrayed some obedience to the natural laws of human existence. All Randy and the group could see after the Checkpoint was the same vast, empty, rocky, endless arid Saharan terrain that runs in the distance interminable with beautiful and natural features of geographical formations. Randy remembered a friend who had trekked very deeply into the desert to beat their checkpoint searchlight and continued along the stretch of kilometres for only God knows how long it took him and whoever must have followed him on the journey to get to Ubari. That friend must have done it purely out of sheer necessity but surely not out of choice. When there is no money and an underpriced job to get on with life, one is forced to do the inevitable to get out of a messy situation. He used the available and risky way that may have hurt his health so badly but was better than not trying at all. The journey made Randy realize why the officers did not allow them to go beyond where they were made to forcibly disembark from the bus the previous day. The distance from the checkpoint to Ubari was far, dangerous, and precariously inhuman to survive. Whoever trekked that distance must have tried to commit suicide or crossed the searchlight and came to the road again and was picked up luckily by any Good Samaritan to Ubari.

After some hours of driving, they reached Ubari and were dumped at the farm roadside on the outskirts of the town. They all scattered and started to trek in different directions but with a common aim to reach the town centre. Randy met many of their kind in Ubari town. The first day passed with everyone finding a place for himself. They passed the night in one uncompleted building that had no doors and went out the next day in search of under-priced jobs that were almost non-existent. The best buildings were the uncompleted and abandoned ones that any new foreigner could have easy access to utilize for his daily existence. Foreigners endured so many unspeakable odds in Libya. The journey to Libya was better not started for once started and one had gone extremely far, there was no letting off the hook. It was like an infection or virus that you went on for some protracted period before weaning of purging oneself of the infection.

The first labourer job Randy, Fenbrabi and his friend Kele had was well digging. It was nice for them. At least they had started somewhere and got their pittance paid in the end. The man they worked for was nice. He had served them some nice meals that made the money they had made for the day a reserve. On the second day of their arrival, there was that Petroleum Company that was exploring the desert for crude oil that came into Ubari town to pick some foreigners for some good, positioned jobs that attracted cheap labour. Randy was lucky to have been among those that had seat to get back with the job scouting agents of the company. Randy's ex-nephew and his friend bade him goodbye. Randy told both that he will be coming back.

They drove for some hours before they reached the company premises in the middle of the desert. The next day, all the workers were assembled and briefed by the company manager before the Sudanese supervisor who understood the local language and English addressed everyone on what the new staff job designations were. Life there was completely different from the norms of what Randy used to know but he adapted easily. They were made to pick Geophones for so many kilometres every day under the burning sun. There was no place to hide even when they had their good lunches. The company was nice to them despite the harsh terrain that was not their fault. After four weeks, Randy opted to leave because he was always thinking about his ex-nephew and his friend. He felt he had gotten enough money that will take them forward. He wanted to surprise them and make them feel happy after they had all wallowed that much in endless sufferings. Randy loved being with them and they all enjoyed the way they related to one another. It was a unity that none of them thought could be broken.

On the appointed day Randy was going back to Ubari town, he was paid off and carried back to town. When he reached the town, he embarked on looking for Fenbrabi and his friend Kele. There was one farm Fenbrabi and Kele had gotten a job and had shown Randy the farm before he left for the same day for the desert job. Randy went straight to the farm on his arrival to reunite and pick both up for the next lap of the journey but could not find anyone there. He returned to the town and started to ask after them through some old faces he had met before going to the desert for the job. Most of the people now were new to Randy. He ran into one of the old faces that knew him with Fenbrabi and Kele. The old acquaintance told him that Fenbrabi and Kele were out of Ubari town but don't know which town they had moved on to. Randy was happy that they could move on but was still interested in being with them. The worst of all was that he did, not know where they had moved on too but he too had to move on. He had thought they must have moved on to Tripoli City as they always talked about it together.

Randy met Ubari new and disappointing altogether with all the attendant predicaments. There was no acting weak like in the situations he had found himself. He thought about the Sabha checkpoint that was the next after Ubari and the last one in Brach. The two checkpoints stood like a colossus respectively and it was exceedingly difficult for any driver to get across with their bulk of customers who were mostly foreigners. Randy started to make enquiries from the people he met newly in Ubari but wanted to see one of the old people because he knew they will be better versed in the news about things that happened in the town than the new entrants. As the day wore on, he went out to reload his intestines still thinking about how he will leave the town at any possible opportunity that came before him. After resting a bit with the day running out gradually, he met one old friend that had come together with them the first day they were dropped off at a farm in Ubari. Both started to talk about what had been going on and what people were doing to get going northwards to any of the coastal towns.

Luckily for Randy, the old friend was planning on how to leave the town the next day, but the driver wanted a full passenger load which at the time he met Randy was yet to be completed. Randy told him how he had gone into the desert and how he had just entered the town and wanted to leave because his ex-nephew and his friend had left for an unknown destination. The old friend did not waste any time meeting the driver with Randy and introduced him as one of the passengers that wanted to leave town the next day. The driver said Randy was the last passenger he needed to make for a full load. The driver asked Randy to pay his money and told them where they will assemble and be picked up at 02.00Hrs of the next day. The driver already knew the fears of foreigners about the checkpoints and assured them he would take them across Sabha and Brach checkpoints. The old friend assured Randy too because he had seen many that followed the same driver to success. The driver was well known and respected by the officers. Randy took refuge in their Blessed Assurance but was still Sceptical about their claims. This was a land you never trusted anything till it had happened or taken place. Randy did not want to be a fool waiting for a promise to materialize but he kept his cool.

Since Randy came into town that day from the desert, he had no place or real friend to get along with. The weather was seething hot and there was that park without a single tree where people slept on the open cement floor. Randy had nothing to give out his personality. He was the same as everyone else and no one will know he had some money on him. He looked haggard like every other person and comported himself gently faking everything he did on that spot. While it was hot during the day the night was directly the opposite like always. Some of the people he met in the open space invited him to come and sleep on their blankets with them. He went to one of them to share his blanket with him. It was very cold, and the blanket did not cover both of them completely. Another man nearby to both offered them another blanket before they felt normal inside the open cold. Randy kept a close watch on his wristwatch to avoid missing the appointed time with the driver. The assembly ground was the same place he was passing the night but will not let anyone know about it. The man who introduced him to the driver did not know where he was going to pass the night either.

At 02.00Hrs, the driver came in his car to pick up his passengers at his house. They were all foreigners and had seen themselves in the day without knowing what the other had in mind except for the man that connected Randy to the driver without connection fees. They drank tea at the driver's house before setting out for the journey in his painted commercial cab. Randy could see that everyone inside the car had not gotten enough sleep before the commencement of the journey. After some hours of driving, they reached one of the most notorious checkpoints in Libya. Sabha. The officers at the checkpoint had a distant chat with the driver and let him through the barrier. With the crossing in mind, Randy felt a bit better and sure of reaching Tripoli that day. The journey continued till a little after midday when they reached Brach. Brach is located at a junction where the road from Niger through Dirkou to Marzuq meets before Sabha. When the driver reached the Brach checkpoint, the officers had a little chat with him and let him through the barrier. Everyone breathed a heave of sigh and looked forward to seeing Tripoli that day. Randy thought he wished he had made the crossing with Fenbrabi and Kele but their whereabouts were unknown and there was little or nothing he could do about it either. They reached Tripoli that evening and had nowhere to go and nowhere to pass the night. They managed to get near to the area where most of the foreign embassies were located and slept on some cartons, they had picked on their way from Medina Qadim on that wintry night in the garden. It was chilly but they had no option other than the only available condition they were open to. It was a dare death, survive and go situation. It was a very harrowing experience Randy prayed never to be caught up with again no matter the circumstances.

15

COASTAL LIFE

AFTER PASSING THE NIGHT IN THE GARDEN, THEY WERE COLD, FIDGETY, AND ALMOST HYPOTHERMIC but moved on as early as possible in the direction of every one of their type. They groped around town to reach an area of the city called Massif. It was the centre of the city with iconic buildings, well-paved gardens and a very beautiful seashore. In between these architectural beauties and their iconic features which they exuded stood most of the foreigners fighting for space and piece of land to wash cars for prospective customers. The job was called *"Lama"* *(to wash) meaning wash and "Lamasiyara" (to wash the car) meant to wash the car while* *Lamasiyara and "jilda" (light animal leather skin for cleaning cars) meant to wash the car* *with leather skin water mopping and drying of the car. Jilda was the leather skin used for* *mopping and drying the water on the body of the washed cars.*

Their fellow illegal dark-skinned people because of sheer selfishness and profiteering chased newcomers like Randy and their group like wandering dogs from one point to the other. They were accused of trying to steal their customers and encroaching on their meagre daily bread by the old ones. On the other hand, the new arrivals needed to survive alongside the old people that already existed before their arrival. Randy and his new group started to fight for someplace among the wild people that will not allow them to exercise their human rights in the status quo. The old people that were there before unashamedly and deliberately ganged up to ostracize them from the status quo. Whichever way was going to be a fight for survival between all parties concerned. There would be grudges and fights to be started and settled with insurmountable obstinacy in the end. The answer was to fight for your place because no one owned the place apart from the government of the day and some of her citizens terrorized the foreigners with no concrete justifiable reason, apart from being illegal immigrants. It existed everywhere on the planet but not all countries treated theirs with the amount of disdain and lackadaisical attitude the Libyan migrants were subjected to. They were only on transit through Libya because of their geographical location to their desired destination. The majority did not want to stay there forever. If there were better ways to avoid the country, the majority of the people would have opted out of the plan to use the country as a transit place. From the reports Randy gathered, the entire Northern Africa areas were hostile countries to all dark-skinned people from mostly West Africa and it is worst when he or she is from an Anglophone country. It is a hard truth to collate and believe but is exactly what Randy had experienced. Randy prided himself as a veritable dark-skinned person. He loves being what he naturally had been endowed with no matter what any other person or persons thought about him.

On the second day that, Randy had arrived in Tripoli city, he met Gozchi at Massif. They exchanged greetings and exchanged experiences as to how they made it through the length of the entire country to be at the coast. Gozchi had been faster to reach Tripoli weeks earlier. Randy had known him as a veritable pauper and mendicant. Randy was sure he must have conned someone to be where he was. Gozchi instead of being friendly and his brother's keeper disallowed Randy from finding a space to do the job everyone was involved in. Randy heard them shout all around *Lama! Lama!! Siyara* which means Carwash. Randy thought how Gozchi the saprophytic Leech of a man he had known from Tamanrasset till the open rocky terrains of the Sahara near Albaraghat had gotten to where he was. He had metamorphosed into a landowner in just a few weeks but had no option but to ask him if he could help him and others out for accommodation that day. He told Gozchi how they had slept in the garden near one of the Embassy located in the town. He agreed to help Randy out with others.

In the evening when he was done with his car wash job, he took Randy and his group to a place in the company of one of his friends Pauledo. On the way, he told Randy and his group that he had gotten the accommodation for them through his friend and that he wanted them to pay the house rent on the spot to enable them to pay the Landlord. The group smelt a rat, but it was dark, and they would not like to spend the next night in the open. The group wanted to see the Landlord themselves but Gozchi and Pauledo will not allow that. The group condescended and paid but something sinister happened when Clemento Machiavelli wanted to fight the injustice both friends were meting out. Pauledo dipped his hand inside his jacket pretending to be bringing out a pistol while Gozchi asked him to hold his intended fire. He begged him as if Pauledo was trying to bring out a handgun from his underarm, but he forgot that the group he was dealing with were not idiots and dummies. It was a threat no one in the group took seriously and did not want to magnify the situation. The group wanted a place to call home and were bent to get out of the street. Randy wanted peace to reign even if he knew the game Gozchi and Pauledo were playing on their former desert counterparts. It showed what some human beings could transform their position and character into when opportunities place them an inch above their peers and friends. Good relationships degenerated into cancerous moral laxity of indescribable magnitude. They were not ashamed of being caught framing their transaction instead they continued to emphasize the importance of their crooked help because it was night. When they finally reached the house, the Landlord came out to get the money from Gozchi and Pauledo. Randy and his group saw that only one-third of the money was paid to the Landlord and the rest was confiscated, embezzled and pocketed by the broad daylight thieves. Randy categorized the money they had stolen from them openly as blood money. Both left boldly but cocooned in shame for the fact that Randy and his group saw them openly in their misdeals and misbehaviour. It was an open robbery through the utilization of the wrong geographical chance to prey on the innocent and friends that knew them when things were completely rough among them. Randy and his group could not fight the open robbery immediately, but they paid for their sins in some other nemesis-drawn-out ways. Gozchi masterminded everything but would meet his waterloo at a later date with his encounter with Mother Nature. He had swallowed karma expecting a thunderous boomerang.

Randy was spending his third day in Tripoli with others in his company. Once they had a roof over their head, everyone started to be on his own, but they all converged at home every evening to tell tales and stories of the day and what everyone must have heard about anything or events of the previous and past times before their arrival to Tripoli. It was a way to know the town better in case anything happened. After all, they did not know what could happen to anyone, any time in a country where foreigners were being chased like rabbits at any point in time without respect and consideration. People's rights were wantonly violated, disrespected, and infringed upon.

On the first day that they will go to Medina Qadim from Tejura, none of them had the money to board a taxi. They thought it was a short distance and could make it there in minutes, but the reverse thought was the case. They trekked almost fifteen kilometres from Tejura to Medina Qadim. When they reached the city and told the people how they had come, everyone was surprised but offered no sympathy for them. It was their private business as they could see that no one cared for anyone about whatever happened to one another. Mercy, respect and all forms of human behavioural modes were neither considered nor respected and will never be in vogue then. Everyone talked hard and acted hard. People's smiles ended in ordinary and unconvinced intolerable leering — hiding all feelings in the abyss. There in Massif, the law enforcement officers regularly came to chase foreigners for arrests. They also went to homes to arrest people for no reason other than to rip them off of their hard-earned money and valuables. They broke into homes for the arrests and sometimes did it on purpose as pre-planned on peaceful streets. Anyone arrested was taken to the government's notorious *Zanzu*. Nobody arrested to the best of Randy's knowledge was charged for any offence. Any arrested person will just remain in prison till fate and luck decided his or her acquittal. People were sometimes transferred from the northern prisons to the southern ones and when a release was to be affected, was done without any consideration of where one was arrested. The freedman starts the northward ascent or travels afresh from the south. It was a type of internal and Libyan national rendition.

The jobs available for them were Shoe making, car wash, pimp and prostitution mostly for women. Randy chose the carwash but could not stand the constant harassment from the law enforcement officers in Massif area of the city centre. Someone else directed Randy to a spot in the city under one bridge where many cars were parked during the day to establish a washing centre there. Randy obliged the directives and was there till he left Tripoli for good. As he was there alone, other people came to join him. He was happy to accept them, but they wanted to edge him out with time.

One of them who wanted to edge him out of the parking area had committed a crime against the land that offered him some life respite. He had carved the country's permanent residence permit, which he used to deceive some people that did not know what it meant to have such a document in one's possession. Those he managed to deceive, he collected some money from for his illegal and criminal services. When he heard he was being sought he left the country in a jiffy and his friend in crime will follow in weeks after him. Randy had been approached by one of his bosom friends about the stamp, but his friend failed to tell him the truth then that it was a forged one. He wanted to appear as a helper to Randy by getting his passport stamped and maybe get some money from the stamp carver as his connection fees. Randy would have gone to prison if he had accepted the stamp on his passport. He preferred to be without any "Ikama" (permanent resident permit) as an illegal immigrant as he and others were known for, than getting a forged Ikama onto his passport.

It is possible to get up and going with some friends' help and equally disastrous to heed the wrong advice or to some insidious assembles by some friends. Some friends are good in some things as you relate with them and corky sometimes to pull you down to their wanted sinister designs with some other things. Friendship is good with lots of verifications attached. Randy remembered how he fell to Bivasco and his brother Biwo because he did not verify the authenticity of their claims. The holocaust survivors said it all: "Never again" and for Randy, it was going to be "Never again" for his survival with friends, but some little mistakes still lurk at the corner for any unsuspecting persons. Most friends will always pull one down while some infinitesimal number will stand aright and sincerely at one's side in times of trials and tribulations. Make friends with some strict vetting controls.

Randy remained alone in the parking area again but not for too long. Some two other better people came again to join him but not for too long too. One of them was arrested when Randy went to fetch some water for the next day's job. Meanwhile, there were chains of arrests going on in every part of the city and countrywide. Randy became selective about where he went and how he got there. The possibility of going out and never coming back home was so rife and troubling. It was continually on and the only news among foreigners was all about arrests and detentions in the Zanzu that went on for an indefinite period. In the Zanzu, men were constantly hanged with their heads upside down and their soles flogged till their manhood started to malfunction temporarily or weakened. People were waterboarded with other assorted chosen and designed types of punishments. The dark-skinned man was used as a guinea pig for any new punishment that was going to be introduced into their "guillotine Gestapo running machines". The outside world never saw what the dark-skinned man saw in the hands of the Arab official powers of disdain and annihilation. Once anyone was not seen, it was assumed that the person must have been arrested for if anyone travelled, he or she always notified those he had left behind. Incarceration in Tripoli took place because of the law enforcement officers' insatiable propensity for peoples' money which they stole from anyone arrested, non-documentation, prostitutes, and illegal and prohibited deals of all sorts. It was a cycle of intimidation, insanity and gross disregard for human life. The citizens were lazy but the foreigners that did ugly and demeaning jobs were robbed and

132

beaten up in some selected alleys around the town. Everyone was a little part that made up the entire reason for the endless chase around the entire city.

There was always noise in the evening where Randy and the other people lived in Tejura. When Randy will advise them to talk silently and personably, he will be shunned and insulted with ignominy. He continually advised everyone every evening, but no one was ready to listen to him. They saw him as a coward, but it did not deter him from calling their abrasive behaviours into order. Randy did not care if any of them listened or not but told them one day that if anything negative was going to happen, he will not be around. They laughed at his forecast and dismissed him with a wave of their hands. They had all assumed the same level of impostor authority that was not going to lead them to a meaningful end in the house. Randy was not happy with the noise but always feared for their collective safety.

Before Randy went to Tripoli, he had heard that his old-time friend in the northern city of his country of origin was living there. He used to be an interesting and wonderful friend. He sent messages to him through some people after someday that he was in Tripoli. He expected his friend Muge to come any day to check on him where he had his belated but honourable car wash office but so many days and weeks had passed by without him coming and he did not know where in Tripoli he could locate him.

One day, Muge suddenly appeared with a car to visit Randy at his working place. They embraced themselves and were so elated at seeing themselves after so many years of not having contact. They exchanged pleasantries and at the end of the day, he came to pick Randy to his place. Randy had an incredibly good shower in his place, and ate before he was driven back to his Tejura abode.

They recalled so much all that had happened in their lives since the last they saw themselves. When they arrived where Randy was living with the other people, Muge accepted the place as being good for any starter in the type of belated life everyone started with in the city. The count of millions starts with a one and so were Randy and his comrades' condition. Muge warned and advised everyone living with Randy to behave more modestly. He advised everyone to talk in a low tone to avoid their voices attracting attention. When Muge left, the noise continued uncontrollably. The shouting and waves of laughter could not subside till when nature set in with her natural sedation. The misbehaviour continued uncontrollably that made Randy remind them again that any day they attracted law enforcement officers to their abode, he was sure he will not be part of the *kalambush* and that if one person was to survive their recalcitrance, intransigence and misunderstanding as it went, that it will surely be him, Randy. He was uncomfortable every day that passed with people that refused to learn and to understand what was right to do. Randy did not fit into their group anymore but had to soft-pedal. He started to look for a place where he could have some peace of mind without letting his friend Muge know about his plans. Randy thought every day something was going to happen but did not know when and how it was going to come. The house was getting uninhabitable every passing day.

Before Randy went to open his "*Lama* ground", he went to an area of the town where so many people stood in their hundreds to beg for any job. People chased any car that passed and took a seat if the owner ever stopped. No one knew why the people wanted anyone and for what. They just went with any person that wanted anyone for anything. It was a complete madness most people involved never weighed the danger of such uncontrolled and not well-thought-out movements with strangers and foreigners. The scene was comparable to the Tamanrasset *travail* ground" but it was called "*Shogol*" (*work*) ground in Tripoli. Hence everyone shouted "*shogol! Shogol!! Shogol* !!!" to all prospective few hours' cheap labour employers. The job-seeking site offered nothing more than degradation of a particular people who were what they were temporarily by chance and not a choice. Randy found it very insulting to see people running as if escaping from a war-torn area, trampling on themselves and sustaining unaccounted-for injuries. Some had one in a million luck and many more came back with woeful tales. Randy stood aside and watched the melee unfold among desperate sons of some healthy nations in Africa. Randy cried silently when a car that wanted to pick up someone among them injured one of them. The driver did not care about what he had done and those that managed to get in urged him to get going for the job that will only last a few minutes or hours and the result will be pittance money received. The money will not buy more than a bottle of iced water. Randy raised his head and cursed their leaders back home. They had reduced the integrity of a Great People and Nation to nothingness in the face of the countries that are supposed to kowtow before them. Too many bad things had eaten deeply and irreparably into the Nation's biological fabrics. What a shame to watch these scenes that should not have been at all.

The next day, Randy went to Massif to eat after work. As he was eating, one Libyan military officer started to move in his direction with some stone face and tenacious steps. Randy sensed danger lurking and stood up with his well-made Semovita-stained fingers and continued eating as he stood. The military officer's steps went faster and faster as he approached those of them that were eating at the time. Randy picked his meat from the plate and withdrew a bit from his position in readiness to run should the man mean evil in the instance. The Egyptian on Randy's left-hand side did not make any movement because he had all the insurance, he felt could protect him from the insane officer as an Arab. When the officer's closeness to them became ridiculously hot and uncomfortable to bear, Randy took some steps away from the food area. The officer asked Randy to sit down but Randy asked him to say that he will not harm him in Allah's name, but he refused to play by the rule. When he refused to swear that he will not harm Randy in Allah's name his intentions became obvious — he was coming for one of those daylight robberies that some of the officers carried out on foreigners in different parts of Tripoli city. Before the officer could utter more words, Randy started to run with his unwashed fingers. The same day was when one of his roommates was arrested in the same Massif. Randy and his other roommates never saw their arrested friend again and whatever became of him wherever he may have been taken to or ended up. The arrests in the town were at a very high point again since their friend had been bundled from Massif. People started to see less of each other. Randy saw one Ghanaian that escaped from *Zanzu* but stepped on mine as he was escaping. One of his legs was amputated and there were many instances of different carnage dimensions perpetrated on people because they were what other people did not like them to be from the Creator. If the world and individuals had the chance to be what their choices are, the world will still have that composition that many would not like to see or cherish.

Randy came to Massif to eat again days later. He met the Egyptian man again there by chance. He declared Randy a bad man. Randy was not worried about his comment because he knew that the Egyptian had acted sheepishly with his stupendous initiative. He was supposed to know when those boots meant peace and war of attrition against foreigners. In secluded areas no one was spared by the disgruntled men in uniform, only when people were many would they play fairly to complement Pan Arabism. The military man in camouflage that made Randy run for his dear life and belongings some days back had collected the Egyptian's money and other valuables before letting him go and yet see Randy as a bad man for escaping the unwarranted attack and daylight robbery. Randy settled down with his eyes revolving like that of a Falcon over a wonderful dish of food for the day expecting the military officer that never came. After eating, Randy told the man that firstly, he was robbed because he could not foresee danger as a Muslim from a fellow Muslim member who in that special case was in military uniform and refused to uphold his tenets of Islamism on request. Common sense would have told him that his Muslim brother meant evil and nothing short of it. Maybe Randy knew it because he was a dark-skinned person and knew what befalls one of them from those who never saw them as humans in the order of life. Secondly that he was stupid for trusting someone because they belonged to the same religion, which did not mean he could not be harmed by his members and thirdly that he was visa-free to the country did not mean that he was insulated or cushioned from dangers. Randy told him that he had run away because there was no one to make any report to when anything happened to any foreigner in Libya and that he should count himself lucky to have escaped unhurt from those rugged boots of that day. The rule of law was only for the citizens and diplomats.

Before the police in Tejura raided Randy's house, Sonnie who had lived with Randy in Albaraghat came to meet him at his car wash office. He was just coming into Tripoli and needed a place to live on. They socialized, and chatted about the past and how they came about being in Tripoli. Sonnie started to relate what he had heard about some people that had travelled from Albaraghat northwards. He said Alhaji Albaraghat had told them back in Albaraghat that some of the travellers carried condoms with them and wanted to know if Randy knew who had carried the condom. Randy was dumbfounded but did not show it. He told him he never knew who did and had no knowledge of anything like that. This was happening months after and was very surprising to Randy. Sonnie had the culture of uncontrolled fulminating loquacity. He was a profoundly serious backbiter that could do anything to denigrate any friend. He did not know that he was reporting an incident that concerned the perpetrator. Randy knew how to handle him with complete deft.

It was after Sonnie's question and news that Randy started to put his jigsaw puzzles into place. Alhaji Albaraghat was a syndicate as Randy had always insinuated about him. He was a member of an inner caucus founded to rip off illegal immigrants like him. Sonnie had opened Ahaji Albaraghat's reason for his continued stay in Albaraghat's dusty border village unknowingly. The law enforcement officers used him as a funnel to siphon money and they in turn shared the proceeds. The officers willfully dropped the illegal immigrants and made their extended caucus carry on to the next town with added proceeds so that by the time the illegal immigrants get to a town like Ubari, they will be left with nothing to proceed thereby making them the temporary slaves they want them to be for their people. It was equally a way to wear the immigrants out and make them find their way back to their different countries. They never knew the secret at the back of every foreigner's mind. Their country was only a stepping-stone to their desired destination. There was nothing they will do to dampen the minds, spirits, and brains of the steadfast illegal immigrants. They could be troubled, locked up in *Zanzu*, beaten up, robbed, raped, name it but can never dampen the will and zeal of the decided foreigners. The caucus changing the laws will not change people's determined minds and hearts. They were mostly law-abiding and hardworking people. They had bad ones among them just like the citizens had theirs too. The foreigners were not saints just as the citizens of the country were not saints either.

Did Randy wonder how something that happened hundreds of kilometres away secretly between the owner of the condom and the officer that confiscated the condom got back to Alhaji Albaraghat from such a distance? Randy had always asked himself why an officer would confiscate a condom in a country that never allowed male-female to contact till married because they believed everyone was sanctified and must be sanctified. They were deceiving and lying to themselves and the outside world. They practised one thing, preached another and got involved in completely something unseen but known. One needs to see most of these pious men gallivanting on other continents with other women and their women too singing hosanna for their temporary freedoms with other men outside their cocooned world. Randy had seen it all in them and laughed at their deceptive unpardonable double life in a free world for the others. They are all humans that are sexually active like any other people anywhere, but their leaders get them locked up in what the outside world sees but is not in any way sincere and true. Humans share the same blood and theirs was not different. Who was fooling who? Alhaji Albaraghat feared moving northwards because he had duped a lot of people who wanted to take vengeance on him. He knew people must have known that he was a brigand illegal immigrant from Ghana serving the wishes of nefarious and uncommitted officers of the law in Southern Libya.

One day, when Randy finished with his daily job, he bought some of his home needs and had some after-job chat with a friend inside the cab they were in. The chat went on for a long time over so many issues and topics that had happened and that were still happening in the city. As they disembarked from the car, they trekked some distance before they separated. When Randy negotiated the corner leading to his flat, he met so many of his neighbours standing around and panting with different indescribable injuries. He asked them what had happened to them. They told Randy that he was lucky that, the entire compound was raided and only those of them talking with him survived the *"Shota Kalambus"* (*police arrest*) onslaught and ambush. The ambush had been planned and executed under the auspices of their Egyptian and Sudanese neighbours. The citizens from those two countries in their compound did not work hard like those of them from West Africa. They were visa-free to Libya, unlike their West African counterparts. They hated their West African counterparts because of mere religious denomination. Randy tried and went inside their room and saw how everything had been scattered and burgled by the policemen and the leftover by their neighbours from Egypt and Sudan. As Randy came out of the house and tried to find out how it had happened, some of his neighbours from Egypt and Sudan beckoned on him to come closer for the explanation he had sought to know the victims. Another neighbour that had run for his dear life shouted from inside the bush to Randy not to ever make the mistake of getting closer to those wicked killers. Randy asked him why he should avoid them, and he continued shouting and warning him to stay clear from them in one of those West African local dialects: "Don't go close to those Egyptians and Sudanese — they wanted to kill me, I managed to escape from them, they stabbed me when the police had gone". Randy went over to him with his shoulders being watched carefully against any attacker. When he met him at the hurriedly made escape route, Randy could not believe what type of injury he had sustained in the hands of their neighbours. He had been beaten and stabbed but managed to escape from their Egyptian and Sudanese neighbours. As Randy sympathized with him, the Egyptians and the Sudanese beckoned on him again to come to them for some explanation. What explanation will be more than what he had seen physically and had been explained in a better language that he understood thousands of miles away from his birthplace? Randy watched their neighbours closely and found that his attacked friend was telling him the truth about all that had transpired in his absence. Their neighbours held daggers and stones in hand to maim those that did not belong to their group of nationality. When they realized that Randy had been convinced not to come to them, they started to pelt him with stones and pursued him all around, but he knew the area better than them. He dodged all their stones with sporting agility and added luck. He left the scene immediately and remembered his warnings and advice the roommates failed to heed. Many had been arrested and must have been thinking about Randy's advice and warnings but giving a second thought that it was too late to listen to the voice of reason.

Randy quickly went back to the bus stop and boarded a cab back to the city. He went to Muge's house to tell them what had happened. Muge said he knew something like that was going to happen because most people he saw there when he went to visit Randy behaved abnormally. He asked Randy to stay put in his place. Randy appreciated his kind gestures. Muge lived in a castle-like building with a few friends. It was the part of a hospital that had not been completed but offered a perfect place to quietly live one's life as an illegal immigrant in a foreign land without hassles. Some spaces could take a village, and everyone would still feel comfortable, but they say that too many hands spoil the broth. He was tactical and stringent in not allowing many people in the complex. Randy acclaimed his righteousness of the decision on the facts that bothered on concomitant factors of safety, the arrogance of any unvetted persons that might generate prying jeopardy checks on the occupants of the property.

Randy was the fourth man to join Muge in the house and the fifth in the line-up. Muge had a live-in girlfriend Eyiat in the complex. They shared one of the rooms happily and Sema held on to one of the adjacent rooms and the other room was inhabited and shared by Randy, Wela and Gagi respectively. They all lived harmoniously, amicably and respected one another. Everyone behaved maturely and sincerely by Randy's reckoning, but the reality was that every person had gotten his or her reservations encysted.

The day Randy's house was raided, one of the men who witnessed the raiding named Jupasa recovered Randy's passport and handed it over to him later after he had informed him. Randy liked his concern and candidness, but the passport was not valid and necessary beyond the first border post of his country. The passport had done her job at the border side of their country and Niger but was just with him as a decoration and will never let him be seen with it anymore if he must advance from that point onwards. Randy was from a country every other national felt his people knew too much because none of them will stoop to being oppressed and hates to see a fellow dark-skinned person abused in any form in their presence. Their country hated colonization, re-colonization, and emancipation standing firm and shoulder high in the comity of nations despite the endemic corruption that had plagued the nation since after her independence.

One family that lived near them in Tripoli invited Wela and Randy for a few hours' jobs. They planned to do the job on the country's free day Friday. After the job, they headed for their house with some friendly chats between them. As they trekked along the sidewalk, some group of people stopped with their car and jumped out shouting *"Girigira! Girigira!! Tahali ni! Tahali Tahali ni Girgira !"* *(blackman, blackman come here, come here, come here)* suddenly accosted them. Randy shouted impulsively, "Weeeeela run, *Shota*". The two of them ran in two opposite directions making it exceedingly difficult for the four men to chase them. The early evening darkness gave them an added cover and advantage to elude the chasers in the street, as both men being chased knew how to navigate the city with ease. Randy was afraid for Wela's safety but knew he must have been home safely because the side he ran to was better for his safety than his. Randy needed more time to get around so many alleys and crisscross other streets to be able to reach home. It took him some time and everyone in the house must have been thinking about the inevitable happening to him. After some time that the people he lived with must have accepted the inevitable happening, Randy surfaced at the gate and was let in. He gave his escape account and heard that of Wela too. They were lucky to have escaped from the plain-clothed policemen. They would have just arrested them and collected their hard-earned money for the day before giving them up to one of their detention centres. Surviving such attacks and ordeals was just by only sheer rare luck and nothing else. They equally would have been what the illegals called *"Asma"* boys who always wanted most foreigners' legs and hands *"kasura" (to break)*. *"Kasura"* was a daily and permanent term on the tongues of the police and *"Asma"* *(a derogatory reference to one as a thug or criminal or simply "hey you")* junks. A word that speaks the volume of anger from most Libyan citizenry toward every foreigner, meaning "break". They liked to break foreigners' legs or hands at the slightest or least provocation. They mostly caused the provocations and ended up venting unnecessary anger on the very innocent, peace-loving and downtrodden illegals.

When the house raids and attacks continued on the streets of the different cities, Sema brought an idea to thwart any possible arrest if their house became a target. Sema suggested that they should all try hiding in the uncommissioned lift in the living room. Everyone laughed and thought it was not going to be possible to hide inside but agreed to try it out anyway. Everyone went in and closed it from behind. It worked but they had to fill out the floor with some planks. They could see the underground floor from the lift. It was very far below and any fall from the height would bring about devastating consequences. No one seemed to mind the dangers associated with the lift but knew that it existed. They had built an exit pipe from the reigning problem in town against illegal immigrants and might need to use it sometime someday. The lift.

As Randy stayed on with his friend Muge, he went out every morning to do his *Lama Siyara* job. No cold weather could keep him away from his only available job choice and necessity, except on Fridays when he went to Church to pray and socialize with other teeming immigrants from different countries that faced the same brutality of the police force.

Some people always came to patronize Randy in his car wash area. After some time, they started to ask him where he was living and how he managed to come to work daily. One day, one of the persons started to sniff cocaine inside his car and told Randy that he wanted some and that if he knew where to get some for him. It was the very first time Randy will see Cocaine and was able to recognize it because he read about it in some crime novels. This sniffing and questioning went on for interspersed days. The final one was when the same man came to Randy and asked him to wash his car. While Randy washed his car, he brought out some Cocaine again and started to sniff and asked Randy to get him some to enable him to get issued with *Ikamah. Ikamah* is the name for a permanent residence permit in their local language as earlier explained. Randy told him distinctively and emphatically that he did not know where the substance was being sold and was not interested in doing so. From that day on the tried but he saw that Randy was not interested and seemed true not to have any knowledge about the substance. Randy could not believe that someone could be doing that in an Islamic country, more so an officer of the law but Randy was only flabbergasted but did not bother as it is his business. Randy only remained friendly with them and extremely cautious when he washed their cars to avoid touching anything that could be incriminating to his personality. He thought that they could plant one pack of any of those substances to implicate him but wished they better spared him of any agony that could bring upon him.

Randy did his car wash alternate and opposite the immigration office. The alternate and opposite depended on the position anyone viewed the location but for Randy, it was both. The officers there knew he was an illegal immigrant but allowed him to do his job they thought must have been better than getting involved in crime and offensive jobs that run afoul of the State laws. He was sometimes invited into their office to pick up something and sometimes to collect his money for any job he must have done for any of the officers. Initially,

Randy did not know the office was an immigration office but just did his job innocently without any fear of the people in the office. They patronized him in measures he appreciated.

Randy got to know it was an immigration officer when he caught a thief in the car park. Since he worked in the park and knew everyone's car, there was no way any new or unknown person could fiddle with another man's car. They all entrusted the security of their cars unto him till that day when he sighted three able-bodied men loosening some extra Tyre from a car, he knew the owner very well. Randy sighted them from afar undertaking their insidious crime and looked closely if it was the owner that was by his car but alas, they were unknown faces. Randy being so sure they were thieves impulsively raised alarm to alert the office and passers-by. He shouted *Klifty! Klifty!! Klifty!!! (Meaning Thief! Thief!! Thief!!!)*. Two of the thieves escaped in their car while Randy got hold of the unlucky third. As Randy held on to him, he tried to escape by warning Randy of the repercussion of his action, but Randy had all evidence of what they had done. He tried to wriggle out of Randy's tight grip on him but had no chance then he tried the worst of his instincts of pugnacity, which attracted a much-undiluted head butt. The head butt got him disengaged from realities around him and floored him temporarily. As the drama unfolded, some people wanted to come to his rescue because they had seen a dark-skinned foreigner mishandle a fair-skinned and more so their citizen without knowing what brought the incident about, but the officers shouted some warning to everyone to step back from Randy through their upper floor opened windows. They even drew weapons to scare but get their message home to the intended intruders. They asked Randy through the window to hold on to the culprit. While some of the officers looked at Randy and the thief through the window for his safety and against being attacked by other people, some trooped out to get the thief arrested from his grip. The officers that came down from the immigration office asked Randy what had happened to warrant him calling him a thief. Randy pointed at the spare tyre he and others had loosened and were about to carry it into their car when he saw them and raised alarm. The officers saw the evidence and arrested the thief. A few minutes later, they called, Randy to come and identify the thief in a lineup. He did not miss the culprit. He was taken to prison immediately since the evidence was there, undeniable, and incontestable. From then on, Randy got respected more than he used to be. The thief episode endeared him to the officers. They trusted him so much and he made sure the trust reposed on him was never betrayed for any reason.

When Randy fell sick at a time, and could not come to work for some days, the immigration officers thought maybe some law enforcement officers must have arrested him. They went from one *Zanzu* to the other looking for him but without any success. After some days, he came to work and was well greeted, embraced and welcomed. They told him how they had searched everywhere for him but could not find him. It was then he told them that he was sick and could not make it to work for the number of days they did not see him. Randy regretted not letting them know when he was leaving Libya for good, but it was the norm. No one ever told anyone when he or she was leaving anywhere. People only heard the news about someone when he or she was long gone out of the country. There were no good and functioning phone services and only very few understood what email meant then.

There were lots of tests where Randy worked. There was that rugged military lady that came to patronize him with incredibly good pay for his services. This lady will leave all her money and identification card in her car and ask him to work on her car. He washed and arranged everything exactly the way she kept them before the commencement of the washing. There was this special day she came and handed over her car key to him to wash her car as usual and walked away. She had taken the road on the southern side of the car park and disappeared into the city. When he started to wash the car, he saw thousands of wrapped Libyan Dinar notes under the car foot mat. He wondered why she should be going about town with that kind of bundled fiduciary notes, which equally could be hers. Randy did his job and arranged everything as she had them before. When Randy finished washing her car and raised his face to start with another car, he saw her emerging from the immigration office. She came over and paid for the services. She was a very great and considerate person. She was Randy's highest paying customer.

The cocaine officers still came to try Randy if he could buy him some cocaine around town. He always wanted to know where Randy came from. He had told the officer for the umpteenth time that he had no idea where he could get the substance, he always requested from him but the officer was always asking for a reason not discernible to him. As Randy worked, he always gave his money to his friend Muge to safe keep for him just in case he was abruptly arrested for the only reason of being an illegal immigrant. If they found nothing on him, the government will be responsible for his daily upkeep and deportation was completely out of the question because no passport existed with him. They could only hold him for some time and let go if he posed no security risk to the state. Randy always knew that but will never get it discussed or talked over with anyone.

Randy had thought his friend Muge had his residence permit to stay in the country because he acted it when they first met but it was a farce and a hollow claim. He had shown Randy his passport with *Ikamah*. It was a forged one.

Randy did not easily realize that his friend Muge had the same status as him even though he pretended to have all it took to be a resident in the country and was equally prone to be arrested any day anywhere like every other illegal immigrant.

As time went on, his friend started to make some triangular business transactions. He would dress up very gorgeously, go out and later come back to the house. The girlfriend worked as a care assistant from house to house. They loved themselves very dearly and trusted themselves deeply. One day, when Muge went out and everyone had returned home from work, Randy and others saw Muge through the window blind being dragged by plain-clothed policemen out of the compound. It was a least expected scene on a Government Hospital premises. The law enforcement officers had ambushed him but before they reached him, Sema had informed him in their home local dialect that plain-clothed policemen were following him. Muge quickly threw away what he had on him into the dirt dump nearby. He was just lucky to have been near the refuse dump when the policemen swooped on him. The evidence may have been thrown away but it was seen when it was being thrown away and so he was arrested for whatever they saw him throw away along with Sema for alerting him where he would have been caught with evidence.

Randy and others saw all that had happened from upstairs. They knew and expected the police to come and search the house. Before it happened, the people that lived with Muge did not know that he was involved in drugs. It was after the arrest that everyone knew what he was doing. Randy and others started to decide on how to hide from the police if they came back. He and others started to wonder how Muge could be involved in such a crime, but it was so and he had carved a niche for himself. Not quite some minutes, three plain-clothed policemen escorted Sema into the complex. Randy and others had seen them through the window blind. They all went into the uncommissioned lift to arrange themselves and locked it from inside. The lift had been unofficially commissioned for self-defence. Meanwhile, the main door to the flat was locked and only Sema held the keys. Randy and others never knew where the keys were if they had wanted to keep the doors ajar for easy entry for the police. On the other hand, it was better to have kept it locked for them to break in with the police. That would show that only both of them lived on the property but as things stood, they must have known how many of them lived together with them. Policemen never acted without a clear-cut survey of the environment. When Sema and the officers reached the door, they heard Sema telling them to open the door from inside, but when no one answered he knew that everyone had hidden properly from him and the officers. Sema broke the door open and came in with the officers. Randy and others who were inside the uncommissioned lift heard them search the entire house but kept quiet. The decorum they all exuded inside the lift was unimaginable. Randy later imagined that what about if any of them had started to cough or the uncommissioned lift gave way, or the planks gave way and all of them get life-threatening injuries or maybe eventually gave up the ghost on top of the jagged metals below? Wow, they were lucky and will always view that day as one of their luckiest days on earth. The police officers that came with Sema said they knew and were very sure that Muge kept nothing inside the house. As they were about to leave, Sema spoke in his local dialect to Randy and others who were inside the lift that "he knows where Randy and others were hiding and that they should not be afraid of anything — lock the door back when we are gone". Randy and others came out of the lift immediately Sema and the officers were gone. They rearranged the scattered house again and watched the gate very closely just in case the policemen reappeared. They came out of the lift after they had heard the main gate jammed and locked.

Sema could come back home because Muge told the police at the station categorically that he was not a part of the crime. When Sema returned, he started to relate how criminal offenders were being beaten up and tortured mercilessly to own up to whatever crime they had committed or did not commit. It was the same way that the *Zanzu* officers treated people for being an illegal immigrants. Undocumented immigrants were compulsory Guinea pigs in Libya. They were defenceless and had nobody to report or run to whenever anything wrong happened to them. Human rights laws for them were rewritten and signed into abusive life of willy-nilly. One hardly knew who was who in Libya. Children and everyone carried a gun. Randy remembered how a small boy went to one of those bombed-out buildings being inhabited by immigrants and started to bluff and threaten them to get some money from them by brandishing a loaded pistol. Under their own-charted freedom called *sawasawa*, one cannot easily get the other disciplined. The meaning of the freedom was taken out of context, but no immigrant dared claim the same right more so when he was an undocumented one.

Randy recalled a scene he witnessed among two Libyans. A driver had made a U-turn in the front of an army garrison gate and the guard questioned him why he would choose an army gate among all free places. The driver jumped out of his car and started to exchange words with the guarding officer who was holding an official weapon in his hand. They argued nose to nose in remarkably high tones. That was the day Randy will believe that *sawasawa"* worked in the country for her citizens. Randy understood at that time what both argued about but wanted to leave the scene quickly to avoid becoming their collateral damage. In the end, both put their swords in their Ploughshares. Randy thought about it for some time when the incident that made both men go nose to nose happened in his own country of origin, the obvious intruder would have been in a very deplorable and messy situation if not dead. Ruthlessness was not the best way to rectify or settle any misunderstanding.

Muge's drug case lasted for so many months but was later released from detention. Randy did not visit him while he was in detention because of fear of molestation and arrest. Muge was right to be angry with him when he was released. Randy's fears were unfounded and mismanaged, but he apologized deeply from his heart to Muge. He later gave Randy back all the money in his possession. Muge started to tell Randy and co that lived with him how he had been followed for eight months by the secret police. He told Randy how he had seen all the narcotic control officers and where their office was situated in the city. Their office was situated right on top of the bridge where Randy washed cars. Randy had passed there several times without knowing it was narcotic police control centre. He did not know that he too had been monitored for months and they knew he lived in the same house with Muge and he did not know what business his friend was involved in. Randy would have sworn for him that he could not do anything like that but since after then did he reconnect properly with what friendship meant. The narcotics officer that always came to Randy at his working place ceased coming after Muge had been arrested. He knew all the private and personal misleading lies Randy had told him about where he came from and where he lived. The narcotic officer must have sought the help of the immigration officers that interacted with Randy to track and report back about him to their narcotic office. They had drawn their physical and evident conclusion that he only lived with the man that perpetrated the crime but did not partake in the crime. Randy must have deeply apologized to Muge but on second thought after so many years, it dawned on him that it was better he did not visit Muge in the penitentiary facility. How would it have looked if those narcotic officers came to the detention centre and found him Randy visiting the person they had tracked along with him for months? Randy thought that he might not be blamed but it will still put him on their narcotic radar for a longer period. Randy said, "It was nice to offend my friend by not visiting him in the detention facility but better not to be seen after all those undeclared interrogations in my car wash car park". Randy knew Muge had helped him and most of all still remembered how he championed the way to the burial ground the day Randy lost his son in Kaduna. It would have been an avoidable death if only Bivasco had lived up to his responsibility as a true childhood friend, but he seized, withheld and starved him of the much-needed fund to continue life when all things temporarily fell apart.

Randy was indeed lucky because of his innocence and knew later why the immigration and narcotic officers asked him some leading questions even when there was nothing to talk about. They knew he was saddled between his jobs and where he lived, and every other fortnight went to the *Souk* to buy food for storage if it was his turn to do so. Randy opined that one's name, character and personality are sometimes saved and play an important role in someone's life. His did. There must be a probable balancing of friendship at some time in one's life. If it were in their home country, Randy would have stuck his neck out because he knew what the laws there constituted and entailed. Despite all that had happened, he still held Muge in very high esteem. Randy never told anyone about his experience with the supposed hibernating undercover narcotics officers and was happy he did not but was only happy he knew them and what they represented later with their location from Muge's after detention stories. He realized later that he was innocently rubbing shoulders with hungry but tamed tigers. Lucky Randy.

Before Muge was released from detention, his friend Basa who supplied him with drugs for sale was also arrested on a tip-off. The main buyer that Muge sold his drugs to had been invited to the house before he was arrested and had been introduced to Basa then. Muge and the customer trusted themselves so much that Basa was co-opted into the business entity. Little did Basa know he was courting a profoundly serious and unavoidable predicament. They started to meet regularly and socialize among themselves. They got used to themselves knowing they were involved in the trade when others were gone to work and sometimes when others had their free day in the week.

Basa was in one of his business travels when Muge was arrested. Before he embarked on his journey, he would read his Koran from cover to cover and believed that he would be saved from any impending dangers and problems. He believed in the Koran getting him safely to and fro his long journeys for the ware he carried through the Sahara Desert. He was so conscientious and had an unwavering Believe in the reading of the religious book. He claimed that the book was his power and defence against all sorts of negative human designs. Randy wondered how he could muster such courage for the international human destruction business. He had all the chances to do other menial jobs like Randy but he chose the fast lane that always had a disastrous dead end.

Since Muge had introduced him to his main buyer before being arrested, he returned from his business travel to hear that he had been arrested. As no one knew what and how the transactions were carried out, he embarked on seeing Muge's main buyer directly.

Before Basa could reach Muge's main buyer, there was a man named Nohj from his country-of-origin Gold coast that he and Muge used as a conduit to deliver his "slow killing guillotine substances" to other buyers. He was a good and trusted errand boy for both. Nohj had unfettered access to the temporary property and acted like an innocent man. Before Muge was arrested, Nohj had bolted away with some quantity of the illegal substance, which he was supposed to have sold to his contact man and made a delivery of the cash. He always did it for them but on this occasion, he took from them, sold and was gone forever. Those of them in the house that were not involved in the trade dared not interlope into what they did and how they did them. It was "look and say nothing in what you know nothing about".

The misplaced trust Basa had in Nohj and the subsequent arrest of Muge drove him into a one-man battalion army. He was now ready to be the importer and distributor after his long-haul travel to get wherever he got them from. With the disappearance of Nohj, he had no middleman again and even though he wanted a middleman, there was no one in the house ready to play his type of kamikaze game of professional suicide mission. Basa could not approach any of the other three men in the house. Already, Sema was in a way involved but had technically been let off the hook. It would have been very detrimental and suicidal for Sema to stick out his neck after such a narrow escape from such an abrasive moment of danger.

The above reasons led Basa to go in search of Muge's main buyer. Randy and those in their room did not know how Basa had arranged to meet Muge's, main man. He left the house confidently when others were at work and was expected back at an unscheduled time. When the time had gone far into the night, everyone in the house thought he must have been nabbed but for what? The thoughts of every one were just for the normal *Kalambush* but they asked if he had gone out for anything or with something incriminating? No one was sure till Sema made it known that Basa had gone out to meet Muge's main buyer. He had gone without negotiations and trusted him from their previous deals. It was after midnight that the occupants of the flat knew that he must have been arrested and probably drug found on his person. Nemesis had caught up with him. Yes, it had.

Sema was more or less the housemaster of the property. He had all the keys for the doors in the complex and knew them instinctively from the pack any time he wanted to use them. He was a very kind man like Muge and so were all the others that shared the property. He was visiting Muge in the detention centre. During one of his visits, he informed him that Basa had been arrested on the same ground as him. Muge told them when he was released that once he knew that Basa had been arrested, he informed the prison guards to take care of his friend who had been arrested and will soon be sent to the penitentiary facility. Basa was not maltreated when he was transferred to the facility because of the groundwork done by Muge before his arrival. The early information was helpful for Basa and made his life in the facility welcome and humanly enduring.

Basa did not stay long there like Muge. He returned to give a breakdown of how he was lured into the house by Muge's main buyer. He said that as he was inside the man's house, he sensed some misbehaviour that could culminate to danger from the man. He had paid him with marked money after getting his cocaine from him. Some men accosted him as he trekked along the sidewalk. He tried to avoid them, but they walked closer and directly in his direction. When the men came on faster and faster towards him, he sensed some danger lurking on his heels. He changed his direction into another street but was blocked by another set of people behaving in the same way as the ones he thought he had left on the other street. He tried to show his physical agility by running but anywhere he ventured to pass was a government mine of human resolve. He ran with his chasers appearing more and more in number with unmatched vigour. He escaped from many of them but could not sustain the tempo and plans of beating the multitude. His time had been well calculated by the law and there was no missing the target. He was finally arrested when he ran out of gas. There was a limit one could beat the law but the law beat him that day.

Randy wondered how Basa graduated into a drug dealer within the shortest possible period he had known him through Muge. He initially was introduced to him as a trolley. He had that connection to buy flight tickets for any prospective passenger and ensured he boarded them through the unscrupulous government agents that dotted the entire line of the official business transactions in Tripoli. Basa always convinced his human cargoes with stories that he had heard from those that had gone out of the country through him. The passengers who do not know him believed him but did not know he was fearful of his leaving the shores of Libya. His human trolley business crashed when the UN-sanctioned the country. He laughed at his passengers for not knowing the truth about the travels they made and about his secrets about what he thought about them. According to him, those who travelled out of the country were fools, he was going to remain in Libya to make his money to the amazement of everyone that knew him. He reinvested into another debilitating business that would see him nabbed and become an ex-convict.

Like what was said earlier: things and chances were gotten through connections. One day, Randy freely without connection fees passed a job interview and was employed. There were not enough telephones then. One Manager of a company came to the church to seek some prospective employees and the information was passed on to him. He asked after the company when he is disembarking at the place he was asked to stop. He could not call the company because the chance never existed, and he could not read nor write the local language that looked like hieroglyphics and cuneiform writings. Randy was learned but educationally blind in the country and so were so many others like him. Despite his shortcomings, he was able to navigate his way across town by remarking buildings and structures. He was able to locate the office and met the manager who interviewed him and offered him the job immediately. He had gone through Randy's credentials and found him very qualified even as an illegal immigrant. It was a job he had undertaken some years back in the Kaduna refinery. One room was allotted to Randy and his name was added to the duty roster. The job was incredibly good, but it was mere daylight robbery and exploitation of his knowledge. The manager knew Randy's onions but degraded him for being an illegal immigrant that was unprotected under the state laws. To him, Randy was not good enough for the corresponding pay packet his fair-skinned counterparts got. Randy on his part took the job up because there was that massive "catch catch" going on in every town and city of the country. The arrests were like declaring a war because something had happened. Randy wondered what type of job he had gotten that the citizens did not like.

The manager knew why and better than the *Kalambush* was going on and being strengthened with best of coordination as such could offer any pittance salary to a very qualified and potential needed worker. People were just rounded up and sent to *Zanzu* and when not so lucky, they will be taken from the place of arrest after some weeks or months driven extremely far into the desert and asked to leave the country. One is given a loaf of bread and little water before being left to those hidden dangers of the Sahara Desert. Randy wished the Citizens had known the ordeals and pains most of the foreigners from other countries had gone through before surfacing in their country. It was no mean feat, and they would never understand. They say, "Who feels it knows it". Randy had not seen anyone that has tried the desert journey among the population, not even for holidays yet they chase those invincible intrepid soldiers of the continent around like what is done to rabbits. People were dehumanized and desecrated in various forms and manners, as against accredited human moral norms of the Geneva Convention. It was sheer man's inhumanity to man that he guessed was at work because the government to his best of understanding was not completely aware of the pilfering and duping some officers were carrying out on some of the foreigners. While most of the officers are mean to the core only a minimal number of them were considerate to do the right things.

There was that bin truck that came to pick some dirt from where Randy worked and ended up picking some cartons, he had kept aside to make his bed look soft at night in his Tejura apartment. By the time he returned from where he had gone to fetch water, he discovered to his amazement that his cartons had vanished. When he raised his head, he saw the truck that had picked them up in the distance negotiating into a compound the gate was always locked each time he passed by there. He ran after the truck and met it inside one compound along the street he used to follow to the church every Friday. He went inside the compound and suddenly discovered everyone in there carrying assorted weapons. It was as if the men were going to war the next minute. The soldiers looked at him with surprise when he entered and asked him gently what he had come for or wanted from the compound. He told them boldly that he wanted his carton the driver of the truck had picked from where he washed cars. Luckily for Randy, the cartons were still on top of the other things they had packed. The soldiers unanimously asked him to pick his cartons with all respect. He did and left without any panic. Randy had always seen these soldiers anytime he was going for church services every Friday but did not know them beyond their facial importance but graded them with their attachment to the official gun values they carried.

One day, Randy and his other flatmates were chatting about issues that had happened and the latest in town, the carton story of the past diverted their attention to the Embassies area of the city. Muge started to smile wryly at the entire story and stiffened his face to ask Randy if he knew the compound, he had entered to pick up his carton? Randy gave an emphatic NO answer. Muge told him he had entered the compound of the second in command for the entire Jamahiriya country, the local name for Libya country. Did Randy exclaim Whaaat? He continued and said: Really? He told everyone present at the gathering that he had always followed the same road every Friday to the Church. On his way to and fro had always seen armed men and exchanged casual greetings with them. He was never questioned nor molested any day. Randy from that knowledge vowed to reroute his Friday itinerary. When it was next Friday and forever, he never ventured to go through that street anymore till he left Tripoli city. What one does not know can never make him fear but what one knows could sometimes make his or her adrenalin run under some coined microcosm. One could endure certain things one truly does not know about but better to duck for safety when it goes the way that it will involve having to swim among people of that constitution from the nation's best-trained guard soldiers who in the event of the unimaginable could be caught in a collateral crossfire one might never live to give his side of the story. The best decision, in that case, was for Randy to stay clear of what he called the King's street. Randy was not fearful because he was not man enough to be intrepid but because his status warranted it and he recognized and respected that, which rightly categorized the fears in him. Other than that, he had no reason to fear anything if he came into any country properly documented but that was not the case at the time. Most illegal immigrants were juveniles and rascals' that had committed one form of a heinous crime or the other before leaving the shores of their different countries. Many had been involved in robberies, cults, and many other crimes they openly confessed to having taken part in or been part of. These were the same people who were trying to get through the iron curtain with their already sharp stained fingers. Randy wondered about the type of Ambassadors those types of people were going to be to themselves and to the people they represented in future.

They were free to make their decisions and follow them up as they wanted. Those of them who thought they were very intrepid, fast, and cunning were always being arrested and getting into troubles that set them back more than those that remained focused but got whatever money that came their way gradually and sincerely. By now, the "money printing machines" and their always well-dressed pimps started to collapse in bits before the law. They made their money hiding and running from the law. They were able to some reasonable extent elude the law with their "ready park and go" system in any of their chosen European countries. Europe was the destination of every foreigner living in Libya but unfortunately, not all of them knew how to make it through the tiny secret outlet. One only left Libya if he had the right connections. The right connections for exit hinged on finance and the person someone knew that was rightly connected with an insider government official that could issue an exit visa at astronomical and loathsome prices. The authorities knew people entered Libya illegally but don't know how and from where the streets of the cities got filled with foreigners and no foreigner ever agreed to say how he or she reached the country. If they ever said it, it was always a misdirection of the truth about them. If ever there was bravery to cross the desert, the authorities expected those that lived in the area to make it not people who were not born there but the reverse was the case. West Africans dominated the foreign population that made desert travel a child's play for those of them that survived it. The bravery did not end with those who came through the desert alone but with some that came in with visas. Randy knew one "Eko akete" *(another name for Lagos city)* man whose visa got expired but he stayed on as a student. He was the only person that had a visa that could read and write the language, but he was equally looking forward to any of the European countries at the least possible chance and opportunity.

It was exceedingly difficult to go into Libya and worse still to be chased like a chicken wanted by its owner. Once one had entered the country, one needed an exit visa to leave the country or else one had to go back the way he came in through. No one wanted to go back the same way he or she came through except some foreigners who after making some dubious money had been converted to dollars. Dollars were hated like a plague by the government of the day but her citizens got them underground through some foreigners that knew how and where to get them. It was *haram* and *mamnual* to be seen with any legal dollar tender or bill as the case might be. It was hypocrisy on the part of the government for they traded on and with the money in question on the international market. Randy always thought about the disinformation of the government to her people over the issue of external trade and international money. The official law of the country against the dollar will get one or more of her citizens to fall prey to some conman ship of some disgruntled illegal immigrants.

One day, some Libyans wanted to change some of their Dinar money into the much-hated dollar bills and had no way of doing so. They wanted to go out of the country to transact some business but their Dinar bills will not make it through the international market except with their Arab neighbours they wanted to go to Europe where it might be highly devalued or completely refused altogether. They sought the help of some foreigners who they thought could help them make the Libyan Dinar exchange into dollar bills. The people concerned got the sack of money from them and went into an embassy, where the owners had directed the changes to be done for them. The sack of money was given to them while they waited outside. The men went into the embassy and betrayed the trust reposed on them. They opened one of the embassy windows on the first floor that was close to the fence of another adjacent building. They all climbed through the window and stepped onto the fence before walking a bit on it. They jumped down from the fence into another compound before hitting the street.

When the people who had sent them waited for too long in vain, they started to ask after them till they were able to talk to the officers of the embassy. The embassy denied seeing those being described, which of course was the truth.

At the time the owners of the money were asking for the men they had given their money, they were on their way back to their different countries through the desert. Their actions were just amazingly fast like lightning. No one was able to know how the men escaped with the money. They raised alarm and a massive search and manhunt were organized in vain to catch them, but it was damn too late. Later in the day, the bad news had gone around and other illegal immigrants in the city braced for the worst-case scenario of other people's sin or crime. A profoundly serious and stringent "catch catch" was put into place against foreigners. Staying in the city became unbearable for every illegal immigrant. People could not get along freely from one place to the other. It was the time Randy had to take up the employment to get a *"Pataka"* *(identity card)* for identifying himself in case the police accosted him. The company was co-owned by Libya and Malta hence the company bore the compound name Libma.

Midday after the incident at the embassy area, one of Randy's friends named Lorko who washed cars in the same car park with him went missing without a trace from the park. Randy had no inkling of his whereabouts and had no one to ask after him. It was an unusual occurrence, but Randy pretended not to be bothered about him. Lorko was a very sincere and nice guy. He confided in Randy and told him almost everything, so Randy asked himself what was amiss with him not being around for work that day. Fortunately, Lorko returned later in the evening of that day and left again as fast as he had come. He was looking very serious, stern and tensed up. Randy asked him what the problem was all about, but he brushed everything aside and asked Randy to be patient with him. When he was gone again, Randy did not see him that day again till the next day morning.

The next day morning, he walked up to Randy and told him why he failed to work. Lorko knew that Randy was a man that will never give another man out for his self-aggrandizement. He called Randy's attention to what had happened the previous day. He continued to relate the incident of the previous day, Randy interjected asking, which incident, please? He said about what had taken place yesterday at the embassy area. Of course, there was no way Randy was going to say that he had not heard the current news involving his illegal peers in the city then. He said three guys masterminded the swindling that took place but two of the guys bolted away with the money involved leaving the other one at the mercy of the owners. The third guy happened to have come from the same place as Lorko and was a juvenile. He cried to Lorko telling him all that had happened and how he was involved. He was going to bear the brunt of a collective crime, which made him jittery and sober. He would be killed if he were ever found in the city. Lorko swung into action to intercept the other two. He was a desert warrior himself and knew what to do in that type of case. The third guy accompanied him and off they went to one of the probable border towns to search for the other two guys. They found them at Ghadamis and out of fear wanted Lorko to take some share of their booty, but he refused to accept. Ghadamis is a Libyan border town with Tunisia and Algeria respectively.Lorko asked the other two guys to share the money equally amongst them and blamed them for the way they had acted. No one apart from Randy knew the part Lorko played in the money palaver and the attendant saga. Meanwhile, the actions of the three guys haunted all the innocent foreigners in the city and elsewhere but in the end survived their ugly onslaughts.

16

CONNECTION CONNECTING CONNECTORS

BEFORE RANDY EMBARKED ON HIS DESERT TRAVELS, HE NEITHER KNEW NOR REALIZED HOW difficult it was to make the journeys with or without documents. Whichever way one looked at it, it was a cumbersome and hard journey to plan into fruition. Once in the city, people start to hear how to make and prepare a journey with all the associated immigration requirements. Most of the corroborations needed to make the journeys sounded laughable but were the real requirements and knowledge needed to have a breakthrough. If anyone knew what was required and followed the rules of engagement, one will luckily be wherever he wants to get to from the continent. It was a matter of having the right connections after one had gotten enough money and the right passport. Nowadays, it is exceedingly difficult to embark on these types of journeys because of biometric designed identities. Despite that, there would be millions of ways to catch the biggest and wisest fish out of water.

Apart from having the money and passports, one needed an exit visa from the Libya country. All foreigners used the country as a stepping-stone to advance their course to European countries. Some illegal foreigners who worked as connectors and acted, as a go-between with some government officials will collect look-alike passports of other countries from their illegal prospective customers that were ready to leave the country to some towns or cities for the issuance of exit visas. It was a closely guarded and well-knitted deal that was away from all that mattered to prying eyes. Randy was equipped and versed in all the required documentation processes but still needed the connection of the best connectors to one of the right "Connectors" in the city.

He read an article that informed him years later that the European Union was giving some States that bordered their continent to the south some money to control the influx of illegal foreigners into Europe from the largest continent and laughed at their financial misdirection. Why? They would have gone to the countries where most of the foreigners came from and made a very tough agreement with the government of the day to create some jobs of any kind that will get most of those travellers who out of desperation had conceived the idea to be absolved before they start thinking about taking some unwarranted but worthy in the end risks across the natural geographical "inhuman" divide, the Sahara Desert. The only saving grace that will minimize but not erase the influx of the crossings is the fear of the new dawn that might get the terrain awash with assorted illegal weapons of different kinds from the North African revolution, which will be used to terrorize innocent travellers and hikers. It will dissuade some, but most too will still dare the terrain and the people. The fear is real and almost insurmountable. The best control would be helping the Sub-Saharan African countries financially to produce jobs through tertiary improvements, then sending huge amounts of money to those leaders that have borders with the southern European countries. The monies they allot to those leaders are only squandered and used for their self-aggrandizements.

After Randy had gotten enough money to make his move out of Libya, he purchased a passport with which he got his exit visa and flight ticket. Those foreigners turned illegal businessmen were the middlemen that connected foreigners like them to those corrupt government officials that milked them dry of their hard-earned money. The unconnected foreigners had no choice but to dance to the tunes of the cheats and dupes. What baffled Randy was that all the connectors had the same status as him, but they wielded unknown and cocooned powers to trivialize him and others. The government knew but pretended to be busy working against the foreigners. Foreigners were only harassed because they could be robbed of their money and other valuables before they are detained and released for another and later detention. It was a type of re-circulation process to keep their pockets heavy and going from the oppression. The conditions that pervaded the entire system never stopped. No lull.

Randy thought very deeply about why the Arabs always called them the dark-skinned West Africans and others of their pigmentation slaves. He knew that if there were any problems within the country, the dark-skinned Sub-Saharan citizens were not going to be spared in the ensuing imbroglio. They saw themselves as masters of the other racial colour divide. The division and discrepancy juggled and made the human strata on their filthy and rotten minds. Their leader had imbibed all hateful and spiteful ideas into their empty heads with religion wrongly used as a target for their wishful wrong thoughts. Every Sub-Saharan African citizen knew he was a target and managed to meander to daily safety. The percentage between the good, when the bad and the ugly, are merged is very infinitesimal. There was that hatred and endless rancour for the dark-skinned people. No wonder the real dark-skinned Libyans were looked down upon as second-class citizens. The living and association dichotomies were so glaring among her population and citizenry. Randy noted one but all-time particularly important behaviour that hardly comes to light. When the Arabs in Africa want the support of other African States, they claim to be Africans but when they align with religion and money, they seek other Arab nations outside Africa. Most African Arabs behave and live bat-like life as individuals and as nations. They hold the soft and easy way to life and politics of hatred and cheating the hollow-hearted and knocked out brains any time they could. They are not steadfast people to be trusted with the way and manner they exhibited and exude their all-time jigsaw human puzzles.

While the government of the day cannot be exonerated from the torments and cheating, some Embassies aided and abetted the rip-off. They knew that most passports that were in circulation were lookalikes, but they issued their transit visa on them because they wanted cheap money from the oppressed and anxious foreigners. The passports were imported from some countries in the continent and could easily be verified and checked but the officers in some of the embassies looked the other way to get some soft money from some soft targets.

Randy thought that the position of the anxious and mistreated foreigners was understandable but for those officers that openly collected more than enough money from what would have cost a pittance was unacceptable and constituted a rape of man's human rights.

The issuance of exit visas to foreigners to leave the country did not guarantee or end it all in Libya. When Randy secured a genuine transit visa from one of the embassies, his friend followed suit. Getting the visas determined how bold one was to stand his ground in documents attestations and accreditations. The foreigners were extremely dogged and professional in their bids and quests to reach their designed destinations and goals. Randy thought that their different documentations were their last bullet as such went hard without entertaining any fear before the authorities concerned. At that point, they did not mind where they ended up but only to be rightly documented for them to face the next Herculean unknown world of human survival. It worked only for the brave at heart and brain. These overcharged documents were not easy to come by hence not everyone was able to dare the Iron Curtain and she closely guarded human-mined-minded gates.

Randy set out from Tripoli to fly to Canada. Those that had made the journey before and failed in their bid had briefed him. It was not a shame but heroic when one tried to travel out and failed to make it. It places one in a better position to make better preparations for his next trial. Those foreigners with big hearts never stopped trying till they were able to get across but those of them that were faint-hearted to face the immigration officer's onslaught tried to dissuade those that had the unalloyed boldness, luck and intelligence needed for the situation's accomplishment. Randy was stamped out of Libya at Abukamash border town and warned not to come back into Libya again. He was happy to have been crosschecked and passed to leave with the cab bound for the Tunisian border of BenGardane.

At the Tunisian border, his passport was checked in a manner that made him feel jittery, but he tried to calm his nerves despite his fears. As he stood, he saw someone he knew in Tripoli and both pretended not to have known each other should any of them get into any type of trouble with the immigration officers. It was an undeclared rule that people played by. The rule was personal and private, but people just played dumb to one another in the presence of law enforcement officers. If one had problems, it was that person alone that faced them. No one was co-opted or victimized, no matter how that person was maltreated as was always the case in that part of the continent where they always called the dark-skinned West African slaves and other derogatory names. No beating could make any foreigner victimize or give away the other.

By the time, the officer finally handed Randy his passport, he was sweating and looking a bit jittery but tried all the time to get himself composed. He felt something was amiss but had no unspoken reason to retreat. He trudged on even in his doubt and disbelief.

Randy arrived in Tunis City in the evening. He lodged in a hotel and left for the airport in the morning. He was corporately dressed in an ashes colour suit and a black shoes to match. He got his boarding pass since his name was already on the flight manifest. He was still overwhelmed with the delay the border immigration officers had made him sense an invincible danger the previous day that something unannounced and unspoken about to him was wrong. He wanted to be boarded before allaying his fears. When his flight was announced, he lined up with others. The immigration officer checking the passengers' passports did not waste time with the other passengers before him. He tried to control his tumultuous and unsettled state and went straight to the man when it was his turn. The officer looked at him and the passport and asked him if he was the rightful owner of the passport. Before he could finish his question, Randy answered in the affirmative "Yes". The officer looked at him again and asked him to stand aside. As he was asking him to stand aside, he was drawing open the passport identification page that easily gave way. The passport had been double laminated and was not made known to him. He had been conned by his fellow illegal immigrant and worse still led him into the trouble he does not know when he would be free from it. If the passport maker had told him the truth and state of the passport, he would not have bought it but it was too late to start gnashing his teeth. He had a deep breath and said he was ready for the associated problems and fallouts that were going to follow or emanate from the present and ongoing immigration discovery. The officer called in some policemen that led him away with his heart thundering and almost finding its way out of his body. He continued to palpitate with fear and thinking of what to say or write a statement to the police when the time came. He had learned that false identity was not a serious criminal case if it does not border on anyone's life. After all, some people and presidents have used it to get through in times of danger when the worst was about to befall them. In his case, he wanted to emigrate to wherever be his destination. They had only done their job by sorting him out because the wrong job done on his passport was too glaring and implicating. Many had gone through the same airport even after being arrested, Randy knew that many would still get through and knew some that had gone through the day he was arrested. He vowed amid the hullabaloo to have better passport construction, body comportment, super journey planning and most of all the human luck effect.

After Randy had been interrogated at the airport police station, he was whisked to the town centre that housed a hidden police station. The building was a bit dark and cold. Randy met some other detainees inside the building that was about to be released after serving their prison terms for the same case he was arrested for. One of the men about to be released Ide asked him in a low tone what had warranted him to be arrested and brought to the station. Randy summarized everything for him, and he advised him briefly about what he should say to avoid a possible long-drawn-out court case and asked him to further stick to whatever he had given as his first statement. He warned Randy to expect some beatings and tortures of some sort from the officers and that despite all; he should not bulge or cave into what they will want to hear. He thanked Ide and got ready for the pressure they will be exerting on him for what they will want to hear to incriminate him more than what they had seen at the airport. He told Randy that he had spent six months and was just about to be released to go. Randy thought about it: same offence, six months jail term, too long but was it what he was destined to go through, if so he was now ready because there was no escape from anything then. He crossed his mind for the worst-case scenario.

On their way from the airport to the hidden city police station, Randy had another identity card, which the policemen had collected from him but out of luck was handed back to him before they boarded the bus. Since he was staying at the back of the bus alone, he tucked the identity card into a small hole where the cardboard paper used for the landing of the vehicle had given way. Randy knew that with that out of his body, there was no way to incriminate him above the passport issue. He was sure the policemen were not going to find the identity card. It was the real document with which they were going to convict Randy for double identity.

When Randy was finally called for more interrogation, he gave a very convincing but dubious story as directed and advised by Ide. Two interrogators were assigned to investigate his case. They both asked Randy questions at the same time to get him confused. He told both officers he could only answer one person at a time. The statement caused revulsion in them to the extent that one of the officers' slapped and kicked him several times in the groin. His baggage was all ransacked and all his money discovered. He had bought some fake dollars before embarking on the journey from Tripoli. The man that sold the money to him went through the same Tunis airport to Frankfurt but was lucky to have gone through. The officers' eyes bulged and rolled like that of an owl when they saw the dollar bills in his possession. Randy knew they wanted the money for the beating to cease and to get a more humanly treatment. Instead of asking him more questions, they started to fiddle with his dollar bills and look into his eyes directly. He asked the officers to have the money to their expected glee, but they warned him not to let anyone know about it. He gave them his words and promise that no one will know that some money changed hands. After getting the money from him, they asked him if he wanted to be deported to Libya or not. Of-course yes. Agreeing to be deported to Libya was the best option while not condescending to that meant being imprisoned for any number of months of their choice. Going back to where he came from will be helpful to recuperate from his financial losses and plan for another travel another day. They say those who fight and run away live to fight another day. He would be ready for another day after his release.

Normally Randy was supposed to have been sent to the court and sentenced to six months imprisonment but was incredibly surprised that on the third day, he was sent to the notorious Beshusha detention centre in Tunis city. While in there, he had no space that could contain his entire body structure. The rooms were filthy; smelled foul, toilets were not flushed, and all her inmates seemed infected with some terrible but contagious diseases. Almost everyone in the detention facility had a terrible cough and scratched their bodies endlessly.

On the second day when everyone was asked to go out for a walk around, Randy found someone who understood the English language. He asked Randy what brought him to the detention facility. He told the new man what had brought him there. Then, the man started to preach Islamic religion to him. He told him how he could be connected to start training for Jihadism in Sudan with plenty of money given to him. The man in question mentioned Osama Bin Laden as the head of the Jihadism from Saudi Arabia living in Sudan. Randy's body's biological connections disentangled and failed to function for some seconds before restarting. He managed to recollect his human value and essence. He knew immediately that Prisons and detention camps were where some of the gate valves for Islamic fundamentalism were being run and controlled for recruitment. His fears were unimaginable, but he pretended to be a novice at what he was being told and engineered into. He thought: passport, flight, arrest, detention and next jihad, Sudan and he asked himself soliloquizing, for what with whatever blood money that might accrue from it? Randy internally said "NO" to submit to another man's way of preaching hatred and atrocious dissemination of lies in the name of the Almighty. At this time, he could communicate effectively in their local Arabic language but he feigned not to understand them for his safety and good. He considered Randy a soft target, but he was wrong. Little did he know that he was convincing a man without any interest in what he wanted him to become. To make his secret job sound interesting, Randy told him he was going to talk more about it with him later, but he became afraid of the man's fanaticism. The man seemed to have had a gang inside the detention centre because many looked in their direction as they discussed. Randy knew he was impenetrable and was going to stay the course of the interlocutions without making him suspect his rejections. He told Randy that someone will be visiting him later in the day and was going to advance his election bid with his visitor. The statement made Randy's face go white. He realized immediately that the detention centre acted as a funnel and recruiting centre for Jihadists and terrorists. He wanted to leave the facility but how was he going to make it out of the detention centre? Only luck was going to pull him out of the place. The clock of sodomy was ticking, and more inconceivable heinous acts could follow. Randy was disturbed and shaky but kept his cool. He reiterated inwardly how he wanted to leave the hell called a cell, Please! Please!! Please!!! He intoned.

They were just out, as usual, the second day when Randy's name was announced and asked to come forward. He stepped forward and saw the officers that had dropped him off in the cell for the past two days had come for him. He was asked to board the bus with his luggage. As he left, he was inwardly happy and pretended not to have seen the Jihadist recruiter and tormentor. Randy did not care where he was being taken to but wanted to leave that cell environment. Leaving "the Beshusha" detention facility behind was remarkable and created ease of mind in him. It was a traumatic experience that, he found so hard to shelve aside to date. It would have assumed a bigger problem of victimization because anyone could be framed and marked for rendition, torture, and unlawful imprisonment that would have arisen to the point of being taken to maybe to most hated terrorist camp Delta in Guantanamo Bay, Cuba.

Nowadays, the entire downtrodden and poor are subjected to all sorts of inhuman treatments at the airports and other points of entry and exit points in some countries because of perceived terrorism. Randy had encountered many forms of racial abuse at many airports. He had spoken vehemently against some and waived some off with discontent. The 911 incidents had changed the world order and lots of the security checks have become racial and biased. Some people's privacy and pride have been invaded, compromised, assaulted, bruised, and desecrated in the name of terrorism checks. Some officers of the law now hide under the guise of the law to disseminate and propagate hatred embedded in chronic hidden racism, all in the name of doing one's governmental assigned job.

Racism has been officially legalized worldwide with the introduction of body scanners. There will always be a selective judgment that will in some situations be misused by law enforcement officers, or those entrusted with the operation of the machines. There was that case of some people scanned and documented against their privacy by some operating officers in Britain. The real case is who will be scanned and who will not be scanned. The answer will be left for anyone's reasoning and judgment.

How could one be scanned possibly at every airport and for how long because of terrorism? What about people who for some reason had undergone some x-ray treatments? They claim the radiation effect on the body scanner is minimal. Whatever grading given to it, radiation is in most cases has gotten cumulative effect with time. The cumulative effect to Randy's understanding is based on health reckoning dangers that could damage the body cells. A body scanner machine is a form of slow death to those that might be forced against their wish and will to go through it. Randy believed he would prefer to be hand searched or body patting even if it was indecent sometimes than submit to the cell-killing machine. He went as far as suggesting that people should be given the chance of making choices, like stripping up to one's birth suit to convince the officers concerned and later be allowed to go unhindered across to the boarding area. So much has been said about the machine not emitting enough radiation to cause any bodily harm but one forgets that no big shot gets scanned, but the ordinary man would be subjected to the inhuman functioning processes of the machines. Everyone is against terror but not at the expense of invented and invincible slow death for the common man. As people could see, sometimes little things assume much and big meanings when they become emblematic of larger truths. Randy would say: "are we listening and is anyone listening up and out there"?

The idea of some government's enactment of "no scanning, no flight" is like taking a horse to the river and forcing it to drink. Any law enforcement officer with racist inclinations could hide as said before under the government's willy-nilly rules and orders to infringe on the poor man's rights. The body-scanning machine is a brazen assault on the weak and downtrodden. The terrorism attachments to these scanning machines are just wrong imposition, wrong wrings of the hand and total legalization of racism without boundaries.

He had a brush with the security personnel at Manchester airport on the 15th of April 2011. He reached the airport well ahead of time and waited for his flight check-in time. After the check-in, he went like every other passenger to the security check-in area. As he was in the queue with other passengers, he inadvertently wanted to pass an open area which would have still taken him through one of the checks-in points but one of the security men asked him to go further away through the queue. He obliged and went ahead as directed by the security personnel. As he was going, the same security man opened the same entrance he had been denied access to another passenger to get through. He found the treatment racial, offensive and a selective judgment. He went back to the security man and asked to be allowed access like the other passengers that had been allowed to get across the barrier that was closed because of him. The security man demanded his boarding pass after allowing him to get across but asked the checker to stay in action on his checking. The security man went to his supervisor to make a false report, which to him did not mean anything in the instance. Suddenly, one man came to him at the hand luggage check-in stand to excuse him for a chat. He was the supervisor. The supervisor asked Randy why he was swearing at his security personnel. Randy was surprised to hear that question put to him. He calmed down and told him what had transpired and that he had not insulted him. He used the word swearing but Randy used the word insult. Randy had always been incredibly surprised at the way the word swearing had been misused by the English themselves. Swearing, cursing and insult were words wrongly used by most of her citizens. The usage is already a cankerworm that will be exceedingly difficult to treat but he believed he would make a difference where almost everyone is going wrong with reckless abandon. The supervisor later asked Randy to go and have a good word with the security man who had treated him with disdain and a sullen approach. Randy had known his plan and what he was up to. He let the sleeping dog lie. He went to the wrong and racially motivated security man to shake hands with him and said sorry to him but deep down him, it was in no way an apology. Randy felt the injustice but wanted to get on with his day and flight. One thing the security supervisor did not know was that Randy was more qualified than him for the job he was giving a wrong judgment because of pigmentation. Randy had a high qualification in security in a country where it mattered most and had the closed-circuit television with security industry authority certificate the supervisor and his personnel were using and applying wrongly with the passengers at the Manchester airport. Randy knew that if he argued with them for his right, he would be framed, and the camera film will be stopped or disabled to suit their intentions. They will gang up against him to disrupt his planned itinerary by calling in the police that will find all the reasons in this world to ostracize the dark-skinned man who knew his right and wanted to exercise it in a country he did not belong and even would not be heard. Right from the hand luggage stand, Randy was ready for the worst-case scenario searching. He knew what they were going to do to him to intimidate him and bring his morals and personality to the lowest ebb, but he had conceived them all and was ready not to sound intimidated. He saw the supervisor talking, using his gesticulations and snake neck methodology to show his personnel who they should deal with apathy and disdain to get him aggravated. It was a commonplace theory and action the police and other paramilitary used on unsuspecting people they hated or wanted to wrongly deal with under the law. He did all he was asked to do till he crossed the metal detector. Apart from his necklaces and pair of eyeglasses, there was not any other iron object on Randy that could set off the metal detector alarm, but it went off when he crossed. At that point, the supervisor was on hand to direct him to enter the most loathed machine of his life. The radiation-emitting body scanning machine. Randy opted for his body to be patted by anyone instead of being scanned but the supervisor told him that he could not travel if he refused to be scanned. He knew what they were out to do and submitted against his wish of being scanned. It did not end there, the supervisor asked him to pull his leather shoes that carried no iron fitting on them off his feet for another separate scanning machine. Randy was smiling inwardly because he had vowed to make them swallow their hatred by not answering or talking to them. He just did what was necessary or asked to do by their edicts and commands. After the body and shoe scanning, he went over to where his hand luggage had come out from the machine to pick up his things but there they were again. Other security personnel had been strictly given the injunction to search his clothes pockets, computer peripherals and every other thing associated with him and his luggage. The supervisor watched with all interest as the commanded security man and woman ransacked his entire belongings that had gone through the scanning machine. They spoke nicely doing their racially motivated and filthy hearts biddings. They had thought of seeing some or any incriminating thing to satisfy their racial wishes but got so disappointed when they could not. They tried from that point when they had finished with their filthy hearts design to sound friendly with him, but he was not in the mood to accept their fake galvanized immediate courtesy. They were openly racist to a man who took it all for that day but will be a vastly different story for them someday somehow should they not mend their ways. They were impugning a gang up with their ill-mannered and half-baked security operational mess-ups on an innocent passenger. The same dress Randy wore through the metal detector the same day through the transit checks in Manchester airport some hours later was what he wore at the Zurich airport transit checks without setting off any alarm and with better human treatment by the Swiss Canton police. He had earlier written how racism has openly been accepted with the introduction of body scanning machines before his encounter with those rotten-headed security personnel who does not understand what body patting as a demand from a passenger meant. Randy said: Aluta continua but the racism had to stop from where they are ordered, their indiscriminate usage without cogent and substantial reasons with their selective judgment reduced with more training to most of the ill-trained, ill-mannered and half-educated security personnel most airports like that of Manchester, Heathrow, Bolognia and Dublin.

The officers picked him up from Beshusha to another detention camp named Wardia deportation camp. Randy had expected a better detention facility than Beshusha, which to his expectation was true. Randy met Ide who had spent six months in the prison before being transferred to the camp awaiting deportation. He was incredibly happy to meet him again. Ide quietly went away on sighting him. There was that man called Charsare that was inside the bus before Randy was picked up at the Beshusha cell facility. He whispered to him that they were lucky that they were going to be deported. Randy asked him where they were deporting them to. They both did not know where they were deporting them, but Randy remembered his bribed interrogators and the dollar bills they had pocketed from him to be spared from more beatings and humiliations in their hands. The probable answer would be Libya. It would be better for him and he later knew that others liked it too — were it to be true.

They spent almost two and half weeks in the camp and had socialized to become a temporary family there. The place was good and forcefully habitable than Beshusha. They were well fed and taken care of in the facility but the idea of not being free made them look emaciated. There was one Jewish man among them that had been tortured and brutalized because of his country of origin. They all sympathized with him and digested his stories. His state was not that good, but they comforted him and asked him to trust every one of them around him. They knew where each one of them came from but kept the truth away from the authorities. They had already made the authorities believe what they had to believe or document about them, but for them, they were extant and going in another dimension and direction. No one could be deported because the Geneva Convention does not constitutionally approve. They all knew that and used it to their advantage, but it was secretly done in Tunisia to some people.

One early morning, some officers of the law went to them after their breakfast and asked them to pick up their belongings and board the bus they had driven to the deportation camp. The Jewish man in their midst had been released or transferred from the camp before they were sent out for deportation. As he left the camp, he thanked them for being good and personable to him as a group and family. They all loved him and his country and had loathed secretly the way and manner he was treated. The torture marks on his fingers and body were healing as at the time they met him in the camp. He was not allowed access to Jewish representatives or consular services in the country. He was most of the time before Randy and others met him there in some sort of solitary confinement.

Randy could not write any secret letter to any embassy that would not be intercepted in that part of the world. He felt too bad about the way and manner the Jewish man was treated and that the world will never get to know the truth except when he was released, and he tells his stories. He felt tired and bottled by circumstances beyond his human control. Randy only relished in the assumption that he was getting better and was going to be released. Randy thought that the man had a big heart when he said that he was Jewish and will die a Jewish man no matter what happened. Randy could not quantify the patriotism he exuded in the face of one of the worst inhumanities to man's treatment in one of the countries that showed her people some of the secret unbearable draconian rules ever recorded in human history. Given the chance then, they would have liked to go with him till they were sure he was safe, but they too were in some very serious trouble they did not know when it was going to end. On the other hand, they were from a different country other than his. They all denied theirs because their countries failed to align with their future, needs, designs and aspirations. They had the choice to make their choices.

The officers drove them on rendition transfer from, Wardia camp to other detention centres in other cities. The rendition centres did not look like the Wardia deportation camp. They were moved around and continuously through Tunis, Sousse, Sfax, Gabes, Medenine and Ben Gardane stations. They slept one night in each of the stations except in Medenine where they had to be sent to the Tunisian border town of Ben Gardane the same day. They arrived at Ben Gardane at midday of the last day and it looked a bit cleaner than other stations they had gone through. Once they were there, Randy knew they were going to be deported to Libya but did not know how it was going to happen.

They were brought out under the cover of darkness like tamed animals from the cell and released back into the wild to fend for themselves once more in a free world where their destiny will be in their hands. They were all asked to go but in the direction of Libya. Randy could not believe he was at last free after some three weeks of an ordeal as against the country's six months of his friend's stated incarceration. His interrogating officers had helped him through the forcible bribery that was requested with ordinary eye contact because he had respected the deal of keeping what they did to him secret all through despite the visible scar and scald evidence on his body. They kept their side of the bargain, which Randy hardly trusted they would respect but was enough for him to be jubilant about momentarily as a free man.

They were four people released from detention at the border post. All four were from two different countries but from the same country by official language.

When the four of them were released, they started to ask themselves how each one of them had gone to Libya in the first place. Three of them had gone into Libya through the hard desert way and the fourth through "the rest and get a relaxed way". The three men that had been into Libya through the desert hard way advised Ide to desist from trying to get into Libya through the desert with them. The trio told him the dangers involved and finally told him that he could end up dying in the desert unreported and missing forever. Ide objected and was determined to follow the trio Randy, Charsare and Smokey. The trio warned him repeatedly and told him that whatever happened to him would be his own making and started walking in the direction of Libya. After they had taken some steps with Ide following them, they suddenly noticed that they were three and that he had heeded their advice without letting them know it. He was lucky to have listened and acted before any major incident took place to his detriment and peril.

Ide's sister had equally been released like her brother. They had both been arrested the same day and served the same punishment. He later found the sister waiting for him at the border's "no man's land". Both managed to enter Libya with some help through the right channel. Some corrupt officers must have acted because they had what it took to get them convinced for any help.

Before the trio stepped into the desert, Charsare made a statement that could get the lily-livered man gnashing his teeth and regret ever finding himself in that type of situation. It was an unforgettable short statement that Randy will always remember. He said "Gentlemen, God for us all and every man to himself". That was when they bade Ide farewell and he stubbornly followed before giving up. The trio disappeared into the desert.

The trio may have trekked through the Sahara Desert but that day brought about a new experience they will not have endured were it not for their previous wealth of experience. They started to walk some meters away from the main road, ducking and taking covers like trained military men. After all, they have accomplished desert warriors of a kind with a wealth of indomitable and unconquerable experiences. They had seen it all before and were ready for it again, no matter the dimension the trekking was taking. They knew what illegal meant and how to circumvent it with their refined understanding. Randy suggested that they should try to stay away from the car light rays that sometimes travelled in their direction with the snaky curving and bending of the road. The reason he suggested that was because movement catches the eyes. They could see the Libya border post in the distance, but they knew how tantalizing the nautical distance was. They walked in the darkness listening attentively and had to develop their human night visor eagle eyes without which movement was impossible. Everywhere around them was peach dark but their eyes were already conditioned to the darkness. There was that bend where it became almost impossible for them to dodge the car light rays coupled with the sound of some desert police patrol jeeps that were too close for comfort for them. As if that was not discomforting and unbearable enough was the added unforgiving sound of some of the desert-groomed dogs that must have sniffed and sensed their positional direction for the police patrol jeeps. Under the circumstance, Randy suggested again that they should cross over to the other side of the road that bordered the Mediterranean Sea.

As he suggested, the sounds of the jeeps, the light rays and the dogs barking increased and got louder and louder as the distance in between diminished. They did not need anyone to tell them that the dogs were reared as sensors and sirens to alert the security officers that guarded the desert at night. The Libyan security officers drove their four-wheel-drive jeeps in the darkness. They failed to use their lights to be able to track and arrest any would-be foreign or illegal intruders from across the borderline. Randy and the duo in his company understood the mathematics and bearings of the border crossings. They were no novices to what was happening around them in the desert. They had drunk all their water but had not made a third of the journey. Only endurance and hope were their last urging spirits.

Charsare and Smokey agreed with Randy but had to wait till the road was free from light rays. The road between both borders was always busy but they managed to find some seconds of respite to make the crossover to the other side of the road. Their crossover happened so fast amid a joint chorus of the barking dogs. When they got to the other side, Randy told the other two guys that they were at the shores of "no man's land but the seashore they were seeing was another part of the truncated iron curtain. He asked them to imagine what would have happened if the seas were not acting as a natural barrier? People would have tried the "ephemeral mission impossible" or the desert daredevil drivers would have taken the divide over and unleashed their contrabands on those that would have hated their crossings most. It was naturally defended from people like them and was naturally justified.

When they crossed over, the barking at the side they had crossed into reverberated. Everywhere was barking and the jeep revved at the other side of the road they had crossed from. It was too disheartening and heartbreaking for them, but they had to live with it and find a way fast to leave them behind without being caught or arrested. The desert government officers did their job in the dark much as the trio had the night for their crossing the long sandy border.

Among the trio, only Randy had a backpack with one extra bag. They were cumulatively heavy with his personal effects, and he could not let go. They continued at the seaside till they felt safe a bit. They were able to leave the barking dogs and the sound of the security jeeps behind.

When they crossed to the Seaside, it was obvious that they were on the wrong side of their escape route. After some hours of trekking on the wrong side, they now decided to conform rightly to their bearing. Before then, Smokey wanted him and Charsare to excuse him to smoke a cigarette. Randy hushed his request down just as Charsare was bearing down on him too. Randy specifically asked him not to make any light in the dark and further asked him if he were in his right frame of mind, he continued and told him that it would be very disastrous if he ever made any fire that will give their position out to the desert police guards and their accompanying dogs. He refrained from making any light comments but was uncomfortable from that point. He was suffering from nicotine jaundice addiction. From that point, no one considered what one another said or did but provided it did not attract any problem for any person in the then divided group. They merely wanted to get across the no man's land borderline into Libya.

They say nothing good comes easy. When they crossed back to the first side of the road they were trekking before, the sandy terrain considerably reduced their trekking pace. It was like walking on the last lap of the journey to Djanet before they boarded their jeep again in the middle of the desert.

All the while they were trekking, Chasare and Smokey had been expecting him to say he was tired from carrying his backpack and heavy bag, but he continued to carry them at ease and followed them equally at their intentionally increased tempo and speed. They had expected Randy to drop the backpack and bag out of frustration, but he continued against their wishes and surprises. Randy clung tenaciously to them because he knew what they were thinking and expecting. He wanted to prove them wrong, show them the tenacity of being confirmed and initiated desert warrior. At that point he ruminated on their thoughts, he was not showing any wobbling or weakness with his heavy bags. They were heavy but he was ready not to let them leave him behind remembering what Chasare had said at the outset of their trekking. They came across many high-layered barbed wires. They were high and had extraordinarily little space in between to make any crossing to the other side of the fence erection. It looked like the real borderline but who was ready to know what it meant at that time of the night and more so at the heat of the trekking without any water to cool down the saddening beats of the revving heart. All they wanted and had to do was to climb the delicate barbed wire demarcations carefully, fast and jump over to the other side of the fence. In that case Randy always threw his bags extremely fast across the high fence and before the others started climbing to cross over, he too was almost at the other side. Randy knew he was surprising Chasare and Smokey with his agility and endurance, but they all kept suspected but known silence together. There were so many of those barbed-wired barriers that could easily injure anyone while crossing. Randy suspected and warned anyone against sustaining a direct injury from the razor-sharp barbed wires, as they could be poisonous from whatever they were prevented from the borderline. They had started the trekking at about 19.30Hrs and were almost 01 .30Hrs at the time they were making these series of barbed wire crossings. They needed to complete the trekking before 06.00Hrs or at worst some few minutes later without which they will be arrested and sent to the most loathed detention *Zanzu* centre in any town or city in Libya.

Of all the distance covered from the long trekking, the most dangerous point was the last long lap that covers the long and wide light beam aperture which was the deciding factor in entering the country's little border town of Abukamash overlooking the Mediterranean Sea. Each one of them had been briefed on how to act when one reached that point of getting into Abukamash. The searchlight was directed into the open desert and riddled with very well-fed wild dogs. As they advanced towards the searchlight, they warned one another to be fast and to ignore the barking dogs, which sometimes could follow any of them for any distance before retreating. They warned again that none of them should attempt or pretend to harm any of the dogs because it was going to make them uncontrollably wild. The last defensive advice they agreed on was to keep away from one another to be able to divert, decentralize and denigrate the powers of the dogs. If they were not in a large group, their powers would be heavily diminished and systematically controlled. The dogs were wild to the core. The barking and growling continued to increase, as they got closer to the light's beam. Once they stepped into the light's beam, they became very visible to the dogs and could be seen equally by the border guards from afar, if only they were awake. Randy thought that they must have done their job very meticulously and officiously to have warranted they're not being awake despite the group barking of the dogs. The doggy alarm did not matter to them as they trudged on inside the beam. The light beam was almost the size of two football fields from the point they crossed it. They had to go extremely far from the border post to keep the barking dogs' noisy voices a bit faint from the sleeping border soldiers. The dogs barked till they started seeing the dogs dance around them but always at the sides. Their noise subsided after some distance. They had gone back to their invaded territory to feel safe once more. After the dogs had gone back, they suddenly hit the road to the amazement of Randy and others. They had trekked all night and reached their desired point at about 06.30Hrs without water for most of the journey. It was their overstretched, unlimited endurance and hope that carried them through the journey.

When they boarded a cab to Tripoli, Randy saw one big can filled with drinkable water inside the cab and asked the driver if he could drink some quantity from it. The driver was generous to accept his request. He took up the can and started to drink like a horse in the river. As he drank, Chasare and Smokey started to complain about the way and manner he was monopolizing the water without any due consideration to their welfare. Randy told them that it was "God for us all every man to himself" and that he was only dancing to the tune of their combined music and their strict rules of laws enacted to their trekking advantage. Then they said jointly that Randy was a confirmed and fully initiated desert warrior. He asked them how they meant it. They said that they had talked in their mother tongue about how they had expected Randy to drop his backpack and bag after some trekking distance, but they were surprised that he held on to them till the end of the journey. They truly never thought he would be able to make it with the bags and heaped praises on him for being able to endure the test of time. Randy smiled and slept for most of the journey back to Tripoli. He was deeply tired and famished.

The worst thing about being an illegal immigrant in any country is that one doe's things differently sometimes from the approved and acceptable norms. One loses everything financially if one failed to make his travels as planned. The success or failure depends on a variety of reasons and the next line of acceptable actions. If one is unsuccessful, expect some people to sympathize and some too to laugh at one secretly. Those that were pathetic learned from other mistakes and got wiser but most pretended to know much when in fact their hollow heads must comprehend what was going on around them. Those that laughed at people are the ones that will relate the things happening in every country but have never been there and cannot muster the confidence and courage to travel out internationally facing and squaring it out with immigration officers before boarding. For Randy, the more people laughed, scorned, gossiped, and made jest of him the more concentrated and focused he was on his planned goals. Whichever way, life goes ahead with all steadfastness. One needs to keep fighting till one achieves his or her aims.

As Randy, Charsare and Smokey reached Tripoli, they dispersed and never saw themselves again. Randy guessed that the border crossing must have made an indelible imprint on each one of them much as it made on him. For him he felt some elation and that he had been goldenly refined and purified ready for further border onslaughts without any fear of arrest. He now knew what he wanted and what precautionary measures he should adopt and avoid.

Randy was now a novice turned professional and would remain so. What he had known is an unseen knowledge embedded in him that no one will ever imagine he had known and can execute satisfactorily. He had seen it all in a very hard way and firsthand. Good and extant experiences will be needed at every point and part of his life.

Randy did not allow the dust to settle before he started his carwash job again near the immigration office. The officers asked him why he was absent from work for so many days, he told them he travelled to another city to visit a friend that had invited him to stay with him for some weeks. He embarked on another trial mission to leave the country after some months of arduous savings, but this time around better equipped financially and mentally to confront all associated tasks that might turn out to be a stumbling block. He had his exit visa ready through an intermediary from Sabha and paid for his transit visa in one of the embassies in the city. Before this time, the dollar seller had gone through the same airport where he was arrested and with the same look-alike documents. This time around, he wanted real dollar notes and planned how he could carry them on his person without encountering any problem, as common people were not allowed to have any of the bills in the country.

He left the country again through Abukamash and Ben Gardane exit and entry points, respectively. He had no problem getting across both borders. He had known both countries very well from his first visit and knew what to do in any situation that might arise. He had deleted all probable and accompanying fears. He lodged in a hotel on reaching Tunis City. He generously gave the hotel service some reasonable tips after he had been allotted a room on the upper floor. The man that documented him called him later and told him that were it not for his reasonable tips, he would have been in some messy situation before their chat. Randy asked him why he had said so. The service man continued: that the police had issued a standing order warning all hotels, that anyone carrying the type of passport he was having should be reported to them immediately for their necessary actions but was not going to make any report against him because of his generosity. He could not believe it but ended up thanking him: *Shukran kati (thank so much)*. He ended the chat with that: "he should be careful when he gets to the airport the next day." He smiled and asked Randy to go to his room unperturbed. He wished him a happy night's rest as he closed the room door behind him. He was a very respectful and personable person. Randy seemed to have had the premonition by opening his hands of friendship based on finance for him.

Randy was uncomfortable throughout the night. He barely slept as he always expected law enforcement agents to come in at any time for his arrest. He quickly checked out in the morning with further tips to mellow his feelings and state of mind. The service man wanted to book a taxi for him, but he declined the offer for the fear of his identity being sold out, but he was also Sceptical if he had not already done it and that the police would just be at the airport waiting with their dragnet to complete their insidious job there. He checked out of the hotel and walked out of the premises and through some streets before he finally waived down a taxi that took him to the airport. The driver asked him where he was travelling to and when he came into the country. Randy quoted dates for him and framed a country as his country of origin. The answers were misleading in case the airport went hot on him. He was too oblivious of the day being mined for him but did not know how things were going to unfold. He reached the airport looking fresh, fearless, and greatly confident.

He remembered his past ordeals when he reached the airport. This time around, he was going to be extra careful, crafty, and faster than usual in everything he was going to do at the airport. He was not going to ask anyone any questions. He knew the geography of the airport and had everything by heart. He went straight to the check-in counter and requested his boarding pass. His name was on the flight manifest. He presented his passport to them. The lady he handed his passport to at the check-in counter asked him to wait for some minutes for her to reconfirm some data. As she went away into another room with the document in hand, Randy later saw the passport being taken by another man through the inner room behind the check-in counter with the passport in a hallway to another direction of the building. Meanwhile, other passengers were being served and checked accordingly. Randy smelt a rat and started to think very fast about how he could rescue his passport and leave the airport. He had been spotted and they were planning what to do with him for coming back into the country again. It was foolhardy to have come back to the same airport after the first encounter of an ordeal, but it was the only nearby functioning airport that could be flown from after the UN embargo on Libya over the Lockerbie bombing incident that exploded in the Scottish airspace. It was a cause worth the trial and advancement from any airport like the one in Carthage -Tunisia or any other that was in proximity to the country. After about twenty minutes, the man came back and dropped the passport at the check-in counter. He spoke in their local dialect and she should ask him to wait till when the police will arrive to question him and possibly get him arrested. The lady only asked him to wait for some minutes before he would be attended to, but she was attending to other people that came after him. Randy pretended not to have understood them and kept his cool. Luckily for him, there was a passenger surge in the next few minutes at the check-in counter. Randy did not need any alarm sounded for the impending and imminent danger. The lady had trusted her instincts wrongly that he did not understand her discussions with the man and had left the only connecting factors that would have made him stay waiting to be guillotined. He had the inkling that things were not fine but turning ugly. He quietly picked up his passport and flight ticket and gently informed the lady he was going to the restroom and would be back in ten minutes. She hastily obliged because she was too busy to understand what was going on around her. She asked him to go quickly and come back. Randy answered her in the affirmative. "Yes, mam."

Randy went in the direction of the restroom but was diverted by the multitude giving him some needed cover. He turned left barely before he reached his target and made straight for the exit door. He saw a taxi that had brought a passenger to the airport with the occupant alighting. He asked the driver quietly but inwardly in frenzy to carry him to a particular garage that if they were to look for him, will facilitate his escape before they had an alternative thought of blocking him. The taxi drove to change direction in another part of the departure hall, which will still make the car come through the same point they were leaving but on a further lane for driving out of the airport. The taxi meandered and came through the same spot they had left. As the driver drove through, he saw the lady, the man that had the passport in his hand and three other plain-clothed policemen he identified two among them raising their heads and trying to Ostrich him from the crowd. He balanced his head to align with the opaque backside of the car so that he would not be easily seen. Randy smiled inwardly. He had survived another detention and still thought they would still be searching everywhere at the airport for him because they were sure the time would not have been enough for him to escape them.

He alighted from the taxi some meters away from the garage and started walking. When he eventually entered the garage, he was the last passenger that will make the driver set off for the travel to the Tunisian border of Ben Gardane. Once inside the bus, he felt very safe till whenever they were going to reach the border. He met one person he used to know in Tripoli on the bus. They both shared seats and more than enough stories all through the journey. He Omona had told Randy that his visa to stay in Tunisia had expired but had no way of extending it. He said he was ready to face them headlong at the border. He had some greedy embodiments attached to his travel to the border which Randy was not interested in. Omona was going to see a trapped woman in the no man's land hotel between Libya and Tunisia to arrange for her to be transferred to Tripoli to enable her to start "printing money" for him as a pimp. Randy told him outright that he was on a mission impossible and should be incredibly careful. Randy wished him good luck.

When they reached the border, the guards came unto the bus to control all the passengers travelling documents. Omona was asked to disembark as was expected but the guards will have no reason to keep him since he was leaving the country voluntarily. Randy had earlier told him to expect the worst but will certainly be allowed to leave the country provided there was no criminal offence recorded against him. They could only bar him from coming back into the country for some years or deny him a visa for some stipulated period. In his case, it did not matter whichever way they acted because all his travelling documents were not really like those of Randy.

By the time he will come back on the bus, he told Randy how he was thoroughly beaten up and abused by the police and immigration for overstaying his allotted period. His face and some parts of his body had swollen up from the beatings and manhandling carried out by most of the officers at the border post. Randy was not surprised to see him in the state he was when he re-entered the bus. He and Omona had jointly half expected what happened and were not surprised at the result. It is the norm in most of the North African countries' military and civil security service personnel to concoct reasons and descend unquestionably at the least or flimsy adduced mistake on any West African. There have been countless deaths of West Africans at the hands of those beasts in government uniforms. They feel superior to their colour which puts them at the bottom of their racial strata and sedimentation. Randy always wondered why they felt the way they did against fellow Africans. They lived happily in every part of the continent unmolested but on their part, most foreigners are unduly subdued and subjugated like Omona experienced that evening at the border crossing and Randy in his first travel to Tunisia at the hands of his interrogating officers in Tunis.

Other Africans accepted it because they had no legal base to fight back against the law. The only way to avoid the inhuman treatment was to find one's way out of the country to countries that have and respected human rights but still maltreated and subjugated their types with minimal effect.

When the bus reached the Tunisian side of the border, Randy trekked over the border to board a cab going to the Libyan border and subsequently to Tripoli. Omona on his own trekked onto the hotel on the no man's land to meet his trapped lady. As the driver of Randy's cab drove on, he viewed the entire no man's land in retrospect. He started to think about the day he trekked the distance they were now driving through comfortably in a cab. He took his time to watch the terrain closely and tears welled up in his eyes. He had undertaken a very precarious journey from the unknown into the unknown. He cleaned his eyes without anyone knowing what was itching and biting his feelings at that moment. It was a distance for driving and at best possibly for Olympic marathoners. The marathon had to be run on a good road, not on a dune type of terrain he had trekked on that fateful day. Human beings who called themselves leaders of a country and a childhood friend he trusted with all love had driven him into the unthinkable acts and messy situations. Both parties have no conscience in their creation of wasted generations of human souls back in their home country. It dawned on him that the risk he took the night he trekked across the no man's land was almost a suicide mission. It was so because there were unconfirmed reports that there were some parts of the land that were mined to prevent invaders from coming through the divide because both countries lived in enmity. Imagine a border where both countries' commuters could not drive through but have to disembark at their sides of the border and catch another cab by trekking across to the other side of the border. There was nothing friendly between both countries to the best of Randy's understanding and knowledge. Nothing was impossible in that part of the world. The news reminded him again about one Ghanaian who lost one of his limbs in a mine accident while trying to escape from Libyan notorious *Zanzu*. He saw the mine victim in Tripoli, and he confirmed what had maimed him. Mine. Randy vowed to stay the course no matter how dangerous and bleak things looked.

Randy reached the Libyan border post after their long drive through the no man's land. He had been warned against coming back to Libya after being stamped out of the country. Randy told the security officers that sometimes people made balancing between projections and expectations. His had hardly worked before now. Furthermore, he had heard one of his friends say that a lie is an abomination unto God, and a very present helping time out of chronic trouble. While illegal immigrants' ways are almost elusive and rare, they are the bravest in every country in the world. They take unimaginable risks and do jobs that are so belated, body damaging and very discomforting. One of the officers involved with checking his documents invited him into their office and asked him why he was coming back into the country again. He told the officer that he had missed his flight and needed to validate his flight ticket with the national airline that had no office in Tunis City. The changes could only be affected in Tripoli –Libya. The officer accepted his cogent reason and allowed him to re-enter the country. He was so happy to have been able to get the officer convinced. He started to beat his chest secretly and vowed to leave the country in his third attempt. True to his feelings and design, he would see his efforts come to fruition sometime someday.

By the time he came back from his second unsuccessful exit trial, Gagi had already gone through the same route where he had failed twice to Canada. He succeeded to reach his destination without any hindrance. They were now four men altogether living with Muge's girlfriend in the flat.

He did not waste time starting his business again and gave the same reason to any of the immigration officers that asked him why he had not been to work for some days. When he had saved enough money, he decided to make his third exit trial. This time around he headed for Turkey after having the usual and necessary travelling documents. He chose that direction because unknown foreign immigrants had polluted all the international airports in Tunisia with regular and unaccountable documentation. The loopholes therein had been abused and plugged. The only way out to exit Libya was to go eastwards and later maybe in weeks or years connect the west that was every man's plan, thought and dream destination. The Western world had become impenetrable through the west. Be that as it may, someone, somewhere, somehow, had to survive in a world plagued by injustice, refined slavery and coordinated deliberate refurbished dehumanizations.

The Birth Of A New Dawn

A sage is out of his hibernation.
Watching the morganatic intellectual horizon
It is a new dawn in the modern world of intellectualism.
Out of distinction, the goldfish has no hiding place.

Optimists and the stoic never ignore agonizing injustices and tragedies.
The good news is here for all to savour and hold to heart without dramatizing.
Good things are the points of synergy to greater heights.
Just act well on your part, than finger-pointing retrogressive solutions

People are embarrassed to own up to irrelevant, trivial, and inane issues.
Self-immolation is part of disastrous seething anger and bitterness.
An aim and risen blames of generations of one before the other.
Sins of arrogance and pomposity are the underlying TRUTH.

Democracy is battered equality above the masses that aid the ruling few.
Democracy leaks like a basket holding ephemeral water content.
Intellectualism needs garnishing and polishing maintenance.
An update, rekindling an upgrade keeps the brain afloat.

In a crowded intellectual world, choice matters for personal improvement.
Let the positives get higher as they look up and ahead to the best!
Never take your intellectual convenience for granted.
Your cerebral productivity and concrete innovations matter to the soul

Knowledge brooks no disruptions when well-guarded and protected.
Knowledge is hotly irrepressible and self-galvanizing to and by the endowed.
The conjunction of juxtapositions and bolsters of the free world at pari-passu
Get judiciously and morally enlightened in a maze of intellectual heaps.

Knowledge helps in understanding yourself and your vicinity.
Possess a solution some see as being far and hard to achieve!
Readership will get you where emptiness debarred you.
A nerdy human aura will not do where titillating subjects abound for good.

Cynicism, dormancy, and hopelessness are alive because many welcome them.
The only way forward in intellectual increment to other things
Marginalized voices are amplified because knowledge is set in, in quantum.
Life is evolving and always revolving around knowledge.

Within and amongst us lies the gold you never expected
Rediscover yourself and tinker better for the once-in-a-lifetime substance
The modern world just handed you your life on a platter of gold.
A deficient world is now full of arrays of golden and glittering opportunities.

Be romantic and sharp with your knowledge and intellectual readership gusto.
New hope and new life are in stock for the best of reasons adduced.
A trade to uplift mankind to heights before so unexpected.
The best of thoughts and adjoining things are published to a better world and improved man.

Personal accountability and inferences are hereby adjudged and sealed.
We feel the moon and sun move as we care less about their importance.
Knowledge is equally perceived so to our detriment.
Let us get wiser and hold our knowledge and intellectual assemblages tenaciously.

EO111414022018MA (ARR) Ex Cathedra Martinet (Enebeli Mike A.O.)

Postscript cum flier: -

*The birth of a new dawn is a poem accompanying the release of **NINETEEN BOOKS** at a time by the author of the under-mentioned books.*

An in-depth perusal and deeper thought will prove the old saying that, "one must never judge a book by its cover".

The good thing about writers generally is the opening and public dissemination of their knowledge to people of intellectual substance, that in turn access and assess these with variable outcomes, to better their already cumbersome ideas, ideals, institutions and honourable intuitions. The contents are educative and will reassuringly make an imprint on the reader's consciousness as his noble choice will be validated by the innumerable advantages of this literary work.

Happy Reading

PENMANSHIP AND WORDSMITH (PAW) BOOKS LISTED BY THE SAME AUTHOR

1. THE PROUD VILLAGER
2. BRAINS OVER BARRIERS
3. "FOES" - FRIENDS OR ENEMIES STANDING (SWEET ARE THE USES OF ADVERSITY)
4. TRUST - THE RIGORS UNDER SADISTIC TRANSGRESSORS
5. THE POCKET PAMPHLET OF WISDOM
6. QUANTICO - MARINES HOME
7. WAMBLING, QUEASY AND HALLUCINATING
8. THE INEQUALITY QUALITY IN EQUALITY
9. QUANTITATIVE EQUATION OF POLITICAL "TAXIDERMISTS"
10. INDELIBLE SINS OF UNFORGETTABLE YESTERDAY
11. GENERATION OF POSITIVE KNOWLEDGE COMPETITORS
12. RIP " ALTERNATIVE FACTS"
13. VAMPIRIC BORN-AGAIN CONSULTANTS
14. CODES OF PRESIDENTIAL IMBECILITY
15. ABOVE THE SUBSERVIENT BREAKING POINT
16. AMAZING AMAZON
17. SYMBOLIC SYMBIOTIC ZERO
18. THE ABUSE OF SILENCE AND DISTANCE
19. SWIMMING IN JAR AND GYRE

Read these books, for they are going to be an extended elevation and opening of your knowledge to new heights. Indeed, a choice not misplaced, but honourably made for positive advancements.

This is not canvassing or proselytizing or convincing for a meaning nonexistent, but feasible for the good of man. Every positive thinker, like the writer, is a new door to a different good world.

The robust and combined epilogue goes into one statement to be inferred and self-processed. An elating one-time summary of edifying assemblages. Thus: -

The Proud Villager with Brains Over Barriers held sway, despite all the FOES (Friends Or Enemies Standing), never deserved the corrosive and anomalous Trust (The Rigors Under Sadistic Transgressors). Things Happen extensively, but you never know till you experience the substance with which the once forgotten and abandoned pamphlet of wisdom contains. It is not just mellifluent, but seriousness that goes with ascertained knowledge and intellectualism aided by amazing unhindered Amazon voice of freedom of expression.

Read, for you will be uplifted socially, culturally, and what have you. Positive readership uplifts you and in no distant time welcomes you into her domains with much that will last a lifetime for you in exchange.

The knowledge they say is power.

Enebeli Mike A. Okwus 22012018

1. Click on: -
2. amazon.de

OR

3. amazon.com
4. And just type in, - Enebeli Mike Alex Okwus
5. Click and there appear the books welcoming you with all respect and dignity.
Happy reading as you patronize me and the voice of freedom given by amazon.com
Thanks, and regards to all.

Signed: - **Enebeli Mike A. Okwus**

Glossary

Shukrankati -	(Arabic) Thanks very much.
Anorexic vegetable -	Marijuana.
Ottogar -	(Turkish) Motor park.
Seseguanto -	(Italian) making love without a condom.
Alupupu -	(Yoruba in Nigeria) Motorcycle/power bike.
Ngwogwolo -	(Ibo in Nigeria) Wooden body constructed truck for commuters.
Epo moto -	(Yoruba in Nigeria) Fuel/petrol.
Janglova -	(Yoruba) Seesaw or Swinging pendulum games played by children on a fulcrum.
Nkeli -	(Ukwuani in Nigeria) Little farms were made by children to practise agricultural science.
Ekuhkuh -	(Author coined from the blues as a child) An involuntary onomatopoeic exclamation to signify positivism leaning and support of a story.
Awoko -	(Nigerian students coined) Reading late into the night and probably till dawn in preparation for examination e.g terminal and final examinations — sometimes, it means "burning the midnight oil".
Asoki -	(College Students coined term) Processed Cassava is usually eaten from a water-soaked state with any chosen ingredient and condiments. It could also be eaten in other countless states or formats.
Oduh -	(Ukwuani Emu in Nigeria) A cultural "statue" blown to assemble people in the village square.
Ije umeh -	(Ukwuani in Nigeria) A recess or temporary adjournment is made after hearing from both parties of any case to ascertain and acknowledge secretly which party was right or wrong — before the spokesperson for the village is authorized by the most senior person to pass judgment publicly same day.

Molue -	(Yoruba in Nigeria) Metal body constructed passenger buses for commuters.
Danfo -	(Yoruba in Nigeria) Minibus for commuters.
Kabukabu -	(Pidgin English Nigeria) Private cars used in place of normal approved vehicles or cars to carry commuters.
Osondu -	(Ibo & Ukwuani) When one has to run for his dear life.
Sa fun iku -	(Yoruba in Nigeria) Run for your life or beware of death (electrocution).
Exbiasojafra -	(Author coined) Ex Biafran Soldier.
Koboko -	(Nigerian term) A deadly instrument of oppression made from dried horsetail that is popularly used by mostly those in the military for flogging civilians.
Sapiloaqua -	(Author/Pidgin coined Nigeria) Locally brewed gin.
Kpotoki -	(Bini in Nigeria) The fair-skinned race.
Muje Muje Soldiers -	(Hausa in Nigeria) Soldiers that understand only forward match or attack orders or commands.
Puree Boys -	(Nigerians coined word in Italy) Very healthy but indolent men converted to serfdom under prostitutes.
Hikihiki -	(Arabic) Doing the right thing(s) for survival but against the status quo and acceptable norms.
Bukoki -	(Unknown but coined by West African foreigners in Niger) Makeshift open air house that looks like where animals are kept (Open air manger).
Bidon -	(Arabic) A plastic water container with sewn old cotton sack around to make the water content remain low in temperature for some time in the desert.
Abrucheri -	(Ghanaian coined term) Ghanaian coined term for going abroad from their country or a been to.
Nta fi Madam -	(Arabic) Do you have a woman?
Kpamu -	(Pidgin English Delta in Nigeria) To be calm, cool and collected in the face of problems or danger.
Ogwugwudada -	(Misrepresented pronunciation by the Berbers visiting Nigeria to sell their native medicines). The word was supposed to read as *"Ogun ti oda"* by the visitors, but because of their inability to pronounce the words rightly, they ended up with *ogwugwudada* meaning "good medicine" but the people started to call them the name for their wares, for them as a people and as individuals to make for the loss of pure communication. In essence the name stood for the Berbers who only visited or visited and sold medicines in Nigeria.

Madiba -	(Xhosa South Africa) Is a title of respect given to the first dark-skinned South African ruler from his Xhosan clan.
Kalambush -	(Arabic) To arrest.
Catch Catch -	(Pidgin English) A term coined by English-speaking foreigners in Libya for arrests through harassment.
Shukran -	(Arabic) Thank you. (Shukran kati) — Thank you very much)
Afon -	(Arabic) Reply for anyone thanking someone e.g my pleasure.
Sawasawa -	(Arabic) Equality before the law of the land.
Mamnual -	(Arabic) Forbidden by law (mostly by the Holy Book of Koran)
Haram -	(Arabic) highly forbidden by the law (mostly by the Holy Book of Koran).
Bara ni -	(Arabic) Get out of here. Mostly used for warnings.
Emshi -	(Arabic) Go away or move.
Walahi Talahi Kasumobilahi -	(Arabic) A constant statement made out of the contest to attract seriousness and belief through religious piety.
Nti(a) misquosh -	(Arabic) You are a bad person.
Nti mafish mok -	one without a brain (idiot or stupid person)
Medina Quadim -	(Arabic) Old City Centre/ downtown.
Shogol ground -	(Arabic with English attachment) An area where foreigners go in search of menial jobs.
Travailler ground -	(French with English attachment) An area where foreigners go in search of menial jobs.
Shota Kalambush -	(Arabic) Police arrest.
Lama Siyara -	(Arabic) Auto/Car wash
Girigira -	(Arabic) Derogatory word for dark-skinned people.
Klifty -	(Arabic) Thief or to steal.
Souk -	(Arabic) Market.
Eko Akete Man -	(Nigeria) Lagosian.
Pataka -	(Arabic) Identification card.
Eesh Varma -	(Turkish sound and meaning) Do you have a job?
Eesh yok -	(Turkish sound and meaning) There is no job.
Eesh, yokma -	(Turkish sound and meaning) There is no job.
Tula -	(Turkish) Block(s).
Biogeographical alloy -	(Author coined) when a situation or object aligns with biology and at the same time reflects a Geographical connotation.
Afromyophobia -	(Author coined) When everything about Africa and Africans is considered bad and unrecognized without due consideration.

Afrotradomedicalism -	(Author coined) African traditional medicine and the belief in African tradition / cultural rights.
Pozholosta -	(Russian) Please.
Bistro -	(Russian) Fast or faster.
Ogoin -	(Rusian) Fine.
Niet -	(Russian) Fine.
Yabanji -	(Turkish) Foreigner.
Siyah -	(Turkish) Dark-skinned (black for objects).
Kara -	(Turkish) Dark-skinned (black for objects).
Egburunise -	(Nigerian coined term in Greece) Roadside, streets and from town-to-town hawking done mostly by foreigners in Greece.
Shoroti -	(Nigerian coined term in Italy) Roadside, streets and from town-to-town hawking done mostly by foreigners in Italy.
Dai -	(Italian) Please.
Scusi -Italian)	Excuse me or excuse me.
Fema -	(Italian) Parking at the side of the road.
Jiro/Njiro -	To go driving around.
Boca –	(Italian) To lick.
Scopare -	(Italian) making love or to make love.
Andiamo -	(Italian) An agreement that calls for both parties to go together to a place.
Quanto -	(Italian) How many/much?
Quanto costa -	(Italian) How much does it cost?
Pagare -	(Italian) to pay.
Piccolino -	(Italian) A special love-making position that allows for a very deep thrust.
Oggi -	(Italian) Today.
Tutti Giorno -	(Italian) Everyday.
Mi dispiace -	(Italian) I am sorry.
Dai mi baci -	(Italian) Please kiss me or kiss me.
Mi amore -	(Italian) My love.
Landkreis -	(Gerrman) County.
Non Anglais -	(French) Short form of saying "I don't understand the English language".
Pizzini -	(Italian) Mafia coded notes or a marked man or member of an association or club.
Cogito ergo sum -	(Latin) I think, I therefore exist.
Varina -	(Botanical term) Botanical name for Cassava.

Apo, Apele, Apokapos -	(student coined fagging names) Derogatory terms used to demean or fag a junior student in the college.
"Conc" grammar -	(English abbreviation of "Conc" as concentrated in chemistry) Using English jaw-breaking words for expressions.
Lama Siyara -	(Arabic) to wash car.
Jilda -	(Arabic) Light animal skin in form of a handkerchief that is used to clean or mop a car after washing.
Ikamah -	(Arabic) Permanent resident permit that allows anyone having it legally to stay in a country.
Shogol -	(Arabic) Work
Jib -	(Arabic) to give (receive)
Ole -	(Nigeria/Yoruba) Thief
L'argent –	(French) Money

ABOUT THE AUTHOR

 The author is an accomplished writer, poet, Information Technologist consultant and many more notations to other fields of endeavour. He is reasonably introduced in his book titled: The Proud Villager, Brains Over Barriers and FOES (Friends Or Enemies Standing).

In this book: Symbolic Symbiotic Zero, he has spoken his feelings through so many poems about all the political traducers and psychopathic sycophants who would not work for the betterment of the downtrodden masses that toiled under all cataclysmic weather to ensure a very smooth and fair extension of positive hearts to their elevations through either democratic voting or riggings through impositions or back door party selections and what have you.

Printed in the United States
by Baker & Taylor Publisher Services